About the Authors

Alison Roberts is a New Zealander, currently lucky enough to be living in the south of France. She is also lucky enough to write for the Mills & Boon Medical Romance line. A primary school teacher in a former life, she is also a qualified paramedic. She loves to travel and dance, drink champagne and spend time with her daughter and her friends.

Kate Hardy has always loved books, and could read before she went to school. She discovered Mills & Boon books when she was twelve and decided this was what she wanted to do. When she isn't writing Kate enjoys reading, cinema, ballroom dancing and the gym. You can contact her via her website: katehardy.com.

Maggie Kingsley says she can't remember a time when she didn't want to be a writer, but she put her dream on hold and decided to 'be sensible' and become a teacher instead. Five years at the chalk face was enough to convince her she wasn't cut out for it, and she 'escaped' to work for a major charity. Unfortunately—or fortunately!—a back injury ended her career, and when she and her family moved to a remote cottage in the north of Scotland it was her family who nagged her into attempting to make her dream a reality. Combining a love of romantic fiction with a knowledge of medicine gleaned from the many professionals in her family, Maggie says she can't now imagine ever being able to have so much fun legally doing anything else!

D0237693

Hot Single Docs

COLLECTION

July 2018

August 2018

September 2018

October 2018

November 2018

December 2018

January 2019

February 2019

Hot Single Docs: Happily Ever After

ALISON ROBERTS

KATE HARDY

MAGGIE KINGSLEY

MILLS & BOON

Published in Great Britain 2018
by Mills & Boon, an imprint of HarperCollins*Publishers*
1 London Bridge Street, London, SE1 9GF

HOT SINGLE DOCS: HAPPILY EVER AFTER © 2018 Harlequin Books S.A.

St. Piran's: The Brooding Heart Surgeon © 2012 Harlequin Books S.A.
Special thanks and acknowledgement are given to Alison Roberts for her contribution to the *St. Piran's Hospital* series

St. Piran's: The Fireman and Nurse Loveday © 2012 Harlequin Books S.A.
Special thanks and acknowledgement are given to Pamela Brooks for her contribution to the *St. Piran's Hospital* series

St. Piran's: Tiny Miracle Twins © 2012 Harlequin Books S.A.
Special thanks and acknowledgement are given to Maggie Kingsley for her contribution to the *St. Piran's Hospital* series

ISBN: 978-0-263-26831-7

09-1118

MIX
Paper from
responsible sources
FSC® C007454

FSC
www.fsc.org

This book is produced from independently certified FSC™ paper to ensure responsible forest management.

For more information visit: www.harpercollins.co.uk/green

Printed and bound in Spain by CPI, Barcelona

ST. PIRAN'S:
THE BROODING
HEART SURGEON

ALISON ROBERTS

CHAPTER ONE

IF LOOKS could kill, Luke Davenport would be a dead man.

Dr Anna Bartlett had finally deigned to join him in Theatre for her assigned job of assisting him in a potentially complicated procedure, and she was clearly less than impressed that he had decided to go ahead without her.

Sure, he'd received a message while reviewing his patient's notes that she was caught up in the emergency department of St Piran's hospital with a chest trauma case requiring a thoracotomy and would therefore be late, but what had she expected? That he would delay the case until she arrived? This patient had already had to wait longer than he should have for his surgery. In any case, if the patient in Emergency survived the aggressive procedure to try and stabilise him, Dr Bartlett would be the only person available to take them to another theatre and that left Luke in precisely the same place—having to find someone else to assist him in surgery. Thankfully, this wasn't that difficult given the talented staff this hospital could boast, and paediatric cardiac surgeon James Alexander had been available and only too willing to assist the returning head of department.

James had joined the staff in the eighteen months Luke had been away. He was not only settled in the area but married to Charlotte, a senior registrar in the cardiology department. Just one of a countless number of changes. So many it was hard for Luke to imagine he'd once been a part of all this. It was frightening how one's world could change in a heartbeat.

Like Luke's had done when the news of his younger brother's death had rocked the seemingly solid foundations of his life and prompted the radical decision to join a military medical unit. Nothing would ever be the same and yet here he was, trying to pick up the pieces of his old life.

If it felt wrong to him, it was no wonder he was an unwelcome disturbance in Anna Bartlett's world. She'd had enough time to become part of this medical community. To stake a claim and make this department her own. Maybe that was the real reason for the resentment he could detect. That he was in charge again.

It would be a bit of a blow to anyone's ego, wouldn't it, being bumped from a position as top dog? Everybody had known that his replacement was temporary but nobody had expected him to return so abruptly. Maybe Anna had secretly thought he might never return from Iraq. To add insult to injury, it wasn't the first time Luke had taken the position from her. He'd been the winner three years ago when he'd been chosen over her for the prestigious role of head of St Piran's specialist heart surgery unit.

Yes. That could well explain the death glare he'd

caught from over the top of the mask as Anna had finally entered the theatre. She stood outside the cluster of staff around the operating table now, gowned and masked, her gloved hands held carefully away from her body. Taller than average, he noted in that split second of noticing her arrival, and her eyes were green. Very cool right now because she was displeased and that made them seem hard—like uncut emeralds. Unusual enough to make a lasting impression. As did her body language. The way she was standing so absolutely still. It advertised the kind of attention to detail, like not contaminating anything, that came from being not only well trained but highly disciplined.

He'd heard that about her from James as they'd scrubbed in together. That his missing assistant was skilled and meticulous. Uncompromising. Single because she chose to be. Or maybe no man could compete with a job that someone lived and breathed to the exclusion of anything else.

'She's good,' James had added. 'Very good. You'll be pleased she's taken on the job of Assistant Head of Surgery. With the reputation she's built here, she could have gone anywhere she chose.'

James obviously respected Dr Bartlett but he'd also said he didn't really know her. Not on a personal level. The way his sentence had trailed off in a puzzled tone had suggested that maybe she didn't have a personal level.

It was James who acknowledged her presence now, however.

'Anna! That was quick.' He gave his colleague a closer glance and frowned. 'No go, huh?'

'No.' The word was crisp. The attempt to save someone in the emergency department had failed. That was
that. An unsuccessful case. Time to move on to the next.
'Want me to take over?'

'If that's all right with Luke. I am rather late to start
my ward round now and I've got my own theatre slot this
afternoon.' James sealed another small blood vessel with
the diathermy rod and then looked up at the surgeon
across the table. 'Luke? Have you met Anna already?'

'No.' His response was as curt as Anna's verdict on
her emergency case had been.

He carried on with the long, vertical incision he was
making in his patient's chest, not looking up until James
moved in to control the bleeding.

She was standing closer to the table now. A mask
covered the lower half of her face and a disposable hat
hid her hair and ears. All he could see were those green
eyes and for a split second the accusation in them hit
home.

Yesterday he had been supposed to meet the woman
who'd looked after his job for eighteen months, but
there'd been that hassle at his house with a burst pipe
and there had been no water supply. There'd been a
problem getting power reconnected as well, after such
a long period of being empty, so he'd had no way of
recharging the battery for his mobile phone when it
had died. The hassles had underscored the fact that he
wasn't exactly thrilled to be back here anyway and…and
she hadn't waited for him, had she? He'd been less than
an hour late but she had gone home and hadn't left any
message other than the theatre list for this morning.

And now she was glaring at him as if accepting her

belated assistance for this surgery was only the first challenge he had coming his way. Well, she could take her attitude and deal with it on her own time.

'If you plan to assist,' he said curtly, 'now's the time to start. I don't like my surgeries being disrupted and I'd prefer to start the way I mean to go on.'

A tense silence fell around them as James stepped back and Anna smoothly took his place. The familiar ache in Luke's leg kicked up a notch but that only served to increase his focus. He turned his head to the scrub nurse hovering over the trolley beside him.

'Sternal saw, thanks.'

The nurse jumped at his tone and handed him the requested item with commendable speed. Then the whine of the saw cut into the silence he could still feel around him. Luke concentrated on splitting the bone beneath his hands. For a short time at least, he had no need—or inclination—to look at the woman now opposite him.

So this was Luke Davenport.

The war hero she'd been hearing so much about in the last few days. Too much. As if it hadn't been bad enough to have her position as head of department cut short, no one hesitated in rubbing salt in the wound by telling her how marvellous Luke was. What a great surgeon. And soldier. How he'd single-handedly saved everybody he had been with when they had come under attack, dragging them from a burning vehicle despite his own badly broken leg and then providing emergency care that had kept them alive until help arrived.

She could believe it. One glance from a pair of the

most piercing blue eyes Anna had ever seen and she knew she was meeting someone just as ambitious and determined as she was herself. Two horizontal frown lines at the top of his nose, between dark eyebrows, added to the intensity of the glance and made her catch her breath. To have him treating her like a junior fresh out of medical school might be unacceptable but it wasn't totally surprising. This man had seen and dealt with things she couldn't begin to imagine experiencing.

'An honourable discharge from the army,' someone had said. 'He's up for a medal.'

St Piran's was so lucky he had come back. The hospital, the patients, the whole damn community was feeling lucky. Anna had had to hide disappointment strong enough to morph very easily into burning resentment. Had to try and smile and pretend she felt lucky that she was being given the opportunity to be the hero's assistant from now on.

No wonder the guy was so full of himself he hadn't even bothered to come and introduce himself yesterday. She'd given him the courtesy of sending an apology for being late for this theatre case and look at his response! He didn't like his surgeries being disrupted. The voice had been deep and the words clipped. This was a man who was not only used to giving orders, he expected them to be obeyed.

Anna's spirits—already well dampened by the unsuccessful struggle to save a life in Emergency—slipped a little further. The only way through this, as she'd discovered with any previous difficult episode in life, was to focus on her work to the exclusion of anything else.

It wasn't hard. 'Good grief,' she couldn't help but comment when the rib spreaders were locked into position and the target of this surgery was exposed. 'Look at that.'

The sac of membrane enclosing the heart had calcified and become a thick, white casing—a kind of scar from the inflammation a virus had caused and so solid it was preventing the heart from beating effectively. Luke was about to perform a pericardectomy and peel this hard layer away from the heart tissue. A tricky, fiddly procedure that Anna had studied but never performed herself.

She would have been happy enough to do the surgery if a better option hadn't been available, but she would definitely have preferred to have the patient on bypass and a still heart to work with. Luke was sparing this man the additional risk of being on a heart-lung machine. He was going to do the procedure with the heart moving beneath his scalpel.

'Your investigations showed the extent of the calcification.' Luke sounded mildly surprised by her exclamation of astonishment. 'Right-sided filling was poor and the stroke volume was abysmal. It's a wonder he's been able to function at all.'

'The first sign that it was anything serious only came when he collapsed at work three weeks ago.'

Anna watched as Luke used a scalpel to cut through the hard, white tissue, his hand large enough to make the small instrument almost invisible. She could see how much pressure he was needing to apply but how careful and controlled that pressure was. He needed to open the scarred tissue but not penetrate the heart beneath.

His response of a grunt to her statement could have actually been satisfaction at the gleam of healthy, pink tissue revealed, but Anna caught something that seemed more like a reprimand that it had taken that long to diagnose the condition correctly and arrange livesaving treatment.

The criticism was unfair. This patient, Colin Herbert, had avoided even going to his GP for years, putting his shortness of breath down to being unfit and his tiredness to the broken nights of helping to parent two young children. Even initial investigations hadn't pointed to a cardiac cause for these symptoms in the thirty-seven-year-old. It had taken a CT scan and then cardiac catheterisation to reveal the rare condition, and that had left Anna having to decide whether to attempt an unfamiliar surgery herself or refer Colin to someone more experienced.

The news of Luke Davenport's return had made it worthwhile delaying the surgery for just a little longer. If Colin could stay in St Piran's, close to his family and friends, it would probably speed his recovery. It would certainly make this period far less stressful for his wife and children.

Luke had now begun peeling the pericardium away from the heart muscle. The anaesthetist, amongst others, was peering into the wound with fascination.

'Looks like plastic,' one of them commented.

Another grunt came from the surgeon and then silence fell in the theatre again. His requests for instruments or responses to updates on monitoring were curt. He barely acknowledged Anna's assistance. Surgery with this man was never going to be a relaxed affair, then. Not that he shouldn't be concentrating fiercely on the task at hand, but that had never stopped Anna from involving her colleagues. Testing their knowledge and sharing her own. Discussing problems and allowing contributions to any trouble-shooting needed. The way mentors had done with her in the past.

Being Mr Davenport's assistant might be like treading water as far as her career was concerned. Demoted to second best but only allowed to learn anything new by observation. Anna could feel the frustration creeping in already. She might well have to bite the bullet and start fighting for the chance to prove herself elsewhere. Having to apply for sought-after positions where most of the applicants, as well as those making the final choice, were male. Skilled, powerful, alpha men like the one working opposite her right now. Men who needed a lot of convincing that a woman was capable of being their equal.

But even as Anna felt the tightening knot of a tension she'd been aware of for her entire career in medicine, something else was pushing into her awareness. The skill Luke was demonstrating here told her that, merely through observation, she could learn from him. His timing was exquisite as he allowed the heart to beat and squeeze out blood, then advancing his scalpel to free the casing a little further in each fraction of time when the heart was filling again and, therefore, still enough to be safe.

The equipment and the technician needed to put the patient on bypass were standing by. Peeling the pericardium

from the back of the heart would be the most difficult
part of this procedure and Luke was keeping the option
of using cardiac bypass available.

He would prefer not to, however, and so far things
were going smoothly. The staff were more than competent and he had no complaints about Dr Bartlett's
assistance. She was good. Somehow she had instantly
tuned in with how he worked, and it was like having an
extra pair of his own hands in action. Smaller hands,
of course. More nimble ones. It was quite possible that
Anna would be better suited to continue this when he
got to the tight patches around the back.

The thought was embryonic. Barely registered, in
fact, because Luke was so focused on what he was doing.
Anna had the edge of the hardened pericardium caught
in a pair of forceps, holding it up and helping to peel it
away as he cut carefully beneath it.

He was using the scalpel with absolute precision.
Tiny cuts as close to the hard casing as possible. There
was less than a millimetre of space to work in. Luke
was vaguely aware that the atmosphere around him was
tense and that he could change it by relaxing a little and
talking more, but he had no desire to do that.

He was being watched in this, his first surgery on
returning to his role as head of department for cardiac
surgery. Being watched and judged. They were wondering if his experience in the army had changed him—as
a surgeon or as a person.

Of course it had. He had honed skills and one of
them was the ability to focus no matter what kind of
distractions were around. What anyone else, including

Anna—no, especially Anna—might be thinking of him
was irrelevant. What mattered here was a good outcome
for his patient. His focus was on that scalpel. Right on its
tip, which was the only part of the blade he was using.

The blood seemed to come from nowhere. There'd
been small bleeders up to now that Anna had dealt with
but this was a sudden gush that drowned his scalpel,
washed over the fingertips of his gloves and began to
form a pool. The beat of the heart made it appear briefly
and then the blood washed over it again, totally obscuring his vision.

Red.

So red.

And warm. He could feel it on his fingers. Sticky
life blood, ebbing rapidly from where it was supposed
to be.

Someone was dying.

He could hear their screams. He could hear the sound
of gunfire, too, and smell something burning.

He had to do something.

But he couldn't move.

Anna saw the moment the small artery got nicked by
the tip of the scalpel. It needed more than diathermy.
Clamping and tying it off shouldn't present more than
a momentary delay. She picked up a clamp, ready to
hand it to Luke, already eyeing up the suture material
he would need.

But he didn't request the clamp. The hand that was
holding the scalpel was as still as stone. Frozen.

And then the surgeon looked up, straight at her,

and Anna's own heart missed a beat. He was looking at her but he was seeing something very different. Something that had absolutely nothing to do with this room or this patient or the surgery he was in the middle of performing.

He was seeing something…terrifying?

Her heart missed only a single beat. With the next one she was moving smoothly. Using the clamp in her hand and then a suture. To those around them, it would look as though Luke had silently requested her control of the nuisance bleeding. Given his virtually silent technique up until now, it wouldn't have surprised anyone. But Anna had been the only one to see the look in his eyes. Had felt the way he had frozen, and it had quite possibly been the most disturbing moment she had ever encountered in Theatre.

It took only moments to deal with the artery and a nurse used suction to clear the operating field again. Anna heard Luke's indrawn breath and looked up to see the way he blinked with such deliberation it gave the impression of a switch being flicked off. And then normal service was resumed. The surgery carried on as though nothing awkward had happened.

But something had changed. Maybe it was an acknowledgment of the way Anna had rescued the situation. Or maybe it was the beginning of the kind of bond that could weld a tight team together.

'If I tilt the heart,' Luke said quietly a short time later, 'you're in a much better position to deal with that patch at the back. Are you happy with what you've seen of the technique?'

'Yes.' The increase in her own heart rate wasn't trepidation. It was far more like excitement. The challenge of trying something new. The idea that she might be on a new journey to learn skills that nobody else could teach so well. There was something like relief mixed in there as well because her future here at St Piran's looked a little less bleak. There was even a letting go of a little of that resentment towards the man who had reclaimed his job. The job she had desperately wanted to keep.

Thank goodness her hand was steady as she took hold of the scalpel. Even better was Luke's quiet praise as he watched what she was doing.

'That's excellent. Keep going. The more of this we can remove, the better the outlook for this patient will be.'

By the time the surgery was complete, the outlook was good and Luke finally stood back from the table and stripped off his gloves, thanking everyone for their contribution to the successful procedure. As he turned to leave, he tugged at his mask, breaking the strings that held it in place, and for the first time Anna saw more than those intensely blue eyes.

She saw a rugged, unsmiling face, with deep furrows from his nose to the corners of a mouth wide enough to balance the size of his nose. He wasn't what you'd call classically good-looking but it was hard to look away. The raw, unpolished masculinity was compelling. Those frown lines were still there at the top of his nose so maybe they were a permanent feature. When Luke started tugging off his bloodstained gown as he neared the swing doors of the theatre, Anna saw the lean muscles of deeply tanned arms. She could have sworn that those doors opened of their own accord, which was impossible but there was something about the commanding height and the way this man moved that made the notion perfectly feasible.

Luke Davenport was a soldier as much as—or possibly more than—he was a surgeon.

Every female in the room was watching as he made his exit, no doubt equally impressed, but Anna knew she would be the only one who found the image conflicting. Downright confusing, really.

Yes, Luke had lived up to his reputation as a gifted surgeon and he was apparently prepared to let her close enough to absorb valuable new skills but…what the heck had happened back when that bleeding had occurred?

Was Luke even aware of the way he had zoned out like that? He certainly hadn't acknowledged her contribution to the situation. He'd been injured during his time on the front line. An injury that was serious enough to prevent his return to his army position. Maybe he'd received wounds to more than his leg? A head injury perhaps that had left him with a form of epilepsy? Absence seizures where the sufferer was unaware of their surroundings and could freeze for up to a minute or so would explain it, but if that was the case, there was no way he should be still holding a scalpel.

That explanation didn't seem plausible, however. A seizure would have someone looking blank and Luke hadn't looked blank at all. He'd looked… *Haunted* was the word that sprang to mind. As though he'd been sucked into a flashback that he hadn't been able to escape from. This seemed far more likely but no less excusable.

What if he'd been close to the pulmonary artery? Or, worse, the aorta? Even a few seconds of delayed response in trying to control the kind of bleeding those vessels were capable of producing could have been disastrous. What really bothered Anna was knowing that she was probably the only person who had noticed the incident, which meant that saying anything might be seen as a form of professional sour grapes. Revenge, even, for the reprimand she'd received because of her late arrival for the case. Everyone knew that she'd missed out on the job as departmental head when she'd first applied. Now they'd be watching to see how she was handling her new role. To make an accusation that could have major repercussions on Luke's career within the first few hours of them working together was unthinkable.

There was only one person who might accept and understand her concerns. The same person who could provide an explanation that could possibly negate the need to take it any further. If nothing else, Luke deserved the courtesy of direct communication but it was also a conversation that needed to happen in private.

Right now her focus had to remain with their patient as he went into Recovery and was then settled into the intensive care unit for monitoring and post-surgical care. She had surgery she was due to perform with a registrar to remove sternal wires from a patient who'd had heart surgery a long time ago but was continuing to suffer pain that was probably a reaction to the foreign material in her body. The procedure wouldn't take too long and she'd planned to use her lunch break after that to talk to Luke and suggest a detailed ward round to bring him up to speed with all the cardiac inpatients.

Maybe she'd better use that time for something rather more personal. To make a judgment call on the integrity of the man she had to be able to trust if she was going to work with him at all. For some reason, the prospect of getting that close to Luke Davenport was more intimidating than anything Anna could remember facing.

She needed to think of it as nothing more than a new professional challenge. Backing away or trying to make it easier was not an acceptable option. She'd take it face on. Anna gave a decisive nod as she followed Colin's bed out of Theatre. She actually found herself almost smiling, having made the decision to confront Luke. If the situation had been reversed she had no doubts at all that Luke would be addressing the issue. He would probably have done so on the spot, with no thought of sparing her the humiliation of an audience.

Maybe this was a subtle opportunity to demonstrate not only her ability to do the job he had reclaimed but that her way of doing it might be better.

The prospect of the private interview with Mr Davenport was no longer simply intimidating.

It was…exhilarating.

CHAPTER TWO

THE need to escape was overwhelming.

And impossible.

Having ripped off the theatre scrubs, Luke had gone straight to the showers in the changing room but he couldn't wash away the aftermath of those few seconds in the middle of Colin Herbert's surgery. Turning the water to lukewarm hadn't brought its recent comfort of familiarity. Even the icy cold blast he finished with couldn't shock it out of his head the way it could chase nightmares away.

His clothes felt wrong, too. His trousers and an open-necked shirt felt too smooth against skin used to the thick fabric of camouflage overalls. At least he didn't have to knot a tie around his neck, like tying a bow on a pretty parcel. How ridiculous would that seem when he would far rather be fastening the Velcro straps of a Kevlar bulletproof vest over his shoulders. Feeling the weight of the armour plating and the bulkiness of pockets stuffed with whatever he might need at a moment's notice.

He felt too light as he strode out of the theatre suite

without a backward glance. Almost as though he was floating.

Lost.

The corridors were full of people going about their business, but it was all so slow. There was no sense of urgency as beds and wheelchairs were propelled to new destinations or staff moved from one task to another. They had time to stop and chat to each other. He saw people smiling and even heard laughter at one point. Someone said hello to him and Luke managed to smile back, but the facial contortion felt grim.

He didn't belong here any more. This was a joke that wasn't the least bit funny. Like the whole of civilian life. It was a game. A pretence. Meaningless.

Going outside was better. A brisk walk around the sprawling, modern structure that was busy St Piran's hospital. A helicopter was coming in to land, no doubt bringing a trauma patient to the emergency department. Luke's eyes narrowed as he watched it intently and soaked in the sound of its rotors. If anything was likely to give him a flashback, surely that was?

It wasn't going to happen. He knew that because he was aware of the potential and he was focused. In control. The way he should have been for every second of that surgery. He kept watching anyway. Testing himself, until the helicopter took off again and disappeared into the distance.

A tempting distance. He could start walking again and just keep going. Stride down the cobbled streets of this picturesque market town until he got to the harbour. Or, better yet, a stretch of beach where he could push himself with the added difficulty of walking in sand. Or hurl himself into the surf with its magic, albeit temporary, ability to numb his body and brain and wash everything away. An effect a thousand times better than a cold shower.

But this was early December. It was freezing and his wetsuit was hanging to dry on his back porch after his early swim that morning. His leg hurt, too, thanks to standing so still for so long in Theatre. And he was here because he had a job to do. A job he had been lucky to be able to come back to. An anchor. Something to build on and the only thing he had, really. Given time, this might start making sense again, giving him the bonus of feeling like he was doing something worthwhile even, though after this morning that goal seemed further away than ever.

At least the patient who had been unfortunate enough to be his first case back here was doing well.

It was nearly an hour later that Luke arrived in the intensive care unit and Colin was awake, though very drowsy. A nurse was by his side and she smiled warmly at the surgeon.

'I've been hearing all about the surgery,' she said to him. 'I wish I could have seen it. I hear you did an amazing job.'

Luke made a noncommittal sound without looking away from the monitor screen giving detailed recordings of what was happening inside Colin's heart thanks to the catheter that had been positioned at the very end of the surgery.

Surgery that could have been a total disaster.

An amazing job? He didn't think so.

The nurse was still hovering. He heard the intake of her breath. She was about to say something else. Possibly another admiring comment. Luke shifted his gaze to give her what he hoped would be a quelling glance. Sure enough, her mouth snapped shut, a flush of colour stained her cheeks and she turned to fiddle with an IV port on her patient's arm.

Colin's eyes flickered open. He saw the surgeon standing beside his bed and smiled weakly.

'I'm still here,' he said, his voice slightly raspy. 'Thanks, Doc.'

Luke returned the smile. 'You're doing fine. We'll keep an eye on you in here for a bit and there's a few tests we need to run later today, but we'll get you onto the ward as soon as possible. Do you have anything you want to ask me about?'

Colin's head moved in a slow shake. 'I think my wife's asked everything already. Dr Bartlett seems to know what she's talking about. I'm still a bit groggy to take it in but I'm alive and that's what matters.' He smiled again, his relief obvious.

'I'll be back later. I can talk to you and your wife then.'

'Dr Bartlett said how well things had gone. What a great job you did.'

'Oh?' That surprised him. Or did Anna not worry about embellishing the truth when it came to reassuring her post-operative patients?

'The wife's just gone to find my mum downstairs

and look after the kids so Mum can come in for a visit. Hey, did I say thanks?'

'You did.'

Luke knew he sounded brusque. He didn't need the nurse to give a look vaguely reminiscent of the glare he'd seen more than once in Theatre from Anna. Did she know? Had word spread that his new colleague had had to leap in and prevent the error he'd made during surgery becoming a potential catastrophe?

'Where is Dr Bartlett?' he asked the nurse as he signed off a new addition to the drug chart and prepared to leave the intensive care unit. 'I need to have a word with her.'

'Back in Theatre, I expect.'

Of course she was. He'd seen the case listed on the whiteboard in the theatre suite. A sternal wire removal. In the same theatre Colin had been in. With the same theatre staff, presumably. Would Anna be checking whether anyone else had noticed the incident and could back up her report on the concerns she now had about the abilities of the returning head of department?

She hadn't said anything at the time. Hadn't even sent a significant glance in his direction, but that said something in itself, didn't it? She hadn't bothered to hide what she thought of him returning to take her job in those early glares. It suggested that she was weighing the implications. Making sure she used the ammunition he had handed her to best effect by choosing the best time and place.

Dammit! How the hell had it happened? He was well used to the nightmares, but to have a flashback like that happen during the day? In the middle of surgery? It was appalling. He wasn't quite sure of how long he had lost his focus but he had no doubts about what could have happened if there hadn't been someone as quick as Anna on the other side of that table.

It wouldn't happen again. He'd lost focus because that had been his first slot back in a civilian theatre. His concentration had been too much on a procedure that couldn't have been more different to the kind of work in an Iraqi field hospital or, more particularly, as a member of the medical emergency response team on a mission on the front line. It had been slow and fiddly compared to the aggressive, lifesaving measures of treating major trauma under circumstances as tough as they got. It had been a mental ambush, triggered by the unexpected amount of blood he'd seen, or the way it had pooled, maybe.

Whatever. It wouldn't happen again because he'd be ready for it and wasn't going to allow a loss of control. Luke was perfectly confident of his ability to do just that.

But would Anna believe it?

A pair of green eyes came to mind. Framed by dark lashes that were unadorned by any mascara. Angry eyes. Accusing and assessing at the same time. What would they be like, softened by trust?

Even more compelling, no doubt, but Luke had to wonder if he would ever witness such a change.

Winning Anna's trust was not even the priority it probably should be because this underlying tension… this waiting for something potentially unpleasant to

happen, was oddly welcome. It made him feel a little
more alive than he had ever felt since he'd been shipped
home.

He was there, in the hospital canteen. Sitting alone near
a window.

Brooding was the word that sprang to Anna's mind.
Hunched over a plate of food he appeared to be toying
with rather than eating. The big room was well popu-
lated and noisy. Was that why the table with its single
occupant seemed to stand out like a beacon? Or was
her glance drawn there like a magnet because so many
other people were eyeing the newcomer and probably
talking about him?

She could understand not wanting to be in there and
either listening to or being the object of the kind of speculation and gossip rife in any group of people as large
as the St Piran's staff was, but why on earth hadn't he
done what she almost always did—buy a sandwich and
some fruit to take back to the privacy of an office?

Was he hoping for company? There must be so many
people there who knew him but there was a hierarchy involved and maybe there weren't any of his peers around.
Anna found herself hoping that by the time she got to
the end of this long queue someone would have joined
Luke. That way, she wouldn't need to feel guilty about
not doing so.

Not that she didn't want the chance to talk to him, but
this was hardly the place to have the kind of conversation she had in mind, and the idea of making small talk
with this man was not appealing. It would be dishonest,

in a way, when they both knew what needed to be discussed—the kind of game-playing Anna had never had the slightest inclination to indulge in. Besides, Luke was making himself look so very unapproachable. Self-contained and cool. If he knew and agreed with all the praise going on behind his back, his self-image would have to be more than a little inflated. Maybe his own company was enough?

Like Anna, Luke had changed out of his scrubs and was dressed neatly. Professionally. Anna slid her tray along the metal bars in front of the food cabinets and found herself running her hand down the side of her close-fitting skirt to make sure it wasn't creased. And then touching her hair to ensure that no tendrils had escaped the sleek knot at the back of her neck. She could do professional, too. Better than anybody, which was no surprise given the amount of practice she'd had.

'Anna... Hi!'

A new burst of hungry staff members was milling behind her, settling into the queue. The greeting had come from Charlotte Alexander, one of St Piran's cardiology staff members, who was behind a couple of nurses who'd stopped to stare into a chilled cabinet containing rolls of sushi.

If Anna made personal friendships among her colleagues, which she didn't, Charlotte would have been at the top of her list. While their relationship was friendly, it was still as professional as Anna could keep it. Even now, when the loose top Charlotte was wearing reminded her that she'd noticed the obvious increase in weight a week or two ago and it had occurred to her that Charlotte could well be pregnant, she wasn't about to ask such a personal question.

Girl stuff, like heart-to-hearts or sharing secrets and especially wedding or baby talk, was never going to happen. They were in the same category as frilly clothes or loose hair or make-up. Badges of femininity. Barriers to acceptance as an equal in a male-dominated profession. How did women like Charlotte manage it? Looking and dressing in a way that accentuated their best features but still having the respect of both colleagues and patients?

It made Anna feel like she had some kind of split personality, but it was so engrained now it was getting hard to know whether it was the Anna at home or the Dr Anna Bartlett at work that was the real her. The only thing she could be sure of was that never the twain could meet.

But sometimes…like right now…it struck Anna that her work persona was simply armour. Concealing anything feminine and vulnerable. Giving her focus and strength. Her gaze strayed of its own accord back to the solitary figure of Luke Davenport. What was it about him that made her even more aware that she didn't look as feminine or, God help her, attractive as she could? Just as well her work persona was so firmly engrained. If armour was what it was, she might need its protection more than ever.

Charlotte had been held up too long. She moved around the nurses who couldn't decide between the teriyaki chicken or smoked salmon.

'Hi.' She smiled at Anna. 'How's it going?'

'Very good. Theatre's over for today and both patients are doing well. I just took the sternal wires out of your Violet Perry. I'm sure the irritation will be gone and she'll be pain-free in no time.'

'That's great.' Charlotte was peering into the sandwich cabinet. 'Hmm. Chicken and Camembert sounds nice. Or turkey and cranberry. No…we'll be sick of that soon. Have you seen how many Christmas decorations are up already?'

'Mmm. Way too soon, in my opinion.' Anna found the seasonal celebrations at work disquieting. Too much of a bridge to personal lives.

'Ham salad,' Charlotte decided, reaching for one of the triangular plastic boxes. 'Oh…weren't you in Theatre with Davenport this morning? Doing Colin Herbert's pericardectomy?'

'Yes.' Again, Anna's gaze strayed towards Luke.

'How did it go?'

For a split second Anna considered confiding in Charlotte. Telling her all about how Luke had frozen and she'd had to take over the surgery. If she did, she'd be taking a step she could never undo. Charlotte would tell her husband, James, and the snowball effect might sweep them all into places they would rather not go. This man was going to be her professional partner from now on. They would be working closely together. Closer than she was with Charlotte or James or any of the other cardiology or cardiac surgery staff. She and Luke would share duties in Theatre, on ward rounds, during outpatient clinics.

As though he sensed her stare, Luke raised his head

to look up. Straight at Anna. Just for a heartbeat she held his gaze and tried to analyse what she could feel in that connection.

Maybe he wasn't bad tempered and brooding, she decided as she looked swiftly away. Strangely, for that moment in time, it had looked more like something deeper. Possibly even unhappiness? What reason could he have?

He had been forced to leave the army early due to his injury, hadn't he? Perhaps Luke didn't want to be here just as much as Anna didn't want him to be.

She looked away but not before she felt an odd squeeze beneath her ribs. She knew what it was like to feel unhappy.

Lonely.

Did she really have to kick someone who might already be down? Maybe she was overreacting. She had stepped in so fast, after all. If he'd been about to move at the same time it wouldn't have been such a big deal at all. Not that she'd had the impression he would have moved that fast, but it wouldn't hurt to think about things a little longer.

'It was amazing,' she heard herself telling Charlotte, absently picking up a pack of chicken sandwiches. 'I've never seen a technique quite that precise. I got to do a patch behind the left ventricle and it wasn't easy.'

'Wish I could have seen it,' Charlotte sighed. 'Did you know he'd ordered the observation deck closed?'

Her disappointment was clear. It was an opportunity to express caution about the man's personality or even say something negative. Curiously, Anna felt the need to defend Luke.

'I guess you wouldn't want too many people watching when you're doing your first case after a long time away.'

'I guess. How's Colin doing now?'

'Really good. We might be able to move him to the ward later today. Tomorrow, anyway, if he stays this stable. We should be well past the danger period for complications from acute dilation of cardiac chambers but his heart's still got to get used to dealing with much more of a blood flow.'

'I'll get up to see him this afternoon. Here's hoping the surgery report won't be far away. I'll be very interested to read it.'

So would Anna, but her agreement was silent. If she'd voiced it, her tone might have suggested that there would be more to read about than Charlotte might expect. They were getting near the cashiers' part of the counter now and she turned her attention to the baskets of fruit. An apple, she decided. The nice-looking green one on the top of the second basket.

The crash that came from somewhere in the kitchens behind the food counters was astonishingly loud. Metallic. Jarring enough for every head in the cafeteria to swivel sharply in that direction and for conversation to cease abruptly.

And in that second or two of startled silence a scream rang out. And then a cry for help.

Jaws dropped as staff members looked at each other

as though trying to confirm the reality of what was happening. Anna heard Charlotte's gasp behind her but she was watching something else. Weirdly, her instinct had been to look away from the source of the sound so she had seen the first movement in the crowd. A reaction time so fast it was hard to process.

Luke Davenport was on his feet. His chair tipped backwards and he pushed at the table in front of him rather than stepping around it. The table also tipped, the tray sliding off to send china and cutlery crashing to the floor but Luke didn't even spare it a glance. He was heading straight for the kitchen.

Access was blocked by the tall, glass-fronted cabinets apart from the space where Anna was, beside the tills and the fruit baskets. There was a flap in the counter beside the last till where kitchen staff could go in and out with the trolleys of used dishes but Luke didn't bother to stop and lift it. Or maybe he didn't see it. He swept the baskets clear to send apples and oranges bouncing around the feet of those still standing motionless and then he vaulted the space, making the action seem effortless.

Kitchen staff were backing away hurriedly, but not quickly enough for Luke.

'Move!' he barked. 'Clear the way. What's happened?'

'Over here,' someone shouted. 'Oh, my God... I think he's dead.'

Luke took several steps forward. Between the tills, Anna could see the blue uniforms of kitchen staff moving. Clearing a space near the stoves in front of which a large man in a white jacket lay very still.

Luke took in the scene. He turned his head with a single, rapid motion.

'Anna!' he shouted. 'Get in here. I need you.'

Someone had raised the flap now but, if they hadn't, it occurred to Anna that she might have tried to leap over it, too. Luke needed her?

The man was obviously one of the chefs. His white hat had come off when he'd collapsed and was lying amongst the pots and pans of an overturned rack.

Luke kicked one of them aside as Anna raced into the kitchen. 'Get rid of those,' he ordered. 'Someone help me turn him. Did anyone see what happened?'

'He just fell,' a frightened woman offered. 'One minute he was cleaning down the cooker and then he toppled sideways.'

'What's his name?'

'Roger.'

The man had been rolled onto his back now. Luke gripped his shoulder and shook it firmly, hunched down so that he could lean close and shout.

'Roger? Can you hear me? Open your eyes!'

He barely waited for the response that didn't come. His hands on Roger's chin and forehead, he tilted the head back to open his airway.

'Does anyone know him?' he demanded. 'Medical history?'

'He takes pills,' someone said. 'For his blood pressure, I think.'

'No, it's his heart,' another voice added.

The few seconds that Luke had kept his fingertips on the side of Roger's neck and his cheek close to his face had been enough to let him know that there was no pulse or respiration to be felt or seen. Anna crouched on the other side of the collapsed man as Luke raised his fist and brought it down squarely in the centre of the man's chest. A precordial thump that was unlikely to be successful but was worth a try.

Ready to start CPR, Anna was thinking fast, compiling a mental list of what they would need. Luke was way ahead of her.

'Get a crash trolley in here. Find a cardiac arrest button. Send for someone in ED or wherever's closest. Anna, start compressions.' He looked up at the silent, horrified onlookers. 'Move!'

They backed away. Anna heard someone yelling into the canteen for the cardiac arrest button to be pushed. If there wasn't one in there, it wouldn't be too far away. She positioned her hands, locked her elbows and started pushing on Roger's chest. He was a big man and it was hard work to compress the sternum enough to be effective.

Ten…twenty…thirty compressions. At least someone would arrive with a bag-mask unit very soon so she didn't have to worry about the implications of unprotected mouth-to-mouth respirations on a stranger.

The faint possibility of contracting something like hepatitis didn't seem to occur to Luke. Or it didn't bother him.

'Hold it,' he ordered Anna, pinching Roger's nose and tilting his head back as he spoke. Then he sealed the man's mouth with his own. One slow breath…and then another.

Anna started compressions again, the image of Luke's lips pressed to someone's face emblazoned in her mind. The kiss of life… She'd seen it before, though it was a rarity in a medical setting. Was that why it was so disturbing this time? Shocking, in fact. She had to concentrate on her silent counting until it was time to warn Luke.

'Twenty-seven, twenty-eight, twenty-nine, thirty…'

By the time they had completed another set of compressions and breaths, there were new voices nearby and the rattle of a trolley.

'Crash team,' someone announced. 'We'll take over now.'

'I've got it, thanks,' Luke growled.

'But it's what we—'

'We just need the gear,' the surgeon interrupted. 'And some assistance.'

Anna could feel the resentment at not being allowed to do what they thought they had been summoned for, but a life pack was lifted from the trolley and put on the floor along with an IV roll, a bag mask and a portable oxygen tank.

She carried on with the chest compressions, pausing only to let Luke rip the chef's jacket and the singlet underneath open to expose the chest and stick the pads in place. On direction, one of the doctors in the crash team secured his airway and attached oxygen to the bag mask, holding it in place until Anna paused again.

Could she ask to hand over compressions to someone else? This was enough of a physical effort to make her aware of perspiration dampening her shirt. No, she wouldn't ask. She was with Luke on this.

He had been the one to respond and identify the crisis, which made this man his patient until he chose to hand him over. And he'd asked for Anna's help. Roger was their patient and they could do this as well, probably better, than the junior doctors assigned to crash-team duties for the day.

'Stop compressions.' Luke was watching the screen of the life pack, waiting for a readable trace to appear. 'V fib,' he announced moments later. 'Charging to three hundred joules. Everyone stand clear.'

The junior doctors inched back, exchanging glances.

'Who is this guy?' Anna heard one of them ask another.

'Luke Davenport,' came the response. 'You know, the surgeon who's just got back from Iraq?'

'Oh…'

In the short space of time it had taken for three stacked shocks to be delivered, the atmosphere in this inner circle around the victim changed. The crash team, who had been busy resenting not being allowed to showcase their skills in managing an arrest, suddenly couldn't do enough to help their leader.

'Do you want an intubation kit, Mr Davenport?'

'Shall I draw up some adrenaline? Atropine?'

'Here's a sixteen-gauge cannula. And a flush.'

'Dr Bartlett? Do you need a break?'

Anna sat back on her heels, nodding. There was plenty of scientific evidence that compressions became less effective after two minutes unless someone else took a turn. She didn't move far away, however. She watched, totally amazed by the speed at which Luke worked. And she noticed things she hadn't noticed before.

Like the streaks of grey in his short brown hair. They had to be premature because she knew he was only a few years older than her and couldn't have hit forty quite yet. He had such neat fingernails too and his hands looked so different without gloves. Far more masculine, which made their speed and cleverness more impressive as he gained intravenous access and secured the line.

His brain was working just as fast. He seemed to be able to think of everything at once and keep tabs on what everybody was doing, but most of all, Anna was caught by the way he'd taken a trolley of equipment and a group of young medics who hadn't been thrilled not to be allowed to take over and forged them into a team that was now working under difficult conditions as well as they could have in a resuscitation bay in Emergency.

It was a team that had achieved success even before Luke had made a move to secure Roger's airway with an endotracheal tube. When the static cleared from the next, single shock delivered, the flat line suddenly gave a blip. And then another...

'Sinus rhythm,' one of the crash team said triumphantly. 'Yes.'

'Have we got a stretcher?' Luke still hadn't relaxed. 'Let's get this man into the ED. Or CCU.'

Charlotte had edged her way to the back of the

kitchen. 'Great job, Mr Davenport. Would you like to hand over now?'

'Call me Luke,' he said, still watching the monitor. The rhythm was picking up steadily and Roger was taking his own breaths now. The chef's eyes flickered and he groaned loudly.

And, finally, Anna saw the grim lines of Luke's face soften a little. He leaned down and gripped Roger's shoulder again with his hand––the way he had when he'd first begun this resuscitation effort. He didn't shake it this time. This was a reassuring touch.

'Just relax,' he told Roger. 'We're looking after you. Everything's all right.'

He looked up at Charlotte and gave a nod to indicate transfer of responsibility. Charlotte moved closer to talk to him, but as she moved, Luke shifted his gaze to Anna.

And something inside her tightened and then melted.

From the moment this incident had started—from when she'd heard the scream and seen Luke's instantaneous response, she'd been aware of his total command of the situation. Of his faultless performance and ability to absorb additional resources and personnel and then… right at the end…an indication that he really cared about this patient.

An impressive mix. If his glance had been in any way smug, it could have driven Anna into a defensive corner she might never have emerged from, but there was no hint of smugness. No self-satisfaction even. The fraction of time he held her gaze sent a message that was more like, We did it. This time, at least.

The triumph that was there was on the patient's behalf. Behind that was the acknowledgment of defeat in other cases and the sadness that they couldn't always win. Shining over both impressions was a kind of promise. A determination to always fight the odds and do the best possible job.

It sucked her right in.

She could work with this man. Could respect him. Like him.

More than that, in fact, judging by the odd ripple of sensation that caressed her spine and sent tingles through the rest of her body.

Dear Lord, she was attracted to him? No wonder she'd been so aware of her own appearance when she'd been standing in line with Charlotte. It explained a lot but it was a reaction that had to be crushed instantly. Allowing something that personal to threaten a professional relationship would be the ultimate play on femininity.

The reason women couldn't be seen as equals in this arena was largely because of the perception that they allowed emotion to cloud their judgment. Or, worse, they put a priority on relationships and undermined their careers by taking time off to have babies.

Not Anna Bartlett. It wasn't on any agenda she'd ever had.

Luke's return and—worse—his attractiveness were roadblocks. Ones she could detour around, which would see her working somewhere else, or deal with if the pull to stay put was strong enough. Either way, getting even remotely close to Luke Davenport would be a mistake.

It was Anna who broke the eye contact.

And turned away.

CHAPTER THREE

THE crisis over, Luke found he couldn't drag his eyes away from Anna.

Not that he hadn't spotted her the moment she'd walked into the canteen. He'd taken a good look then because he hadn't been sure it was her. Something about the height and body shape of the woman had seemed familiar but he'd only seen her eyes before this so it could have been anybody.

Just an attractive female member of staff. A senior member, obviously, because of the way she held herself. The way she moved with the confidence of someone who knew she was very good at what she did. And maybe he recognised something in the way this woman was dressed. Power dressing, really, with that pencil skirt and neat shirt. She probably had a matching jacket that would make the outfit the female equivalent of a man's suit. And what was that horrible thing she'd done to her hair? It was all scraped back into a round thing that made her look like a cartoon version of a librarian or frumpy secretary. All she needed was some thick-rimmed spectacles to complete the picture.

When her head had turned to scan the room, he hadn't

needed to be close enough to see the colour of her eyes
to recognise that this was, indeed, Anna Bartlett. While
she wasn't radiating resentment right now, there was an
air of containment about her that suggested she didn't
change her mind easily. A reserve that could well morph
into an arctic-type chill when she saw him. A woman
that knew her own mind and woe betide anyone that got
in her way. Like him.

Luke almost sighed as he dropped his gaze back to a
meal he wasn't particularly interested in. He wasn't enjoying this lunchtime experience much at all, in fact. He
knew that many of the people around had to be talking
about him. Gossiping. The happy chatter and laughter
going on around him, even the smell of abundant, hot
food all seemed irrelevant. Superficial.

The crash and then the scream had been real, though.
He'd reacted on autopilot. He wasn't sure what had made
him demand Anna as an assistant. Possibly because she
had been the only staff member nearby that he could
call by name. Or maybe it was the memory of how well
they had worked together in Theatre only a short time
ago.

It had been a good choice. The crisis had been dealt
with and a life had been saved and it had only been then,
when it was virtually done and dusted and he was handing his patient into the care of a new team, that Luke
had allowed anything else to enter his head. It was then
that he'd had his first close-up look at Dr Bartlett and
he'd had the curious impression that he'd been looking
at something he wasn't supposed to be seeing.

No wonder! The cool professional he'd seen queuing

for her lunch was absent. This woman, standing in the canteen kitchen with a creased skirt and a shirt that had come untucked on one side, was…wrong, somehow. Even more disconcerting was that a thick lock of dark blonde hair had escaped the bun thing and lay against a long, pale neck.

Her cheeks were flushed. From the exertion and stress of doing CPR or was she embarrassed at being dishevelled? Even her eyes looked different. Enlarged pupils made them seem softer. Warmer.

Good grief…she was rather lovely.

Any impression of warmth vanished, however, as Luke stared at her, unable to drag his gaze away.

And then she dismissed him! Simply turned on her heel and walked away.

How rude. No genuine warmth there, then. Anna Bartlett was clearly a career woman through and through, and she probably saw him as nothing less than an obstacle in her scramble to the top of that ladder. Any hope that she might discuss this morning's incident with him before reporting it to a higher authority faded and disappeared.

Charlotte, the cardiologist, was saying something to him, he realised. Something about whether he'd like to come with them to the emergency department to see what the investigations Roger needed would reveal.

'Yes,' he said. 'Please.'

'You'll remember Ben Carter?'

'Of course.'

'And have you met Josh O'Hara? No, you wouldn't

have. He joined the A and E staff while you were away.'

Luke kept up with the pace set by the people pushing the stretcher, heading away from the canteen and any areas that his assistant was likely to be heading for.

He'd see Anna again soon enough. Doing a ward round later today or perhaps in the departmental meeting scheduled for early tomorrow morning. Given how he felt about her in the wake of that dismissal, it might even be too soon.

The aura of the war hero already surrounding the return of Luke Davenport to St Piran's had evolved into something far more tangible by the time Anna was halfway through her ward round later that afternoon.

He had become a living legend.

Thanks to the crowd in the canteen at the time, accounts of the incident would have spread like wildfire and reached every corner of this institution in no time flat. Spilling into ears eager for the smallest details.

The junior nursing staff on the cardiology ward were discussing it when Anna paused outside the central station to collect some patient notes she needed.

'It was like something in the movies,' someone was saying in awed tones. 'He just pushed everything off the counter and jumped over it.'

'I heard he did mouth-to-mouth without even using a face shield.'

'Yeah...'

'Is the guy still alive?'

'Apparently he's in the cath lab right now. He'll

probably get admitted in here or CCU when they're finished.'

'Do you think Mr Davenport will come down with him?'

'Ooh…I hope so.'

The giggling from the young nurses was irritating. Anna decided it was because her own participation in the incident had been totally eclipsed by the actions of St Piran's new superhero. Except that she couldn't convince herself to be that petty. The irritation was really there because part of her was as star-struck as everyone else seemed to be. The man was intriguing. Compelling. Apparently trustworthy. And that was disturbing because Anna felt that she knew something about him that no one else knew. Or would believe.

If she wanted to discuss her concerns with someone, the obvious choice would be Albert White, the CEO of St Piran's. He would listen to any concerns she might have about Luke's abilities. He might even believe her and, if he did, he might set some kind of probationary programme in place. Things like that did not remain confidential. Eventually, it would leak. Given his performance in the canteen and new status amongst the staff, nobody else would believe Anna.

She might find herself more alone than she'd ever been in her struggle to break through the glass ceiling of her gender. It could affect how well she was able to do her own job. She stood to lose the trust and possibly even the co-operation of the people she worked with and teamwork was vital in this line of work.

Tread carefully, she reminded herself, even when her

demotion from being team leader had been rubbed in when a flurry of activity had heralded the new arrival in the coronary care unit adjacent to the ward and more than the necessary staff numbers flocked to greet both the patient and the new head of department.

Roger the chef was made comfortable and wired up so that every beat of his heart could be monitored, the trace and its extra information like blood pressure and the level of oxygen in his blood appearing on one of the screens flanking the central nurses' station. It was there that Luke caught up with Anna.

'He needs urgent revascularisation,' he informed her. 'I'm hoping you can fit him in on your list for tomorrow.'

Anna closed her eyes for a split second as she groaned inwardly. She opened them to find herself under intense scrutiny.

'Is that a problem?' Luke asked. 'You don't have any elective patients on the list?'

'I do, but I've just been talking to a Mrs Melton and reassuring her. She's stable but has severe triple vessel disease. This is her third admission for surgery because she's been bumped off the list for urgent cases on the last two occasions.'

'Has she had a major infarct? An arrest?'

'No.'

'Come and look at Roger's films and then we can discuss it. Have you got viewing facilities in your office?'

She did, but Anna was aware of a strong reluctance to take Luke there. She had chosen not to take over his office in his absence and her space was relatively small. It was also the most personal space she had here at work.

She was already a little too aware of this man. His size and reputation and…and whatever it was that was exerting a tugging sensation on something emotional. Not to mention the danger that frisson of potential attraction had represented. She didn't want him invading a personal space. Not yet. Not until she felt a lot more confident in her interactions with him and that wasn't going to be until she'd resolved the dilemma she was in.

'The seminar room's closer. Where we hold the departmental meetings.'

'Of course. Have you got the time now?'

'Yes. I've finished the ward round.'

The round Luke had been supposed to join her for, but if he noticed any reprimand in her dry tone he gave no indication of it. He led the way down the corridor, his pace fast enough to keep Anna a half step behind. The hint of asymmetry in the way he moved had become a noticeable limp by the time they reached the lifts but Luke didn't pause. He pushed open the fire-stop doors and headed up the stairs.

Commenting on something as personal, not to mention physical, as the aftermath of his injury seemed inappropriate. In the same ball park as asking Charlotte if she was pregnant, and this wasn't remotely like the far more social setting of the hospital canteen with its 'time out' from work atmosphere. This was work and Luke's focus was entirely professional. He had no difficulty using the computerised system to bring the images from the catheter laboratory onto the large screen in the meeting room.

'As you can see, there's a seventy to eighty per cent stenosis on the left anterior descending and diffuse disease over a significant segment of the vessel. And that's not all. There's a critical stenosis in the circumflex. Here…see?'

'Yes.' Anna watched and listened. It was quite obvious that Roger was in more urgent need of surgery than her Mrs Melton. As the head of department, Luke would have been within his rights to simply order her to juggle lists but instead he was taking the time to put all the information in front of her, presumably with the intention of giving her the opportunity to make the call.

Exactly the way they should be interacting as colleagues. There was every reason to take a moment to admire the way he was dealing with the situation but there really shouldn't have been any space in Anna's head to be so aware of the way Luke moved his hands as he spoke. Of how elegant those movements were for those large hands with their clever, tapered fingers.

It was quite reasonable to appreciate the way he spoke so clearly too and the transparent speed with which his mind worked, but that didn't excuse the enjoyment Anna found she was getting from the timbre of that deep voice. She brushed off the visceral reactions. So he was intelligent and articulate. She should have expected nothing else in someone who had beaten her in a job application.

But perhaps that underlying awareness of him as a

person and not simply a surgeon made her more aware of his physical issues. When they had finished coming to a mutually agreeable compromise on theatre lists, which would see Mrs Melton staying on as an inpatient until her surgery could be scheduled, Luke stood up. His face was grim and he blinked with slow deliberation, as though he was in pain but determined to ignore it. Or switch it off. The action took Anna straight back to their time in Theatre that morning and she knew she couldn't avoid broaching the subject.

'How's your leg?' she found herself asking. 'I understand you suffered a fairly serious injury?'

'I survived.' Luke's tone told her it wasn't a welcome subject for discussion. 'It's improving all the time.' His stare was expressionless. 'Why do you ask?'

Anna had to fight back the urge to apologise for asking a personal question. His eyes were so blue. So intense. No way could she simply dismiss that sharp squeezing sensation occurring deep in her belly. It might have been a very long time since she'd experienced a shaft of desire but it was all too easy to recognise. She looked away.

'I've taken on a position as your assistant. If you have problems that I could help with, please don't hesitate to tell me.'

Luke made an incredulous sound, as though Anna would be incapable of giving him any assistance. That she had no idea what she was talking about. The sound rankled. She looked up to meet his gaze again.

'If, for example, you find it hard to stay on your feet for a long theatre session.'

A corner of his mouth lifted. Just a fraction. A sardonic twist but enough of a curl for Anna to realise she had yet to see Luke smile. He certainly wasn't about to now. His expression was anything but friendly or relaxed. Her heart skipped a beat and then sped up but it was too late to swallow any words that had been spoken and try to get back onto safe ground.

She had seen his pain when Luke knew how good he was at hiding it, and it seemed like he was exposing a physical flaw. Almost as bad as that loss of focus in Theatre that morning had been. Anna had been the only person to pick up on that, as well.

He'd barely met the woman and yet it felt like she was inside a very personal space. As for offering to help with his problems. Ha! She didn't know anything.

No one here did.

And yet the idea was appealing. To have someone in his corner who was prepared to listen even if they couldn't begin to understand.

To have someone to hold at night…

Whoa! Where the hell had that come from?

Luke could manage being alone. He had to. Just as well he'd learned to bury the kind of emotional involvement that could make reality too hard to deal with. He might be back in a very different reality now but the ability to remain detached at some level was just as important. More important, maybe, given that he felt the despair of a meaningless existence pressing in on him from all sides.

He was looking into a future that had only one bright

spot. His work. And Anna was trying to undermine it. Something like fear made him straighten and defend himself by attacking.

'Are you suggesting I'm physically incapable of doing my job?' He had her pinned with his gaze. 'Hoping that it might prove too much and I'll quietly go away and let you take over again?'

He saw her eyes widen and felt a flash of remorse at being so harsh. He also heard the swift intake of her breath but he didn't give her time to speak. He couldn't afford to back down. Admitting defeat wasn't something Luke Davenport did willingly.

'This is my home,' he continued. 'Where I live and where I work. Where my future is. I'm back and I have no desire to go anywhere else.'

Which one of them was he trying to convince here?

'I wasn't suggesting anything.' Anna's tone was clipped and very cool. 'Maybe I was hoping there might be a satisfactory explanation for what happened in Theatre this morning. For your slow response to a significant bleed.'

A moment's silence hung heavily between them. Not that Luke had any intention of denying the accusation or trying to excuse himself.

'I lost focus,' he admitted simply. 'It won't happen again.'

He saw the way her features softened at his honesty. She wanted to believe him. But he could also see confusion in the depths of those astonishing green eyes. What had he been thinking, attacking her for asking what had been a perfectly reasonable question? No wonder she felt torn.

'Are you intending to report the incident?'

She held his gaze. She had courage, this woman.

'Would you?'

'Yes,' Luke responded without hesitation. 'Sloppy performance is never acceptable.'

Anna tilted her head in agreement but said nothing. They left the meeting room in silence. There seemed to be nothing more to be said.

So that was that. The subject was out in the open and he'd all but told her he expected it to be reported. All he had to do now was wait until someone, presumably Albert White or one of the other hospital administrators, came to have a little chat with him.

It didn't happen the next day.

If anything, Luke got the impression that Anna hadn't said anything at all about him that wasn't complimentary, judging by comments made in the departmental meeting the next morning.

More than one member of the cardiology and cardiothoracic surgical staff said admiring things about Colin Herbert's surgery. The congratulatory buzz when Roger's case came up during the discussion on revised theatre lists was actually embarrassing.

Luke cut it short. 'I had some very able assistance from Dr Bartlett,' he told the group briskly. 'And she's the one with the real work to do with his CABG today.'

That coronary artery bypass grafting was well under

way by the time Luke left his administrative tasks and headed for the theatre suite. He didn't don a gown or mask and enter the theatre. Instead, he slipped quietly into the observation deck and sat, probably unnoticed, in the far corner. You could see what was going on and hear what was being said and, if you wanted, you could focus on one person and make judgments about their ability. Their personality even. That was why he had requested that the space be closed during his surgery yesterday. An unusual case would have attracted as many people as could have squeezed in here and, on some level, he would have been aware of it.

Anna wasn't aware of him. He could watch every movement and hear every comment. He could feel the time and care she took with every meticulous stitch as she took the veins harvested from Roger's legs and used them to make new conduits to take blood to where it was needed in the heart muscle. Her voice was as calm as her movements. She was polite in her requests and prepared to discuss anything with the anaesthetist or bypass machine technicians. She spoke frequently to her registrar as well, asking questions and explaining her own decisions. A natural teacher, then.

With a voice that he couldn't imagine getting tired of listening to. Not when it was coupled with a brain that was clearly as focused but as flexible as her hands were. An impressive mix.

He stayed where he was only until the blood flow in the new coronary arteries was deemed acceptable and Roger was successfully taken off bypass. He would see Anna again today and maybe she would let him know who she had decided to speak to. He couldn't pre-empt her by speaking to someone himself because that would make it a bigger issue than it actually was. It wasn't going to happen again because he was in control now. Of every waking moment, at least.

But nothing more was said about it despite their paths crossing frequently when they shared a busy outpatient clinic and more than once during ward rounds and departmental meetings. By Friday, both Colin and Roger were on the ward and recuperating well and finally, late that afternoon, Luke got a call to the office of St Piran's chief executive officer.

'Luke.' Albert White shook one hand and gripped Luke's other shoulder at the same time. 'I'm so sorry this has taken so long. It's been a hectic week that included a day or two in London. Welcome back. It's good to see you.'

'It's good to see you too.' And it was, except that he could feel the distance between them. He'd been on another planet since he had last worked here. But Albert was a familiar face. Part of the anchor that Luke hoped to use to stabilise his life.

'How's the family?'

'All well when I last heard any news.'

'I was astonished to hear that your parents had taken off to New Zealand, of all places. I hear they're living on a military base in North Island?'

'They are indeed. Dad's taken an administrative position. He calls it a semi-retirement but I can't see him ever not being full-time army.'

'No. And your older brother?'

'Currently in Australia. Helping train their SAS.'

Albert shook his head. 'Army family through and through. At least we've got one of the Davenport boys back again.'

'Yes.' The word was clipped. Luke didn't want to discuss the 'Davenport boy' who would never make it back.

There was a moment's silence, which seemed appropriate, and when Albert spoke again his tone was more serious, acknowledging so many things that were not going to be said.

'How's the leg?'

'Oh, you know. Still attached. Still works. I'm not complaining.'

Albert chuckled. 'Works pretty well from what I've been hearing. What's with the commando techniques in the canteen? Leaping tall buildings on the agenda, too?'

Luke summoned a smile. 'I don't think so.'

'Well done, anyway. I hear the chap's doing really well.'

'He is. Dr Bartlett did a quadruple bypass on him. She's an excellent surgeon.'

'She is indeed.' The glance Luke received held a hint of relief. Any awkward subjects were being left well behind. 'So things are working out, then? You two going to be able to work as a team?'

Luke couldn't detect even a hint that the CEO might be fishing for any confessions regarding a bumpy start. Maybe he should say something about it himself but if Anna had chosen not to, perhaps he should respect her decision. Albert didn't seem to notice that his silence was covering a moment of confusion.

'Not that I expected any problems, but it was good to hear Anna singing your praises the other day. A pericardectomy, I hear?'

'Um...yes. First case. What did she say?'

'That you did the entire procedure off bypass. That she was delighted to have the opportunity to learn something new.'

About the procedure? Or about him?

This meeting was nothing more than touching base. A welcome home.

'Come and have dinner some time soon. Joan would love to catch up.'

'Sure. Maybe when I've had time to find my feet properly.' Luke hoped his vague acceptance would not seem rude but he wasn't ready to get drawn into a segment of the St Piran's community that knew his family so well. He wasn't here because of the family connection. He was here because he'd had nowhere else to go.

Besides, he was getting into a routine now. An icy swim in the ocean at daybreak to chase away the night's demons. As many hours as possible focused entirely on his job and then exercise and work-related reading until he was hopefully exhausted enough to sleep for more than a few hours. He didn't want to tamper with what seemed to be working. Or remind himself of the past, which would only emphasise too clearly how different life was now. Control was paramount.

Control could be undermined by confusion, however.

Anna had had a whole week to decide how to present her concerns about his skills but she hadn't done so.

Why not?

Not that Luke wasn't grateful but he was definitely puzzled. She'd agreed that the matter should be reported. That sloppy performance wasn't acceptable. And yet she had apparently accepted his.

Why?

He would have spoken to her about it before leaving work that day but it was late and she had already gone. It wasn't hard to use his influence to find her contact details but Luke discovered that she was living well along the windy coast road that led to Penhally.

A phone call to thank her for making his first week back smoother than it might have otherwise been seemed too impersonal. What he said might even be taken the wrong way—tacit approval for not reporting the incident perhaps. Taking a fifteen- or twenty-minute drive to what was quite possibly only a small collection of dwellings and knocking on her door after dark was a long way too far towards the other end of the spectrum, however. Far too personal. Why was he even considering it?

It didn't seem nearly as inappropriate on Saturday morning. Especially as the world in general seemed a brighter place. Days and days of grey skies and inter-mittent rain had been blown inland by a stiff sea breeze and the sun was making a determined effort to raise the temperature by at least a degree or two. The surf had been high enough that morning to make his swim an adrenaline rush, and his leg hadn't collapsed under him when he'd attempted a slow jog on the softer sand.

Yes. For the first time since arriving back, Luke felt that things were a little less bleak. Some time out on a day like this to drive up to Penhally and revisit old haunts was an attractive idea. He might have intended to wait until Monday to give Anna the excellent article on restrictive cardiomyopathy he'd come across in one of the journals he'd been reading until the early hours of that morning but if it was in the car, he'd have the perfect excuse to drop in at her house on his way past if he chose to.

He did choose to.

Maybe because the signpost to the lane she lived on was so easy to spot. Or perhaps because the house he found at her address was so unlike what he might have expected. Not even a house. More like a cottage with its latticed windows and some kind of evergreen creeper scrambling along the faded shingles of its roof. The small garden was overgrown and…it had a picket fence, for heaven's sake!

If someone had asked him where he thought Dr Bartlett would be living, he would have imagined a modern apartment. Streamlined and minimalist. Devoid of personality—hers or its own. This cottage probably had tourists stopping to take its picture and a name somewhere under the tangled, prickly branches obscuring half the fence. Bay View Cottage perhaps, given the glorious sweep of Penhally Bay on display. It was only a short walk down the hill to get to a beach and, given the rocky coves he had noticed just before turning off the main road, the coastline was due to provide one of those gems that surfers searched for.

Sure enough, when he left the car and went a little further uphill towards the front door of the cottage, he could see a stretch of white sand beyond the boulders. This cottage might be rundown but it was sitting on valuable land. Any closer to Penhally or St Piran and it would be worth an absolute fortune. Was that why Anna had chosen it? As an investment?

That made far more sense than a desire to inhabit what had to feel like an alien space. Having come to terms with the apparent contradiction, Luke was now hesitant in knocking on her door. Had he passed a letterbox? He could leave the article in there and then explain it on Monday.

He might have done exactly that if it hadn't been for the sudden loud noise from inside the cottage. A crashing sound not dissimilar to the one he'd heard in the canteen earlier in the week.

No scream followed the sound but he could hear the dismay in Anna's voice.

'Oh…no!'

CHAPTER FOUR

'ANNA?' Luke didn't bother knocking. He tried the doorhandle and found it turned, so he shoved the door open. 'Are you all right?'

There was no response. Cautiously, Luke advanced along the narrow hallway. He could hear Anna's voice again. It was much quieter now. Soft and soothing.

'It's all right,' she was saying. 'Poor baby, you gave yourself a big fright that time, didn't you?'

Maybe he was in the wrong house.

'Anna?'

'Who's there?'

'Me,' Luke said as he stepped into a doorway on his right.

'Luke? Good grief! What on earth are you doing here?'

She sounded surprised. No, more like appalled. Luke opened his mouth but no words emerged. This was Anna?

She was sprawled on the floor, her arms around a large dog that was virtually in her lap and making enthusiastic attempts to lick her face. There were newspapers spread around them both, a collection of paintpots and an aluminium stepladder lying on its side.

'I was just on my way to Penhally. I heard the crash.'

'From the road?'

'No...I...er...had an article I wanted to give you.' It was weirdly hard to string a coherent sentence together so Luke gave up. He stared at Anna instead, trying to take in the faded, ripped denim jeans she was wearing. The paint-stained jumper. The soft waves of her loose hair that reached her shoulders. Those amazing green eyes that were staring at him in utter bewilderment right now.

Luke dropped his gaze. The dog was staring at him too. Warily. Pressing itself further into Anna's arms and visibly shaking.

'What's wrong with the dog?'

'He's scared.'

'Of what?'

'You.'

She should probably be scared herself, Anna thought. A large man she hardly knew had just come into her house uninvited. Into her bedroom. Well, it would be her bedroom again when she'd finished renovating it. Right now it was just a mess.

Like her head.

Luke was wearing some jeans that were probably as old as her own. He had a black woollen jumper on with the sleeves pushed up to reveal bare forearms. His hair looked windswept and there was a tension about him that suggested he could leap into action at any moment. To save a life or rescue a damsel in distress.

He'd thought she was in distress.

He'd come into her house to rescue her.

And here he was, looking rugged and grim and… and…gorgeous.

Thank goodness she had her arms full of warm, shivery puppy. She hugged him more closely.

'He's a rescue puppy,' she told Luke. 'I've only had him a couple of weeks. My neighbours, Doug and June Gallagher, own a farm and they found him in the creek. In a sack. They would have kept him but they've already got a lot of dogs and he was terrified of Doug. June reckons he's been badly treated by a man.'

'So you took him? You're going to keep him?'

He sounded as though she'd just informed him that she intended to fly to the moon. Anna almost laughed but she felt absurdly close to tears. This wasn't supposed to happen and the earth had just tilted beneath her feet.

Dr Bartlett didn't do feminine or personal. She didn't do attraction to her colleagues.

Mr Davenport wasn't supposed to meet Anna. And there were no rules about Anna feeling attracted to a man. There hadn't needed to be for too long to remember.

This was threatening to do her head in completely so she dragged her gaze away from the towering figure by the doorway and buried her face in the expanse of woolly hair in her arms.

'You're all right,' she soothed. 'He's not going to hurt

you.' The reassurance seemed to bounce back at her and it sounded good. The warmth and smell of her dog was good too. Comforting. Anna raised her head to find that Luke was closer. He had dropped to a crouch and he was looking at the puppy.

'What is he, exactly?'

'We're not sure. The vet thinks he's about four months old. She reckons he's part poodle because of the wispy hair. Or maybe there's some wolfhound in there. A designer dog gone wrong, we decided, and that's why nobody wanted him.'

'A poodle and a wolfhound?' Luke seemed to be making a valiant attempt to imagine such an unlikely combination.

He looked intrigued and, with his focus so completely on the puppy, Anna got the chance to look at him.

He looked so different. Was it the casual clothing or the fact that he was here, in her home? No. It was more than that. The grimness she was getting accustomed to in his face had lightened. The puppy had distracted him and caught his interest. Was it possible it might even amuse him? Make him smile?

Anna really wanted to see Luke smile.

'It could be possible,' she said, her tone deadpan. 'As long as they'd had a staircase handy.'

Luke's gaze flicked up. He gave a huff of sound that could have passed for laughter but there was no matching curl to his lips. Instead, there was an incredulous expression in those amazingly blue eyes. As though he was seeing someone he didn't recognise at all.

Because she'd cracked a fairly pathetic joke?

Or because of the reference to parentage? Canine sex.

Sex...

Oh, Lord! Anna closed her eyes. She couldn't hold the puppy any more tightly because she could feel his ribs too well already. Poor thing, he'd had a hard time in his short life so far. At least he'd stopped shaking, though.

'What's his name?'

'I can't decide. Every time I come up with one, I try using it but it doesn't feel right. Herbert was my last effort.' To her dismay, Anna realised that Luke would make the connection. That the surname of his first surgical case had seemed like a good name for her pet. How unprofessional would that seem?

Probably not as bad as talking about dogs mating on the stairs.

And did it really matter? This wasn't work. It was home. Different.

Confusing.

'He's got big feet.'

'Mmm. He's growing fast, too. I think that's why he's so clumsy. He got underneath my ladder and tried to turn around and that's how it tipped over.'

Luke was silent for a moment but then he looked at Anna and she saw that the grim lines were still missing from his face. There was a hint of amusement there but it was lapped by a sadness she could feel all the way to her bones.

'I knew someone once,' he said quietly. 'He grew

too fast and looked a bit goofy, with his hands and feet always looking a bit too big for him, and he was such a clumsy kid we all called him "Crash". He grew up, though. Into the strongest, bravest guy I knew.'

He was talking about someone important. A fellow soldier, maybe? Someone he had loved who had died? Why was he telling her something so personal?

'I heard a crash,' Luke added. 'That's why I came inside.'

Anna swallowed. Luke's lips were moving. Slowly but surely they were curling into a smile. A real smile. One that changed his whole face, deepening those furrows to his nose but adding a sparkle to his eyes that made him seem so much more…alive.

It faded all too quickly and instinct told Anna that she had been given a glimpse of something normally well hidden. The real Luke? A letting down of some guard that not many people got to see, anyway. A real smile and he had chosen to bestow it on her.

Something deep inside her was captured. Something huge and warm and wonderful. Anna knew she would remember this moment for ever.

'It's a great name,' she said softly. 'Crash?'

The big pup wriggled in her arms and looked up at her. He tried to prick up his ears but they were too heavy and stuck out sideways. Liquid brown eyes were full of trust and a long tail gave a thump of approval.

'Crash it is,' Anna announced. She smiled up at Luke. 'Hey, thanks.'

'No problem.' But the smile had well and truly vanished from Luke's face and he stood up.

He was leaving. Something oddly like panic made Anna's heart skip a beat.

'Would…um…would you like a coffee or something?'

'No. You're busy and I'm on my way to Penhally. I'll leave the journal.' He dropped it onto a chest of drawers by the door. 'There's a good review of restrictive pericarditis in there. I thought you'd be interested.'

The reminder of work was timely. She had to work with Luke. Work and home couldn't mix. Professional and personal couldn't mix. What had she been thinking, blathering on about her rescue puppy? She scrambled to her feet.

'Thank you.' There wasn't a thing Anna could do about what she was wearing or what her home looked like, but she could summon as much as she could of Dr Bartlett. Lifting her chin, she could feel the shell of professionalism beginning to enclose her. Protect her.

'That was thoughtful of you. I did do as much research as possible when Colin was admitted but it might well be something I didn't come across.' She looked pointedly at the door. 'I'll see you out, shall I?'

'No need.' Luke turned to leave but then paused. 'Actually, there was something else.'

'What?'

The hesitation was almost imperceptible. 'You don't seem to have reported that incident from Colin Herbert's surgery. Or not that I've heard about.'

'No. I decided not to.'

'Why not?'

'Because you said it wouldn't happen again.' *And I*

believe you, Anna added silently, looking away so that he wouldn't see any crack in her newly formed shell. *I trust you.*

Luke didn't say anything. After a long moment he broke the eye contact and gave a single nod.

'Thank you,' he said, the words somewhat curt.

And with that he was gone.

Anna stood very still. She listened to the sound of her front door closing. And then the sound of a car engine starting up and a vehicle moving away.

Even then she didn't move. Standing like this, she could feel that shell cracking and falling away, exposing something tender. She could almost feel Luke's presence still in the room. She could still see that amazing smile.

And, heaven help her, but she wanted to hang onto it for just a little longer.

The sound pierced his eardrums, his body rocking from the force of the impact. Through the painful buzzing that came in the wake of the explosion he could hear the cursing of his companions. The screaming.

'Get out!'

'Get down!'

The ping of bullets ricocheting off the metal of their armoured vehicle came faster. An unearthly shriek from someone who had been struck ripped through the sounds of chaos.

Of panic.

He could feel the heat now. Not just the normal strength-sapping attack of the desert sun but the kind of heat that could sear flesh. A lick of flames that could bring death with far more suffering than a bullet.

The dust was thick. Getting thicker. The chop-chop-chop of a nearby helicopter was stirring the ground. Bringing assistance, but it was going to be too late. It was getting hard to breathe. He could smell the dust. Taste it. Dust mixed with blood to become a suffocating soup.

His companions needed help. The driver was slumped over the wheel, others bleeding. The young paramedic was crying. Facing death and terrified.

He could feel that terror reach out and invade his own mind. He was frozen. Becoming aware of the pain in his own leg. Terrible, unimaginable pain. He couldn't breathe. Couldn't move...

They were his brothers, these men. All of them. And he was going to watch them die.

He was about to die himself. He could see the enemy emerging from the clouds of dust, their bodies shrouded with the clothing of the desert, their faces disguised by heavy, dark beards. He could see the cruel muzzles of the weapons they were pointing at him but he couldn't move.

Couldn't even breathe...

The sound of his own scream was as choked as the air around him.

Arghhh!

The desperate, strangled sound that finally escaped his throat was, mercifully, enough to wake him. Even as his eyes snapped open, Luke was throwing back the covers on his bed, swinging his legs over the edge so that it was a continuous, flowing movement that had him sitting, hunched on the side of his bed, his head in his hands as he struggled to drag in a breath.

The feeling of suffocation—of imminent death—was still there.

He couldn't afford to stay still. He knew what he had to do.

The warm, fleecy trackpants were draped over the end of his bed. His shoes were right there to shove his feet into. Running shoes.

It wasn't real, he reminded himself as he pulled the laces tight. It hadn't even happened that way. He had never seen the enemy. He had been able to move. To drag his companions to shelter behind the vehicle as the helicopter hovered overhead. He had staunched the flow of blood and kept airways patent. None of them had died.

But the nightmare was always the same.

He was watching his own brother die. Feeling the fear. Unable to help.

Matthew. Mattie. The clumsy kid with the happy grin who'd had to tag along with his older brothers and do everything they did. Crash.

Oh…God! What on earth had possessed him to suggest that Anna Bartlett use that precious nickname for that skinny, ridiculous-looking dog?

What was she doing with a dog in the first place? How could she keep a pet that needed so much time and love with the kind of hours he already knew she put into her career? She did love it. He had seen that in the way she held it and soothed it. The way her face had brightened with joy at finding a name she really liked.

He had now pulled on the coat hanging by the door. Within seconds he was lurching down the rough track that led to the beach. It didn't matter that it was the middle of the night. His night vision was better than most people's and he was getting very familiar with this route.

Maybe it didn't matter that he'd given his brother's name away to a dog. It wasn't as though he was planning to visit that unlikely little cottage again and they were hardly likely to be chatting about it at work because they never talked about anything remotely personal.

In fact, he was having enormous difficulty reconciling the woman who was his assistant head of department with the person he'd found on the floor of that room cuddling...Crash.

Sea air so fresh that it bit into his lungs and numbed his face barely penetrated his awareness. He could feel the shifting of sand beneath his feet and hear the sound of the surf crashing in right beside him but his mind had fastened onto that picture of Anna on the floor.

With her hair in a soft tumble of curls. Her arms holding a vulnerable creature. Comforting it. Protecting it. He had felt the love. That was what had hit him in such a poignant place. What had reminded him of the kid brother who had never come home.

He'd reached the end of the beach now. Turned to go home again. He might even manage another couple of hours' sleep before daylight came. Usually, by the time he had done this punishing circuit, the nightmare had faded.

And it was only then that Luke realised he hadn't had to fight the remnants of that terrible dream the way he always did. From even before he'd left his house, all he'd been thinking about was Anna.

Or rather the two Annas.

Now that he'd seen her at home, he'd be able to recognise what he'd missed at work so far, surely? Some signs that hidden beneath that power-dressing, uber-professional, calm, cool and collected surgeon was… the most compelling woman he'd ever met in his life.

He was watching her. And he was puzzled.

Anna could feel the unasked questions hanging in the air between them.

Had it been real? Had he really found her wearing scruffy clothes, with her hair in an untidy mop, living in a shambolic house with a rather large and definitely unhygienic animal? Did she really have a sense of humour?

It was easy to emanate denial because that wasn't who she was at work. She'd also had years of practice in deflecting any line of communication that threatened to become personal. Patients could be so useful.

Like first thing on Monday morning when the anticipation of seeing Luke for the first time since he'd been in her house was making Anna feel more nervous than she had since her junior years as a doctor when she'd had to perform in front of some eminent consultant.

Luke hadn't looked any different.

'Good morning, Anna. How are you?'

'Very good.' She wasn't going to return the query. Luke wasn't one of her patients.

'How's—?'

Crash? She knew that was coming next and she had to stamp on that topic of conversation before it could start. The temptation to talk about her puppy was too strong. She wanted to tell Luke that Crash had learned to sit. That he had stepped on an overturned lid of a paint tin and made a giant pawprint on her wooden floor and it had been such a perfect signature she'd been reluctant to clean it off. Would that make him smile again? She couldn't afford to find out.

'Mrs Melton?' She interrupted smoothly. 'Finally getting to Theatre, thank goodness. I know it's your slot this morning but I'm more than happy to do the surgery. Or assist.'

'It's a long time since I did a CABG.' He knew exactly what she'd done in changing the subject. She could see him taking it on board that her private life was not up for discussion. Could see the focus as he let it go. 'Might be a good idea if you assisted.'

Was this a challenge? To see if she did trust him to operate safely on his own? A sideways glance as Luke fell into step beside her made her notice that his hair was damp. Just out of the shower? That image was disturbing. Anna dragged in a breath, only to catch a whiff of something fresh and clean. Like a sea breeze. Good heavens, she could almost imagine Luke had just been for a dip in the ocean. In the middle of winter? Who would be that crazy?

Her senses were threatening to override her train of thought. What had he asked? Oh, yes… Was he offering her the opportunity to observe and judge his capabilities in Theatre or might he want her company for an entirely different reason?

'I can't imagine that you'll have any problems,' she said calmly. 'But I am a little concerned about the quality of her saphenous veins. I'm wondering about harvesting the lesser saphenous or possibly upper extremity veins, in which case I could probably be more helpful than a registrar.'

Your choice, she threw at him silently. I'm available.

He simply nodded. 'Excellent. Have we got time to review her films? I'd like to have a word with her as well and introduce myself.'

'Sure. I'm heading to the ward right now.'

Mrs Melton was thrilled to hear that the head of department would be doing her surgery. She beamed at Luke.

And he smiled back. Anna was watching and she could see that it was a purely professional sort of smile. It still softened his face and reminded her of when he'd smiled at her but it wasn't anything like the same. It didn't make his face come alive. It didn't come anywhere near his eyes.

She found herself watching him just as intently as she suspected he was watching her. She saw him smile in greeting colleagues. She saw him smile in satisfaction when he was informed of how well a patient was doing. He even smiled directly at her on one occasion. All mechanical gestures. Done because it was expected and it would be impolite not to.

Anna wanted to know what those shadows in his eyes were from and why they were dense enough to smother real smiles. She wanted to know who the real 'Crash' had been and why talking about him had cracked open the armour Luke wore.

For that was what it was. Anna could recognise it because she had her own. By the end of their second week of working together, she had the weirdest sensation that they were like actors. Playing their part on stage but with each of them knowing perfectly well that the role the other was playing was not the real person.

Even more disturbing, Anna was becoming obsessed with wondering about the real Luke. The man that had really smiled at her. Why did he come to work each day with his hair damp and smelling of the sea? The temptation to ask was becoming unbearable. Or maybe it was the desire to touch his hair...to press her face against it and see if that was where the impression of the outdoors and punishing exercise came from.

She wanted to know why he refused to admit that his leg hurt even when it was obvious it did. When there were lines of pain in his face at the end of a long day that she could feel herself. She could smooth those lines away. With her fingers. Or her lips. If he let her.

If she let herself...

The intrigue refused to go away. The pull became stronger but Anna was fighting it. Anyone seeing Mr Davenport and Dr Bartlett together would see nothing more than a purely professional association. Reserved but respectful. Discussions might be animated but they were only about their patients. Their work. Current research. New technologies. Endless topics to talk about.

A seemingly endlessly fascinating man to talk to.

If it wasn't for the puzzle that Anna represented, Luke might have been tempted to admit defeat.

Every day was the same. Enclosed within the walls of an institution that sometimes felt like it was filled with people who had created their own illnesses. Heavy smokers who seemed surprised that they'd had heart attacks because of their damaged blood vessels. Morbidly obese people who still expected lifesaving surgery.

What for? So they could carry on with their meaningless lives? Lie in bed and keep eating junk food?

'I'm not going to operate on Walter Robson,' he informed Anna after a ward round late that week. 'I refuse to spend my time patching someone up just to give them longer to indulge in slow suicide by their appalling lifestyle choices.'

If he'd hoped to get under her skin with such a terse and controversial statement, he was disappointed.

'I agree he's a poor candidate for surgery,' she said calmly. 'Maybe that will be enough of an incentive for him to stop smoking and lose some weight. If we can reduce his level of heart failure and get his type-two diabetes and cellulitis under control, it will reduce the surgical risk.'

Luke almost exploded. Thumped the wall beside

them or walked away from his colleague. Told Anna what he was really thinking.

That she knew nothing about risk. Real risk—the kind that young, healthy people took for the benefit of their brothers-in-arms, if not for the much bigger human-rights issues. That patching them up was the kind of lifesaving surgery that had some meaning.

But that would open floodgates that had to remain shut. It would take Anna into a life that didn't exist for him any more except in his nightmares, and winning freedom from those nightmares was the hurdle he had to get through to survive.

He had discovered a new way of dealing with both the terrors of the night and the feeling of suffocation he could get ambushed by at work. He could distract himself by thinking about Anna. Just for a few seconds. Like a shot of some calm-inducing drug.

Her voice became a background hum as she talked about dealing with Walter Robson's anaemia and whether his chronic lung problems would improve if he carried through his vow to quit smoking.

Luke let his gaze stroke the sleek hair on top of Anna's head and then rest on the tight knot nestled at the nape of her neck. That clip thing would be easy enough to remove. The hair might still be twisted and squashed but he could bury his fingers in it and fluff it out until it bounced onto her shoulders.

His breath came out in a sigh. It was enough…the feeling of desperation was fading again.

'Luke?' Anna had caught the sigh. Fortunately, she

misinterpreted it. 'The decision has to be on medical grounds, not moral ones.'

'Of course.'

This wasn't the place to discuss the ethics of what represented a significant part of their careers. Much of the workload was genuine and worthwhile. He knew that. He used to get more than enough satisfaction from it.

Why did everything have to be so different now? So difficult?

And why couldn't he see what he knew was there—hiding behind the person Anna was within these walls?

She wouldn't let him. That was why. The boundaries had been marked and were being reinforced every time she changed the subject if he tried to talk about something personal, like the puppy he had named for her. Or had she even kept the name?

No wonder James had sounded puzzled back on his first day when they had been scrubbing in together. As though he had no idea of what Anna was like out of work hours.

Maybe Luke was the only person here who'd had a glimpse of that side of Anna.

He liked that notion.

He liked it a lot.

CHAPTER FIVE

'I'M HAPPY to cover Christmas Day.'

'So am I.' Luke's nod was matter-of-fact. 'Thanks, Anna. That's the holiday roster issues sorted, then. Let's get on with the rest of the agenda.'

Anna couldn't help but notice the look that passed between James and Charlotte Alexander, who were sitting together in this departmental meeting. No mistaking the look of relief. Joy even at the prospect of spending a special day together with no danger of being called in to work.

The movement of Charlotte's hand was probably unconscious. She seemed to be listening carefully to Luke as he introduced a new grading system for cardiac patients.

'It's hoped that this will be brought in nationwide to try and standardise criteria and address the increasing numbers of people that are dying while on waiting lists for surgery. We've been asked to implement this at St Piran's as of the first of January as part of a multi-centre trial, so your feedback is going to be important.'

Anna was listening, too, but she'd already read the proposal and she and Luke had discussed it at length.

It was hardly surprising that she caught that movement from Charlotte in her peripheral vision. A hand that gently smoothed the loose fabric of her top, gathering it up as it came to rest cupping her lower belly. There really was no doubt now that she was pregnant. It would be a special Christmas for them, wouldn't it, with the extra joy and dreams that came with knowing they were about to become a family?

'As far as degree of valvar dysfunction goes, we're staying with the New York Heart Association functional classes. As you can see, mild is class one and scores two. Severe is class three and scores fourteen. If there is coronary artery disease present as well, it puts it into class four and we can add ten to the overall score.'

Luke had the score sheets projected onto the wall. He was going to cover all the non-coronary revascularisation type of patients like valve replacements and then he'd run through the more complex scoring system for patients who had arterial disease. He was being clear and methodical and making sure everyone understood. People were nodding approvingly. A system like this could make prioritising people on the waiting lists much more straightforward.

Charlotte was one of those nodding. As though she would be only too happy to be filling in the score sheets on her patients and adding her comments to the feedback that would be required. But how long would she be around to be doing that?

It was all very well having secrets but it was also annoying. When were they planning to share the information and allow arrangements to be made for Charlotte's absence for maternity leave? For James to be covered at the time of the baby's arrival? For a new member of staff to be advertised for, if necessary?

No wonder there was such prejudice against women in top positions. Imagine if she was pregnant herself? Even if she worked up to the last possible moment and then took minimal maternity leave, the disruption to the department would still be huge.

Unthinkable. It always had been.

So why was she watching Charlotte surreptitiously right now instead of focusing on the information Luke was presenting? Wondering what her colleague was thinking and how she'd come to the conclusion that having a baby was more important than her career. What it might be like to feel a new life growing and moving within your own body. To face the enormous responsibility of caring for that baby when it was born.

The disturbing niggle was annoyance, not envy. Luke needed to know. He had quite enough on his plate settling back into running such a busy department and working the kind of hours he did with the extra stress of recovering from a major physical injury. Maybe it wasn't her place but Anna wanted to warn Luke. She could help him put arrangements into place to make sure they could cope with the inevitable disruptions.

Her gaze was on the head of department now. He was talking about the Canadian Cardiovascular Society's criteria for grading angina.

'The class is assigned after appropriate treatment, not at the time of admission or diagnosis.'

Luke stood tall but relaxed and his voice was clear

and authoritative. What was the X factor in the way he presented himself that got people on side so easily? Anna found herself biting back a smile. It certainly wasn't his warm and friendly countenance. He was always so serious, often looking grim, and he could be downright impatient with staff who couldn't get up to speed quickly enough. He was utterly closed off on a personal level and yet he drew everyone in.

Already this department felt more cohesive than it had under her own leadership. There was enthusiasm for all sorts of projects that might otherwise have been seen simply as more paperwork and stress. In the space of just a few short weeks they had a new rostering system in place, had been chosen for this pilot centre for an important national initiative and several new research projects had been kicked off.

Maybe that X factor was because of the sense that Luke was driven, despite—or perhaps because of—the physical challenges it now incorporated. Anyone could see how hard it was for him to be on his feet all day and keep up with such a demanding schedule. This job was his life and he was going to do it so well that anyone who chose to get on board would have an unexpectedly satisfying ride.

And she was one of them. Funny how the resentment she'd felt at Luke returning to take his leading role in the department had faded so quickly. Perhaps it had been pushed away completely because she'd been watching him so carefully and the more she saw, the more compelling this man was becoming. Had she really thought she wouldn't learn from him? It wasn't just his technical excellence in Theatre. Apart from that momentary wobble on his first day back, Anna hadn't seen anything that would have undermined her opinion that he was one of the best in his field. It was rare for someone so good on the practical side to be so competent at administration, but Luke really seemed to enjoy the challenge of running a large department effectively.

Yes. The closer she could stay and work with Luke the more she could benefit. She wanted them to be a close team.

How close?

The odd question came from a part of her brain that was normally closed off at work. The kind of disruptive thought that had never been a problem in the past but, curiously, had started to plague her out-of-work hours lately. She couldn't distract herself easily right now either. She was trapped, motionless, and she had already been distracted by the people around her.

'Scores for the ability to work or give care are a little more subjective,' Luke was saying. 'Especially the middle category when it's threatened but not immediately.'

Anna's concentration was certainly threatened. She didn't need a sideways glance at the Alexanders to remind her of married couples amongst her colleagues. It happened all the time. Didn't they say that you were most likely to meet the person you were going to marry amongst the people you worked with?

It wasn't going to happen to her. The desire for a husband and family—if it had ever been there—had been dismissed long ago. About the time she'd discovered the passion she had for surgery and it had become obvious that if she was going to have any chance of getting to where she wanted to be, it had to be the only thing that mattered in her life.

Adopting a puppy had been extraordinary enough. A substitute baby? No. You couldn't leave a baby in the house for a helpful neighbour to collect and care for while you were at work. Or leave a pile of newspaper on the floor so you didn't have to get up in the middle of the night to deal with toileting issues. She still had to factor in collecting Crash every day from the yard he shared with June and Doug's dogs. To take him for a walk on the beach and spend time training and playing with him. To listen to the snuffles and odd whimpers in the night from his bed in the corner of his room. All in all, it was a major upheaval in her life. Not that she wasn't getting a lot of pleasure from it. And if it was a substitute child it was as close as she ever wanted to get, that was for sure.

No family, then. And what was the point of a husband if you weren't planning on having a family?

A partner was something different, however.

A lover.

At this point in the meeting Anna very uncharacteristically stopped listening to anything being said around her. She was watching Luke's hands as he shaped the size of whatever it was he was talking about. Strong, tanned, capable hands.

She couldn't stop herself imagining them running down the length of her spine. It would be no effort to fit the curve of her bottom into their grip and he would be able to pull her against his own body with no more than the slightest pressure. It would feel lean and hard, like his face.

And he would have turned that blinding focus onto her. Those incredible blue eyes would be on her face. On her lips as he dipped his head…slowly…to kiss her.

Oh…dear Lord… With a huge effort, Anna managed to tune back into her surroundings just as the meeting was wrapping up. People were closing diaries and starting to chat. Charlotte pushed back her chair and stood up.

'Just before you all go…'

The buzz of conversation died. Here we go, thought Anna, but the announcement wasn't what she expected.

'I've been involved in organising the staff Christmas function,' Charlotte said with a smile. 'It's in the canteen on the twenty-second, seven p.m., in case you haven't seen the flyers. There's going to be lots of nice food and plenty of non-alcoholic drinks if you're unlucky enough to be on duty. It's a chance for everybody to get together in the spirit of the season, so I hope you can all make it. Partners and families are welcome. There's going to be a Secret Santa. Bring a small gift and put it under the tree and then you'll get one yourself at the end of the night. Or just bring one for any children that might be there and if they're not needed they can go to the children's ward.'

Anna looked away from Charlotte. Towards Luke. Their senior cardiology registrar should be talking about her upcoming maternity leave, not a Christmas party. Luke had an odd expression on his face. As if he couldn't believe that something so trivial was being announced in a departmental meeting.

As though a party or celebrating Christmas was absolutely the last possible thing he would have any desire to do.

Did he ever relax? Let his guard down and enjoy something social?

Something intimate?

She gathered up her folder of papers and stepped around the table. Towards Luke. She couldn't stop herself. The wanderings of her mind during the meeting might be under control now, thank goodness, but they'd left an odd kind of physical yearning and it was like a magnet, pulling her towards Luke. She did her best to disguise it. Her professional mask was quite intact, on the outside at least.

'Good presentation,' she offered. 'I think we'll have full co-operation in the trial period.'

'Yes.' Luke was shutting down the program in his laptop. 'I'm hoping so.'

Anna's thoughts were tripping over each other. She had a strong urge to engineer a way to spend some time with Luke and it would be easy enough if she asked to discuss something professional, like the planned research project she was taking on to analyse post-operative infection rates in cardiac patients.

But something new and rather disturbing was happening. She could actually feel the war going on between her head and her heart. She didn't want a professional kind of interaction. She wanted…

Oh, help… Was she actually thinking of asking him for some kind of a date?

No, of course not. She didn't do work relationships. Of any kind. This was Anna getting rebellious, trying to claw her way through Dr Bartlett's armour. It simply wouldn't do.

Her thoughts might be running with the speed of light but she had been standing there for a shade too long judging by the quizzical set of Luke's eyebrows when he glanced up at her.

Anna was aware of the final staff members exiting the meeting room, including Charlotte. She hoped her smile was offhand.

'You planning to go to the Christmas party?'

'No. Are you?'

Anna couldn't look away. Her mouth wasn't going to wait for her brain to mull over what seemed to be a perfect compromise between professional and personal. It just widened its smile and opened to say something extraordinary.

'I will if you will.'

Something flickered in Luke's eyes. Astonishment? Interest?

'I don't like parties,' he said.

'Neither do I,' Anna agreed. She could have left it there. What was wrong with her today? 'But this is a staff function. It's polite to put in an appearance. Especially for HODs.'

Luke was frowning now. 'You think I should go?'

'I think there must be a lot of people in St Piran's who would enjoy the chance to welcome you back.

Good relations both within and between departments are useful.'

Luke grunted. He looked up as the meeting door swung shut behind the last person. 'Did you know Charlotte Alexander's pregnant?'

Was he trying to change the subject? 'I guessed. How did you know?'

'She told me. We need to look at possible replacements amongst the registrars we have available. Or get in a locum.'

'Yes. How much time have we got?'

'We should look at getting it sorted next month.'

'It's going to be a busy start for the New Year. Which reminds me…' The rebellious part of Anna had finally been quelled. Maybe it was just as well Luke was so good at sticking to professional. 'I wanted to have a chat to you about the parameters for this infection study. How retrospective do you think we should make it? I've got my registrar primed to start digging through records.'

'Let's have a look at our diaries. We should be able to squeeze in a meeting. You can bring anyone else you want involved along as well.'

'I will.'

Not that it was likely to help, Anna thought, her heart sinking. If she was capable of having totally inappropriate thoughts about her boss when there were a dozen or more members of the department around her, what hope did she have by flanking herself with a couple of junior doctors?

She needed to escape. To get home and get a grip. Heading purposefully away from work, Anna barely registered the huge Christmas tree in the hospital foyer with its twinkling, coloured lights but she thought of it again as she turned her car towards her cottage.

This was the silly season, she reminded herself. Everything would settle down, including whatever it was that making her feel so...unsettled.

The Christmas party was well under way by the time Anna managed to get there.

The canteen was noisy and crowded, warm with the inviting aroma of hot, savoury food and people determined to enjoy themselves. There were bright balloons and streamers and huge, shiny silver stars hanging from light fittings. There were flashes of even brighter colours as well. Where on earth had people found their accessories?

A trio of nurses wore headbands with big yellow plastic stars that flashed on and off. Steffie, the staff nurse from the cardiology ward, had earrings and a matching necklace that had red and green twinkling lights. Anna spotted a set of glowing reindeer horns and Santa hats made of shiny red sequins. She passed a registrar who wore a large badge. Rudolph's nose was flashing and a tinny version of a Christmas song could be heard competing with the background carol music in the room. More than one person rolled their eyes as the owner of the badge reached to push the nose as the song finished.

'Not again, Peter. Please.'

A very young-looking nurse was dressed in a naughty Santa costume, the rim of white fluff on the bottom of her dress barely reaching her thighs. Anna groaned inwardly. This really wasn't her scene at all. She knew she must look as out of place as she felt. Prim, in her skirt and jacket. It was getting harder to respond to the smiles and greetings of people when she was completely sober and they were clearly making the most of the party drinks available to those not on duty.

She felt like an island. A rather barren, rocky one, moving through a sea of festivity. She had to be the only person there who didn't have at least a string of tinsel tied on to signal that they belonged.

And then she spotted Luke.

Another island. Even rockier, given the tight body language and an almost desperate look on his face as Anna edged through the partygoers to join the group of familiar faces.

'Anna. Merry Christmas!'

'Thanks, Ben. Hi, Lucy.' Anna smiled at Ben's wife, her gaze dropping to the bundle snuggled against the front of her body with a sling. 'I heard you'd had another baby. Congratulations.'

'Thanks. Yes, this is Kitty. She's ten weeks old now.'

A small girl was peeping out from behind Lucy's legs.

'This must be Annabel.' Anna searched her memory. 'It's her birthday soon, isn't it?'

'Christmas Eve.'

'Just as well she's a party animal.' Ben grinned. 'She's loving it.' He was holding Annabel's little brother, Josh, but he reached down to touch his daughter. 'Tell

Dr Anna how old you're going to be on your birthday, darling.'

'Free,' Annabel said shyly. Ben tickled her head and made her giggle.

Who could help smiling at the joyous sound? Glancing up, Anna saw Luke's lips curve and it was, almost, the kind of smile he'd given her that day. Poignant. Real.

But not happy. The sound of laughter around them was virtually constant and Anna wanted to hear Luke laugh. To see and hear him forget himself in a moment of happiness. The feeling that he might never do that was heartbreaking. She tore her gaze away swiftly. Towards another smiling face.

But Josh O'Hara's smile looked forced and the petite, blonde woman standing beside him wasn't smiling at all. She was draining a glass of wine.

The A and E consultant noticed the direction of her gaze. 'Anna? You won't have met my wife. This is Rebecca.'

Charlotte and James Alexander joined the group, along with another man whom Anna recognised as Nick Tremayne, head of the Penhally medical centre.

'Has anyone seen Kate? I told her to pop in while I was upstairs visiting my patient but I can't find her anywhere in this crowd.'

'Nick!' Ben stepped closer to the newcomers. 'So you got in to see Mrs Jennings?'

'Yes. The surgery went well. She should be up and about with her new hip in no time. Home for the new year.'

'How's Jem?' Anna asked. 'He was the talk of the hospital there for quite a while.'

'He's great. Started senior school in September and seems to be loving it. Still gets a bit tired but it's been a big year for all of us.'

'Sure has.' Charlotte smiled. 'It's going to be a special Christmas this year. Your first together as a new family.'

'It's going to be wonderful. If I can find my wife, that is. Excuse me. Carry on enjoying yourselves. Oops!' Nick almost collided with a waiter bearing a tray of brimming champagne glasses.

Anna caught Luke's gaze and there was a moment of connection there. Neither of them was enjoying themselves in this setting.

It might be better somewhere else, Anna's response of a smile suggested. Somewhere without any of this crowd and noise. Somewhere they could be alone. Together. It had to be her imagination but Luke seemed to be silently in agreement. If nothing else, he certainly recognised the connection.

'Drink, Anna?' someone asked.

'No, thanks. I've still got patients I want to check on before I head home.'

'Definitely not for me,' Charlotte said happily.

'Or me,' James chimed in valiantly. 'I've climbed on the wagon with my wife.'

'Oh?' Ben's smile broadened. 'For how long, might I ask? Seven or eight months, perhaps?'

'Um…actually, there's something we probably should have told everyone quite a while ago now.'

The tray was still within reach and Josh's wife swapped her empty glass for a full one. Anna caught the expression on Josh's face. He's embarrassed, she thought in surprise. He doesn't want her drinking any more. No. The tension was deeper than that. It was hard not to get the impression that he wasn't comfortable having his wife there at all.

She took another glance at the woman she'd never met before. Rebecca had the kind of grooming that came, in her experience, with women who had plenty of money and too much time to spend on how they looked. Flawless make-up. Shoulder-length hair that was beautifully cut and exquisitely highlighted. Her nails sported a perfect French polish and her figure might be curvy but it looked well toned.

Rebecca had also caught the look from her husband. 'What?' she snapped. 'You think I've had enough?' A tiny snort suggested that an unhappy exchange was nothing new to this couple.

It was Anna's turn to feel embarrassed. She looked away to where Lucy was giving Charlotte a one-armed hug that wouldn't disturb the sleeping baby in the sling. Ben and Luke were both offering their congratulations to James and they all seemed unaware of the sudden atmosphere Anna was separating them from.

'Maybe I have had enough,' Rebecca said, too loudly. 'Of everything.'

'I'll order a taxi for you,' Josh said. 'I've still got some work I need to do tonight.'

'Of course you do.' Rebecca's laugh was brittle.
'Let's go.'

'When I've finished my drink. It's not as if I have any reason not to, is it?'

Josh's voice was too low for anyone but Anna to hear. 'I think we should go now. This isn't the place.'

'But it never is, is it, Josh?' Rebecca raised her glass but, to her dismay, Anna saw that the woman's lips were trembling too much for her to take a sip and tears were filling her eyes. Debating whether she should say something when it was obviously none of her business, Anna was relieved to see Rebecca blinking hard. Making a determined effort to control herself.

But then she shifted her gaze to where Lucy was standing with her tiny baby and Charlotte had pulled her top tight to show off her rounded belly, and Rebecca's face just crumpled. She pushed her glass at Josh and turned, tears streaming down her face as she fled. The others all turned in surprise.

'Oh…God,' Josh groaned. 'Sorry about that. I need to… Would you…?'

'Give it to me.' Anna took the champagne glass and Josh elbowed his way through the throng in pursuit of his wife.

'What was that all about?' Lucy looked worried.

'What happened?' Charlotte looked bemused.

'Josh and his wife. They didn't look very happy.'

Oh, no. Was this social occasion about to become the kind of gossip session Anna refused to engage in?

'Not everyone appreciates Christmas,' Luke said levelly.

'That's true.' Ben nodded and went along with making

the subject about generalities. 'Look at the increase we see in A and E for things like self-harm.'

'The hype doesn't help.' Anna was more than happy to direct conversation away from colleagues and their probable marriage woes. She gave Luke a grateful glance and then waved her hand to encompass the party and all the decorations. 'There's this huge expectation put out that it's going to be the happiest day of the year. Brimming with fun, family times and the best of everything. No wonder it just serves to underline what some people aren't lucky enough to have.'

There was a moment's silence and Anna could have kicked herself. Had she been responsible for the atmosphere in this group going from joy at James and Charlotte's news to entirely unnecessary gloom? She bit her lip.

'I'm just hungry,' she said apologetically. 'Take no notice. I might go and find a sausage roll or something.'

'And I'd better take these guys home,' Lucy said. 'We need to pace ourselves to get through all the parties lined up for the rest of this week.'

'And I...' Luke was obviously trying to think of a reason to excuse himself as well.

No surprises there. The noise level around them was increasing. Music had been turned up to compete with the laughter and happily raised voices, and there was a new sound mixed in with the general hubbub. A sharp cracking. People cheered and then there were more muted bangs. Someone was handing out Christmas crackers and people were pulling them with gusto.

The sound was not unlike distant gunfire. Anna's gaze flicked back to Luke. He didn't like parties anyway. How much worse would this be when it couldn't fail to remind him of being in a war zone? She could see his tension escalating. Instinctively, she found herself moving closer. Wanting to protect him. He looked straight at her and she had never seen him look so grim.

James was handed a cracker. 'Here we go.' He laughed, holding it out to Charlotte.

This bang was much louder. Charlotte squeaked in surprise, Annabel buried her face in her father's shoulder and little Josh burst into tears.

But Anna was still watching Luke. She saw the exact moment he stopped seeing her. When his face took on the same expression it had had in Theatre that first day. One of horror.

'Luke.' Anna put her hand on his arm and she could feel muscles as unyielding as steel beneath her fingers.

'Luke.' Her tone was more urgent now. She had to get through to him. Snap him out of this flashback before anyone else noticed.

But he didn't seem to feel her touch. Or hear her. He started moving away and seemed unaware of the people in his path. Someone got jostled and spilled their drink.

'Hey! Watch where you're going.'

Ben and James were watching where Luke was going. Anna caught the glance the two men exchanged. Frowning, Ben opened his mouth to say something but Anna shook her head.

'I'll go,' was all she said.

It was quite easy to follow Luke. People were stepping aside like a wave as they saw him coming. Smiles faded from faces to be replaced with dropping jaws. Anna didn't catch up with him until he was well past the doors of the canteen. She barely noticed Josh coming in the opposite direction. Good grief, this party wasn't proving very enjoyable for more than one person.

Finally, she got close enough to catch hold of Luke's hand but he didn't stop. He towed her along until he reached the end of the corridor. The noise from the canteen was muted now, like the lighting in this junction that contained the lifts. Two big pot plants on either side of a bench seat had some tinsel draped over their leaves.

Luke stopped and his head turned swiftly from one side to the other. At some level he was making a decision on what direction to take next. He still felt just as tense. Just as distant.

Anna had to distract him. Bring him back to the present. She stepped in front of him and reached up to hold his face with both hands.

'Luke…' She tilted his face, forcing him to look down at her. 'It's me. Anna.'

He was still caught somewhere else. A long way away in time and place. Somewhere dark.

Anna had to do something. Without thinking, she stood on tiptoe, still holding Luke's face.

And then she kissed him.

CHAPTER SIX

LUKE knew that Anna was kissing him.

Just as he'd known that she had followed him from the canteen and had caught his hand. He'd heard the urgency in her voice.

But it had all been on another level of his consciousness. Maybe that was what it was like for people in a coma. Or coming out of one, anyway. They could hear the voices and feel the touch but there was a transition period before they were able to enter the same reality.

Something had snapped inside him with the sound of that cracker and he'd known he was getting sucked into a flashback. He'd tried to fight it off as he'd stormed out of the canteen. Tried to shut down the even louder cracks of the real gunfire he could hear. The explosions of landmines. The screams of dying men. But the pull had been huge. Even the smell of savoury food became acrid. Like smoke. Rusty. Like blood.

By the time he was in the corridor all Luke had been aware of had been the need to escape. To find somewhere he could be alone and bury his head in his hands until, somehow, he could wrestle the monster into submission and regain control. And then he'd felt Anna's grip on his hand and heard her voice calling his name.

He tried to clear his head. Tried so hard. He wanted to get back to her. He was caught in the horror of a battlefield and she was there but not there. If he could just reach her, everything would be all right. Couldn't she hear him shouting? That he was trying, dammit. Doing his utmost to get to her.

Maybe she had heard. Maybe that was why she was holding his head and pulling it down. Pressing her lips against his with such intensity.

God…he recognised this form of escape. Distraction. Release. An affirmation of life. Passionate sex that carried no strings because if you got involved you only risked more of exactly what you were using it to escape from.

How did Anna know?

It didn't matter.

Luke could feel the force that had taken over his mind receding. He was in control again but instead of pulling away his lips moved over hers and his arms went around her body. He drew them both into the shadowy area between the bench and the giant pot plant.

He let his hands shape her body. Feeling the trim curve of her waist and the neat rounds of her buttocks and then up, beneath the layer of the tailored jacket. Up to the solid anchor of her shoulder blades and then around to the softness of her breasts. He cupped them and brushed his thumbs across the nipples that he could feel like tiny pebbles beneath the silky fabric of her blouse.

And all the time his lips moved over hers. Encouraged when they parted beneath his. Excited when his tongue made contact with hers. Aroused beyond belief when she responded, her tongue dancing with his and her hands touching his body.

This was Anna, for heaven's sake! At work. The place where she had no personality or, at least, no personal life anyone was allowed to encroach on. Had she been drinking? No. She'd refused alcohol at the party because she had work she still needed to do. They were both sober. Sober enough to realise that this was totally inappropriate.

How long had they been standing here, locked in each other's arms, lost in a flash of physical release that had exploded like a cork from a champagne bottle?

Too long. Not nearly long enough.

Had anyone seen them?

He had to stop but it was too hard not to taste her for just a moment longer. To hold her against the length of his body and imprint the feel of her into his brain. He would need that memory and it was too important not to make sure that it stuck.

He was kissing her back.

Anna had only intended to distract him. A brief, hard kiss that was supposed to have the same kind of shock effect that a slap on the face might provide to someone in the grip of hysteria.

But after that first stunned beat of time he had kissed her back. His lips had softened and moved beneath hers and his hands had touched her body and something inside Anna had simply melted.

He hadn't seemed to hear her voice or know she was there as she'd followed him. Maybe he didn't actually know who he was kissing. She could be anybody so she didn't have to be Dr Bartlett, did she?

She could just be Anna.

An old version of herself, even. One that had been lost too many years ago to count. The young girl who had dreamed of finding true love. A prince who was going to think she was the most wonderful person on earth. Who would love her for being exactly who she was. For ever.

And layered on top of that dreaming girl were flashes of everything she'd discovered about herself later. The yearning for a soul mate. The ability to give love and the need to receive it. Wild things like a need for physical release. All the things that had had to be buried so that they couldn't become a torment.

For just a few seconds Anna let herself sink into this astonishing kiss because she knew she would never experience anything like this ever again and she wanted to remember it, but the insanity began to fade and maybe she transmitted a tension that had nothing to do with desire. Something changed, anyway. She couldn't have said who actually broke the kiss and pulled away.

Maybe they both did.

For a long, long moment they stood there, still close enough to touch but not doing so. Staring at each other. Anna could see it was Luke looking down at her, not a tormented soul who was caught in a different reality. He knew who he was. Where he was.

And who he had been kissing.

Oh…Lord…

Anna swallowed hard. How on earth was she supposed to handle this? And not just the kiss. She'd witnessed another flashback incident. He'd said it wasn't going to happen again but it had. OK, so he wasn't in the middle of surgery and it hadn't endangered anyone, but there was no way her conscience would allow her to make excuses or ignore the implications of this.

She had a professional responsibility here and she had just complicated it to the nth degree by not thinking and by doing something as outrageous as kissing her new boss.

Then again…maybe that gave her a way in. An opening to talk about what had happened and what they were going to do about it.

She took a deep breath.

'Feeling better?'

She knew.

Too much.

Luke could feel himself closing off. Slamming mental doors in an effort to protect himself. To protect her?

'Maybe I should ask you the same thing,' he said coolly.

'Sorry?'

'You kissed me.' He managed to sound offhand, as though it hadn't blown him away. Like it hadn't meant anything at all.

He could see the way her eyes widened in shock as though he'd physically slapped her. The way she collected herself and looked away.

'You needed distraction.'

She couldn't know. Not everything. Not that she was already a distraction that he held onto every single night. That she represented a kind of rope that he could use to haul himself back to where he needed to be. A link that he had now tied firmly into the horrors of the past but one that led back to the present. To the future. A rope that he just needed to run his hand along to save his sanity. He would get where he intended to go eventually, as long as he could feel it running beside him.

The rope had been formed largely due to the intrigue that the contrast between what this woman was like at home and at work had sparked. Appreciating the fact that she was an attractive woman had woven another strand into it. But this…this blinding demonstration of what physical passion she was capable of did more than thicken the rope. It had come alive. It was warm and soft and he could stay glued to it with no effort at all. He didn't even need to touch it because a part of his mind could see it. Glowing.

'It was the Christmas crackers, wasn't it?' Anna asked. 'That sound like gunfire. You had some kind of flashback, like you did that day in surgery.'

'Nonsense.' It was. It had to be because if it wasn't, it would mean he would lose his job and that was all he had to fill his future.

And if he lost his job, he would lose Anna.

'I didn't like the noise,' he admitted stiffly. 'I told

you I didn't like parties. I left because I'd had enough. The noise of the crackers was just the last straw.'

'Do you actually remember leaving the canteen?'

'Of course I do.' And he did, in a vague, dream-like way. A background that had faded rapidly as he'd got sucked into the flashback. He remembered that Anna had been following him and... 'I...bumped someone,' he said aloud. 'They spilled their drink.'

That surprised her. 'You didn't look like you were aware of what you were doing.'

'I was...angry.'

'Why?'

'The party. The noise. All that food and drink and the silly costumes. It's all such a waste of time and money.'

She wasn't convinced. 'You didn't stop, Luke. You didn't hear me calling you. I kissed you because I couldn't think of anything else that might shock you enough to get you off whatever planet you were on.'

'And I hope you plan to include that little gem in whatever report you're obviously intending to make.'

A spark flashed in Anna's eyes. 'For God's sake, Luke. This isn't about reports or jobs or whether someone gets embarrassed. This is about the fact that if there's any chance of you "losing focus" or having a flashback or whatever the hell that was really all about that you're obviously not prepared to talk about, then you can't operate on people.'

Luke watched the play of expression on Anna's face. Her distress was all too easy to see in the frown lines framing her eyes. In the way her lips trembled.

'I'm not out to get you,' she said fiercely. 'I want to help you.'

It was more than that, Anna realised as the words left her mouth. Had it been growing within her all the time she'd been watching Luke so carefully? Hoping to see him smile? Thinking so often about that short space of time when they'd been alone in her house and tumbling ever further into the confusion of her response to him. She could see the shadows that clouded his life and his eyes. There were things that haunted him and closed him off but she'd had a glimpse of the man he'd once been. Or could be.

She wanted, more than anything, to dispel those shadows. To get close enough to be allowed to help him.

She cared about him, Anna realised with something like dismay. She couldn't pinpoint when it had happened. Maybe the evidence had been there for days and days. A sum of everything she had seen or imagined. Elements that had floated in an uncoordinated fashion until the fear she had felt in seeing Luke virtually run from the canteen.

Something else had been added in when she had felt him respond to her kiss. A confused medley of caring and attraction. Not something she wanted to try and analyse and she certainly couldn't possibly tell him about any of it. Not when it was beyond the realms of possibility that he could feel anything like the same connection. Or that someone like him would want help from someone like her. He was more qualified than she was in so many ways. He was older. More skilled. He had seen and done things she would never want to do.

No wonder he was looking at her in a stony silence that took a little too long to be broken.

'Help me?' The words were bitten out scathingly. 'How do you propose doing that, exactly, Anna? By spreading a rumour that I might be unfit to do my job?'

'No.' Anna tried to catch his gaze but Luke was looking at the blasted potted tree they were standing beside. 'I think if you have the time, you'll get on top of whatever it is or find the help you need from someone a lot more qualified than I am.'

The snort of sound was incredulous. 'A shrink, you mean? Cheers, Anna.'

She ignored the rejection. She'd be angry, too, if someone suggested she couldn't handle her own issues. 'What I was going to suggest is that you don't operate unless I'm assisting you. For the protection of everybody involved.'

'You think I need supervising? By you?'

Anna flinched, biting back the observation that he had needed her during Colin Herbert's surgery. Something told her that Luke was trying to turn this into a confrontation he could feel justified in dismissing. She had to find a way to rescue this discussion or she would lose him. For ever.

The lift suddenly pinged into life close by. The doors slid open.

'Oops, wrong floor,' a masculine voice said. 'Hey… sounds like there's a party going on.'

'Yeah. Staff do, mate. Doctors and nurses. Security wasn't invited.'

'Shame. Wanna crash it?'

'Nah. More than our jobs are worth. Come on. Push the damn button.'

The doors slid shut again but a single word of the exchange lingered in Anna's ears.

Crash.

The kiss seemed a very long time ago. Hard to believe it had happened, even. But it had and for a brief time Anna had felt the same kind of connection she had that day he'd told her about his friend 'Crash'. It was possible to find a chink in the armour he wore.

'Actually,' she told Luke quietly, 'I was thinking of it more in terms of it being beneficial to both of us.'

'So I get a supervisor. What do you get?'

'A mentor,' Anna said. 'The chance to learn from someone whose work I already respect.' She managed a smile as Luke finally made eye contact again. Had she also managed to placate him? 'Think about it. I'm going to go back to that party for a bit. I need some food.'

Going back into the canteen was the last thing Luke wanted to do but he found himself following Anna after a brief hesitation. He needed to prove he could. To Anna and to anyone else who might have raised their eyebrows at the manner in which he'd left. Most of all, he needed to prove it to himself.

He could see Anna walking well ahead of him.

He didn't need a babysitter. Or help.

He didn't need somebody kissing him because they thought he was on 'another planet' either. Because they felt sorry for him?

No. Anna had said she could learn from him. That she respected his work. That didn't suggest she felt sorry for him. That kiss hadn't held any hint of unwillingness. Quite the opposite.

She'd kissed him because she'd wanted to kiss him. And what's more she'd wanted to keep on kissing him. It wouldn't have been difficult to pull away as soon as he'd responded. What she was saying was at odds with her behaviour. As much of a contradiction as her smart suits and paint-splattered old clothes. It was a puzzle and Luke liked that. He liked having Anna to think about. To ponder over. He was like a boat being tossed on a stormy ocean and Anna was his anchor. Maybe he could get to his future without her but it would be hard.

Lonely.

Luke was walking slowly. He could see the brightly lit interior of the canteen now, beyond the doors that were propped open by chairs. Anna had vanished into the crowd.

A couple stood on the shadowy side of the doors, partly screened because one of the chairs had shifted. A man and a woman. He wouldn't have taken any particular notice of them except that he could feel the atmosphere as he got closer.

A palpable tension. Maybe he recognised it because the air had the same charged feeling as it had had in those stunned moments after kissing Anna.

Sexual tension.

The man raised a hand to shove his fingers through his hair and then rub his forehead with the palm of his hand.

It was Josh O'Hara, Luke realised with astonishment. The A and E consultant he'd met the day he'd accompanied Roger into the emergency department after his cardiac arrest. The man last seen going after his distressed wife when she'd fled the Christmas party.

This woman was definitely not his wife.

She was quite tall and very beautiful, with long dark brown hair tied loosely into a ponytail.

'I saw her leave,' the woman was saying. 'She looked dreadful, Josh. You should go home. Talk to her.'

'I know. I will. But she had gone by the time I got outside and I just had to… Oh, God, Megan…'

It was only a snatch of conversation that he overheard and Luke wished he hadn't. There was something going on and he didn't need to know about it. It was none of his business how difficult or miserable other people were making their lives.

He had more than enough to deal with in his own.

Something made him turn his head again, however, as he pushed himself back into the party.

He saw Josh move his head. Tilting it further into the space behind the door that no one in here could see. Luke could sense the intent. Josh was planning to kiss this Megan. But almost at the same moment his head jerked backwards and he saw the shadowy figure ducking from reach as she emerged. She was shaking her head and she walked away without a backward glance.

Almost ran away, in fact.

That's what he should have done when Anna had gone to kiss him. Ducked the gesture and gone.

So why did he feel relieved that he hadn't even thought of doing so at the time?

Sleep proved elusive for Anna that night.

She couldn't close her eyes without thinking about that kiss and thinking about it brought it unerringly back to life.

She could still feel it.

The way his lips had moved over hers. Exploring them. Claiming them.

The strength in his hands. Their sure grip when he had pulled her close.

That incredibly gentle touch of his thumbs on her breasts.

And every time she relived that particular moment, her nipples tingled and a shaft of desire pierced her belly. And every time it got stronger. Feeding on itself. Taking on a life of its own. Becoming so intense it was physically painful.

With a groan, Anna shifted her body, turning over in her bed yet again. She had to stop thinking about it before day broke and she found herself on duty having had no rest.

Becoming aware of an odd thumping sound a moment later, she dragged her eyes open to find another set of eyes disturbingly close to her own. A long, wet tongue emerged to lick her face and the thumping accelerated when Anna laughed and wiped her face on her pillow to dry it.

'You're supposed to be asleep, Crash. On your bed.'

The puppy wriggled with delight at hearing her voice.

He obviously had no objection to being awake in the middle of the night.

'It's all right for you.' Anna pulled her hand out from under her pillow and reached to stroke the dog. 'You can sleep whenever you want to in the daytime. I need to sleep now and I can't.'

Crash leaned against the side of the bed, his chin tilting up against the mattress.

'He made out it was all my idea,' Anna informed Crash indignantly. 'And maybe it was, to start with, but you know what?'

Big ears twitched into their endearing sideways position and Anna smiled as she stroked them.

'He liked it as much as I did, that's what. He could have backed off and he didn't. He kissed me back.'

And how!

Anna let her breath out in a long sigh. A release that was partly pure pleasure at the memory but it also held a good whisper of frustration and more than a hint of anxiety about the implications of it all.

Silence gathered around them both as Anna's thoughts drifted on the breeze of that sigh. Her hand stilled and finally Crash heaved a sigh of his own, folding himself into a lumpy shape on the floor. He didn't go back to his own bed. He was still there, right beside her, prepared to share any vigil.

But Anna's eyes had drifted shut. One thing was certain. That kiss couldn't be undone and it put her and Luke on new ground. Unexplored, potentially dangerous but undeniably exciting territory.

Was Luke awake right now?

Would he remember that kiss?

Oh, yes. Anna was as certain of that as she was about the fact that the kiss couldn't be undone. Curiously, the knowledge was comforting and sleep finally came, but it didn't quite erase the tiny smile curling her lips.

CHAPTER SEVEN

IF LOOKS could kill…

Anna had to bite back an ironic smile as she pressed her foot on the control to start the water flowing and reached for the small, soap-impregnated scrubbing brush.

She'd probably been glaring at Luke in a very similar fashion that first day they'd been in Theatre together. Resenting his presence. Resenting him. Knowing that she was perfectly capable of doing the job without him being there. Feeling demoted in some way.

Now it was his turn. This was his first theatre slot following that little talk they'd had after she'd chased after him out of the staff Christmas party. The issue had been ignored for the day or two since then. In fact, Anna had had the impression that Luke had been avoiding her and that had been fine because any embarrassment lingering from the kiss had been somehow watered down until it didn't exist any more. Maybe he was hoping she would also forget her intention of scrubbing in with him for the safety of everyone involved but she hadn't forgotten. She hadn't waited for an invitation either, she had simply arrived.

Luke was apparently focused on scrubbing his hands and forearms with commendable thoroughness. Under his nails and between his fingers. Carefully angling the water flow so that it chased soap from the wrists up to his elbows and then dropping his hands to rinse from the wrists to his fingertips.

He muttered something under his breath as he reached for a sterile towel to dry his hands. It sounded like, 'Blackmail'.

'Sorry?'

'Nothing,' Luke growled. He stepped towards a theatre nurse waiting to help him don his gown and tie it. He cleared his throat and raised his voice. 'Good that you had the time to join us this morning, Anna.'

'Wouldn't have wanted to miss it,' she responded calmly. 'Pretty complicated case. I'm sure I'm going to learn a lot.'

The nurse made an approving sound. 'We all are,' she said admiringly. 'The gallery's a very popular place today. Full house.'

Anna looked up and smiled at Luke.

See? the smile said. Nobody's going to blink an eye at me being in Theatre with you. We are the only two people who know the real reason I have to be here and we both know why it has to be this way. Her smile faded but she held his gaze. Get used to it, she advised silently. You don't have to like it but you do have to deal with it.

Not that she expected him to deal with it in quite the way he did. By making her the lead surgeon. Talking her through the more complex aspects but only taking over for a few minutes at a time. It was a long and complicated surgery. The middle-aged female patient had a tumour in one lung that had spread to send tentacles around the major vessels that returned blood to the heart. The diagnosis had not been made until the reduction in blood flow due to the compression had given her heart failure. Swollen ankles and shortness of breath had finally made her seek medical help.

Fortunately, they found no cardiac involvement, but the dissection needed to remove as much of the tumour as possible was tricky. The patient was on bypass for nearly five hours as Anna and Luke worked to free the blood vessels and remove a lobe of her lung. By the end of the procedure Anna was exhausted. It wasn't until their patient was off bypass and her heart was beating again effectively that she could relax at all and it was then that she realised how Luke had 'dealt' with what he'd taken to be her supervision. He'd made her do the work and put so much pressure on her that she hadn't had time to even think about how focused he had been.

If that was how he wanted to play this, it was fine by her. Brilliant, in fact. In order to watch her and challenge her to improve her own skills, he was having to focus just as intently as he would if he was doing the procedure alone. More so, in some ways, because he had to think ahead in several directions so that he could troubleshoot if she wasn't on exactly the same wavelength.

Not that any major discrepancies in thinking had occurred. They had been amazingly in tune. So much so that Anna would have noticed instantly if Luke had lost focus. He hadn't. She had been challenged. She'd learnt a lot. To outward appearances they had worked as a close, harmonious team. The initiative had been a huge success as far as Anna was concerned and not only from a personal perspective. The patient's quality of life had been improved immensely and, if she was lucky, the length of it might be well beyond current expectations.

While Luke might not be prepared to recognise it yet, there had also been an additional, albeit secret bonus. He had done more than save face. Nobody watching—and there had been plenty of them—would have thought there were any undercurrents. They would have seen a head of department using exceptional skills in both surgery and teaching. His kudos had probably been raised by several degrees.

She might be exhausted now but she was also delighted. This could work.

And maybe it was a good thing that Luke was grumpy about it. Anna found she was frequently the recipient of glares over the next few days. Surprisingly often, and not just when she might have expected to cross paths with her senior colleague on ward rounds or in meetings.

It was getting so that she could sense that brooding, intense look from a considerable distance. From the end of a corridor, for instance, when she got out of a lift. Or from across the canteen when she joined a lunchtime queue. He seemed to be everywhere. All the time. It didn't matter how late she stayed at work to catch up on paperwork or how early she arrived to get ahead with whatever her day held. He was always there. Or was it just that she was so much more aware of it?

Too aware.

So, yes, it was good that he was grumpy. It meant that he wasn't thinking about that ill-advised distraction of kissing him. Or, if he did think about it, it didn't make him happy. Either way, he wasn't going to want a repetition of anything like that and that was exactly what Anna needed to push herself forward. To get over it and get on with her career and her life.

It was good.

It was. And if she reminded herself of that often enough, it would be true.

It should have been a relief to get Christmas and the start of the new year over with.

To get back to business as usual and away from all the forced cheerfulness of so many people trying to spread the joy of the season. Even patients were wishing him a happy new year, and there'd been far too many invitations to social events to find plausible excuses to avoid. So many smiles to produce.

Theatre had been the best place to be, of course. No tinsel allowed in there and nurses had to remove any silly seasonal earrings. He didn't tolerate small talk either so he didn't have to hear people talking about how excited their children had been as they had counted down the sleeps or what people were planning to do to see in the new year.

The only downside of being in Theatre had been that Anna had followed through her threat of supervising him. His response had been a form of attack in a way. If she wanted it to be like this and pretend she was there to improve her knowledge and skills then she could jolly well put the hard yards in instead of watching.

To his surprise, Anna had embraced the perspective and anyone in the gallery would have been convinced that that was the only reason she was in Theatre with him. Even more surprising was how much he enjoyed teaching her. At some point during that first operation on the woman with that nasty tumour threatening her cardiac function, Luke had stopped watching like a hawk to catalogue things he could be doing better than Anna and, instead, began channelling his knowledge and watching how quickly she understood what he was saying and how deftly the information was put into use.

He not only enjoyed the session, if he was really honest with himself, it had also been a relief to have her there.

Just in case.

Having watched Anna so closely during that surgery, Luke found himself continuing to watch her. He justified the scrutiny by telling himself he was watching her to see whether she was watching him. He watched her on ward rounds and in meetings. Even in the canteen. It was easy to create any number of opportunities to watch his assistant. He could find patients in the intensive care unit whose condition needed review. Departmental issues to discuss. Research projects to plan and monitor.

He discovered that Anna spent almost as much time in the hospital as he did. Way too many hours to have any kind of life away from a career. How did she find time to work on renovating that small cottage she lived in or to give her pet the attention it needed? Not that it was any of his business.

Or was it? At one point, he had to wonder if Anna's willingness to put in so much extra time was purely due to her dedication to her career or whether it had something to do with him still being in some kind of probationary period. Was he just aware of it because he was trying to keep one step ahead of her?

Or…was he watching for a signal of some kind that she remembered that kiss?

That she might find herself thinking about it as often as he did? Sometimes he would catch her gaze and he'd feel an odd buzz. A hint that she might remember.

That she might be wondering if it would be as extraordinary if it happened again.

Wanting it to happen again…

On one of the first days of the new year, Anna was with Luke and one of her registrars in his office. They were discussing one of the new research projects due to get under way.

'The main causes of prolonged hospital stay, morbidity and mortality following cardiac surgery are haemorrhage and infection,' Luke was reminding the young doctor present. 'And, quite often, infection is one of the sequelae of haemorrhage.'

Anna was listening quietly. This was an occasion when she was in Luke's company but his attention was on someone else. Even when he involved her in the discussion, he would forget to glare at her and the simmering undercurrent that she was waiting on for further evidence that Luke was unfit for the position of responsibility he held vanished. She could interact with—and enjoy—the company of an intelligent and stimulating colleague.

Bask in it even.

The registrar was nodding. 'Is that because they're more susceptible to infection due to a low cardiac output?'

'That's one of the parameters we need to keep in mind. There's also the issue of how long the chest has been open, whether they've been on bypass or whether hypothermia has been employed. There's a lot of stuff that's been written on aspects of this in other studies. What we're aiming to do is possibly challenge their findings with more current information or testing methods and/or add in any other significant parameters. Here, I've printed off some of the articles for you.'

The registrar's eyes widened. So did Anna's.

How long had Luke been in here already today to search out and print off this stack of material? And this was supposed to be a day off for him. Didn't he have other places he wanted to be? Or other people he wanted to be with?

And why was the thought that he'd rather be here, having a meeting with her, a cause for a rather pleasant internal glow? Not that Anna was going to analyse her reaction. She didn't get a chance to, anyway, because her pager sounded.

The disruption earned her a sharp look from Luke and Anna sighed inwardly. 'Can I use your phone?'

'Of course.'

She found Ben Carter on the other end of the line and listened intently.

'I'm on my way,' she said a short time later. 'Luke's here as well. We'll both come.'

'What's going on?' Luke demanded as she put the phone down.

'Helicopter's due to land any minute bringing in a thirteen-year-old boy. He's hypothermic and unstable. Ectopic activity increasing so he could arrest at any time. Ben wants us on standby in case rewarming via bypass is necessary. He's put a theatre on standby as well and called in a technician.'

'You're the one on call. I'm not even supposed to be here today.'

Anna was at the door already. She turned to see the registrar looking slack-jawed at the potential case and Luke looking…good grief…wary? Or hopeful? Why?

She didn't have time to consider any personal issues. There was a child's life at stake here and if it came to trying to rewarm him by using cardiopulmonary bypass it was new territory for her. She'd read about it but never even seen it done. A flicker of something like panic had to be crushed.

She held Luke's gaze for a heartbeat despite—or perhaps because of—knowing he could probably see that flash of fear.

'But you are here,' she said quietly. The presence of

the registrar in the room ceased to matter. 'And I need you, Luke.'

They both followed her but it was Luke's tall form striding beside her that gave Anna confidence. They moved fast enough for him to be limping by the time they reached the emergency department but they were still side by side.

A team.

The main resuscitation area in Emergency was crowded. Helicopter paramedics in their bright overalls and helmets were there with the medical staff, transferring their patient with great care. There was a bustle of activity and a buzz of urgent instructions.

'Gently! Don't bump him. Cardiac function is fragile.'

'Is the Bair Hugger on?'

'Dextrose, not saline. Get some more in the microwave to get warmed.'

'Make sure that oxygen is warmed and humidified.'

'Get some more dots on. We need a twelve-lead ECG.'

'What's his temperature now?'

'Nineteen point five degrees Celsius.'

Luke whistled silently.

'The lowest ever temperature that someone's survived without neurological impairment was around thirteen degrees, wasn't it?' Anna kept her voice low. The boy's mother was on the other side of the room, looking terrified.

Ben Carter was leading the resus team and he wasn't

happy with the oxygen saturation level of the boy's blood.

'I'm going to intubate,' he decided. 'Anyone who's not directly involved step back a bit, please. It's critical we do this with minimal movement.'

One of the paramedics stepped well back, close to where Anna and Luke were watching. Standing by.

'What happened?' Anna asked.

'Kid got ice-skates for Christmas,' the paramedic said quietly. 'They live on a farm up north a bit and there's a dam. He and his brother went skating and he hit some thin ice and went through. Took his brother about thirty minutes to find a branch big enough to get him out and another half an hour to run home and raise the alarm. Probably ninety minutes before we arrived on scene and the wind chill was significant. First temperature we got was eighteen degrees.'

'Cardiac rhythm?' Luke was watching Ben and his team securing the boy's airway but he was listening to Anna's conversation with the paramedic.

'Slow atrial fibrillation. Marked J waves.'

Anything below a core temperature of thirty degrees was enough to put someone at risk of cardiac arrhythmias and arrest. This boy was dangerously cold but there was still hope. Anna remembered a lecturer at medical school talking about hypothermia.

'You're not dead until you're warm and dead,' he'd said.

The Bair Hugger was a blanket designed to force a current of hot air over the patient's skin. Intravenous fluids were warmed to try and raise blood temperature but these methods might be too slow to help someone with such severe hypothermia.

'Luke.' Ben had finally stepped back from the initial flurry of making sure their patient was as stable as possible. 'Didn't think you were on today.'

'I'm not.' Luke flicked a sideways glance at Anna and there was a hint of a smile on his lips. He was here because she wanted him to be but it seemed like he wanted her to know he was happy to be here.

'Well, I'm glad you're here. Both of you.'

'What's the plan?'

Ben looked grim. 'External exogenous rewarming is only going to achieve a rate of about a two point five degree increase per hour. He's too cold to wait that long. With full cardiopulmonary bypass we could get a rewarming rate of seven point five degrees an hour.'

'We can't justify something as invasive as bypass unless he's arrested. What about pleural lavage?'

The cardiothoracic registrar was looking bemused. Anna leaned closer. 'That's using an inter-costal catheter to pour large volumes of warmed water into the chest cavity.'

'Still pretty invasive,' Ben was saying. 'And possibly less effective. Right now we'll keep ventilator support going and monitor his rhythm. We should get results on the bloods we've drawn soon. I want to see what his acid-base status is. At least slow A fib isn't a malignant rhythm.'

'We need an arterial blood gas as well,' Anna put in. She stepped forward to retrieve the sheet of paper emerging from the twelve-lead ECG machine but she didn't get time to analyse the trace. An alarm sounded on one of the monitors at the head of the bed.

'He's in V tach,' someone warned. 'I can't find a pulse.'

'V fib now.'

'Start CPR,' Ben ordered, moving to the side of the bed. He looked back at Luke, who gave a terse nod.

'One shock. If that doesn't work, bring him up to Theatre under CPR.'

'Theatre 3's on standby. Bypass technician was paged when I called Anna.'

'Charging,' someone announced. 'Stand clear.'

Luke gave another nod and touched Anna's arm. 'Let's go. Better if we're scrubbed and ready by the time they come up if we're going to be needed.'

A cold, still heart.

This lad was technically dead and here they were thinking they could play God and bring him back to life.

Luke could see the lines of strain around Anna's eyes. He knew that her lips beneath that mask would be pressed tightly together. And, despite how subtle it was, he saw the way she flinched when her hands touched the chilled flesh in the small chest they had just opened.

'We need to work fast,' he reminded her quietly. 'Standard bypass. Arterial cannula in the ascending aorta. Right atrial cannulation with a single, two-stage cannula.'

Anna nodded. She was already placing a purse-string

suture around the major vessel that took blood from the heart to the rest of the body.

Within minutes, with both surgeons working together in a tense atmosphere, the cannulae had been positioned and the boy's blood was now being circulated through the heart-lung bypass machine instead of his frail-looking body. Circulated and being carefully warmed.

There was nothing more they needed to do surgically until it was time to take him off bypass and repair the vessels currently holding the thick tubes. Then they would—hopefully—restart his heart, close his chest and wait to see if he woke up. Wait to see whether his brain function had survived this terrible insult.

Hours later, Luke found Anna in her office. She had been pacing back and forth between the intensive care unit and the wards. Between the canteen, where she'd eaten nothing at all, and the ICU. Between her office and the ICU.

'It's taking too long,' she said when Luke appeared through the door.

'He's in a good rhythm. Body temperature is within a normal range. The hyperglycaemia has been corrected. Renal function is looking good.'

'I know, I know.' But Anna was still pacing, her arms wrapped around her body as if for comfort. 'Blood gases are fine, too, and I'm happy with cardiac pressures. But what about possible complications like thromboembolism? Or disseminated intravascular coagulation?' She dragged in a breath. 'Have you met his mum, Janet? Did you know his big brother is six years older and that she had two late miscarriages before Jamie came along? What...what if he doesn't wake up?'

'Anna...' Luke stepped in front of her, forcing her to stand still. He gripped her upper arms. She was so wrapped up in this case, so desperate for them to have succeeded, she was losing her perspective. He'd never seen her like this.

So involved.

Caring so much.

'The sedation is only being lightened slowly. It'll take time for him to start breathing on his own and he's not going to wake up before then.'

'But what if—?'

'Stop,' Luke commanded.

He was still holding her. Looking down at Anna's pale face. Those astonishing green eyes were locked on his. Hanging onto his words of reassurance. Believing what he was telling her. And then his gaze dropped to her mouth and he saw the tiny tremble of her lips and that undid something deep inside him.

'What you need, Dr Bartlett,' he said very softly, 'is distraction.'

She caught the meaning of his words as soon as he'd uttered them. Her gaze dropped to his mouth and he found himself running his tongue across his lower lip. Slowly. Deliberately.

Time came to a standstill.

'Mmm.'

The sound Anna made could have been agreement but it sounded more like need. Desire.

It was all the permission Luke needed. His hands left

her arms. He used one to cradle the back of her head and with the other he cupped her chin. Then he bent his head.

He was initiating this kiss. He was in control and he intended to make sure Anna was aware of nothing but the sensations he was going to provide with his lips. And his tongue.

This was going to be a kiss that Anna would have no chance of forgetting. Ever.

Anna kept her arms wrapped around her body even after that first touch of Luke's lips.

She'd needed to keep hold of herself in those seconds leading up to that kiss. Feeling the way his fingers splayed and claimed control of her head and her chin. Sensing the intent of this being far more significant than the last time they'd kissed.

She'd kept her eyes open as she watched his face dipping to meet hers. So slowly. And she'd held herself even more tightly with her own arms then because she'd been sure she was falling.

Desire had sucked her into some kind of vortex and she was spinning wildly. Totally out of control.

And then his lips had touched hers and moved over her mouth. Questing. Claiming. Giving. Demanding her involvement and response.

Sensations rippled through Anna and unlocked the awful tension that had been building from the moment she'd touched Jamie's small, cold heart. Her skin tingled and seemed to melt and then her muscles gave up conscious control. Her arms let go of her own body and, instead, moved to hold Luke's. She could feel the strength of his muscles and the steady thump of his heart and all the time his mouth was doing such amazing things to hers. Her bones were melting now. He could just scoop her into his arms and lay her down on the floor of this office and she'd willingly—

Luke pulled away and for a dazed moment all Anna could think of was holding on more tightly. Pulling him back.

'Phone's ringing,' he said gently.

'Oh...' Anna put her hand to her mouth and took in a shaky breath. 'I—I'd better answer it, hadn't I?'

Luke was smiling at her.

Really smiling. His eyes were crinkled and the corners of his mouth had disappeared into those deep furrows beneath his cheeks.

'Yes.' He nodded. 'I think you had.'

She actually stumbled moving towards her desk. Heaven only knew what the intensive care consultant on the other end of the line thought of her initial stammered response but the content of the call was more than enough to bring her back to the present and reality. She put the phone down a moment later.

'Jamie's breathing on his own,' she told Luke. 'He squeezed his mum's hand.'

To her horror, Anna felt tears gather in her eyes. She never cried. She most certainly never cried in front of a male colleague.

But Luke didn't seem to mind. He reached out and pulled her into his arms. Not to kiss her this time but simply to hold her. For long enough to be more than a celebratory hug. Long enough for Anna to know that he understood exactly how she was feeling. Long enough for her to take several deep breaths and get her brain working properly again.

'If we get up there soon, we might see him wake up and then we'll get an idea of what kind of neurological impairment he might be left with.'

An hour later they were part of the group around Jamie's bed in the intensive care unit as the young boy's eyes flickered open. His father and older brother were there now, too, but it was his mother who was closest. The first person Jamie saw.

He blinked a few times. Opened his mouth and moved his lips but his brow furrowed as though he couldn't find a way to make his mouth do what he wanted it to do. He stared blankly at the woman leaning so close to him, with tears running down her face.

Everybody present was holding their breath.

Luke and Anna were standing side by side. So closely their shoulders were pressed together. Unseen by anyone else in the cubicle, Luke's hand moved just enough for his fingers to tangle with Anna's.

Jamie tried again.

'Mum?' The word was croaky but clear. 'What's the matter?'

Anna felt her hand gripped so tightly it was painful but all she moved was her head. Just far enough to meet Luke's gaze.

To see the triumph at the back of his eyes.

He let go of her hand before anyone could notice but

that didn't break the link. It was still there in his gaze. A connection that had taken them way beyond being merely colleagues.

He would come home with her tonight. Or she would go home with him. It didn't matter. It wasn't even a decision that needed to be discussed because it had already been made. Back in her office. Or maybe well before that but neither of them had taken that step forward.

Now they had taken that step and they both knew there was no going back.

CHAPTER EIGHT

CRASH stayed at the farm up the road from Anna's cottage.

'He often does,' she assured Luke. 'That way I don't disturb the Turners by collecting him if I have to work late. June loves him to bits. She would have kept him except that Doug put his foot down.'

She was talking quickly, Luke noticed, as the glow of realising she had kept the name he'd suggested for her puppy wore off. Was she nervous? Unsure she was making the right choice here, a passenger in his car as they drove away from St Piran's hospital that evening?

He was feeling a bit uptight himself. Sex in an army camp was a lot easier than this. You got attracted or desperate for distraction and a tent or somewhere private was never far enough away to allow for second thoughts. No awkwardness. No pressure. No strings afterwards.

This was different.

There was danger here. For the peace of mind he was struggling to achieve. For the relationship with an important colleague that could get damaged. And for Anna…because she might get hurt. She might want something that he couldn't give her.

Like commitment.

Curious that the prospect of hurting Anna outweighed the more personal ramifications this step could represent. He wanted to protect her. To turn his vehicle round and take her back to the hospital. Let Anna drive home to her small cottage. Alone.

Luke flicked a sideways glance at his passenger as he turned onto the road that led to his beachside house. She'd pulled out whatever it was she used to restrain her hair and it tumbled to her shoulders. Her hands were clasped in her lap and she was still wearing her power-dressing clothes.

Not for long, though. Luke found he had to lick suddenly dry lips. There was still time, he told himself. He could turn round. Tell her that he'd changed his mind and maybe this wasn't such a good idea after all, given how closely they needed to keep working together.

But Anna seemed to sense that quick glance and she turned her head as well. Her eyes seemed huge in a pale face as they drove under a streetlamp. Her lips were parted a little and maybe she was experiencing the same kind of dry mouth he was because she mirrored his own action and licked her lips. The action rendered Luke helpless to act on any good intentions. Almost ashamed of himself, he cleared his throat and it came out in a kind of growl.

Anna sighed, assuming the sound was related to the conversation she was using to fill the awkward journey.

'I know, I was crazy to take on a puppy with the kind

of hours I have to work but when I am at home he's wonderful company.'

Oh, God…was she lonely?

The urge to protect this woman from being hurt morphed into something very different. He might not be able to offer commitment or any kind of a future but he could step, temporarily at least, into that void in her life and give her some companionship. The kind of closeness that would make her feel like she wasn't alone in the world. That someone cared enough to give her pleasure.

That someone cared at all.

She wasn't the only one here who needed that.

Anna was pleased that Luke didn't draw the curtains in the bedroom he led her into. His house was almost on a beach. Not one of the rocky, dangerous coves that dotted this coast but a sandy stretch with enough width for smooth waves. The kind of gem tucked amongst the rocky ones that surfers loved to try and keep secret. She could see it because it was a clear, cold night and there was enough moonlight to not only show her the view but to mean that harsh electric lighting was unnecessary inside. That pleased her, too.

She had already declined an offer for any food or drink. That could come later. Or not. They were there for one reason and that was to continue the kiss that had begun in her office. To finish what had been started.

Standing here was different, however. Anna was too nervous to look at the bed so she stood in front of the big window that had the view of the beach and stared out. Luke came to stand very close behind her. His hands brushed her arms. A slow stroke from her elbows to her shoulders and back again and there his hands lingered.

'Are you sure about this, Anna?' he asked quietly. 'It's OK if you want to change your mind.'

She turned and it was suddenly very easy. As though his body warmth was an irresistible magnet. Her breast brushed his hand as she moved and the sensation blitzed any final nerves.

'I don't want to change my mind,' she said softly. 'Do you?'

By way of response, Luke bent his head and his lips touched hers. The chill of the evening outside was coming through the uncovered glass beside them and the pale light of the moon offered no pretence of warmth, but Anna had never felt heat like this.

Scorching her lips as Luke claimed her mouth. Trickling over her body with the touch of his hands as he undid the buttons of her blouse and undressed her. Building inside as she watched him strip and stand there, bathed in moonlight. Tall and lean and powerful. Magnificently male.

She wanted him to catch her in his arms and throw her onto the bed but, instead, he came to stand in front of her. Skin to skin. Her breasts pressed into the hardness of his chest and she could feel his arousal against her belly. He wanted her. As much as she wanted him. His arms came around her then and their lips met. In a kind of slow dance, moving as one person, they somehow made their way from the window to the bed and then they were lying together. A tangle of limbs and passionate kisses and a consuming need that brooked no delay other than Luke fishing in a bedside drawer for protection.

The few seconds of watching him was like being suspended in time and space for Anna. The piercing anticipation had to be the most delicious sensation she had ever experienced and she clung to it, knowing that it would end very soon. Wanting it to end so that she could feel Luke inside her. Touching parts of her body that had never felt so hollow. Reaching places that weren't even physical.

She just knew he would be able to touch her soul.

Passion so intense had to explode and burn out in a dramatic climax and if that had been the end of it, it would have been incredibly satisfying on a physical level. Even better was that Luke smiled at Anna when they finally caught their breath.

'Now we can really get to know each other,' he promised.

And they did. A slow exploration of each other's bodies. A shaping of muscles on Anna's part with a compliment on how fit he must be. A tracing of Anna's breast with a single finger that ran across the flatness of her stomach to her belly button.

'You are beautiful,' Luke told her.

She found the scars on Luke's leg and he tried to move her hand but she resisted.

'They're part of you, Luke,' she said gently. 'Don't hide. Please.'

He went very still as she touched the misshapen muscle of his thigh and the lumpy ridges of the scars.

'Ugly, isn't it?' he ground out finally.

'No. They tell me that you have courage. That you're different.' Anna propped herself up on one elbow to look down at Luke. Even in this half-light she could see the shadows in his eyes that were part of the scars she had just been touching. What she could feel on his leg was nothing compared to the scars that had to be still hidden.

'Special,' she added in a whisper, leaning down to kiss him. She tried to put what she couldn't put into words into that kiss. To tell him that she accepted him for who he was. With scars. That she had courage too. That she could be trusted.

They made love again and this time it was slow and sweet and, in its wake, Anna fell asleep in Luke's arms, drifting off in a cloud of utter contentment. Of promise. Of a hope so compelling it was safer to go to sleep than contemplate the notion that it might be unjustified.

She woke some time later to find herself alone in a strange bed. She lay there, listening, but the house had that peculiar kind of silence that told her she was alone within these walls. Turning her head, she caught the glow of a digital, bedside clock. It was 3 a.m. Where on earth was Luke?

Taking the rumpled sheet with her to wrap around her body, Anna climbed from the bed. Instinct took her straight to the window and she stared out, the way she had when she'd first entered this room. For a long minute it was too dark to see anything. Then the moon emerged from thick cloud and she saw him. On the beach.

Running.

How could he be doing that? Not just because it was the middle of the night and it had to be well below zero out there, but how hard would it have to be to do that, in soft sand, on a leg that was damaged enough to make him limp at a fast walking pace or put him in noticeable pain when he had to stand for any length of time?

He was more driven than Anna had suspected and it was disturbing. Maybe he wasn't driving himself towards something. Maybe he was trying to run away.

He came back to the bed a while later, warm and fresh from a hot shower, and when he reached for Anna, she was happy to sacrifice further sleep to make love yet again. This time, however, there was an edge that hadn't been there before. Concern for Luke. The knowledge that she was with a deeply troubled man.

When daylight broke, Luke was absent from the bed again but Anna knew where to look. He wasn't running on the beach this time. She could see the dark shape striding into the surf. Diving into a breaking wave further out and then surfacing to swim, with a strong, steady stroke, parallel to the sand.

She had showered and dressed by the time Luke returned to the house. She saw him coming up the path in his wetsuit, carrying dripping flippers in one hand. His face registered surprise.

'You're not going to stay for breakfast?'

'I'd better not. I need to collect Crash and I've got a huge list of things I want to get done on my day off. If I can finish the painting and get the windowsills sanded and varnished, I can put my bedroom back together properly tonight.'

'Shall I come over after work and give you a hand?'

Anna hesitated. She could decline the offer and send a signal that she wanted to slow down whatever was happening between them. If she accepted, it would take them to a new level. The start of a relationship instead of a one-night stand.

Luke was pulling the zipper on his wetsuit. Peeling it away to reveal his bare torso, and Anna's body instantly reminded her of exactly what it had felt like to have those hands peeling away her own clothing. The sound of the nearby surf reminded her of watching him in the night, punishing his body by pounding over the sand. Enduring the pain in his leg because he was driven. And courageous.

And she…loved him for it?

Oh, help!

'I—I'd love a hand,' she heard herself say aloud. Good grief, what was she doing? She couldn't stop herself. 'I'll cook you some dinner. Do you realise we totally forgot to eat last night?'

Luke looked more surprised than he had on finding her dressed and ready to leave.

And then he smiled. 'Sometimes food can be over-rated. I had everything I needed.'

Anna actually blushed as she smiled back. 'Me, too.'

A day at home was important for Anna.

By throwing herself into the renovations of her

cottage and spending time playing with Crash, she could banish Dr Bartlett and let her recharge her professional batteries. Usually the door between work and home was firmly closed but today there was a wedge preventing that. She found herself wondering where Luke might be and what he might be doing.

He wouldn't be in Theatre. Although the tacit agreement that they would act as a team for surgery was still new, it was working and Anna trusted Luke not to break it. If something extraordinary happened, like Jamie's case had presented yesterday, he would call her in.

How was Jamie today? Anna peeled off her gloves and discarded the sandpaper she had been using, intending to make a call, but the phone rang as she walked towards it.

'I thought you might like an update on Jamie,' Luke said. 'We're transferring him to the ward this afternoon. He's bouncing back from his surgery remarkably well and I think we'll find he'll end up showing little effect from being virtually frozen to death.'

Anna listened to Luke's voice and absorbed the welcome news. The call ended, she went back to varnishing her windowsill. Thoughts of Luke were there as pervasively as the smell of polyurethane. Catching sight of Crash ripping her sandpaper to shreds with his tail thumping, she made a mental note to get to the supermarket so that she had something to feed Luke for dinner tonight. What did he like to eat? What would he like to do when they'd finished eating?

Oh, Lord. She could only hope that Luke wasn't in his office, struggling to concentrate on important paperwork, getting ambushed by memories of their astonishing night together. On the other hand, maybe she hoped he was. This was all as confusing as it was wonderful.

She put a roast of beef in the oven to cook slowly and fill her cottage with a welcoming aroma. She wanted Luke to feel welcome. She purchased wine, too. She wanted him to relax and feel comfortable. This was another new step. A chance to get to know each other better on more than a physical level. A chance to talk about things other than work. A chance to test these newborn feelings she was experiencing. To see if there was a chance of finding ground that might nurture them or whether they needed to be ruthlessly weeded out.

Except that turned out to be harder than Anna had anticipated. Luke seemed happy to be in her home and he clearly appreciated the meal, though he declined any alcohol. He was polite but unforthcoming when it came to any personal conversation.

'What was it like?' Anna asked at one stage. 'Working in a field hospital?'

'Basic. Fast and bloody.' His tone was detached enough to signal a lack of desire to go into details. 'These Yorkshire puddings are fantastic,' he said into the moment's silence that fell then. 'Where did you learn to cook like this?'

'My mother was adamant that a girl had to be able to cook. So was my father, come to that.'

'And you weren't.'

It was a statement, rather than a question. Delivered with a quizzical edge that made Anna think he could see right into places in her heart that even she didn't peer into too deeply any more.

'Things that boys were allowed to do were more important. I jumped through the girl hoops but it wasn't enough.' Anna looked down at her plate. 'My father wanted a son that he never got.'

She heard Luke's fork clatter as he put it down. Then she felt him touch her hand. 'He got something better, then, didn't he? They must be very proud of you.'

Anna shrugged. 'Surprised might be closer to the mark. Disappointed, maybe, that I didn't become a teacher or a nurse and shower them with grandchildren. Grandsons,' she amended with an attempt to lighten the revelation with a smile. 'What was your family like, Luke? You weren't an only child, were you?'

'No. All boys in my family but if there had been a girl she would have been expected to do the boy things. She wouldn't have had a choice, really, being dragged from one military post to another. I was the one to break the family tradition and become a doctor instead of a soldier. Even then, I was expected to aim for a career as an army medic. I rebelled.'

'You went in the end. I'm sure your parents are proud.'

'They're in New Zealand,' Luke said, as though that answered the unspoken question. And then he steered the conversation away from himself again. 'What's the next project you've got lined up for the cottage?'

He helped her clean up after the meal and then he helped her move the bedroom furniture back into place. And then, as Anna had hoped he would, he took her into her own bed and made love to her. He wouldn't stay the night, however.

'I've got so much reading to catch up on,' he excused himself in the early hours. 'You've got no idea how out of date you can get by taking a year or two off. I've got to keep up my exercise program, too, and I can't miss my early swim.'

Too many good reasons not to stay.

'Don't you ever sleep, Luke?'

'Sleep's overrated.' He bent to kiss Anna again as he took his leave. 'Life's too short to waste it.'

Maybe sleep wasn't so overrated.

Fatigue was like a form of anger. Something that simmered and bubbled occasionally to splash in unexpected directions.

'That is a surgical mask, not a damned bib. Don't come into this theatre unless you're going to wear it properly.'

The junior theatre nurse went pale and fled. Luke looked away as Anna glanced up from the meticulous stitches she was placing in preparation for a mitral valve replacement. He knew there had been no real reason to snap at the nurse. She'd been delivering some new IV fluid supplies, not planning to come and lean over the operating table.

'I've got all the anular sutures placed and tagged,' Anna said.

'Let's get the valve seated, then, and tie them off.'

'OK,' Anna said as the procedure continued. 'I'll have the aortic needle vent now, thanks.'

Luke watched as she removed more air and then re-started the heart.

'Can you elevate the apex of the left ventricle?' she asked him. 'If those adhesions are too dense, I'll go for clamping the aorta. I'd like to follow up with an echocardiograph to check.'

Would she say something when this was over? Reprimand him in some way for his irritation with the junior nurse? He probably deserved it, given that this wasn't the first time.

Ripping off his mask and the disposable hat as he left Theatre, Luke pushed his fingers through his flattened hair. What was wrong with him?

It wasn't simply fatigue. Insomnia had been a part of his life for many months now and he had coped. Maybe the difference was that he was choosing to stay awake when he craved sleep. Night after night. It had been nearly a week now. He would hold Anna in his arms after they'd made love and feel the way her body softened and her breathing slowed. The blissful temptation of sleep would pull at him in those moments, too.

Taunt him.

When he needed sleep and was ready for it, it wouldn't come. If offered itself at times like this, when he couldn't accept. He just couldn't go there because he had no control over what his sleeping mind chose to do. While it could be the saving of him to have Anna to hold close in the wake of a nightmare, he had to spare her from sharing that part of his life, because then he'd have to talk about it and he wasn't going to do that with anybody.

If he could bury it, it would go away.

Eventually.

Luke fell asleep the next night Anna stayed at his house.

Maybe that was what had woken her—the change in how he was holding her. It was more like she was holding him right now. With a careful tilt of her head, she could see his face and it looked so different she was shocked. He looked so much younger. Unguarded.

Vulnerable.

Those piercing, intense eyes were shuttered. His lips were soft and slightly parted and she could hear his soft, even breaths. Even the furrows at the top of his nose had softened. Anna willed herself not to move. She didn't want to wake him. Heaven knew, he needed the sleep. Nobody could keep up the kind of pace Luke did without coming to physical harm. It was no wonder he snapped at the people around him occasionally.

So she stayed awake. Holding this man she was coming to feel more deeply for every day. Wanting to protect him and give him the healing rest that only sleep could provide. That was probably why she felt the moment the nightmare started. The way the muscles beneath her hands and arms became so tense. She could hear the way his breathing became shallow and rapid. His heart was pounding beneath his ribs and she could feel the rumble of his moan even before it reached his lips.

'No-o-o-o…'

'Luke. Wake up.' Anna held him more tightly. 'It's all right. It's just a bad dream.'

She couldn't hold him now. The strength in his body was frightening as he twisted and fought whatever demons had come in his sleep. Anna could see the sheen of sweat on his body. His breath came in choking gasps now—as though he was suffocating.

'Arghhh!' The sound was one of agony.

The covers were hurled back from the bed and Luke swung his legs over the side. He was almost crouching there and he covered his face with his hands.

Anna scrambled to her knees and across the bed. Kneeling behind Luke, she wrapped her arms around him.

'It's all right,' she said, hoping her voice wouldn't betray how shaky she was feeling. 'I'm here, Luke. You had a nightmare.' That's all, she wanted to add, but bit the words back. This wasn't something that should be belittled in any way.

His breathing was slowing now. For a moment he leaned back into Anna's embrace but then he lurched to his feet.

'I need some fresh air,' was all he said. He began dragging on clothes. Fleecy track pants. Running shoes.

She couldn't make him tell her anything about the nightmare if he didn't want to. Anna closed her eyes. Waiting. Hoping.

'You…' Luke paused as he got halfway across the room but he didn't turn round. 'You weren't… I didn't want you to see that.'

'It was a nightmare, Luke. Don't go. You don't have to run away from it.'

The huff of sound from him was angry. She knew nothing. And he wanted it to stay that way.

'Would you rather I went home?'

'Up to you. I won't come back to bed. I've got some work I may as well do now that I'm awake. After my run.'

And with that he was gone.

Anna didn't want to wait. There was no moon tonight so she wouldn't be able to see him down on the beach. She didn't want to watch either. Luke had his own way of dealing with whatever was bothering him and it didn't include her.

What was she to him? With a sinking heart Anna found her clothes and then the keys to her car. Was this just about the sex?

Distraction?

When she arrived home to her cold cottage, Anna put an electric heater on and made a pot of tea. It was nearly 4 a.m. and she was far too wound up to go to sleep again. She missed Crash.

Opening her briefcase, she got her laptop out and connected to the internet. With no emails that caught her interest, she idly clicked on a search engine and stared at the flashing cursor.

'PTSD', she tapped in on impulse.

So many sites. She opened the one that had been given first place in the queue and within minutes she was totally engrossed.

Post traumatic stress disorder was a syndrome that

could develop following any traumatic event. Things like natural disasters and car crashes, violent assaults or even medical procedures, especially for children. Top of the list, however, as she'd known quite well, was war.

Traumatic experience put the mind and body into a state of shock, she read, but most people could make some sense of what had happened, process the resulting emotions and come out of it eventually. In PTSD, the person remained in psychological shock. There was a disconnection between the memory of the event and how the victim felt about it.

Anna read on, almost feverishly, skipping a few paragraphs to the heading of 'Symptoms'.

Nightmares.

Flashbacks.

Difficulty falling or staying asleep.

Irritability or outbursts of anger.

She found herself nodding at that one. She hadn't said anything about the way Luke had snapped at that poor theatre nurse the other day but other people were talking about it. And about the way he had avoided all social invitations outside the hospital over the Christmas and New Year period. Some were keen to remember his odd behaviour at the one event he had attended and the way he'd stormed out of the canteen.

Her eyes drifted further down the list. Not that she needed any more information to confirm what she was already convinced of.

Depression was common. So was guilt. People often attempted to numb themselves through substance abuse. Luke obviously avoided drinking but wouldn't his exercise regime fit into the same category? How numb would you get, running or swimming in the middle of winter? And physical pain could override mental suffering.

The victim could also feel detached from others and emotionally numb. They would have a sense of a limited future and wouldn't expect to live a normal life span or get married and have a family. PTSD would harm relationships, the ability to function and their quality of life.

There were treatments suggested, of course, but they came with the background rider that the sufferer had to be willing to confront it and not see the admission as a sign of weakness. Luke had been brought up in a military family. Was it the kind of thing that didn't get mentioned? That he wouldn't be able to allow himself to admit? He'd denied having flashbacks. Pushed her away in the wake of that nightmare. He 'hadn't wanted her to see it'. Had he ever, in fact, gone to sleep before when she'd been in the same bed?

Maybe her intrusion into his personal life was making it worse. Removing opportunities he might have otherwise had to sleep. Putting stress on him by making him think he had to factor her into a future that might already seem too difficult.

It was so clear to her that Luke was suffering from PTSD. It was also very clear that the only way to conquer it was to confront it. Somehow he would have to learn to accept it as part of his past. Numbing it or pushing the memories away would only make it worse and it was more likely to emerge under stress.

The sound of a distant beeping finally intruded on Anna's thoughts and she realised her alarm clock was going off. Her huff of laughter was ironic. It was time to get up and get ready for work. With a heavy heart she went through the motions, but she couldn't stop thinking about the pieces that had finally fallen into place and created a picture so much darker than she had feared.

As far as she was concerned, she was a part of that picture. She was in far too deep to escape. She didn't want to.

For better or worse, she had fallen in love with Luke Davenport.

She wanted to help him.

But how?

CHAPTER NINE

'WHAT's this?' Anna had stooped to pick something up from the floor of Luke's office.

He glanced at the scalloped, gilt-edged card she was holding. Damn, he hadn't noticed he'd missed his aim.

'Nothing,' he said. 'It was supposed to go in the bin.'

'But…' Anna was reading the fancy calligraphy and then she looked up with a stunned expression on her face. 'Luke…this is an invitation to a medal ceremony, isn't it? Returning Heroes. With a ball to honour the recipients of the medals.'

'I'm not going. I hate parties.' Luke swivelled his desk chair so that he could drop a file into the cabinet behind him. 'Was there something you wanted to talk to me about?'

'Yes.'

Another file tab caught Luke's eye and he pulled it out. It took several seconds to register the silence. Anna wasn't going to talk to him until she was confident he was listening.

Fine. He swung the chair back around. 'What do you want to talk about?'

She was still holding the card and looked down at it again. 'This.'

'That's not why you came in here. You didn't know it existed.' He could feel his eyes narrowing as he sighed. 'What was the real reason you came in?'

'This isn't even an invitation. It says you're "required to attend". That sounds pretty official. Will you get into trouble if you don't go?'

Luke gave a huff of laughter. 'What can they do? Kick me out of the army? Give my medal to someone else? That's fine by me. I don't want the damn medal.'

'Why not?' Anna sank into the other chair in his office but her gaze was unwavering. Fixed on Luke. She wasn't going to let this one go.

He felt trapped. Angry. The way he had ever since he'd woken from that nightmare to find Anna in his bed. This was becoming a problem. OK, the sex was great. She was great. He loved seeing her like this, at work, in her neat clothes and with her hair all scraped back. Being completely professional in their interactions while all the time they both knew what it would be like after, away from work.

When the clothes came off and the communication came through touch and not words. When they could both escape to a place that promised only pleasure.

But maybe it had run its course. It wasn't going to work. Not long term.

She was already too close. Had seen too much. She didn't represent a rope that he could use to help him into his future any more. She was starting to resemble a roadway. With traffic in both directions. He didn't want to go back. He couldn't. Because if he did, he would be taking Anna with him and she would see who he really was and then she would be the one to go.

And that might finally destroy him.

Anna could see the play of emotion on Luke's face. The annoyance that she was pushing when he'd made it clear he wasn't interested in either going to this ceremony or talking about it. She knew perfectly well she was stepping over a boundary here. She could almost see him weighing up whether she was worth the trouble.

Would he tell her to get out? Push so hard she had no choice but to leave? He'd been holding her at a distance ever since that nightmare. They hadn't been to bed together for three days now. They hadn't even spent that much time together at work. He was avoiding her because he didn't want to talk about the nightmare. Probably didn't want to admit how often he had them. Or that they happened at all, like the flashbacks. Talking about this medal ceremony and what it had to remind him of might tip them over the edge and it would all be over, but it was a risk Anna had no choice but to take.

Maybe Luke needed a push himself to recognize that he had PTSD. He had to be willing to confront his past. She was quite prepared to help him and be with him through any rough patches but only if it was part of a healing process. Otherwise she would just be locking herself into a miserable cycle of watching the man she loved suffer. Getting pushed away and hurt herself and then crawling back for more of the same.

She wasn't going to do it. If she did, she would only

be allowing Luke to stay locked in that dark space permanently and he was worth more than that.

'Why not, Luke?' she asked again. 'Why don't you want to get the recognition you deserve? It's your name that's right at the top of that list. Does your family know about this? Will they be there, hoping to be part of the honour?'

'I don't want the damned medal.' The words burst out in an angry rush as Luke leaned forward on his desk, both hands clenched into fists. 'I haven't told my family because I don't want to celebrate what happened. Or to glorify war. To pretty it up for the media with everyone in nice, clean uniforms and rows of shiny badges. Dancing, for God's sake! That's about as meaningless as everything else in civilian life.' He lowered his voice and it became rough. Totally compelling. 'War is about blood and guts and people. People who can be terrified they're not going to get back to the ones they love. Who can die, in agony, a thousand miles away from the people who love them.'

He tipped his head back, closing his eyes. 'Yes, I survived. But what about all the others?'

Slowly, he brought his gaze back to Anna's. His eyes were dark. So shadowed they were blank of emotion. Like the rest of his face. 'I don't want a prize for being one of the lucky ones.'

Anna swallowed. Hard. She was part of his civilian life. Meaningless.

The silence stretched on. Tense and horrible. She had to say something. To try and defuse this awful distance escalating between them.

'Yes, war is about people,' she said finally. 'That's how they generally start, isn't it? You have a group of people, including innocent children, who lose their lives or have their rights as human beings threatened or taken away. Most people have to try and close their minds to the atrocities that go on because it doesn't affect their lives and they can't do anything about it, anyway.' She drew in a breath, the words coming more easily now. 'But some people are brave enough to put their hands up and say, I'll help. I'll go into horrible places and endure terrible things. Not because I might end up getting a medal for it but because it might—eventually—help to make the world a better place.'

Was he listening? Anna couldn't tell. She was talking hard and fast now, barely forming the thoughts before the words tumbled from her mouth. Desperately trying to let Luke know, somehow, that it was all right to have this as part of his past. That she accepted it. And if she talked enough, maybe by some miracle she could say something that would get through to him. Stop him from shutting her out and pushing her out of his life.

'If enough people didn't avoid even thinking about wars, maybe something could change without people having to die,' she continued. 'And maybe the publicity that comes from something like this is what makes them take notice. It's the heroes that people can't help taking notice of. That they listen to.'

Luke was staring at her now but his face was still devoid of emotion.

'Maybe the people who take the most notice are the

ones who've lost someone they love. Because they have to try and make sense of it all.'

Which was exactly what Luke needed to do himself, wasn't it?

'Or maybe it's the people who will feel lucky for the rest of their lives because someone they love has come home. Thanks to one of those heroes. I'll bet the families of all the soldiers you saved would love to give you a medal, Luke, but they don't have to, do they? The army is going to do it for them.'

Still no reaction. Anna felt a flicker of anger. 'How do you think they'll feel if you can't be bothered to show up?'

That did it. Luke's face finally moved but it was only to turn away from her. 'Are you finished?'

'No.' Anna's mouth had gone dry. This was it. She had failed. He wasn't going to let her into this part of his life. Her breath came out in a ragged sigh. She closed her eyes in defeat. 'The party wouldn't be so bad,' she said dryly. 'At least nobody would be wearing reindeer horns.'

Opening her eyes, she found Luke had turned back to face her. For a heartbeat her flippant comment hung in the air and then she saw a change in Luke's eyes. A lightening of those shadows. A vaguely incredulous expression that took her back to...

Oh, help. Back to that day when Luke had come to her cottage and discovered Anna instead of his colleague, Dr Bartlett. When she'd made that stupid joke about unlikely dogs using a staircase to become mates. So she was no good at cracking jokes? Did he have to look at her as though he was seeing someone he didn't even recognise?

Someone stupid, maybe, who said meaningless things that made him wonder why on earth he'd ever been attracted to her?

But Luke's lips were moving now.

Good grief! He was smiling. Virtually grinning.

'OK,' he said. 'I'll go. On one condition.'

'What's that?' The relief that he wasn't shouting at her or physically throwing her out of his office was enormous. It was making her feel light-headed. Ridiculously happy.

Hopeful, even.

'That you come with me.'

Anna's head cleared astonishingly quickly. An image of a military ball sprang into her head. Men in dress uniform. Luke in dress uniform. He would look impossibly gorgeous. And she would have to be dressed up and feminine. No way would she be on ground where she could feel like an equal. But they weren't equal, were they? Even here. Not on emotional grounds, anyway.

She would be so proud of him if she went. She would be getting herself in ever deeper.

But wasn't that what she wanted? Needed? Or was it that she knew she should fight it but just couldn't help herself?

Anna shook her head, trying to clear the confused jumble of her thoughts. Luke misinterpreted the gesture as reluctance.

'You think I should go,' he said. 'And you're probably correct.'

Another memory was niggling at Anna now. She'd persuaded Luke to attend the staff Christmas function by telling him that heads of departments would be expected to attend. Look what had happened there. How much more likely would a flashback be when he was surrounded by army uniforms and by people wanting to talk about why he was being honoured as a hero?

'I won't go unless you come with me,' Luke said quietly. 'Please, Anna. I…need you.'

Three little words. Possibly the only three she'd ever hear from Luke but maybe they were enough.

'All right,' she said with a catch in her voice. 'I'll come with you.'

Why had he been so determined not to attend this event?

So bad-tempered about having to put on his dress uniform 'Blues' and act like a soldier? Gritting his teeth as he'd accepted all the congratulations that came with the medal now pinned to his tunic.

Hating it all so much he'd barely spoken to Anna, even though he could see how much effort she'd put into this on his behalf. Buying a new dress and having her hair done in some fancy way. Putting up with his foul mood for the whole of their drive to London. All those long stretches when the only sound in the vehicle had been the windscreen wipers trying to cope with the sleet of the January evening.

He'd only asked her to dance because it was the last duty he had to perform tonight. The recipients of the medals and their partners had been invited to take the floor first and people were watching. Clapping.

One dance and then he could escape. Drive back to St Piran, apologise to Anna and then forget the whole excruciating business.

The lighting was softened as the orchestra began playing a waltz. Chandeliers still sparkled overhead and the reflection of the crowd present could be seen in the glass of the floor-to-ceiling windows that filled one wall and afforded a spectacular view of London beyond. Diamonds glistened on women and the buttons on dress uniforms gleamed on the men.

Holding out his hand to Anna, Luke had the sudden, awful thought that he hadn't bothered to find out if Anna knew how to dance something formal. He'd had lessons as a teenager, along with all his brothers, and the skill was automatic. Not that he'd had either the opportunity or the desire to use it for a very long time. But Anna took his hand and came into his arms willingly. The dark, emerald fabric of her long dress shimmered in this lighting and he gathered her into a formal dance hold. Stiffly at first, until the steps came more easily. It was only then that he noticed how light Anna was on her feet and how well she was able to follow his lead.

More couples came onto the dance floor but Luke didn't even notice. In his relief that he wasn't embarrassing Anna and making her evening even worse than he had already by assuming a skill she might not have, he relaxed a notch. Another notch or two got added when he remembered that the evening was almost over. He was going to get through it. And that was when he finally looked down and really noticed the woman in his arms.

Her hair had been scooped up in some clever fashion to make coils that sat sleekly against the back of her head. Little bits had been pulled free, however, so that tiny soft spirals framed her face and drew attention to the lovely length of her neck. The style was formal and precise—like Anna was at work—but it was those free tendrils that Luke really liked. They reminded him of the way Anna was when she wasn't at work. Softer. Surprising.

Pure woman.

The fabric of her dress was silky under his hands. Almost as delicious as he knew her bare skin to be. The colour was sheer brilliance. How had it taken him this long to notice how it was a shade or two darker than her eyes and made them so…luminous.

So extraordinarily beautiful.

Mesmerising.

The music altered tempo as the orchestra started something less classical. Something moody and sweet. It was the perfect opportunity to make an exit from the dance floor but Luke had lost any desire to do so. Instead, he drew Anna closer. He wasn't following any routine steps now, just moving to the music that surrounded them. Holding an amazingly beautiful woman who followed every move he made so easily it was like holding an extension to his own body.

She looked and felt so lovely. She even smelled so wonderful that Luke bent his head to get closer. Was that perfume coming from her hair or her skin? Or was it just

Anna? It was hypnotising. A new space. An escape that was better than sleep. Better than sex, even, because he could keep this up for ever.

He certainly wasn't going to be the one to suggest stopping any time soon.

Anna had been very close to tears by the time Luke asked her to dance.

Wishing she'd never agreed to accompany him. A million miles away from this would have been too close. She'd tried so hard to look the part and he'd been so closed off and angry from the moment he'd arrived at her door to collect her.

The drive had been awful. Full of silences during which she had nothing to think about except the distance between them. That she was no closer to imagining a way out of this for Luke that could offer the promise of a happy future for him.

For them both.

Watching him during the ceremonial part of the evening had been even more grim. He looked just as gorgeous as she'd expected in the crisp, dark blue uniform with its braid and insignia, but she'd been able to see how much he'd been hating it. Tension so great it seemed like he could simply snap at any moment. Luke hadn't wanted to be a part of any of this. He hadn't wanted any of it to be a part of his past.

Could no one else see what she could see? That the event that had led to him being here tonight was what had scarred him so deeply. That he was determined to escape the memories and he couldn't see that the only way to stop them haunting him to the point of ruining his life was to turn round and confront them.

The tension had been contagious. All Anna had wanted was for the evening to end. To get through that long drive home somehow and then…what?

Admit defeat and see what she could do about putting her life back together the way it had been before Luke had come back to St Piran?

It had been the thought of trying to move on without him that had been what nearly brought her to tears in public. But then Luke had held out his hand when the medal recipients had been invited to take the dance floor first. It had been the first time he'd touched her in what felt like a very, very long time, and as soon as Anna had felt that contact she'd known exactly where she really wanted to be.

Not a million miles away at all.

Right here.

In Luke's arms.

He could dance. When the initial awkwardness wore off, Anna was astonished to find he could actually dance beautifully. The music was soothing and the rhythm of the waltz easy to follow even from long-ago lessons. Glancing up, she found Luke's face still grim and turned away. He was going through the motions here, but in reality he was hunting for an escape route.

Dropping her gaze, Anna stared at the medal pinned to his tunic, awarded for an act of outstanding bravery during active operations against an enemy. It was a beautiful silver cross mounted on a wreath of laurel leaves with a crown in its centre. The ribbon had narrow stripes of dark blue on each edge and a central stripe of crimson. What would he do with it when he got home? Shut it away in its box and hide it along with the memories of why it had been bestowed?

Looking up again, Anna was startled to find Luke's gaze on her face. An intense gaze but one she was getting used to. As though he was seeing her properly for the first time. Looking…amazed.

The waltz ended and Anna knew this would be when Luke suggested they sit down or go to supper perhaps. Or just go home.

Instead, he drew her closer and she could feel some of that terrible tension leaving his body. They were so close. She could feel the length of his body against hers. Leading her. So powerful and yet it felt gentle, probably because she was so willing to follow.

And then she felt his cheek against her hair and Anna closed her eyes, sinking into the delicious knowledge that Luke wasn't just dancing now.

He was dancing with her.

Another medley of tunes began. And then another, but Luke made no move to take her away from the dance floor and Anna certainly wasn't going to be the one to break this connection.

She wanted it to last for ever.

The start of the fireworks display startled all the guests. The wall of windows provided a great view of the city lights on the other side of the Thames but nobody had noticed the grassy bank-side area until the impressive display got under way.

It began with a sound like a cannon firing. A huge silver rocket shot up into the blackness of the sky and then exploded into a shower of tiny silver spheres that drifted down slowly.

Not that Anna was watching them. At the first sound Luke had stiffened so abruptly that she had tripped on his foot. Then he moved again, so sharply Anna could swear she felt him snap. He dropped his arms from her body and turned swiftly, weaving between couples who had also stopped dancing to see what was happening. They began to move towards the windows.

Anna moved in the opposite direction. Following Luke. All the way out of the ballroom. Through the area where a buffet supper was being served. Through the vast foyer where staff were now stacking all the chairs that had been used for the initial ceremony. Down a wide flight of steps. She could feel the sting of sleet on her skin. Gathering up the folds of her dress, she raced after Luke. Around the corner of the building. As far away as he could get from where the fireworks were happening.

And there he stopped. When Anna came around the corner she saw him, his head on his arm, leaning against the stone wall. She could hear him gasping for breath in the same way he had when he'd been having that nightmare.

'Luke!'

'Go, Anna.' The plea was hoarse. 'Get out. While you can.'

She came up to be right beside him. 'I'm not going anywhere. Talk to me.'

'I can't.'

At least part of him was there and aware of her. He'd been like that in the canteen too, hadn't he? Having a flashback he couldn't control but still aware of things around him, like bumping into someone and spilling their drink. Maybe, if she tried hard enough, she could get through to him.

'Why not?' she begged. 'Why can't you talk to me, Luke?'

'My problem. If I told you, it would become your problem.' The words were staccato. Agonised. 'I won't do that to you.'

'It's already my problem.'

'No. You can go. I want you to go.'

'I can't do that, Luke.'

'Why the hell not?' His head turned and the expression on his face broke her heart.

'Because…because I love you, that's why.'

Luke buried his head again and he groaned. It was a sound of such distress but was it due to her confession or because of whatever still had him in its grip?

Fireworks were still going off, muted a little by the vast building between them but still loud. Possibly loud enough that he hadn't heard what she'd just said. Or maybe he had chosen not to hear it because he already had too much to deal with.

'It's the noise, isn't it?' She had to touch Luke. To get closer. 'Where are you, Luke? What do you see?'

A moment's silence and then Luke spoke in a low, desperate voice she barely recognised.

'We're under fire. We're on our way to a village. There's children hurt by a landmine but we don't get there.' The words were rushing out so fast it was hard to hear them clearly. 'It's an ambush. Another mine. And artillery. The truck's tipped over. Everybody's hurt. I…I felt my leg snap.'

He dragged in a breath. 'We need to get out. Danny's unconscious. His airway's blocked. There's a chopper coming. I can smell the smoke and the blood. The guys are screaming. I'm trapped. I'm trying to get them out and I can't move. I can't breathe…'

Anna was gripping his arm. 'Yes, you can, Luke. You did get them out. All of them. That's why you got the medal tonight. You saved everybody in that truck. You saved their lives.'

'But I didn't…' Luke groaned again. Or was it a sob? 'Not the life I wanted to save.' Yes, it was definitely a sob now. Torn from somewhere deep inside. 'I couldn't save Crash, Anna. I…wanted to…so much…and I… couldn't…'

Racking sobs took hold of Luke's body now. All Anna could do was to hold him as hard as she could and be there. Saying nothing. Letting him hold her so tightly it was impossible to take a deep breath and letting him rock her as he rocked himself.

And eventually, as she became aware of how damp and cold they were both going to be, Luke quietened.

'Let's go home,' she said.

Luke waited outside while she collected their coats and the car keys.

'I can drive if you'd like.'

'No. I'm all right.' Luke's voice was sombre. 'Better if I'm doing something. I'm sorry about that.'

'I'm not,' Anna said, but Luke didn't hear her. He was striding ahead to where the car was parked.

Sleet was still falling and got thicker as they left the outskirts of London but the road was still clear enough. Anna listened to the windscreen wipers. They sounded different now. Maybe because the atmosphere inside the car wasn't as charged as it had been coming in the opposite direction. The tension was gone. Luke seemed tired but calm.

'Who was Crash?' Anna asked softly. 'A friend?'

'My brother. His real name was Matthew. Mattie.'

'Oh...'

Anna was searching her memory. She'd known that name had come from something special. A kid who'd grown too fast, he'd said, and looked a bit goofy with big feet. So clumsy he'd earned the nickname of Crash. He grown into...what had Luke said? Oh, yes. The strongest, bravest guy he knew.

And then he'd given her that first smile. The one that had melted her heart.

'He was younger than you?' The question was tentative. It seemed too good to believe that Luke was finally talking to her.

Letting her in.

'Yeah.' Luke's gaze was fixed on the road ahead. He was driving a little below the speed limit. Taking it carefully.

Anna felt safe with him but did he feel the same way?

'There's an older brother, too,' Luke said after a

moment. 'The Davenport boys, we were called. A collective troop. A mini-platoon. Nobody questioned that we would do anything but take after our dad and join the army.'

'It must have been hard for you, then.'

'Yeah.' The word was heartfelt. 'I felt guilty. Especially after Crash joined up. I'd always tried to look out for him, you know? In the end, though, he was looking out for me. He was the only one who understood why I wanted to be a civilian. A doctor.'

Anna couldn't ask the obvious question but it was hanging there and Luke could sense it.

'He got killed in action in Iraq,' he said very softly. 'And it just broke me up. I owed him so much. I missed him so badly. In the end, the answer seemed easy. I joined up to honour his memory. To do what I should have done all along. I thought it would make me feel less guilty. That it would somehow help fill the horrible, empty, useless feeling I had.'

A long silence this time and then Luke sighed. 'All I really achieved was to screw up the rest of my life. I'm not fit to do my job any more. I'm not a viable proposition to be in any kind of a meaningful relationship. I meant what I said, Anna. You should get out. Relatively unscathed. While you still can.'

'And I meant what I said,' Anna whispered. She wasn't going to tell him again that she loved him. It was enough to know she had said it aloud and it was true. Instinct told her he wasn't ready to hear those particular words but she could remind him of something else she'd said. 'I'm not going anywhere. We all need courage to face the future,' she added carefully. 'It's not a sign of weakness if you have to ask for help sometimes.'

Maybe she could remind him of something he'd said, too. 'You're the strongest, bravest man I know,' she said, deliberately using the words he'd used to describe his brother. 'You'll make it.'

This wasn't the time to talk about finding the help Luke needed or how to find it. They'd made enough of a breakthrough tonight. All Anna wanted now was to get home and go to bed. With Luke.

And sleep. She was so tired. The windscreen wipers flicked in a steady rhythm. Swirls of tiny white flakes zoomed towards them in a hypnotic pattern. Anna could feel her eyes drifting closed.

She was sound asleep, Luke noticed, as they finally left the main roads behind. The snow began falling more thickly and he slowed their pace. He didn't like the deteriorating conditions but he could take his time getting them home. Funny, but he felt like he had all the time he needed now. For anything. He couldn't remember when he'd last felt this…peaceful? Maybe he never had.

He stole another glance at Anna. He would get her home safely. He knew the road and he could cope with the weather.

What he couldn't control was the other traffic on the road that night. Especially when he had no warning of what was coming around the corner. The driver of the big truck probably didn't realise how far his wheels were over the centre line of the coastal road because the snow was starting to settle in patches and the road markings were fading.

The jolt of leaving the smooth road surface and then hitting a fence post woke Anna and all Luke could hear as he fought desperately to prevent the car tipping into a roll was her scream of fear.

CHAPTER TEN

ANNA'S scream was cut off abruptly with the first impact of the rolling vehicle but the sound of metal shearing and scraping on rock was another kind of scream. Airbags deployed with a blast and shockwave that was indistinguishable from gunfire.

Luke was inside his nightmare but he knew he was awake and that made it so much worse. So confusing. His mind was being rocked and jolted as viciously as his body. One moment hanging in the straps of his safety belt, the next jarring on solid ground. A maelstrom of fear and desperation. The past, the present and things that had never been real, and never would be, existing only in his imagination.

He was in an army vehicle again but not the one in which he'd met the end of his time at war. In one that he'd never actually seen or touched. Just imagined. The one his brother, Matthew, had been driving. And each time they hit solid ground, they were hitting the mine that had destroyed the person he loved most in the world. Once, twice…three hits and he was still alive and awake.

This time, he had to save him.

Or he would die himself.

The violent churning of the landscape, vehicle and people probably lasted no more than thirty seconds but it felt like for ever. And then there was silence. A broken headlamp flickered for a second or two and then died.

It was pitch black and utterly silent.

Luke had been convinced that the worst sound he could ever hear were the screams of frightened and dying men, any one of whom could be his brother. Even the terrified sound Anna had made had become the last breath Crash had expelled.

In that instant, however, he knew the real truth.

That silence was far worse.

Crash.

Blindly, Luke reached out. His fingers caught in the limp, metallic folds of airbags that had erupted from the steering-wheel, the centre console and the dashboard.

'Can you hear me?'

A tiny sound in the silence as he strained to listen. An indrawn breath. Tentative and ragged.

'Y-yes.'

It wasn't Crash. It was Anna.

Of course it was. He'd known that all along. Hadn't he?

And she was alive, thank God. 'Are you hurt?'

'I…I'm not sure…'

He had to move. To find a source of light and then check Anna out. He had to get her out of this and make sure she would be all right. Any other course of action or result was unthinkable.

But his head swam when he tried to move. Impossible

to tell which way was supposed to be up. Had the car ended up on its roof instead of its wheels? Was it really Anna?

Luke found the catch of his safety belt and released it. His body didn't start falling so he wasn't upside down. His head started to clear.

'Take a deep breath,' he told Anna. 'As deep as you can.'

He listened to her comply with his request.

'Is it difficult? Does anything hurt?'

'N-no…'

'Can you move your arms? God, it's so dark. I can't see anything. Does your neck hurt? Don't move your head if it does.'

He could hear Anna shift position. Could see a change of shape in the darkness.

'I…I can move.'

So could Luke. He turned and began to lean sideways so that his hands could reach Anna's huddled figure on the far side of the vehicle. She was lower than he was. The car was on some kind of slope.

And then he froze.

It wasn't his head swimming this time. It was the car that was moving.

Rocking gently.

There was a scratching, scraping sound coming from somewhere beneath them. Metal on rock. And Luke became aware of another sound. He hadn't noticed it before because it could have been the rush of his own blood pulsing in his head.

Somewhere, far below, waves were rolling onto rocks.

They had been on a coastal road that often came close to clifftop. There had been a fence of some kind. A farmer's field or a barrier that was there to prevent anyone getting too close to a dangerous place? Like one that had a sheer drop to rocks that would not be survivable?

Perhaps it was just as well it was too dark to see anything outside.

Cold, damp air was coming in with the sounds of the night. Luke's door seemed to be missing or crumpled to leave an open space. Survival instinct was trying to kick in. The upward ground was on his side and he had an escape route. Even if the car was teetering on the top of a cliff, he could make a dive for it and roll free.

But that would change the weight distribution dramatically and that might be all that was needed to tip the vehicle and send it plunging over the edge.

With Anna still inside.

He would rather die himself.

The car was still rocking. Scraping.

'Luke?' Anna's whisper was terrified. 'What's… happening?'

'Don't move,' he said softly. 'Give me a sec. I need to think.'

Fear was clawing at him now. A dense cloud that contained a kaleidoscope of images and emotions that paralysed Luke for a moment. Sucking him into the place he couldn't allow himself to go.

No.

He couldn't smell blood. Or smoke. Or dust. Nobody was screaming.

They were in a car, not an armoured vehicle. This was Anna. Not Crash.

So why was it just as important that she was going to be all right? Crash was the person he had loved with all his heart. The one he would have given his own life to save.

It had taken a split second for Luke to understand the truth that silence could be more dreadful than any scream.

The truth he now learned arrived with similar, blinding clarity.

He had only been confused about the person he needed to save because of an emotion he hadn't allowed himself to entertain.

He loved Anna.

A different kind of love than he'd had for Crash but it was just as powerful. More so, even. He'd been kidding himself thinking of her as his rope. Or anchor. Or any other kind of tool to help him find his own future.

She was that future.

From that first moment when he'd found himself under her resentful glare she had entered his consciousness. His mind and—slipping somehow under a defensive radar—his heart.

'Luke…' Anna was crying. 'Talk to me. Are you hurt?'

'I'm fine.' He moved his hand carefully, just far enough to grip hers. 'As long as you are.'

'What happened?'

'We've had an accident. There was a truck. It came

around a corner on the wrong side of the road. I had to swerve and... Oh, God, I'm sorry, Anna.'

The grip on his hand tightened. 'That doesn't matter. We just need to get out.'

'We have to be careful. I'm not sure how stable the car is and I don't want it to move.'

'I'm scared.'

'I know. I am too but we'll get through this, Anna. Together.'

'Are you sure you're all right? It's not... I mean... You know...like a flashback thing?'

Oh, yes. The flashbacks he'd never admitted to. He couldn't admit to loving Anna either, could he? What did he have to offer her? He was broken.

'I want to get out. I want to get home.'

'I know. We will. I'll get you out, Anna. I'll take care of you.'

There was a light outside now. Coming closer. A powerful torch that filled the interior of this battered car in a sweeping motion. For a heartbeat Luke could see Anna's face clearly. The way she was looking at him.

She wasn't going anywhere, she'd said—way back before the accident had happened. She'd said she loved him.

He could see that love in her eyes. He could fall into it. Return it? How much courage would that take? What if he failed her, as he had failed his brother? If he lost her...

'Anna...I—'

The light got brighter. Steadier. A man's voice called out. 'Whatever you do in there, don't move. I've got a chain in the truck and I'm going to get it onto the back of your car. Help's on the way.'

Luke didn't want to move. Neither, it seemed, did Anna. The grip on his hand was tight enough to impair circulation.

'Don't let go of me,' she begged. 'Please. Not yet.'

'I won't,' he vowed. I can't, he added silently, because I love you.

The nearest hospital was St Piran's.

Ben Carter was astonished to find Anna and Luke turning up in the emergency department, dressed up to the nines, in the early hours of the morning but he was more amazed to be able to give them a medical all-clear not long afterwards.

'You're both incredibly lucky. A few bumps and bruises but nothing that a good sleep won't help.'

Anna caught Luke's wry glance. As if a good sleep was remotely likely for him even when he hadn't been through such a traumatic few hours. It was a private exchange. Ben didn't see it because he was shaking his head.

'I can't imagine what it must have felt like, seeing your car going over that cliff when the chain broke. The rescue guys are going to be talking about their good timing for years to come.'

'So will we,' Anna said. She smiled at Luke. 'Let's go and see if that taxi's here yet.'

They went to Luke's house because it was closer and Anna was still worried about the effects the accident might have had on Luke that no X-ray or examination would have picked up.

To have had this happen today, of all days, when he had been starting to open up to her about the past that haunted him so badly. No wonder he was so quiet now. And why he made no move to make love to her when they went straight to bed. They were both utterly exhausted but Anna was determined to stay awake. To be ready to hold Luke when he had the nightmare she was sure would come.

At some point, however, she fell asleep because it was impossible not to. When she awoke to find winter sunlight warming the room, she gasped in horror. Had she slept through Luke waking? Going to outrun his demons on the beach or dispel them with an arctic swim? He never missed his dawn swim.

But he was still there. Beside her. One arm draped over her body. Her gasp must have woken him because his eyes were open.

'You OK?'

Anna nodded. 'I'm sorry...'

'What for?'

'I must have slept through you getting up. I didn't mean to. I wanted...'

Luke was staring at her with an odd expression.

'What?' she breathed. 'What's wrong?'

'I didn't get up,' he said slowly. 'I didn't even wake up.'

'You slept through the whole night?'

'What was left of it, anyway.' He blinked at her, disbelief still etched on his features. 'That's hours. Hours and hours and hours.'

Anna's lips trembled as they stretched into a smile. 'How do you feel?'

'Different...' Luke's gaze dropped to Anna's lips and then dropped further. 'Hungry.'

'You want breakfast?'

'No.' He looked up again and smiled. 'I want... you.'

Anna snuggled closer, raising her face to meet Luke's kiss. 'I want you, too.'

'You're not too sore or anything?'

'A bit stiff and achy. Nothing that a walk on the beach in some sunshine won't cure.'

'Soon.' Luke's lips brushed hers gently and then came back as he sighed. 'Or maybe not that soon.'

His mouth claimed hers this time and Anna surrendered willingly. The walk could wait.

The last day of January found them walking on the beach.

A dawn walk that had become a firm habit now. Crash was with them, loping around on his big, puppy feet with a stick of driftwood clamped between his teeth.

'You're supposed to bring it back,' Luke called.

'He wants you to chase him.'

'That won't help his retrieving training.'

'No.' Besides, Anna didn't want to let go of Luke's hand. She loved this time of day with him. In the soft light and breathing the fresh, cold air. Walking so close they often leaned on each other as well as holding hands. And sometimes, as they did right now, they would stop and watch the waves rolling in for a minute or two.

'You haven't been for a swim since the accident.'

'No. I don't need to any more.'

Anna gave Luke a questioning glance but he was still staring at the waves.

'When I came back from Iraq,' he said a moment later, 'it seemed like I had no connection here any more. Or anywhere. Part of me was still over there. Caught up in the frenetic battle to save lives. To stay alive. Civilian life seemed empty. Meaningless.'

Still Anna said nothing. She couldn't. She remembered Luke saying something about that and she hadn't forgotten thinking that she had been included in the things that had no meaning. She knew that wasn't true. Maybe Luke hadn't told her as such but he was showing her. Every day. In so many ways.

'It made me numb, swimming in a freezing sea and getting tossed around by the surf,' Luke continued quietly. 'And it helped…then. I don't need to be numb now. I don't want to be, even for a moment.' He turned his head and looked down at Anna.

'Because even if it was just for the length of time it took to have that swim, it would be too long to feel numb. I don't want to give up a second of the most amazing feeling I could ever have.'

Anna's breath caught. She knew the answer but had to ask the question. To hear the words spoken aloud. 'What is it…that feeling?'

'My love for you.'

His kiss tasted of the sea and it was slow and exquisitely tender. Anna stood on tiptoe and wrapped her arms around his neck. It took the impatient bark of a large puppy to bring them back to the present moment. Luke laughed, stooped to pick up the stick that had been placed right beside his feet and threw it again. Then he took Anna's hand in his and they began walking again, a triumphant Crash making wide circles around them with the stick back in his jaws.

'I love you, Anna,' Luke said. 'You are the reason I want to get up in the mornings and the reason I can't wait to get to bed at night. I hope I never have to have a night or day without you to share it with but...' He took a deep breath and let it out in a sigh. 'I'm not going to ask you to marry me. I can't.'

Anna's feet stopped without any such instruction from her brain. Her hand tugged at Luke's a heartbeat later and he had to stop, too. She stared at him. The shadows in his eyes had begun to lift in the last week or so but the sadness she could still see in his face was heartbreaking.

'I can't offer you anything,' Luke said. 'I've lost my job.'

Anna gave her head a slow shake. 'You didn't lose it. You had the courage to go and talk to Mr White about everything and he had the good sense to persuade you to go onto the board of directors for St Piran's. You're going to be a brilliant administrator, Luke, and it's not as if you're not going to be part of the department for teaching—'

'Your department now,' Luke interrupted.

Anna looked away. It was so weird to think she had wanted to hang onto that position so badly that she would have preferred Luke to have never come back to St Piran's.

'I have PTSD,' Luke said into the silence. 'An official diagnosis from a qualified shrink.'

'An eminent psychiatrist who specialises in cognitive-behavioural therapy,' Anna corrected with a smile. 'Someone who thinks you're making amazing progress already.'

She watched a wave roll in. And then another. And then she turned to face Luke again.

'All you ever need to offer me is your love, Luke.'

He was watching her face with that intent gaze of his. Listening carefully. Waiting to hear what she would say next.

'And I don't want you to ask me to marry you,' she said.

She saw him swallow hard. Saw a flicker of doubt—fear, almost—in his eyes.

Anna smiled. 'Because I'm going to ask you.'

She took a deep breath. This shouldn't be so hard, should it? She'd been competing in a man's world for long enough to be able to tackle anything.

'I love you, Luke Davenport. With all my heart. I don't want to have a single night or day without you in it either. Will you marry me?'

He was still staring at her. One of those looks—as if he was seeing her for the very first time.

'Um… Please?' she added.

His arms came around her with such speed that

Anna squeaked as she felt herself grabbed and lifted. She was being whirled round and round and the world was spinning.

'Yes,' Luke said. 'Yes.'

He stopped whirling her but was still holding her well off the ground, his hands around her waist. Her hands were on his shoulders as he slowly lowered her enough for their lips to touch.

A new wave came in, leading the incoming tide further up the beach, and it reached far enough to swirl around Luke's ankles and splash Anna's legs with pure ice.

Luke dropped one arm to catch Anna behind her knees. He scooped her into his arms and carried her through the still foaming wave to dry sand but he didn't put her down. Crash followed as they left the beach to go home and get ready for their new day. And still Luke hadn't put Anna down.

And that was just fine by her.

She was exactly where she wanted to be. Moving into her future, cradled in the arms of the man she would always love.

ST. PIRAN'S: THE FIREMAN AND NURSE LOVEDAY

KATE HARDY

For the St Piran's mob – especially Caroline,
Maggie and Margaret, who kept me sane

CHAPTER ONE

THE familiar warble flooded through the fire station and the Tannoy gave a high-pitched whine.

Was it a drill, Tom wondered, at 2:00 p.m. on a Friday afternoon?

And then he heard the words, 'Turnout, vehicles 54 and 55. Fire at Penhally Bay Primary School. Query trapped children.'

Joey's school.

Fear lanced through him. Please, God, let this be a drill.

Except he knew it wasn't. Their drill was always a fire at 3 King Street, St Piran—which just so happened to be the address of the main fire station in the area. Which meant that this was real.

He headed straight for engine 54, where the rest of the crew were already stepping into their protective trousers, jackets and boots. Steve, the station manager, was in the front seat, tapping into the computer and checking the details.

'What have we got, Guv?' Tom asked as he swung into the seat next to Steve, the doors went up and the engine sped down the road towards Penhally Bay.

Steve checked the computer screen. 'Explosion and fire at Penhally Bay Primary.' He gave the driver, Gary, the map reference, even though everyone knew exactly where the school was, on the hill overlooking the bay. 'Called in by Rosemary

Bailey, the headmistress. The fire's in a corridor by a store-room and it's blocked off three rooms. Two of the classes were out, so that leaves the quiet room and the toilets. They're still checking off the kids' names, so they're not sure right now if anyone's in there or not.' He paused. 'The storeroom contains all the art stuff, so we're talking about flammable hazards and possible chemical inhalation from glue and what have you. Tom, you're lead. Roy, you're BAECO.' The breathing apparatus entry co-ordinator kept the control board with the firefighters' tallies in place so he knew who was in the building, how long they'd been in there, and when he needed to call them out because their oxygen supplies would be starting to run low.

'The rest of you, follow Tom's lead. We'll start with the tanks in the appliances, then we'll set the hydrant and check the supply.'

'Right, Guv,' the crew chorused.

'Who's our back-up?' Tom asked. Two engines were always sent out for an initial call, and then more would be called as needed, staggering their arrival.

'King Street's on standby,' Steve said. 'And the paramedics are on their way.'

All standard stuff, Tom knew.

'Nick Tremayne is going to be there, too,' Steve added.

Tom had attended fires with Nick in attendance before, and knew that the GP was unflappable and worked well in a crisis. 'That's good.' And Tom was really relieved that his crew was taking the call, so he could see for himself that his nephew was fine.

And Joey *would* be fine.

He had to be.

Joey was all Tom had left of his big sister since the car accident that had claimed her life and her husband's just over a month ago, at New Year. Losing her had ripped Tom's heart to shreds; the idea of anything happening to his precious nephew, the little boy his sister had entrusted to his care...

His mind closed, refusing to even consider the idea. Joey couldn't be one of the trapped children. He just *couldn't*.

But, all the way there, Tom was horribly aware of the extra problems that small children brought to a fire. Physically, their bodies couldn't cope as well as an adult's with the heat of a raging fire. And then there was the fear factor. Everyone was scared in a fire—you couldn't see your hand in front of your face, thanks to the choking thick smoke, and the heat and noise were incredible. Children found it even harder to cope with the way their senses were overwhelmed, and sometimes got to the point where they simply couldn't follow directions because they were too frightened to listen.

Please, God, let Joey be safe, he prayed silently.

Please.

'Hello, Tommy,' Flora said as Trish Atkins, the teacher of the three-year-olds, brought the next of her charges through to the quiet room where Flora was giving the routine vaccinations. She smiled at the little boy. 'I know Mummy told you why I've come to see your class today—not with my magic measuring tape to see how tall you all are, but to give you two injections to stop you catching a bug and getting sick.'

Tommy nodded. 'Will they hurt?'

'You'll feel a bit of a scratch,' she said, 'and it's OK to say a big "Ow" and hold Trish's hand really tightly, but it'll be over really quickly and I'll need you to stay still for me. Can you do that?'

'Yes,' he lisped.

'Good boy.' She gave him the choice of which arm and where he wanted to sit; he opted to sit on Trish's lap.

'Mummy told me you're getting a kitten.' Distraction was a brilliant technique; if she could get him chatting about the new addition to their family, he wouldn't focus on the vaccination syringe and he'd feel it as the scratch she'd promised, rather than as a terrifying pain. 'What's he like?'

'He's black.'

'What are you going to call him?'

'Ow!' Tommy's lower lip wobbled when the needle went in, but then he said, 'Smudge. 'Cause he's got a big white smudge on his back.'

'That's a great name.' She smiled at him. 'What sort of toys are you going to get him?'

'A squeaky red mouse,' Tommy said. 'Ow!'

'All done—and you were so brave that I'm going to give you a sticker. Do you want to choose one?'

The distraction of a shiny rocket sticker made Tommy forget about crying, just as Flora had hoped it would. She updated his notes, and was about to put her head round the door of the quiet room to tell Trish that she was ready for the next child when she heard a huge bang and then fire alarms going off.

She left her papers where they were and headed out to the main rooms of the nursery. The children were all filing out into the garden, some of the younger ones crying and holding the hands of the class assistants. Flora could see through the large windows that Christine Galloway, the head of the nursery, was taking a roll-call of all the staff and children.

'I think everyone's out, but I'm checking nobody's been left behind,' Trish said from the far end of the room.

'Do you want me to check the toilets?' Flora asked.

'Yes, please.' Trish gave her a grateful smile.

Once they were both satisfied that everyone was out, Flora grabbed her medical kit and they joined Christine and the other teachers. Two fire engines roared up, sirens blaring and blue lights flashing, and they could see smoke coming over the fence from the primary school next door.

'I'd better get next door in case anyone's hurt and they need medical help,' Flora said, biting her lip. She knew all the children in the school, from her work as the school liaison nurse, and the idea of any of them being hurt or, even worse… *No.* It was unthinkable.

'Let us know if there's anything we can do,' Christine said. 'I'll put your notes in my office when we can go back into the building.'

'Thanks.' Flora gave her a quick smile, then hurried next door to the primary school.

The first person she saw was her boss, Nick Tremayne, the head of the surgery in the village. 'Nick, what's happened? I was next door doing the vaccinations when I heard a bang and the fire alarms went off.'

'We don't know what caused it—only that there's a fire.' Nick gestured to the firemen pumping water onto the building.

'Is anyone hurt?'

'Right now, we're not sure. The head's getting everyone out and ticking off names.'

Flora glanced at the building and saw where the flames were coming out. 'That's the corridor by the art storeroom— it's full of stuff that could go up.' And she really, really hoped that everyone was out of the block. The corridor led to the storeroom and three prefab rooms. Two of the rooms were used as Year Five classrooms and the third was used as the quiet room, where teachers took children for extra reading practice or tests.

The firefighters were already working to quell the blaze. Some had breathing apparatus on, and others were putting water on the blaze. She could hear one of the fire crew yelling instructions about a hydrant.

Before she could ask Nick anything else, two ambulances screamed up. The paramedic crew and two doctors headed towards them. Flora recognised one of them as Megan Phillips, who lived in the village, though she didn't know Megan's colleague.

'I'm Josh O'Hara, A and E consultant,' the unknown doctor introduced himself. 'And this is Megan Phillips, paediatrician.'

Josh was simply gorgeous, with black tousled hair that flopped in his indigo-blue eyes. Right now he wasn't smiling; but no doubt when he did, any woman under the age of ninety would feel her heart turning over. And that Irish brogue would definitely melt hearts.

Although Flora knew who Megan was, she didn't know the doctor well at all; Megan kept herself very much to herself in the village. So Flora was relieved when Nick stepped in and spoke for both of them. 'Nick Tremayne, head of Penhally Bay Surgery—and this is Flora, my practice nurse and school liaison. Luckily she was doing the MMR vaccinations next door and she's brilliant with kids. Flora, you know Megan, don't you? Can you work with her and I'll work with Josh?'

'Yes, of course,' Flora said.

Though she also noticed that Megan and Josh didn't glance at each other, the way that colleagues usually did. The tension between them was obvious, so either they hadn't worked together before and weren't sure of each other's skills, or they knew each other and really didn't get on. Well, whatever it was, she hoped they'd manage to put it aside and work together until everyone was safe. In this situation, the children really had to come first.

Megan gave her a slightly nervous smile. 'Shall we go and see what's going on?'

Flora nodded. 'The fire drill point's at the far end of the playground, on the other side of the building.'

'We'll start there, then, and see if anyone needs treating,' Megan said. 'As you're school liaison, you must know everyone here?'

Flora felt colour flooding into her cheeks, and sighed inwardly. If only she didn't blush so easily. She knew it made her look like a bumbling fool, and she wasn't. She was a good nurse and she was fine with the children—and the teachers, now she'd got to know them. She just found herself shy and tongue-tied with adults she didn't know very well. Stupid, at her age, she knew, but she couldn't help it. Pulling herself together, she said, 'I know all the staff and most of the children—I've either worked with their class or seen them for the usual check-ups.'

'That's good—you'll be a familiar face and that will help them feel less scared,' Megan said.

As they rounded the corner, they could see a woman leaning against the wall, her face white, nursing her arm.

'Patience, this is Megan, one of the doctors from St Piran's. Megan, this is Patience Harcourt. She teaches Year Three,' Flora introduced them swiftly. 'Patience, what's happened to your arm?'

'I'd gone to the storeroom to get some supplies. I'd just switched on the light when it went bang—I went straight for the fire extinguisher, but before I could do anything the whole thing went up. I got out of there and closed the fire door to contain it.' She grimaced. 'Thank goodness one of the Year Five classes was doing PE and the other was in the ICT suite.'

'Was anyone in the quiet room?' Flora asked.

Patience shook her head, looking white. 'I hope not, but I don't know.'

'Let's have a look at your arm,' Megan said, and sucked in a breath. 'That's a nasty burn.'

Patience made a dismissive gesture with her other arm. 'I can wait. Check the children over first.'

'Your burn needs dressing—the sooner, the better,' Megan said gently. 'Will you let Flora do it while I check the children?'

The children were shivering because it was cold outside and the teachers had taken them straight outside away from the fire, not stopping to pick up coats; some were still wearing their PE kit. Some were crying, and all were clearly frightened.

'We need to get them huddled together to conserve warmth,' Megan said. 'Under that shelter would be good. And then I can see if anyone needs treating. Flora, when you've dressed Patience's burn, do you want to come and help me?'

'Will do.' Again, Flora could feel the hated colour flood her cheeks. She was glad of the excuse to turn her face away while she delved in her medical kit; then brought out what she needed to dress the burn and make Patience more comfortable.

Tom was training one of the hoses on the flames. He didn't have a clue whether Joey was safely in the playground with the other children because he couldn't see. Although he was frantic to know that Joey was all right, he had a job to do and his colleagues were relying on him not to let them down. He had to keep doing his job and trust his colleagues to do theirs.

I swear if he's safe then I'll do better by him, he promised silently to his sister. *I'll change my job, give up firefighting and concentrate on him.*

And then the headmistress hurried over towards them.

'Is everyone safe?' Steve asked.

Rosemary Bailey looked grim. 'There's still part of one class missing. Some of the Reception children.'

Tom, overhearing her, went cold. *Joey was in the Reception year.* 'Is Joey all right?' he asked urgently.

Rosemary bit her lip. 'He's not with the others. There's a group of children who'd gone to the quiet room at the end for extra help with reading. He must be with them.'

Tom swallowed hard. 'The quiet room. Is that the room at the end of the corridor?' The room that was cut off, right now, by flames.

'Yes.'

'It's near the storeroom where the fire started. Right now, it's structurally unstable,' Steve said. 'How many children are there?'

'Five, plus Matty Roper, the teaching assistant in R2.'

R2. Definitely Joey's class, Tom knew. And he knew Matty—he'd had twice-weekly meetings with her about Joey since he'd become Joey's guardian. Joey had been struggling at school for the last month, just shutting off, so Tom and Matty had been trying to work out how they could help him settle back in.

Ice slid through his veins. The children were stranded. *Including Joey.*

CHAPTER TWO

'Right, I'm going in,' Tom said. 'Gary, can you take this hose from me?'

Steve grabbed Tom's shoulder to stop him. 'You're not going anywhere.'

'My nephew's trapped in that room. No way in hell am I leaving him there!' Tom snarled back.

'Nobody's saying that you have to leave him, Tom. But nobody's going into that corridor until we've stabilised the area—otherwise the whole lot could come down. And we can't afford to let the flames reach the really flammable stuff.'

Steve was making absolute sense. As an experienced fireman and the station manager, he knew exactly what he was doing. Tom was well aware of that. And yet every nerve in his body rebelled against his boss's orders. How could he just wait outside when his nephew was trapped inside that room?

'Tom, I know you think Joey might be in there, but you can't afford to let emotion get in the way.'

Ordinarily, Tom didn't. He was able to distance himself from things and stay focused, carrying others through a crisis situation with his calm strength. But this was different. This was Joey. The last link to his elder sister. No way could he let the little boy down.

'You either keep doing your job as lead fireman and getting

the flames under control,' Steve said softly, 'or you're off duty as of now, which means you go back to the station.'

And then it would be even longer before he could find out if Joey was safe. Waiting would drive him crazy. Tom dragged in a breath. 'Right, Guv. I'm sticking to my post.'

The fire crew that had arrived as back-up started to get the supports up; Tom forced himself to concentrate on damping down the blaze. Abandoning his job wouldn't help Joey. Focus, he told himself. Just *focus*.

It felt like a lifetime, but at last the area was stabilised and they were in a position to rescue the trapped children and their teacher. Steve had already vetoed the door as the access point; although the flames were out, the corridor was still thick with smoke, and until the fire had been damped down properly it could reignite at any time. The window was the safest option, now the area was stabilised.

But there was no way Tom's muscular frame would fit through the window. His colleagues, too, were brawny and would find it an equally tight fit.

'Um, excuse me?'

Tom looked down at the woman standing next to him. She was a foot shorter than him, and her face was bright red—whether through embarrassment or the heat from the fire, he had no idea.

'I'm the school nurse,' she said. 'Look, I know I'm a bit, um, round...' her colour deepened and she looked at the floor '...and I'm not as strong as you, but the children are only little. Matty and I can lift them up between us and pass them through to you. And I can check them over while I'm in there and make sure they're all right.'

'I see where you're coming from,' he said, 'but you're a civilian. I can't let you take that risk.'

'But I know the children,' she said, her voice earnest—though she still wasn't looking at him, Tom noticed. 'It'll be less frightening for them if I go in to help.' She bit her lip. 'I know it's dangerous, but I won't do anything reckless. And we need to get the children out quickly.'

True. And, the faster they did that, the sooner he'd see Joey. That was the clincher for him. 'All right. Thank you.'

She nodded. 'I'm sorry I'm, um, a bit heavy.'

He looked at her properly then. Yes, she was curvy. Plump, if he was brutally honest. But there was a sweetness and kindness in her face, a genuine desire to help—something that he knew had been missing from the other women he'd dated. Sure, they might have been tall and leggy and jaw-droppingly gorgeous, but they would've fussed about chipping a nail. And he knew who he'd rather have beside him in this crisis. Definitely the school nurse.

And she had the sweetest, softest mouth. A mouth that made him want to…

Whatever was the *matter* with him? His nephew was missing, he had a job to do, and he was thinking about what it would be like to kiss a complete stranger? For pity's sake—he needed to concentrate!

'You're fine,' he said, and proved it by lifting her up to the window as if she weighed no more than a feather.

She scrambled through, and Tom almost forgot to breathe while he waited. Were the children all right? Was Joey safe?

And then Matty Roper and the school nurse came to the window and started lifting the children through, and there just wasn't time to ask about Joey as he took the children one by one and passed them over to the team of medics lining up behind him ready to check over the children.

Three.

Four.

He swallowed hard. The next one would be Joey.

Except the next person to come to the window was Matty Roper.

'Where's Joey?' he asked urgently. 'The head said there were five children missing—that they were in the quiet room with you.'

'Only four,' Matty said. 'And Joey wasn't one of them.'

'But he *has* to be. There were five children missing. He was one of them.'

'I'm sorry, Tom. I only took four children to the quiet room with me and they're all accounted for.'

Panic flowed through him, making every muscle feel like lead. How could Joey be missing? How?

'Please, Matty. Check again. Just in case he came in and you didn't see him.'

'Tom, I know he didn't,' Matty said gently. 'I'm sorry.'

'Then where the hell is he?' Tom burst out in desperation.

'I don't know.' She looked nervously at the supports against the wall. 'Is this going to hold?'

This was his job. He had to get Matty and the school nurse out. And then he could start to look for Joey.

Please, God, let it not be too late.

Grim-faced, he helped Matty through the window, and then the nurse.

Once they were both standing on safe ground, he leaned through the window. 'Joey! Joey, where are you?'

No answer.

Was he trapped in one of the other classrooms? 'Joey!' he bellowed.

'Do you mean Joey Barber?' the nurse asked.

'Yes.' She'd seen the other children, Tom thought, so maybe she'd seen his nephew. 'Have you seen him?'

She shook her head. 'Not today.' Again, she didn't meet his

eyes. 'He's the little boy who lost his parents just after New Year, isn't he?'

'My sister and her husband,' Tom confirmed. And it was beginning to look as if Joey might be joining his parents. No, no, no. It couldn't happen. He couldn't bear it. 'The head said there were five children missing. Now it's just Joey. Oh, hell, can't he hear me? Why isn't he answering?' He yelled Joey's name again.

The nurse squeezed his hand. 'The noise of the explosion will have scared him and probably brought back memories of the car crash. Right now, even if he can hear you, he's probably too scared to answer.'

He thought about it and realised that she was right. 'Not that he speaks much anyway, since the accident,' Tom said wryly. 'He barely strings two words together now. It's been so hard to reach him since Susie and Kevin died.' He dragged in a breath. 'If anything's happened to him, I'll never forgive myself.' He'd never be able to live with the guilt: his sister had asked him to look after her precious child, and he'd failed. Big time.

'This isn't your fault,' she said softly. 'You can't blame yourself.'

'I need to find him.' He handed over his damping-down duties to one of his colleagues and went in search of the station manager. 'Guv, Joey's still missing. I need to find him. Please.'

'All right.' Steve looked at him, grim-faced. 'But you don't take *any* risks, you hear me?'

'I won't,' Tom promised. He wouldn't put anyone in danger. But he'd take the buildings apart with his bare hands if he had to, to find his nephew.

'I, um, could help you look for him, if you like.' The nurse was by his side again. 'He knows me, and a familiar face might help.'

'Thank you.' Tom looked at her. 'I don't even know your name,' he blurted out.

'Flora. Flora Loveday.' Her face reddened again. 'And I know it's a stupid name. I'm not a delicate little flower.'

'No.' He was beginning to realise now that she was shy, like the proverbial violet—that was why she blushed and couldn't quite get her words out and found it hard to look him in the eye—but he had a feeling that there was much more to Flora Loveday than that. She'd put herself in a dangerous situation to help the children. 'No, you're like a…a peony,' Tom said, thinking of the flowers his mother had always grown in summer. 'Brave and bright and strong.'

Her blush deepened to the point where she seriously resembled the flower.

'I'm Tom. Tom Nicholson.'

She nodded but said nothing and looked away.

With Flora by his side, he checked with Rosemary Bailey and the rest of the fire crew. All the areas had been cleared, and nobody had seen Joey.

He eyed the wreckage. Fear tightened round his chest, to the point where he could barely breathe. Where was Joey? 'Maybe he's in the toilets,' he said.

Flora shook her head. 'They've been checked.'

'He has to be here. He *has* to be.' Desperately, he yelled Joey's name again.

'If he's scared already, shouting is only going to make him panic more,' she said quietly. She paused. 'When I was Joey's age, I hated going to school. I used to hide in the cloakrooms.'

Tom hardly dared hope that Joey would've done the same. But it was the best option he had right now. 'Let's have another look. I know they've been checked, but…' He glanced over to the huddled children at the far end of the playground.

'Joey's tiny. If he was sitting among the coats and didn't reply, whoever checked might have missed him.'

Together, they went over to the Reception cloakrooms.

'I'll start this end—can you start that end, Flora?' Tom asked.

'Sure.'

He'd checked under every coat at his end when he heard Flora call out, 'He's here.'

Huddled up at the far end of the cloakroom, beneath piles of coats, his nephew was white-faced. And Tom had never been so glad to see him in all his life. He dropped to his knees and hugged the little boy tightly, uncaring that he was covered in smoke and smuts and he would make Joey's clothes filthy.

Joey squirmed. 'You're hurting me,' he whispered.

The soft sound pierced Tom's heart. Of course. The little boy didn't like being touched, not since his parents had died. As a toddler, he'd adored riding on his uncle's shoulders and playing football and going down the huge slide in the playground on Tom's or his father's lap, but since the accident he'd put huge barriers round himself.

Tom let his nephew go. 'Sorry, Jojo. I didn't mean to hurt you. It's just I was very scared when I couldn't find you. I'm so glad you're all right.'

Joey stared at him and said nothing.

'I know this afternoon's been scary, but it's all going to be just fine,' Tom said softly. 'I promise. I'm going to have to stay here until the fire's completely out and everything's safe, but maybe Mrs Bailey will let you sit in her office and do some drawing until I can get in touch with the childminder and see if she can take you home.'

Joey said nothing, and Tom had absolutely no idea what the little boy was thinking. Did he feel abandoned, or could he understand that other people relied on Tom to do his job and keep them safe and he had to share Tom's time?

Flora was sitting on the low bench by the coat rack. 'Or,' she said, 'maybe you could come home with me until your uncle's finished here. I live on a farm, and I've got the nicest dog in the world.'

Tom looked at her. 'But I've only just met you.' Did she really think he'd let his precious nephew go off with a complete stranger—even if she had been brilliant and helped to rescue him?

She bit her lip. 'I know, but Joey knows me. And my boss is here—I take it you know Nick Tremayne?' At Tom's curt nod, she said, 'He'll vouch for me. And it's no trouble. I just need to pick up my paperwork from the nursery next door—the children will all have gone home by now, so I'll have to finish the clinic next week anyway.'

So she *did* think he'd let Joey go home with someone he didn't know.

Then again, Tom was usually a good judge of character and he liked what he'd seen of Flora. She was kind, she was brave, and she'd thought of the children before herself.

'Is that all right with you, Joey?' Tom asked.

Joey looked wary, and Tom was about to refuse the offer when Flora said, 'You can meet my dog and see around the farm.'

'Dog,' Joey said.

And, for the first time in a long, long time, he gave a smile. A smile that vanished the second after it started, but it was a proper smile. And it made Tom's decision suddenly easy.

'Do you want to go with Flora and see her dog, Jojo?' Tom asked.

This time, Joey nodded.

'I can borrow a car seat from the nursery—they have spares,' Flora said. She took a notepad from her pocket and scribbled quickly on it. 'That's my address, my home phone and my mobile phone.'

'Thank you.' Tom dragged in a breath. 'This is going to sound really ungrateful. My instincts tell me to trust you, but—'

'I'm a stranger,' she finished. 'You can never take risks with children. They're too precious.' She bit her lip and looked away, and Tom felt like an utter heel. She was trying to help and he'd practically thrown the offer back in her face.

'Talk to Nick,' she said. 'And then, if you're happy for Joey to come with me, I'll be next door at the nursery.'

Somehow, she'd understood that this wasn't personal—that he'd be the same even if the offer had come from a teaching assistant he didn't know. 'Thank you,' Tom said and, making sure Joey was right by his side, went to find Nick Tremayne.

At half past seven that evening, Flora heard the car tyres on the gravel and glanced across at Banjo, who was standing guard over the child asleep on the beanbag. 'All right, boy. I heard him. Shh, now. Let Joey sleep.'

She'd opened the kitchen door before Tom could ring the doorbell. 'Joey's asleep in front of the fire,' she whispered. 'Come in.'

He'd showered and changed; out of his uniform, and with his face no longer covered by a mask and soot, Tom Nicholson was breathtakingly handsome. When he smiled at her, her heart actually skipped a beat.

Which was ridiculous, because he was way, *way* out of her league. He probably had a girlfriend already; though, even if he didn't, Flora knew he wouldn't look twice at her. Looking the way he did, and doing the job he did, Tom was probably used to scores of much more attractive women falling in a heap at his feet. He wouldn't be interested in a shy, plump nurse who spent most of her time looking like a beetroot.

'He's absolutely sound asleep,' Tom whispered, looking

down at his nephew, who was lying on the beanbag with a fleecy blanket tucked round him.

'It's been a long day for him—and a scary one.' She glanced at Tom. 'Um, I've already fed him. I hope that's OK.'

'That's great. Thanks for being so kind,' Tom said.

'I could hardly let him starve.' Flora shrugged it off. 'Poor little lad. He's had a lot to cope with, losing both his parents. I know what that's like.' She'd had to face losing both her parents, the previous year, so she had an idea what he was going through—though, being twenty years older than Joey, at least she'd had an adult's perspective to help her cope. She looked more closely at Tom and saw the lines of strain around his eyes. 'You look exhausted.'

'Once the immediate danger's passed, the real work starts—making sure we keep the site damped down so the fire doesn't flare up again.' Tom grimaced. 'Sorry I've been so long. And I took time out for a shower, because if I turned up covered in smuts and stinking of smoke it might scare Joey.'

He'd put his nephew first; and no doubt the shower had been at the expense of taking time to grab a meal. It was good that he could put Joey first, but the poor man must be starving as well as tired. And if she made him something to eat, she could keep herself busy doing something practical—which was a lot easier than sitting down and having a conversation where she'd end up blushing and stumbling over her words and getting flustered. She'd learned the hard way that being practical and doing something was the best way of dealing with her hated shyness. 'He's perfectly safe and comfortable where he is, so why don't you sit down and I'll make you a hot drink and something to eat?' Flora asked.

'I can't impose on you like that.'

'You're not imposing. I made a big batch of spaghetti sauce this afternoon. It won't take long to heat it through and cook some pasta—that's what Joey and I had.'

'Thank you.'

The next thing Tom knew, he was sitting at the table with a mug of coffee in front of him and Flora was pottering round the kitchen.

The kindness of a stranger. Tom was used to women offering to cook him things—it was a standing joke at the fire station that, almost every day, someone dropped by with a tin of home-made cookies or cakes or muffins for Tom. Old ladies whose cats he'd rescued, young mums whose toddlers he'd got out of a locked bathroom—and even the hard-nosed local reporter had seen him in action, rescuing someone from a burning building, and had joined what his crew-mates teasingly called the Tom Nicholson Fan Club, turning up with a batch of cookies for him on more than one occasion.

Even though he'd explained gently that he was simply doing his job, he could hardly be rude enough to turn away things that people had spent time making personally for him. So he accepted them with a smile on behalf of the fire crew, wrote thank-you notes—again on behalf of the entire fire crew—and secretly rather enjoyed them making a fuss over him.

But Flora Loveday was different.

There was something about her—a kind of inner peace and strength that drew him. Here, on her home ground, she glowed. He'd been too frantic with worry about Joey to notice properly earlier, but she was beautiful. Soft, gentle brown eyes; her hair, too, was soft, all ruffled and curly and cute. And the warmth she exuded made him want to hold her close, feel some of that warmth seeping into him and taking the chill of the fear away…

And then he realised what he was thinking and slammed the brakes on. Yes, he found her attractive—dangerously so—but he couldn't act on it. In his job, it wasn't fair to have a serious relationship with someone. He worked crazy hours and did dangerous things; he'd seen too many friends die and leave families behind. And there was Joey to consider, too. He'd had too many changes in his young life, just recently. The last thing he needed was his uncle being distracted by a new girlfriend.

But Tom also knew that he could do with a friend. Flora was the first person who'd seemed to understand or who had managed to start to reach Joey. And he really, really needed help reaching his nephew.

'So what have you and Joey been up to?' he asked.

'I took him to see the chickens.'

'Chickens?' He hadn't expected that.

She went pink again. 'My dad started Loveday Eggs.'

He'd seen their boxes in the shops. 'So you have chickens here?'

She nodded. 'The hens are free range, so we went and collected some eggs. And then we made some brownies.' She smiled. 'There are some left. But not that many.' She placed a bowl of pasta in front of him.

'This smells amazing. Thank you.' He took a mouthful. 'Wow. And it tastes even better than it smells.'

'It's only boring old spaghetti and sauce.' She looked away.

'It's wonderful.' He ate the lot and accepted a second bowl. And then he grimaced. 'Sorry. I've just been horribly greedy.'

'You've just spent hours sorting out a fire. You must've been starving.'

'I was,' he admitted. And then he accepted her offer of helping himself to the brownies. 'Wow. These are seriously good. And you made them with Joey?'

She fished her mobile phone out of her handbag, fiddled with it and then handed it to him. There was a picture of Joey, wearing a tea-towel as a makeshift apron, stirring the chocolatey mixture in a big bowl—and there was almost as much chocolate round his face.

And he looked happy.

Tom couldn't speak for a moment. Then he gulped in a breath. 'I didn't know Joey liked cooking.'

'Most kids love messy stuff,' she explained, her colour deepening. 'And cooking's better still because they get to eat what they make.'

In one afternoon, she seemed to have got far closer to his nephew than he'd managed in a month. And he knew he needed help. Flora might be the one to help him reach Joey— and there was just something about her that made Tom sure that she wouldn't judge him harshly. 'It never even occurred to me to try doing something like that with Joey.' He raked a hand through his hair. 'Don't get me wrong, I like kids. I'm always the one sent on school visits, but I just don't seem to be able to connect with Joey—and I'm his uncle. Everything I suggest us doing, he just stares at me and says nothing. I can't reach him any more. I feel…' He shook his head, grimacing. 'Hopeless. Helpless. I don't even know where to start.'

'Give it time,' she said. 'It's only been a month since the accident—and he was one of the quieter ones in the school even before then.'

Tom blinked in surprise. 'So you work at the school? I thought you said Nick Tremayne was your boss?'

'He is, but I'm the school liaison,' she explained.

'So you visit the local schools?'

She nodded. 'I spend half my time at the local nursery and schools, and half my time at the practice. I do a health visitor clinic at the primary school for mums one morning a week, a clinic at the high school, and I do the vaccinations and preschool health checks in the nursery. Plus I take the personal development classes—I get the little ones thinking about healthy eating and exercise and how they can get five a day, and how they can look after their teeth properly.'

It was the most he'd heard her say in one go, and she looked animated; clearly she loved her job and felt comfortable talking about it. 'So I take it you like your job?'

She smiled. 'I love it.'

Just as he loved his: something else they had in common. Tom paused, remembering what she'd said when he'd first walked in. 'I'm sorry about your parents.'

'And I'm sorry about your sister.' She bit her lip, looking awkward. 'I didn't know her very well, but she seemed nice.'

'She was. My big sister.' Tom sighed. 'And I feel worse because I was meant to go to France with her, Kevin and Joey to see our parents for New Year and I bailed out. Maybe if I'd been driving the crash wouldn't have happened.'

'You don't know that,' Flora said. 'And think of it another way—if you *had* been in the crash, Joey might've been left without anyone at all.'

'Mum and Dad would've stepped in to help, but they're nearly seventy now, and it's not fair to drag them back to England and make them run around after a little one. Dad's arthritis really gives him gyp.' He rubbed his hand across his forehead, but the tight band of tension refused to shift. 'I loved spending time with Joey when Susie was alive—I used to see them most weekends. I've always tried to be a good uncle and we used to have fun—but since the accident he's just put all these barriers up and I don't know how to get them down again.'

'Give it time,' she said again, her voice kind.

'Did he talk to you this afternoon?'

'A bit. He was a little shy.' She shrugged and looked away. 'But so am I, so that's OK.'

And that was one of the reasons why Flora seemed to

understand Joey better than he did: she knew what it was like to be shy, and Tom never had. And he couldn't help wondering what Flora was like when she wasn't shy. He knew she was practical and kind—but what did she look like when she laughed?

Or when she'd just been thoroughly kissed?

Oh, for pity's sake, he really needed to keep his libido under control.

Luckily his thoughts weren't showing on his face, because Flora continued, 'I read him some stories after we'd eaten—he chose them from the box I take to clinic—and then he fell asleep on the beanbag.'

'Bless him.' Tom bit his lip. 'I think he's had a better time with you than he would've done at the childminder's.' He sighed. 'I feel bad taking him to the childminder's for breakfast and then not picking him up until after dinner for half the week, but I work shifts—it's the only thing I can do. I was trying to avoid any more change in his life, but she told me the other week I'm going to have to find someone else because she's moving.'

'Would your childminder be Carol?' she asked.

Yet again, she'd surprised him. 'How did you know?'

'I know all the local childminders, through work,' Flora explained. 'Carol loves it here in Cornwall, but her husband's been promoted to his company's head office in London so that's why she has to move.'

'So if you know all the local childminders...' Tom brightened. 'Do you happen to know anyone with spare places who'd be good with Joey and could take him from half past six in the morning until school, and then after school until a quarter past seven or so? I can hardly take him with me to the station, in case we have a shout.'

'Nobody's got any spare places right now,' Flora said. 'The

ones who did have are already booked up from taking on Carol's clients. But I can ask around again, if you like.'

Yet another example of his failure at being a stand-in parent. 'Susie would've had that sorted out on day one,' Tom said grimly. 'When Carol told me she was leaving and I'd have to find someone else to look after Joey, I was still trying to get my head around what had happened and learning to fit my life round my nephew. I didn't have room in my head for anything else. And now I *wish* I'd made more of an effort.' He blew out a breath. 'Sorry. I shouldn't be dumping on you like this.'

'Not a problem. It's not going any further than me.'

'Trust you, you're a nurse?'

'Something like that.' Flora smiled at him, and Tom realised that she had dimples. Seriously cute dimples. Dimples he wanted to touch. Dimples he wanted to kiss.

Though now wasn't the time or the place. 'Thank you. You've been really kind. Can I impose on you and ask you what's your secret? You've got through to Joey when nobody else can, not even his teachers.'

She shrugged. 'I think he likes Banjo.'

The dog wagged his tail at hearing his name. The sound of Banjo's tail thumping the floor woke Joey, and he sat up, rubbing his eyes. For a moment, he stared wildly round him, as if not knowing where he was.

'Hey, Jojo, we're at Flora's. At the farm,' Tom said, going over to him and squatting down so that he was at his nephew's level. 'You fell asleep, sweetheart. I hear you've been running about with Banjo here and seeing the chickens and making brownies.'

Joey nodded.

'Did you have fun?'

Joey nodded again.

'That's good.' Tom smiled at him. 'The fire's out now so

your school's all safe again, ready for Monday morning. And
we ought to let Flora get on. Shall we go home to Uncle Tom's
upstairs house?'

Joey just looked at him.

Home.

Clearly Joey didn't think of Tom's flat as home. Maybe
he should've moved into his sister's house instead of taking
Joey back to his place, but he simply couldn't handle it. Every
second he'd been in the house, he'd expected Susie to walk
into the room at any time, and it had to be even harder for
Joey. Right now, Tom was caught between the devil and the
deep blue sea, and he hated himself for not being able to make
Joey's world right again. For being a coward and escaping to
work whenever he could, losing himself in the adrenalin rush
of his job.

'Shall we say goodbye to Flora and Banjo?'

Joey yawned, then made a fuss of the dog, who licked
him.

'You can come back any time you like and play with him,'
Flora said. 'He liked playing ball with you this afternoon.'

Joey said nothing, but there was the ghost of a smile on his
face.

'Thank you for having us,' Tom said, knowing that his
nephew wasn't going to say it.

'My pleasure. Come back soon, Joey,' Flora said with a
smile.

Tom tried slipping his hand into Joey's as they walked
to the front door, but Joey twisted his hand away. Tom was
careful not to let his feelings show on his face. 'Bye, Flora.
Thanks again.'

He opened the car door, and Joey climbed onto his car seat.
The little boy allowed Tom to fix the seatbelt, but Tom could

see by the look on his nephew's face that Joey had retreated back into his shell again. He didn't even wave to Flora.

If only he could find a way of getting through to Joey.

He was just going to have to try harder.

CHAPTER THREE

DESPITE the fact that he'd lain awake half the night, worrying about Joey, Tom's body-clock was relentless. He didn't even need to look at his alarm to know that it was six o'clock. For pity's sake, it wasn't even light. And it was the weekend. Why couldn't he just turn over, stick the pillow over his head and go back to sleep?

Ha. He knew the answer to that. Because Joey woke early, too, and Tom needed to keep the little boy safe. His life had changed completely. Nowadays, he couldn't stay up until stupid o'clock watching films or playing online with his friends on a game console, or sleep in until midday on his day off. He had responsibilities.

Coffee, first. Tom dragged himself out of bed, then pulled on his dressing gown and headed for the kitchen. He blinked in surprise when he switched on the light and saw Joey sitting at the table in the dark, all dressed and ready to go out. Joey's long-sleeved T-shirt was on back to front and he was wearing odd socks; Tom couldn't help smiling. Cute beyond words. Part of him was tempted to ruffle his nephew's hair, but he knew that the little boy would only flinch away, so there was no point.

And that hurt.

'Why were you sitting in the dark, Jojo?' he asked gently.

Joey said nothing, but glanced over to the doorway.

Of course. He couldn't quite reach the light switch. Tom's flat wasn't designed for a four-year-old.

'I'll get a light put in here you *can* reach,' Tom promised. An uplighter would be the safest. Or maybe one on a timer switch. 'You look all ready to go out.'

Joey nodded.

'Where do you want to go?' And please don't let him say 'home', Tom begged silently.

'I want to play with Banjo.'

Flora's dog had clearly made the breakthrough that none of the adults had been able to make, because this was the longest sentence that Joey had strung together since the accident.

It would be an imposition on Flora, Tom knew, but this was the most animated he'd seen Joey since the little boy had come to live with him. He couldn't afford to let the opportunity slip away. Though going to visit Flora at this time of the morning would be a little too much to ask; he needed some delaying tactics.

'OK, sweetheart, we'll go and see Banjo.' *And Flora.* Awareness prickled all the way down Tom's spine, and he squashed it ruthlessly. This wasn't about his attraction to the sweet, gentle school nurse who had the most kissable mouth he'd ever seen. This was about his nephew. 'But it's a bit early to go and visit anyone just yet; it's still dark outside. I'm not even dressed—and I don't know about you, but I really could do with some breakfast first. How about we make something to eat, then go and buy some flowers to say thank you to Flora for looking after you yesterday, and a...' What did you buy dogs? Tom's parents had always had cats rather than dogs, and he hadn't had the space in his life to look after an animal properly so he had no pets. 'A ball or something for Banjo?' he finished.

Joey nodded.

Tom put water in the kettle and switched it on. 'What do you want for breakfast?'

Joey shrugged.

'Juice? Cereals?' Flora had got through to him yesterday by baking. Tom didn't bake. He did the bare minimum when it came to cooking: stir-fries, pasta and baked potatoes were pretty much his limit. Anyway, suggesting cake for breakfast wasn't exactly healthy.

But there had to be something they could do.

'How about a bacon sandwich?' he asked. 'We can make it as a team. How about you're the chef, in charge of buttering the bread and squirting on the tomato ketchup, and I'll grill the bacon?'

Joey gave him a tiny smile, and went to the drawer where Tom kept the tea-towels. Without a word, he tucked a tea-towel round himself like an apron, the way he had in the photo Flora had shown Tom the previous evening, then fetched the butter and tomato ketchup from the fridge.

This was good, Tom thought. A positive step.

Joey buttered the bread while Tom grilled the bacon. Tom carefully laid the cooked bacon on the bread, then looked at Joey. 'Over to you, Chef.'

Joey squeezed tomato ketchup over the bacon—a bit too much for Tom's taste, but he'd wash it down with coffee and a smile because no way was he going to reject his nephew's efforts. 'Excellent teamwork. High five, Chef.' He lifted his palm, hoping that Joey would respond.

For a moment, he didn't think Joey was going to react— and then Joey smiled and touched his palm to Tom's. Only momentarily, but in Tom's view it was huge progress from the way things had been. And it gave him hope for the future.

'Can we see Banjo now?' Joey asked when they'd finished, his face eager.

'Once you've washed your face and changed your shirt—

because they're both covered in ketchup—and cleaned your teeth,' Tom said. 'And I need to wash up the breakfast things. Then we'll go to the shop on the way.'

'My singing isn't that bad, you horrible dog,' Flora said, laughing as Banjo started barking.

But then he went over to the kitchen door and barked again.

'Visitors?' Odd. She wasn't expecting anyone, and it was too early for the postman. But there was no other reason why her dog would be barking by the front door. She switched off the vacuum cleaner and went to answer the door.

'Oh—Tom and Joey! Hello.' She hadn't expected to see them today, despite telling them the previous evening that they could come round at any time. And it was incredibly early. Barely after breakfast.

'We wanted to bring you something—didn't we, Jojo?' Tom said.

Joey nodded, all wide-eyed.

'These are for you.' Tom handed her the biggest bunch of flowers she'd ever seen. 'We weren't sure what colour you like, but Joey thinks all girls like pink.'

And there was every shade of pink. Bold cerise gerberas, tiny pale pink spray carnations, even some blush-pink roses.

Flora couldn't remember anyone ever buying her flowers before—except her parents, on her birthday and when she'd qualified as a nurse—and it flustered her. 'I, um…' She felt the betraying tide of colour sweep into her cheeks. 'Um, they're lovely. I, um…' Oh, help. 'Do you want to come in?'

'This is for Banjo.' Joey was carrying what Flora recognised as a squeaky toy bone.

'Thank you. He loves those.'

Just to prove it, when Joey squeaked the bone, Banjo

bounced into the middle of the room, bowing down and wagging his tail to signal that he was ready to play.

Be practical, Flora told herself. Don't make an idiot of yourself. 'I'll put these lovely flowers in water,' she said. 'Would you like a coffee?'

'I'd love one.' Tom smiled at her, and she felt her toes curl. Which was crazy. She didn't react to people like that. Anyway, he wasn't here to see her...was he?

To cover her confusion, she turned to the little boy. 'Joey, would you like some milk or some juice?'

Joey shook his head and continued playing with the dog.

Tom glanced at the vacuum cleaner. 'Sorry, you were busy.'

'It's OK. I was only vacuuming. And you brought me those gorgeous flowers.'

'It was the least we could do. You were a total star yesterday. We wanted to say thank you.'

He'd brought her flowers to say thanks for helping with Joey. No other reason. She squished the ridiculous hope that he'd bought them for the usual reason a man bought a woman flowers. Of course not. She already knew she wasn't the kind of woman who could make men look twice; she was way too short, thirty pounds too heavy, and on the rare occasion she wore a skirt it was usually six inches below the knee rather than six inches above. Plus she spent most of her time with a red face, tongue-tied. No way would someone like Tom be interested in her.

As always when faced with a social situation involving adults, she took refuge in practicalities, gesturing to Tom to sit at the scrubbed pine table in the centre of the kitchen, then busying herself arranging the flowers in a vase. Once she'd put them on the table, she made two mugs of coffee, took the remaining brownies from the tin and put them on a plate, then sat down with Tom and slid the plate across to him. 'Help yourself.'

'Thanks…' he smiled at her '…but, lovely as those brownies are, I'd better pass. We've just had breakfast. Chef Joey there makes a mean bacon sandwich.'

She raised an eyebrow. 'I assume you grilled the bacon.'

'But he did the important bit—he buttered the bread and added the tomato sauce.'

Joey clearly wasn't paying attention to anyone else except Banjo, but then Tom lowered his voice. 'I'm sorry we turned up unannounced. He told me this morning that he wanted to come and play with Banjo—and it's the longest sentence he's said in a month. I feel bad about taking up your spare time, but this was a chance to get through to him. I just couldn't turn it down.'

'It's not a problem,' Flora said, keeping her voice equally low. 'I wasn't doing anything in particular, just the usual Saturday chores.'

'I don't want to make things awkward with your boyfriend.'

She felt the betraying colour heat her cheeks again. 'I don't have a boyfriend.' The boys at school had never looked twice at her, she'd never been the partying type as a student nurse, and she knew that she wouldn't even be on the radar of a gorgeous firefighter like Tom Nicholson. Then a really nasty thought hit her. 'Is it going to be a problem for your girlfriend, Joey coming here to play with Banjo?'

'There's nobody serious in my life—just Joey.' He smiled wryly. 'Let's just say my last girlfriend found it a bit hard to share my time. The way she saw it, I should've made my parents come back to England to look after him.'

'How selfish of h—' Flora clapped a hand to her mouth. 'Sorry, it's not my place to judge.'

'No, you got it right first time. And she told me that the day after the accident.' For a moment, he looked grim. 'Apart from the fact that we hadn't been dating for very long, it wasn't a hard choice to make. Joey comes first.'

'Well, of course he does.'

Tom gave her an approving smile that made her feel as if she were glowing from the inside.

'I've been thinking about your childminder issue. I could help out, if you like.' The words tumbled out before Flora could stop them. 'I finish at five, the same time as the after-school club—so I could meet him from there if you like. There's only me and Banjo to please ourselves, and it's as easy to cook for two as it is for one, so if you're out on a shout or something he can have his tea here with me—if you think he'd like that,' she added swiftly.

Tom looked surprised at her offer. 'That's really kind of you,' he said carefully.

Oh, no. He'd obviously taken it the wrong way. She'd better explain. 'Look, I just know what it's like to lose both parents,' she said. 'And that wasn't me trying to—well, you know.' She blushed again.

Trying to come on to him? From another woman, Tom wouldn't have been so sure. But with Flora, he knew she was genuine; he hadn't known her long, but it was obvious that she was the type to wear her heart on her sleeve. She was offering to help because she was kind, because she cared, because she'd lost her own parents and she could understand exactly how Joey felt—and she wasn't emotionally hopeless with the boy, the way he was.

'I know it was a genuine offer,' he said softly, 'and I'm not trying to come on to you, either.' Though he knew that wasn't strictly true. He couldn't put his finger on it, but something about Flora Loveday drew him. And it was completely unexpected because she was nothing like the women he usually dated. She wasn't sophisticated, fashionable or glamorous. But there really was something about her that made him—well, just *want* her.

Though, right now, he knew he couldn't think about dating anyone. His life was too complicated. He pulled himself together. 'It's always good to make a new friend. Especially one as kind as you.'

She blushed even more, and Tom couldn't help smiling. Flora was so sweet. And there was a vulnerability about her that made him feel protective. Strong.

'And it's really all right for you to help me with Joey?'

'I wouldn't have offered if I didn't mean it.'

Tom closed his eyes for a moment. It seemed as if his prayers had all been answered. 'Flora, thank you. I have no idea what I would've done if you hadn't offered to help.'

Looking embarrassed, she glanced away. 'It's not a big deal. Joey's a nice little boy. But he might not want to come here.'

Tom smiled. 'Considering that he was up before I was, this morning—and I always wake at six—and he'd got himself dressed, with odd socks and his shirt on back to front, ready to come and see you and play with Banjo…I think he's going to say yes. But you're right—we do need to ask him first.' He looked over to where his nephew was busy making a fuss of Banjo, rubbing the dog's tummy while the spaniel had his eyes closed in bliss.

'Joey—can you come here a moment, sweetheart, please?'

Joey eyed the dog, clearly torn between making a fuss of him and doing what his uncle had asked, but eventually trotted over.

'How would you feel about Flora picking you up from after-school club in future?' Tom asked.

Joey frowned. 'Carol picks me up from school.'

'I know, but Carol has to go to live in London very soon,' Tom said gently. 'It's a big change for you, I know, but I've been trying to find someone you'd like to stay with while I'm at work.'

Joey's hazel eyes turned thoughtful. 'Would Banjo come, too?'

'Banjo's normally here during the day,' Flora said. 'But he'd be here to meet you when we got back from school. You could help me take him for a walk. Would you like that?'

Joey considered it, then nodded shyly.

'And then I'll come and fetch you as soon as I've finished work,' Tom said.

'Can I play with Banjo again now?'

Tom smiled. 'Sure.'

Joey raced back to the dog and found the squeaky bone.

'When do you want me to start picking him up?' Flora asked.

Tom thought about it. 'Carol's right in the middle of packing everything now. It's pretty disruptive for Joey, and I'm trying to keep things as calm as I can.' Calm and relaxed, like it was here at the farmhouse, Tom thought. Everything was neat and tidy, though it wasn't the kind of house where you'd be scared to move a cushion out of place. It was more that everything felt *right* just where it was, warm and welcoming and organised and comfortable. Just what Joey needed.

As for what Tom himself needed…he wasn't going to examine that too closely.

'I've got a day off on Monday. I don't have anything planned, so I could start then, if you like?' Flora suggested.

'Actually, I'm off myself on Monday and Tuesday—I work four days on and then four days off,' he said. 'But if you can do Wednesday to Friday this week, that'd be brilliant.'

'What time does your shift start?'

'I work seven until seven.'

'So what happens in the mornings,' she asked, 'if you have

to be at work at seven and school doesn't start until a quarter to nine?'

'I'm still working on that,' Tom admitted. 'I've been dropping him at Carol's at half past six.'

She shrugged. 'Well—I don't start work until nine, so you can do that with me, too. I'll have plenty of time to take him to school on the days you're at work.'

Tom stared at her. 'Really?' Usually, if something was too good to be true, it usually was. It couldn't be possible to sort out his hours and Joey's so easily—could it? 'Half past six is really OK with you?'

She smiled. 'I'm used to being up with the chickens, even though I don't have to feed them myself any more. And it'll be nice to have breakfast with someone in the mornings.'

She was so calm about it, so serene. Did she know what an angel she was? Tom wanted to hug her, but he had a feeling that she'd find it as awkward as Joey did. Something told him that Flora wasn't used to people hugging her. Except maybe some of her younger patients—he'd already noticed that she had children's drawings stuck to the door of her fridge with magnets.

'I'll need your contact numbers. And you'll also need to tell the school,' Flora added.

'Sure. If you have a piece of paper and a pen, I'll write my numbers down for you.'

Flora handed him her mobile phone. 'Better still, you could put them straight in there.'

Her fingers brushed against his and a wave of awareness swept down his spine. Not that he'd dare act on that awareness. Apart from the fact that she was shy—with him, not with Joey—if he messed this up, he'd lose a friend as well as help that he badly needed right now. He needed to keep a lid on this. Trying not to think about how soft her skin was and wondering how it would feel against his mouth, he keyed in his home number, his mobile and the number of the fire station. 'I've already got your numbers. I assume if I need to get you at work I should ring the surgery?'

'Yes, or try my mobile—I don't answer if I'm driving, though, so it'll go through to voicemail,' she warned.

'Good—that's sensible. I've had to cut too many people out of cars when they've been trying to talk on the phone and drive at the same time. Why they couldn't just pull over and make the call safely, or use a headset...' He rolled his eyes. 'Sorry. Preaching to the converted. And, as a medic, you know all that already.'

Flora smiled. 'Yes.'

She went quiet and shy on him again once they'd finished with the practicalities, but Tom was aware that he was eking out his coffee, putting off the moment when he'd have to leave here. Scared of being on his own with his nephew and failing to connect with him yet again? Or something else? He didn't want to analyse that too closely. And this really wasn't fair to Flora, taking up her day. 'Come on, Joey. Remember we said we'd go and play football in the park?'

'Can Banjo come?' Joey asked.

'No, Flora has things to do,' Tom said, before Joey could suggest taking up even more of Flora's time.

'Can we come back tomorrow?'

Tom was searching for an excuse when Flora said, 'I don't mind. I don't have anything much planned.'

'Tell you what, maybe Joey and I can take you out to lunch.' The words were out before he could stop them and he could see the surprise on her face—and the wariness. Help. He needed to take this down a notch. Make it clear that he was inviting her out with both of them, not on a proper date.

Though he was horribly aware that he'd like to have lunch with Flora on her own and get to know her better—a lot better.

'I mean, you fed us on Friday so it's our turn to feed you—right, Jojo?'

Joey nodded.

'And I know a place that does a really good Sunday roast, just down the road from here.' Tom smiled at her. 'So, can we take you to lunch tomorrow?'

'That'd be lovely. Thank you.'

'Great. We'll pick you up at half past eleven.'

It wasn't a proper date, Flora told herself as she stood in the doorway, waving as Tom's car headed down the driveway. They were just acquaintances who were on their way to becoming friends. Nothing more than that.

And she'd better not let herself forget it.

CHAPTER FOUR

DESPITE her resolutions to be calm and sensible, Flora found herself changing her outfit three times the next morning. She really should've asked Tom whether she needed to dress up for lunch.

Then again, they were going out with Joey, so the restaurant was more likely to be a family-friendly place. Which meant smart-casual rather than trendy—and besides, she didn't do trendy clothes. In the end, cross with herself for minding, she opted for a pair of smart black trousers, a long-sleeved cerise T-shirt and low-heeled sensible shoes. Hopefully this would strike the right balance.

She was relieved when Tom turned up wearing black chinos and a light sweater. And she suppressed the thought that he looked utterly gorgeous, like a model. He was her *friend*. Right?

Joey's seat was in the back of the car, but she noticed that Tom included Joey in the conversation, even though the little boy barely answered much above yes, no and—from what she could see in the rear-view mirror—a shrug.

Lunch was as excellent as Tom had promised. Flora noted that Tom helped Joey cut up his meat without making a big deal about it, just a soft, 'Can I give you a hand with that, sweetheart?' Tom really was a natural father figure, even though he clearly didn't think he was good enough. And they all had fun with the ice-cream machine; Tom helped Joey make a huge mountain in his bowl, and the little boy looked really happy as he added sprinkles and sauces from the toppings bar. He decorated Flora's and Tom's ice cream, too.

'That,' Flora said, 'is the best sundae I've ever seen.' She smiled at the little boy. 'Thank you, Joey. I'm really going to enjoy this.'

'Me, too,' Tom said. 'You're really good at decorating ice cream, Jojo.'

Joey's smile said it all for him: right now, all was right with his world.

Flora exchanged a glance with Tom, and her heart did another flip. This felt like being part of a family. And the scary thing was that she liked it. A lot.

'I think,' Tom said solemnly, patting his stomach afterwards, 'we need to walk off all that ice cream. It's really sunny outside, so how about we go to the park?'

Joey nodded, and Tom drove them there. Even though it was a chilly February afternoon, there were plenty of people walking through the gardens, pushing a pram or with a toddler running on the grass beside them. At the far end of the park, there was a playground with swings, slides and climbing frames; even from this distance, Flora could see that it was busy.

'Hello, Flora! Fancy seeing you here.' Jenny Walters smiled at her; she glanced at Tom and Joey and her smile turned speculative. 'Out to the park for the afternoon?'

'I, um. Yes.' Flora felt colour bursting into her face. Oh, no. The last thing they needed was gossip. But how could she explain that she and Tom were just friends, without it sounding like a cover story? 'You, too?' she asked, hoping that it would distract Jenny.

'Just me and Rachel. Damien's at home watching the football.' Jenny glanced at her daughter, who was holding her hand. 'Actually, I'm glad I've caught you. I know I'm probably worrying about nothing, but Rachel's got this thing on her foot and I don't like the look of it.' She bit her lip. 'Sorry, I can see you're out with your...' she paused '...*friend*, and I know I shouldn't ask outside clinic or the surgery.'

But it would only take a moment and would stop her worrying. And Flora always felt more comfortable when she was doing something practical. At work, she wasn't shy because she knew who she was: Flora Loveday, nurse. Plus looking at Rachel's foot might take Jenny's mind off the fact that she was accompanying Tom and Joey. She glanced at Tom and Joey. 'Would you mind if I took a look? I'll only be a couple of minutes.'

'No, that's fine—isn't it, Jojo?' Tom said.

Joey nodded solemnly.

'Thanks.' Flora smiled at them. 'Jenny, would you and Rachel like to come and sit down on that bench over there? Then, if you don't mind taking your shoe off, Rachel, I'll have a swift look at your foot.'

'It looks like grains of pepper on the bottom of her foot,' Jenny said. 'I thought it was maybe a splinter but she hasn't been running around barefoot in the garden, not at this time of year. I've tried putting mag sulph paste on it with a plaster on top, just in case it was a splinter, but nothing happened.'

From the description, Flora had a pretty good idea what it was, but she needed to see it for herself, just to be sure. 'Wow, that's a nice sock, Rachel,' she said as the little girl took her shoe off to reveal a bright pink sock with black pawprints. 'Those are pawprints just like my Banjo makes.'

'I like dogs,' Rachel said. 'What sort is yours?'

'He's a springer spaniel, and he lives up to his name because he bounces about everywhere,' Flora said with a grin. 'Guess what colour he is?'

'Black and white?'

'Half-right. Guess again.' Flora kept the little girl distracted by chatting while she inspected her foot.

'Brown and white?'

'Absolutely. Hey, do you know a song about a farmer's dog that almost sounds like Banjo?' she asked.

Just as she'd hoped, Rachel began singing, 'There was a farmer had a dog...'

And, to her surprise, when Rachel got to the bit where a letter in the dog's name was replaced by a clap, Joey joined in.

Tom looked transfixed. And, even though she'd seen enough to have her suspicions confirmed, Flora let Rachel and Joey finish the song before she asked her next question.

'That was brilliant singing, Rachel—and brilliant clapping, Joey.'

Both children looked pleased.

'You can sing us another clapping song, if you like,' Flora said. 'But first—Rachel, does it hurt when you walk?'

'A bit,' Rachel said. 'It's prickly.'

'OK. Well, the good news is, we can do something about that. Sing me another song, and I'll have a quick word with Mummy.' She smiled at the little boy. 'Joey, can you help Rachel with the clapping bits?'

Rachel was clearly delighted to have a younger child join in and, while she explained to Joey what they needed to do, Flora explained to Jenny what the problem was.

'It's a verruca,' she said.

'But I thought that was like a single big black spot?'

'Sometimes you get a cluster together, like this one,' Flora said. 'It's actually a wart on the bottom of the foot, so you might hear it called a plantar wart. Because of where it is, it gets trodden into the foot, so that's why it looks like spots rather than a growth. It's really common and nothing to worry about; my guess is, she picked it up at swimming.'

'I had a verruca when I was a kid,' Jenny said. 'I remember my mum taking me to the hospital, and this woman put a thing on my foot that burned and really hurt—and she told me off for making a fuss.'

Flora curled her lip in disgust. 'That's awful! You can still do the freezing treatment, but you can get something at the pharmacy so you can do it at home, and it's a special liquid so it shouldn't hurt. Or you can try duct tape.'

'Duct tape?' Jenny looked surprised.

'It works fairly well, but it's a little bit more long-winded. What you need to do is cut the tape just to the size of the verruca and put it on—it stops air getting to the skin and so it dies off and lets you get to the verruca,' Flora explained. 'Keep it on for six days, then take the tape off, soak Rachel's foot in a bowl of warm water for five minutes, then dry it and rub the area with a pumice stone to get rid of the dead skin. Then you put more duct tape on, and keep following the cycle. Usually it goes in three or four weeks.'

'I'll try that,' Jenny said.

'It's really infectious, so make sure you don't share towels,' Flora warned.

'And I'd better stop taking her swimming for a while.'

'Nowadays, the advice is just to cover it with waterproof plaster when you're swimming and use flip-flops in the communal areas,' Flora said with a smile.

Just when she'd finished explaining, Rachel and Joey sang and clapped the last bit of their song.

'That was brilliant, Rachel and Joey.' Flora applauded them both. 'Rachel, I've told Mummy what she needs to do, and you'll be pleased to know it won't hurt and you can still go swimming.'

The little girl beamed. 'Yay!'

'We'd better let you get on. Sorry we interrupted.' Jenny

gave Tom an apologetic smile, then patted Flora's shoulder. 'Thanks, Flora. You're such a star.'

Absolutely right, Tom thought, though he noticed how Flora shrugged the praise aside.

'Sorry about that, Tom,' Flora said as they headed towards the playground again.

'No, you're fine. I guess that's one of the perils of being a medic—everyone always wants to stop and ask your advice instead of going to the surgery.'

'I don't mind,' she said.

No, he thought, because she was special. She made a real difference to people's lives. 'Actually, that was fascinating. I learned a lot from that.' As well as reinforcing what he'd already guessed: that Flora was patient, was instinctively brilliant with children, and was great at reassuring worried parents, too. And he'd noticed that, even though Flora clearly knew Rachel's mum, she'd been shy with the woman until she'd actually been treating the child: and then the professional nurse had taken over, pushing the shyness away. Flora clearly had confidence in herself at work, but none outside. And he really couldn't understand why. Not wanting her to go back into her shell, he kept her talking about work. 'I had no idea about verrucas. I can't remember having one as a kid.'

'You must've been about the only child who didn't get one,' she said with a grin. 'Does Joey like swimming?'

He had no idea. 'Susie used to have a paddling pool for him in the garden, but I don't know if he ever went to a proper pool or had lessons. Probably not, or the swimming teacher would've got in touch with me by now, through Carol or something.' He sighed. 'I doubt if Joey will tell me himself, so I'll have to ask Matty Roper.'

'It might help you get a routine going, if you do things together on certain days—well, obviously depending on your shift,' she said. 'Maybe your first day off after a shift, you could go swimming together. And putting stickers on a calendar will help him remember what you're doing and when—that might make him feel a bit more secure with you.'

'I would never have thought of that.' Tom said. 'You're a genius.'

She shrugged. 'I'm no genius. I work with children, so I pick things up from the teachers and childminders.'

Hiding her light under a bushel again, Tom thought. Why did she do that? Why was she so uncomfortable with praise? Had her parents been the sort who were never satisfied and kept pushing? Or was it something else?

They reached the playground, and Joey made a beeline for the swing.

'Shall I push you?' Tom asked.

Joey shook his head, and proved that he could manage on his own.

Flora was sitting on the bench near the swings where she could watch; feeling useless, Tom joined her.

'OK?' she asked.

'Sure,' he lied. Hell. He needed distraction. And Flora was really, really good at being distracting.

Not that he would ruin things by telling her that there were amber flecks in her brown eyes. Or that her mouth was a perfect rosebud.

Pushing the thoughts away, he said, 'Did you always want to be a nurse?'

'I wanted to be a vet when I was small, and I was always bandaging up the dogs and the cats,' Flora said.

He could just imagine it, and couldn't help smiling.

'But I knew I wouldn't be able to handle putting animals to sleep, and Dad said I was so soft-hearted I'd end up taking in every stray brought in for surgery and I'd have to buy a

thousand acres to house them all—and he was probably right,'
Flora finished with a smile.

'But the medic part of it stuck?' he asked.

She nodded. 'I was going to take my exams to be a children's nurse when I'd qualified, and work at St Piran's.'

'So why didn't you?'

She shrugged. 'I realised Mum and Dad were struggling a
bit. I couldn't just leave them to it, so I came home to look after
them and did some agency work. The job as school liaison
nurse came through last year—ironically, not long after Mum
died. She would've been so pleased.'

'Was she a nurse, too?'

Flora shook her head. 'She and Dad, their life was the farm.
Loveday's Organics. Dad believed in it well before it became
trendy, and he worked with the Trevelyans on sorting out a veg
box scheme. Though I didn't really want to take the farm over
when I left school.' She gave a wry laugh. 'Whoever heard of
a farm girl being scared of chickens?'

'You're scared of chickens?' Tom asked.

'Not any more, but I was for years, even as a teen.' She
blushed prettily again, and Tom had to stop himself leaning
over to steal a kiss from that beautiful rosebud mouth. Did
Flora really have no idea how lovely she was?

'I think they knew I was nervous and it made them nervous, too, so it made them flap more. And that in turn made
me more nervous, and it just got worse. Nowadays, it's not so
bad. Toby taught me how to keep them calm, and I can even
go in and collect eggs now.'

Tom was surprised to feel a flicker of jealousy at the other
man's name. She'd said she didn't have a boyfriend... 'Who's
Toby?'

'He manages the farm for me. He's worked with us for the
last four years—he was Dad's assistant, but I know he took
as much as he could off Dad's shoulders. His wife's a real

sweetie, too. Their little boy's a couple of years older than Joey.' She looked thoughtful. 'Actually, they live in the cottage at the bottom of the driveway. It might be nice for Max and Joey to play together.'

'Maybe.' Tom was even crosser with himself for being pleased that Toby was clearly committed elsewhere. He had no right to be jealous and no right to dictate who Flora saw. 'Though Joey doesn't make friends very easily. He keeps himself to himself.'

'Max is a nice little boy. He'd be kind. Maybe we could do a play-date in a couple of weeks, when Joey's used to me and has settled in.' As if she could sense the knot of worry in his stomach and wanted to head him off the subject, she said, 'So what about you—did you always want to be a firefighter?'

'No, I was going to be an arctic explorer or drive a racing car.'

She laughed. 'So it was always going to be something dangerous, then?'

'Sort of.' He sighed. 'I think Dad was always a bit disappointed that I didn't go to university, but I'm taking my firefighter exams and I'm ready to move up to the next level, so I've proved to him that it's a career and not just a whim.'

'So what made you decide to be a firefighter?'

He could lie and give an anodyne response, but he had a feeling that Flora would know. And she deserved better than that. He took a deep breath. 'My best friend at school died in a house fire when I was thirteen.'

She winced. 'Sorry. That must've been hard for you.'

His world had been blown wide apart. Until then, it had never occurred to him that people his own age could die. Stupid, because of course they could. But he'd never known anyone die who wasn't really, really old and really, really sick. 'Yes. I found it pretty hard to deal with. And I couldn't help thinking, if I'd been a grown-up, one of the firefighters,

I would've been able to save Ben.' He shrugged. 'I know the fire wasn't my fault, but I guess becoming a firefighter was my way of trying to make up for what happened to him.' He'd never actually told anyone that before; he risked a glance at Flora, and to his surprise she wasn't looking at him as if he was crazy. She actually seemed to understand. 'Ben's the reason why I almost never lose anyone.' Why he drove himself past every barrier, no matter how scary. 'I remember how hard it was for his parents, when he died, and I don't want anyone else to go through that.'

'It takes someone very special to be that dedicated,' she said softly.

He shrugged. 'I've done the work for long enough to have a fair idea what I'm doing when it comes to fires, even though they can be unpredictable.' He probably took more risks than others, but he didn't really have a family at home to worry about.

Until now.

And that was a real struggle. He'd been thinking about his job, whether he ought to change to something with more child-friendly hours and less danger so he could protect Joey. Yet, at the same time, being a firefighter was all he'd ever wanted to do. He couldn't imagine doing anything else. And he found it hard to be a stand-in father; work was an escape for him. Which, he thought wryly, made him a really awful person. 'But being a parent to Joey…that's something I don't think I'll ever be able to get right,' he admitted.

'Probably because you're trying too hard.'

He frowned. 'How do you mean?'

'It's impossible to be the perfect parent,' she said gently. 'I see new mums breaking their hearts because they can't get it right and everyone else seems to get their babies to sleep and eat much more easily than they can. But then they come to realise that you can't be perfect and your best really is good enough. And that takes the pressure off and stops them trying so hard, and then the babies relax too and it all works out.' She took his hand and squeezed it. 'And it's even harder when you're suddenly dropped into a parenting role—when you're expecting a baby you have a few months to get used to the idea, and your confidence grows as the baby does. Joey's four, already thinking and acting for himself, and you just need to give yourself a bit of time to catch up with him.'

He thought about it.

And, to his shock, he realised that she was right. He *was* trying too hard. Trying to make up for Susie and Kevin not being there any more, trying to be the perfect stand-in and getting frustrated with himself and Joey because the barriers between them seemed to grow every day; and then feeling guilty because he'd escaped into work to forget his problems outside.

'You're a very wise woman, Flora Loveday.'

She just smiled.

They sat in a companionable silence, watching Joey on the swings, until they heard a scream. They turned round to see a woman cradling her child on the ground by the climbing frame.

'That's Maisie Phillipson and Barney,' Flora said. 'Tom, would you mind if—?'

'Go,' he cut in softly, knowing exactly what she was going to ask. He was beginning to realise that Flora just couldn't stand by and do nothing if there was a crisis and she knew she could do something to help. And he recognised that this was her way of dealing with her shyness, too; doing practical things meant that she didn't have time to think about what was going on and to feel self-conscious.

'Maisie, what happened?' Flora asked as she reached the climbing frame.

'One minute, Barney was climbing—the next, he was on

the ground.' Maisie bit her lip. 'I should've been watching him, not chatting.'

'Even if you'd watched him for every second, you wouldn't have been able to catch him,' Flora said. 'Do you want me to take a look at him?'

'Flora, you're an angel. Yes, please,' Maisie said, giving her a grateful smile.

Flora sat on the sand next to the little boy. 'Hi, there, Barney. Mummy says you fell off the climbing frame. Does anything hurt?'

'No-o.' Barney looked torn between braving it out and showing just what a tough six-year-old he was and bursting into tears.

'That's quite a big fall, and you're being really brave,' Flora said with a smile. 'Did you hit your head at all?'

'I think so.'

'Did everything go black after you hit your head?'

'No.'

That was a good sign. 'Can I just look into your eyes with my special torch?' Flora asked.

'All right.'

She took the torch from her handbag. Both of Barney's pupils were equal and reactive, to her relief. 'Righty. And now I need you to do something else for me.' She took a thimble with a bee on it from her handbag and slipped it onto her forefinger. 'Can you follow the bee with your eyes?'

He did so, and she checked his eye movements as she moved the bee from side to side.

'That's brilliant. I haven't got a sticker on me, but I'll bring you one when I'm in school next week,' she promised.

Barney looked hopeful. 'Can it be a rocket sticker?'

'Absolutely a rocket sticker,' she said, smiling back.

'Can I go and play now?'

Maisie sighed. 'All right. But *not* on the climbing frame. And be careful!'

'He'll be fine, Maisie,' Flora reassured her. 'You can give him some infant paracetamol when you get home, if he says anything hurts, and just keep an eye on him. If he still has a headache in six hours' time, or he's sick or passes out, or he feels really dizzy or can't see properly, or goes to sleep and you can't wake him, then take him straight to hospital.' She smiled ruefully. 'I really ought to keep a bumped-head leaflet in my handbag.'

After saying goodbye to Maisie, she returned to Tom.

'Everything OK?' Tom asked, standing up as she neared the bench.

'Bumped head. He'll be fine.'

'You must see that all the time.'

'Pretty much every session at the primary school,' she agreed with a smile. 'I know the advice off by heart.'

They walked over to the swings; Joey had slowed down and was just letting the ropes rock him back and forth.

'Shall we go down the slide, Jojo?' Tom asked.

The little boy shook his head. Before Tom could ask anything else, he slid off the seat and headed for the seats on a spring. He chose the one like a frog, and sat bouncing on it with his shoulders hunched and his back turned to Tom.

'Are you OK?' Flora asked.

'Yes.'

She could see on his face that he wasn't. And she knew that male pride would get in the way of him telling her what was wrong. But he'd confided in her earlier about his best friend as a child, and something in his eyes had told her that it wasn't something that most people knew about. She was pretty sure that it was the same as whatever was upsetting him now; but he needed to get this out in the open to let him deal with it. Which meant pushing beyond her own boundaries, not letting her shyness get in the way of helping him. She took a deep breath. 'Don't fib.'

Tom sighed. 'I guess no, then.'

And now for the biggie. She forced herself to say it. 'Want to tell me about it?'

He was silent for so long that she thought she'd gone too far. And then he bit his lip. 'Joey used to love the slide. On Sunday mornings, if Susie was cooking Sunday lunch for us, Kev and I used to take Joey to the park for a kickabout with a football, and we always ended up on the slides and the swings afterwards. He used to love going down the slide, sitting on my lap or his dad's, when he was really tiny.'

And she could see on Tom's face how much he missed it. And how hurt he was that his nephew didn't want to do that any more; what he could see was Joey's rejection, not the scared little boy behind it.

'He's probably remembering that, too, and it probably makes him miss his parents, but he just doesn't know how to tell you,' Flora said softly, taking Tom's hand and squeezing it. 'It might even be that he's scared to tell you, in case you're upset too.'

'Upset with him?'

She shook her head. 'Grieving. Missing his parents the way he does. I can remember my grandmother dying when I was about four, and my mum crying, and I felt helpless because I didn't know how to make things better for her. And because I felt helpless, I hid in my room and avoided her until she'd stopped crying and she was Mum again. I wasn't rejecting her—I just didn't know how to deal with it.'

He returned the pressure of her fingers and didn't drop her hand. 'You're right, and it's stupid of me to feel rejected because he doesn't want to go on the slide with me.' He swallowed hard. 'It's just that now he hates being touched. I can't even give him a hug or ruffle his hair because he really doesn't like it—he pulls away every time. He never used to hate it. He loved playing rough-and-tumble games with me and his dad. He used to run to me and give me a huge, huge hug hello whenever he saw me. And now...' Tom shook his head. 'He's quiet and still and...I just can't reach him.'

'It's a hard situation for both of you, Tom,' she said gently. 'Give yourself a break. You're doing your best.'

'And it's not good enough. I don't know how to be a dad.'

Flora had the strongest feeling that Tom hated failing at anything, but this was even harder because he loved the little boy and wanted to make Joey's world all right again.

'You're doing better than you think you are,' she told him. 'You spend time with him, you talk to him, you take him out— that's a lot more than some kids get from their parents.'

'I guess so.' Tom looked haunted. 'I just wish...'

'Wish what?' she prompted.

He shook his head. 'Never mind.'

Obviously he felt he'd already let his guard down too much with her. But Flora also noticed that he was still holding her hand. Taking comfort from her.

Well, it was what a friend would do. Slightly less ostentatious than a public hug. And, if it made him feel better, she was perfectly happy to hold his hand.

As for the awareness flickering down her spine, the tingling in her skin—well, she'd just have to ignore it. This wasn't about them. It was about Joey.

Eventually Joey stopped bouncing on the frog seat.

'Shall we go and have a hot chocolate to warm us up?' Tom suggested.

Joey nodded. Although he didn't hold his uncle's hand, he did at least fall into step beside him; and Flora noticed that Tom shortened his stride to make it easier for the little boy to keep up. He was sensitive to the needs of others and she liked that. A lot.

When they'd finished their hot chocolates—which Tom insisted on paying for—he drove them back to the farmhouse.

'We'd better let you get on,' Tom said, before she had the chance to invite them in.

'OK. Well, thanks for lunch. I really enjoyed that—and the park.' She smiled at Joey. 'Uncle Tom has a day off on Monday and Tuesday, so he's going to pick you up from school. But I'll see you on Wednesday for breakfast, and after school we'll take Banjo for a walk and collect some eggs, yes?'

Joey nodded.

'Thanks, Flora. You're a gem,' Tom said softly. 'We'll see you on Wednesday.'

CHAPTER FIVE

'FLORA?'

Even without the caller display showing the number on her phone, she would've recognised Tom's deep voice.

'Yes?'

'Are you busy right now?'

'I was about to go out,' she admitted.

'Never mind, then. I'll catch you later.'

'Tom?' She paused. Why would he be phoning her mid-morning? 'Is everything OK? I mean, have you been called in to work? Do you need me to pick up Joey?'

'No—nothing like that. But I did want to talk to you about Joey.'

He needed her. And somehow that made it a lot easier for her to push the hated shyness away. She made a swift decision. 'I'm going to the church to put flowers on my parents' graves. I won't be long. I could meet you in the coffee shop in half an hour, if you like?'

'Are you going to the church at Penhally?'

'Yes.' She frowned. 'Why?'

He sighed. 'That's where Susie and Kevin are buried. I ought to put some flowers on their grave. I know I should take Joey with me, but I haven't been able to face going to the churchyard yet, and I don't want him to see me all choked up.'

'The first time's the hardest,' Flora said. 'Why don't you

come with me? I'm putting flowers there myself—but, if you find you could do with talking to someone, I won't be far away.'

'Are you sure? I won't be in your way or anything?'

'Of course you won't. Look, I've just picked some daffodils from the garden. I'll split them with you.'

'Really?'

The relief in his tone decided her. 'Really. See you at the church in ten minutes.'

She drove to the church and parked on the gravelled car park outside the churchyard wall. It was such a quiet, peaceful spot, overlooking the bay; her parents had enjoyed sitting on the bench on the cliffs on Sunday afternoons.

Tom was waiting for her in the little lych gate, and her heart skipped a beat as he smiled at her. 'Thanks so much for this, Flora.'

'No worries.' She handed him half the flowers.

He stared at the daffodils and swallowed hard. 'Susie used to love spring flowers. The first thing she did when she and Kevin got the house was to plant spring bulbs. I remember she was so excited at having her own garden instead of just a window-box in her old flat in St Piran. I didn't get it at all because I was happy with my flat and not having to bother with weeding or mowing the lawn, but...' He grimaced. 'I guess I still can't believe she's gone.'

'I know what you mean. I find myself talking about my parents as if they're still here,' Flora said softly.

He rested his hand on her shoulder; even though she was wearing a sweater and a coat, it was as if she could feel the warmth of his skin against hers, and it sent a ripple of pure desire all the way down her spine.

'I really appreciate the way you've been here for me,' he said.

'Hey, that's what friends are for,' she said lightly, and turned away before she did something really stupid. Like standing on tiptoe, reaching up and brushing her mouth against his. 'Have you got something to put the flowers in?'

'No.' He looked horrified. 'It didn't even occur to me.'

'If Susie and Kevin are the first people you've lost, then of course you wouldn't think about it. It's something you find out the hard way.' She'd guessed he hadn't had a chance to think about the practicalities. 'Don't be too hard on yourself.' She produced a jam jar and a plastic bottle of water from her tote bag. 'The local florist sells cone-shaped vases that you just push into the ground for fresh flowers, but this will keep the flowers nice for now.'

'Flora, thank you.' He looked surprised and relieved in equal measure. 'I can't believe you thought of that, too.'

She shrugged off his praise and patted his shoulder. 'I'll come and find you when I've finished, shall I?'

She took the previous week's flowers from her parents' grave, tidied up the area, arranged the new daffodils, and then went to join Tom. His face was set and she could see that his eyelashes were damp. She remembered the first time she'd visited her parents' grave; she'd gone alone, and ended up bawling her eyes out on her knees in front of their grave, really wishing she'd had someone to hold her. Right now, Tom needed that same strength. And this was something she could do.

'Come here,' she said softly, and slid her arms round him, holding him close.

Tom closed his eyes, wrapped his arms round Flora, and rested his face against her hair. She smelled of roses and something else he couldn't quite pin down. And something of her warmth and strength seemed to flow into him as she held him, to the point where he was able to cope again.

'Sorry about that,' he said. 'I'm not usually that weak.'

Though, for the life of him, he couldn't let her go. He needed to feel her arms round him.

'It's not weak to admit you miss someone,' Flora said.

Wasn't it? He was a firefighter. He was meant to be in control. Someone who coped brilliantly in the worst kind of emergencies. Why was he going to pieces now, after putting flowers on his sister's grave? 'It feels it.'

'It's grief,' she reminded him gently. 'And it makes you feel all kinds of weird things. You might feel angry that the ones you love have left you, you might feel as if it's your fault and you're being punished for something, you might feel numb— and it's all OK. You get through it eventually.'

'It feels never-ending,' he admitted. 'Work's easy. I know what I'm doing there. But home… I never would've believed it's so hard to be a parent. How much worry there is.'

'It's not an easy job at all, especially when you're on your own,' Flora reassured him. 'And what you're feeling right now is perfectly normal. Give yourself a break, Tom.'

'Maybe.' He dropped a kiss on the top of her head. 'Do you mind if we get out of here?'

'Sure.' She paused. 'A walk on the beach might help.'

'The sea always makes me feel grounded,' he agreed. 'I loved coming to the bay when I was a child. It didn't matter if it was summer or the middle of winter—the wind would blow my worries away and the sound of the sea would silence all the doubts.' And with her by his side, it made him feel as if he *could* do things. As if he wasn't making a total mess of his life, outside work. Her warmth and her calmness soothed him even more than the sound of the sea.

They headed down the cliff path to the beach. The tide was half-out and the sea was calm, the waves rumbling onto the shore and swishing out again. They walked in silence for a while, and eventually Tom turned to Flora.

'I've been thinking—you and Joey. Are you really sure it's all right for you to have him for so long?'

'Of course it is.'

'I feel I'm taking advantage of you. And I need to sort out paying you.'

She shook her head. 'I don't want any money, Tom.'

'But you're looking after my nephew and you're giving him breakfast and dinner. I can't expect you to do it all just out of the goodness of your heart. That's not fair.'

'I don't mind,' Flora said. 'If anything, it's going to be nice to have a bit of company.' She still found the house a bit empty in the mornings, half expecting her dad to come in from seeing to the chickens or her mum to come in from the garden with some herbs or some flowers. Not that she could tell Tom that without sounding needy, and she didn't want him worrying that she wasn't stable enough to care for Joey properly.

'Then thank you.' He bit his lip. 'Poor Joey's finding it hard to adjust to change.'

'It must be hard for you, too.'

He nodded. 'And I can't even bring myself to go over to my sister's house and sort out her stuff, even though I know I should. I did a kind of grab raid when Joey was at school, the first week. I went there with a suitcase and got his clothes and his toys from his room. I've probably missed something important, something that really matters to him, and I know I shouldn't be so selfish—but I just can't handle it. I kept waiting for Susie to walk into the room and she just didn't, and it all felt so wrong…' He shook his head, grimacing. 'Sorry, I'm being really self-indulgent and you've had it harder than me, losing both your parents.'

She took his hand and squeezed it. 'It always hurts to lose someone you love. Look, I could come with you if you like, and help you sort through the stuff. It really helped me not to be on my own when I had to sort through my parents' things—Kate Tremayne from the surgery was really kind and helped me. It made a huge difference.'

'I might take you up on that.' His fingers tightened round hers. 'Thanks.'

'I've been thinking. Something else that might help Joey— you could try inviting one or two of his friends home for tea, when you're on a day off.'

'I don't think he has any friends,' Tom said. 'He did get a couple of invites, the first week back at school, but when I tried inviting the kids back the mums made excuses, and there haven't been any invites since.' He sighed. 'I don't know whether it's because he's so quiet and hardly talks, and they find that hard to deal with; or whether the other kids see Joey as being "different" because his parents died and they don't like him.'

She nodded. 'Other children can be cruel.'

Tom raised an eyebrow. 'That sounds personal.'

'Probably,' she admitted. 'My parents were elderly—Mum was forty-three when she had me, and Dad was ten years older than her. Everyone else's parents were around twenty years younger than them, so the kids at school always wanted to know if they were my grandparents, and refused to believe me when I said they were my parents. Then they used to say I was weird because my dad had grey hair.'

'That's horrible.' And that, Tom thought, was what was really at the root of her shyness. The way the children at school had made her feel like an outsider, rejecting her and mocking her; something like that would stick and make you worry about how other people saw you. And it would make you wary of others as you grew older. 'And you're not weird. Not at all.'

'It was just childish nonsense.' She shrugged. 'It doesn't bother me now.'

He wasn't so sure about that, but held his tongue. 'Did you lose your parents very long ago?' he asked.

'Last summer. Dad had a stroke. He was the love of Mum's life and she just gave up after he died—I know physiologically there's no such thing as a broken heart, but I honestly think that's why she died. Without Dad, she couldn't carry on. I buried her the month after.' She dragged in a breath. 'I hate just having a little wooden cross and a plastic pot I stick in the ground for flowers, but the stonemason says he can't put the headstone on for another couple of months.'

'So you understand exactly how Joey's feeling right now.' Guilt flooded through Tom. 'I'm sorry, I didn't mean to rub salt in your wounds.'

'You're not. And you,' she said softly, 'I know how you're feeling now, too. What you said about your sister's house—it was like that for me at the farmhouse. I guess I could've sold up, but I didn't want to—it's my home. So in the end I painted the walls a different colour and moved the furniture around and changed the colours of the cushions, just to get it into my head that things were different now and Mum and Dad aren't coming back.' She paused. 'It's going to take a while until you get used to it, Tom, so be kind to yourself.'

He was still holding her hand and he rubbed the pad of his thumb over the back of her hand. 'Can I buy you lunch? As a friend,' he added swiftly.

Not that he needed to say that, Flora thought. It was pretty obvious Tom wasn't going to be interested in her as anything other than a friend; she was way too mousy and boring. 'That'd be nice,' she said.

'If I follow you back to your place, we can drop your car off and I'll drive us,' Tom suggested.

They ended up at the Smugglers' Rest, just up the coast; and over a leisurely lunch they discovered that they had a lot in common. They both enjoyed the same kind of music and both were fans of historical crime novels—though Flora found out that Tom preferred action movies and hated the romantic comedies she enjoyed. And she couldn't remember the last time she'd enjoyed someone's company so much. When he'd opened up to her in the churchyard, it had made her feel close to him—to the point where she'd actually stopped feeling shy with him. They'd gone past that. She felt as comfortable with Tom now as she did with the people she worked with; and the fact that he seemed to listen to what she said, was interested in her views, made her feel more confident than she'd felt outside work since…since for ever, she thought.

Eventually, Tom glanced at his watch and gave a start. 'I've got to pick Joey up from school in a quarter of an hour! I can't believe how fast time's gone. I've really enjoyed having lunch with you, Flora.'

'Me, too,' she said, meaning it.

He tipped his head slightly on one side. 'Come with me to meet Joey?'

Flora pushed away the tempting thought that Tom might want her company for a bit longer. He was simply being practical; if he dropped her home first, he'd be late for school. 'OK.'

Joey was the last one out of the classroom and, although several of the children were lingering in the playground while their mums chatted, nobody made a move to speak to him. Flora's heart went out to him; poor little mite, he was having such a tough time.

Joey was silent on the way to the car, but when Tom strapped him in he asked, 'Are we going to see Banjo?'

'I do need to drop Flora back at the farm before we go home—but, if Flora doesn't mind, we can stay for a few minutes.'

Joey's faint smile said it all for him.

Tom stayed long enough to have a cup of tea with Flora,

and Joey accepted a glass of milk and a cookie; but then Tom called his nephew over from playing with the dog. 'We need to let Flora get on, and I have to cook you something for tea. We need to go, sweetheart.'

Joey nodded, but said nothing.

Tom's eyes were sad as he glanced at his nephew, and Flora's heart contracted. If only she could wave a magic wand for them. But they were going to have to muddle through this together and learn to bond and talk to each other and trust each other.

'We'll see you on Wednesday morning, then, Flora,' Tom said, and, to her surprise, kissed her on the cheek.

She felt the betraying wash of colour flood into her cheeks. Obviously Tom was a fairly tactile person; the kiss didn't mean anything at all, and this was just friendship. Yet she could feel the touch of his lips against her skin all evening, and it sent a mixture of warmth and excitement bubbling through her.

Tuesday was busy, thanks to a cold snap. Flora was on duty at the surgery all day on the minor injuries clinic, and there was a steady stream of people coming in to see her after falling over, most of them with hands that hurt. Several of them had very obvious signs of Colles' fractures. 'I'm going to have to send you to St Piran's for an X-ray and backslab,' she explained to the first of her patients. 'Everyone puts their hands out to save themselves when they fall, and if you land awkwardly you can end up breaking your wrist. You'll be in a cast for a couple of weeks until it heals. The good news is that casts are lightweight nowadays, so it won't get too much in the way, but the bad news is that you're going to have to get someone else to do all your lifting and carrying until your arm's healed.'

It felt odd not to see Tom and Joey in the evening. Flora was cross with herself for getting too involved, too fast. For pity's sake, she knew that Tom had other demands on his time. His job was incredibly difficult, and he had to get used to being a stand-in dad to his nephew. He wasn't going to have time to keep coming over to the farm and seeing her. And, unless she was looking after Joey, he didn't really even have a reason for coming to see her. 'I'm being ridiculous about this,' she told her dog. 'Worse than a teenager with a crush—and I haven't got a crush on Tom Nicholson.'

Banjo regarded her steadily, as if he didn't believe her.

She sighed. 'All right, so I think he's gorgeous. And it's not just the way he looks. He's a nice guy and there's something about him that makes me feel more...well, confident. He listens to me, so I don't feel like a bumbling idiot when I'm with him. I like the way his mind works, I like the way he puts other people first, and I like the way he's trying so hard to fit his life round Joey, rather than making Joey fit round him.' She bit her lip. 'But I've got to be practical about this, because he's way out of my league.'

But all the same she was pleased the next morning to hear the crunch of the gravel as Tom parked outside.

'Have you had breakfast yet?' she asked as she met Tom and Joey at the door.

He shook his head. 'I'll get something at the station.'

'It's as easy to make breakfast for three as it is for two.'

'Thanks, but I need to get going or I'll be late for work.'

Of course. And she was being ridiculous, feeling disappointed that he wasn't staying. At her age, she should know better. 'See you tonight, then.' She smiled at him. 'Have a nice day.'

'You, too. Bye, Joey.' Tom ruffled his nephew's hair awkwardly, and Joey gave him a pained look. Tom was clearly careful not to react in front of the boy, but Flora saw his shoulders slump as he headed back to his car. Every time Joey rejected him, she had a feeling that it cracked Tom's heart that little bit more.

'So what would you like for breakfast, Joey? I was thinking about French toast. Have you ever had French toast?'

The little boy shook his head.

'Do you fancy playing chef?'

His face lit up and he went to fetch a tea-towel from the drawer. Flora couldn't help smiling as he tucked it round himself to keep his school uniform clean. 'Good boy—well remembered.'

Joey seemed to thoroughly enjoy helping her beat the egg with vanilla essence and dip the bread into it. While the French toast was cooking, she sliced up some fruit onto two plates, then put the cooked French toast next to it.

'Nice?' she asked after Joey had taken a bite.

He nodded.

'Score out of five?'

He thought about it, then held up his right palm with all four fingers and thumb outstretched.

'Five? Excellent.' She beamed at him. 'We make a good team, Joey Barber.'

She washed up the breakfast things, then took him to school. 'Now, Joey, I know you don't like holding people's hands very much, but there's a fair bit of traffic here and I need to know you're safe, so I need you to hold my hand from the car to the playground, OK?'

He nodded and let her hold his hand.

For one crazy moment, Flora thought, This is what it would be like to take my own child to school. Then she shook herself. How silly. She didn't even date, so marriage and children were hardly an option.

But, oh, how she missed being part of a family. How she'd love a family of her own, somewhere she'd be accepted for herself. She adored Banjo, but the dog could only listen to her, not talk back, and she wasn't quite soppy enough to believe that the dog understood every word she said to her. Right now, she was rattling around on her own in the farmhouse. Lonely. As an only child, she didn't even have nieces and nephews to spoil—not now, and not in the future. So, unless she could do something to overcome her shyness and start dating, it was pretty unlikely that she'd ever have a family of her own again.

Though where did you meet people? At work wasn't an option for her; apart from the fact that the male doctors in the practice were already married, most of her patients were children. Even if she did end up treating an adult male who happened to be single, there was no way she'd be unprofessional enough to ask him out on a date.

And she wasn't one for parties or going clubbing. Which left a dating agency—and no way would she be able to meet up with a complete stranger. She'd spend the whole evening beetroot red, fumbling for words and feeling too awkward and embarrassed to relax, wishing herself back safely at home. It wouldn't be like the other day, when she'd sat in the Smugglers', chatting to Tom. Or like this morning, when she and Joey had made French toast.

She glanced at the little boy. Joey stood apart from the other children in the playground; he'd always been one of the quiet ones, but he was really cutting himself off. Was he scared that if he let someone close, he'd lose them, the way he'd lost his parents? That would explain why he was refusing to let Tom hug him or ride on his shoulders, the way Tom had said he'd done while Susie and Kevin had still been alive.

Maybe playing with Banjo would help. Bonding with the dog might help him bond with his uncle again, and gradually he'd learn to open up to other people.

The doors opened and the classroom assistant stood there to welcome the children in. 'See you at five, sweetheart,' Flora

said, and watched him walk in through the doors before she
headed off to work.

She texted Tom to let him know that Joey was safely at
school, and got a brief text back saying just 'Thanks'. Well, he
was at work, and he was busy. She'd been an idiot to hope that
he'd send a personal message back. That kiss on her cheek the
other night had been completely platonic, and she was acting
like a teenager. She put it firmly out of her mind, got on with
her work, and then met Joey from after-school club at five.

'How was your day?' she asked.

He shrugged and said nothing.

OK. She'd try something less emotional and see if he responded to that. 'Do you like drawing?'

He nodded, to her relief.

'Great. You can draw some pictures when we get back, if
you like.' She'd popped to the shops at lunchtime and bought a
sketchpad and pencils; she'd also picked up some more books
from the library. Joey drew pictures and played with Banjo
while she prepared dinner; then she read him some stories
while the veg steamed and the shepherd's pie cooked. Over
dinner, he told her shyly that a policeman had come in for
show-and-tell and he was the daddy of Mitchell in his class,
and Flora had a lightbulb moment: this was something that
might help Tom and Joey bond.

Finally, at a quarter past seven, Tom rang the doorbell.

He tried to make a fuss of Joey, but the little boy was having
none of it; he turned away and concentrated on turning the
pages of his book.

Seeing the hurt in Tom's face at the rejection, Flora switched
on the kettle. 'How was your day?' she asked.

'Pretty eventful. I had to break into a house to rescue a
family,' he said.

'Was it a fire?'

'No—it was carbon monoxide poisoning.'

'What happened?' She put a mug of coffee in front of him.

'The husband thought he had a bug or something. He felt a bit dizzy and sleepy, but he didn't have a temperature so he went in to work. He felt a bit better during the day, so he rang home—he knew his wife had been feeling a bit rough, too, and had stayed at home with the youngest because she had a vomiting bug, but then his wife didn't answer the phone or her mobile. He was worried in case she'd had to take the little one to hospital or something, so he rang their neighbour and asked him to take a look. He could see her car outside, but there was no answer when he knocked on the door. He looked through the window and saw her collapsed on the floor, so he called the emergency services.'

Flora winced. 'Lucky for them that the neighbour was there.'

'We broke in and got them out; then the ambulance arrived and the paramedics put them on oxygen.'

'Was that enough, or did they have to go to hospital?'

Tom couldn't remember talking about his job to a girlfriend before; it felt odd, chatting to someone who understood where he was coming from, but he rather liked it. 'The oxygen was enough,' he said. 'The paramedics put them on an ECG monitor and the trace was OK, so they're going to be fine. We took a look in the house and could see that the flames in the gas fire in the living room were yellow, not blue.'

'Which I take it is a problem?'

'Very much so,' Tom said. 'They called in a gas engineer to sort it out, and it turned out there was a blocked flue as well as the dodgy gas fire. It's all sorted now, and he rang us to thank us for saving his wife and youngest child's life, and to let us know what had happened.' He smiled. 'I like days like today, where I can actually fix things and make them right. How about you?'

'I was doing routine vaccinations today—back at the nursery, finishing off the ones I didn't do on Friday—and I was at the surgery this afternoon. Joey and I have had a nice evening together. We read some stories.'

Tom took the hint. 'Which was your favourite, Joey?' he asked, hoping that this time his nephew would respond.

'The one about the dog,' Joey said.

'We're going to choose the next ones together, so I don't pick ones he's already read,' Flora explained.

'I drawed Flora a picture. Me and Banjo,' Joey said.

'It's on the fridge.' Flora removed the magnet and handed the picture to Tom.

Tom suppressed the wish that his nephew had drawn him a picture, too. Flora was doing so much for him; it was churlish and ridiculous to be envious of her. Yet she seemed to be able to get through to the little boy where he couldn't, and he really wished he knew her secret.

'Can I get you something to eat?' Flora asked.

'No, you're fine. Thanks for offering, but I get a meal at work before the end of my shift.' He could see that she was taking it as a personal rejection and smiled to soften it. 'But this coffee is fabulous. Just what I need.'

There was another awkward silence while Tom wondered what he should say next to his nephew.

Flora, as if sensing his dilemma, stepped in. 'Joey had show-and-tell in class today,' she said.

'What did you see, Jojo?' Tom asked, picking up her obvious cue.

'A policeman.'

'Did you try on his hat?'

'And his handcuffs,' Joey said solemnly.

So Joey had enjoyed that, Tom thought. Would he, perhaps, like a firefighter to go in for show and tell? His gaze met Flora's, and she nodded very slightly, as if guessing what was in his mind. 'Have you ever had a firefighter in for show-and-tell?' he asked.

Joey shook his head.

'I'll have to check the schedule with my boss, but if you want me to I can maybe arrange to bring the engine and the crew out and show your class around. Obviously, provided we don't have to go off to put out a fire.'

Joey's eyes went wide.

'Would you like that, Joey?' Flora asked softly.

Joey nodded, and Tom felt the muscles of his shoulders relax. 'I'll have a chat with my boss and your teacher, then.' And maybe this would help Joey bond with him again. It would be something he could talk to his classmates about, maybe.

Tom meant to kiss Flora on the cheek again when he took Joey home, but somehow he ended up brushing his mouth against hers instead. Her mouth was soft and sweet and she tasted of vanilla. He had to resist the temptation to kiss her again; her eyes had gone wide and the amber flecks were even more obvious, and she looked utterly adorable.

And he really shouldn't be doing this.

'Flora, I—'

'It's OK.' She shook her head, clearly not wanting to discuss it. 'You'd better get Joey to bed. See you in the morning. 'Night, Joey!'

The little boy waved, and Tom mentally called himself all kinds of a fool. Flora was a lifesaver for him, right now, and he'd better not do anything to jeopardise it.

CHAPTER SIX

THE next morning, Tom looked wary when he dropped Joey off. Flora strove to be cheerful and polite and breezy so he wouldn't think she was still thrown by that kiss—even though she was, and her lips were still tingling at the memory of his mouth against hers. She knew how pathetic it was, having a crush on the most gorgeous firefighter in the crew. Of course he wouldn't be interested in boring, mousy her. They were just *friends*.

'Joey, do you like porridge, like the Three Bears had?' she asked.

He nodded.

'You can help me chop the fruit to put on top,' she said, 'and then we'll have a story while the porridge is cooking. I found a really good one where the bears get their revenge on Goldilocks; would you like to hear that one?'

He nodded again.

'Say bye-bye to Uncle Tom,' she said with a smile.

'Bye-bye.' Joey gave a tiny wave.

'See you later, Tom. Have a nice day,' she said brightly.

That was definitely a fake smile, Tom thought as he drove to work. Flora was clearly wary of him—and no wonder. He'd really messed up last night. Fancy kissing her like that. Why on earth hadn't he controlled himself? But he found her irresistible. And he hadn't been able to stop thinking about her ever since that hug outside the church.

When he'd kissed her on the cheek it had been spontaneous. Friendly. But last night's kiss—though equally chaste—had thrown him. He'd even dreamed about Flora last night. Dreams that set his pulse racing and made his body surge when he thought about it.

But she clearly didn't think the same way. So he needed to keep himself strictly under control in future.

Tonight, he'd bring flowers when he picked Joey up. He'd apologise, tell her that she had nothing to worry about—and he'd keep it platonic in future.

Thursday morning was Flora's clinic at the high school, where anyone could drop in and talk to her privately if they had any worries. She was also doing the second of the three-stage HPV vaccinations of the Year Eight girls. She could hear them chattering in the queue; one of them was talking about how her boyfriend had kissed her for the first time, and Flora thought of the way Tom had kissed her last night and how it had sent heat all the way through her body.

Oh, how juvenile. She really, *really* had to get a grip. She was twenty-four, not fourteen.

She'd just finished vaccinating one class when the school receptionist came hurrying through. 'Flora, there's been an accident. The fire brigade are on their way, but two of the Year Eight lads decided to skip lessons and go skating on the pond—they went straight through. Luckily one of the sixth formers decided to go to the library halfway through private study and heard them yelling for help; she had the sense to call the emergency services on her mobile phone and then came to tell me.'

The pond had had a reputation as a skating rink in Flora's days at the school; and, no matter how often the children were warned not to do it, there was always at least one every year willing to take the risk. As the boys had fallen through the ice and must have been there for a while, they were severely at risk of developing immersion hypothermia; they might even need hospital treatment. 'OK, I'm on my way. There are space blankets in the PE department, aren't there?' At the receptionist's nod, she said, 'Can you get someone to bring some through—and some spare clothing and towels, please?' As soon as the boys were out of the pond, the first thing she needed to do was to get them into dry clothes and start warming them up, heads and torsos first.

'I'll ring through now,' the receptionist said.

Flora took her medical bag and hurried over to the pond, pulling her coat on as she went. It was barely above freezing; why on earth had the boys been so daft? She could see the fire engine there; the crew had ladders out and one fireman was crawling along it towards the boys so he could pull them out. Her heart missed a beat. Even though she couldn't see the fireman's face and she knew that several of the fire crew were just as tall and brawny as Tom, she knew instinctively that it was him.

Please, let him be safe.

Rob Werrick, one of the PE teachers, came out with a space blanket, spare tracksuit bottoms and sweatshirts, and towels. 'It's Danny and Harry from Year Eight,' he said as he glanced at the pond. 'When I heard what had happened, I should've guessed those two would be involved.' He rolled his eyes. 'What on earth did they think they were doing?'

'In my day, there were stories about people skating on the pond. They probably thought it sounded like fun,' Flora suggested.

'Taking a huge risk, more like.' Rob sighed. 'They've all been warned to stay away from the pond. But do they ever listen?'

'Teenage boys,' Flora said ruefully. 'I think they have selective hearing.'

She could hear Tom talking to the boys, explaining how he was going to get them out and what they needed to do. He brought the first one back with him across the ladder, and kept the other one talking as he did so—no doubt, Flora thought, so he could keep a check on the boy's level of consciousness.

'Hi, Flora.' He smiled at her. 'Well, young Danny, I'm handing you over to safe hands now to get you checked over while I go and fish your mate out of the pond.' He winked at Flora, then headed back to the ladder.

'Come on, Danny, let's get you inside and get you out of those wet clothes and warmed up.' She hurried him into the nearest building.

'I can't get undressed in front of you. You're a girl,' Danny mumbled.

Usually Year Eight boys managed to make her blush or stutter; most of them were as tall as she was and it took her right back to her schooldays, when she'd been awkward and painfully shy and just hadn't fitted in. But Tom's words had bolstered her confidence: he'd treated Danny as a child and made it clear he was handing the boy over to someone whose opinion he respected. To *her*.

'You're a child,' Flora said crisply, 'and I'm a nurse. I'm not interested in your naked body. You're wet and very, very cold, and I need you to get into dry clothes before I can assess your breathing and your heart, OK?'

Danny muttered something she couldn't quite catch and didn't look her in the eye.

She rolled her eyes. 'If it makes you feel better, I'll turn my back. Dry off and get dressed, please—and don't rub your skin, pat it.'

Tom came in, a few moments later. 'What are we going to do with Harry?'

'Same as Danny. Wet clothes off, blot your skin with a towel—don't rub,' she warned, 'and then dry clothes on and a space blanket round you.'

Harry looked as embarrassed as Danny. 'I can't—'

'I've already had that conversation with Danny. I'm turning my back,' Flora said.

She could see the amusement in Tom's eyes but, to his credit, he didn't laugh.

Once the boys were dressed in dry clothes and had space blankets round them, she blotted their hair dry and then put woolly hats on them.

'Why do we have to wear hats indoors?' Harry asked, his teeth chattering.

'Because you lose the most heat from your head—the hat stops you losing the heat,' Flora explained. 'And you're both shivering, which is a good sign.' It showed that their bodies were trying to bring their temperature up again rather than just giving up.

'Is there anything else you need?' Rob Werrick asked.

'A mug of hot chocolate each would be good—not boiling hot, but warm so it helps to get their temperature back up,' Flora said.

'I'll make you both a coffee at the same time. Milk, sugar?'

'I'm fine,' Flora said.

'Just milk for me, please,' Tom said.

After the warm drink, Danny and Harry finally stopped shivering. Flora took their pulse and blood pressure, and listened to their hearts. 'You're going to be fine,' she told them. 'You were incredibly lucky this time, but for pity's sake *never* do anything like this again. It really isn't worth the risk. And nobody's going to think you're cool or clever if you end up in hospital.'

'Ice needs to be at least twelve centimetres thick to bear

your weight,' Tom said, 'and this wasn't anywhere near thick enough.'

'It looked thick enough,' Danny said, looking mutinous.

'But it wasn't. You went straight through it.'

'Dad said he skated on the pond when he was here,' Harry said.

'Your dad might have been teasing you.'

'No, he really did it.'

'Then he took a very big risk. The pond's too deep for you to haul yourself out onto the ice once you've gone through it. And you two are very lucky that someone heard you yelling for help. If you'd been stuck in that water for thirty minutes, you might not have survived,' Tom said grimly. 'Your body temperature would've dropped so low that you could've died—and think of how your families would've felt, losing you.'

Danny and Harry looked at each other, but said nothing.

'Are our parents going to have to know about this?' Danny asked eventually.

'Of course they are,' Flora said. 'Your parents need to know what happened. I'll be the one speaking to your mums and reassuring them that you're both OK and you haven't got hypothermia.'

'Mum's *so* going to ground me,' Harry said. 'And she's going to ban my games console for a month.'

'Me, too,' Danny said. 'It's not fair.'

'And it was fair of you both to skip lessons, go onto the ice to show off to your mates, and end up risking the lives of the fire crew?' Flora asked.

Harry's cheeks reddened. 'I s'pose not.'

'Danny?' she prompted.

He pulled a face. 'No.'

'Is there something you both want to say to Mr Nicholson

here, then?' Flora asked. Both boys hung their heads. 'Sorry,' they mumbled, their faces bright red with embarrassment.

'And?' she prompted.

Danny looked at her. 'What?'

'He saved your life,' she pointed out quietly. 'Which I think might be worth two little words your parents probably made you say when you were little—and you've clearly forgotten.'

They both went even redder and muttered, 'Thank you.'

'Right. Better get back to your lessons.' Flora folded her arms. 'And you might find life an awful lot easier if you stop to think things through before you act next time, OK?'

The boys nodded, looking ashamed, and shuffled out of the room.

'So you have a stern side, Flora Loveday,' Tom said, sounding amused.

'When people do really stupid things and put others at risk, then yes.' She shrugged. 'You don't need to shout or swear to get your point across.'

'No, somehow I don't think they're going to forget what you said to them.' He sighed. 'I wanted to shake the pair of them, I admit. It was a really stupid thing to do. Ice can vary in thickness across a pond—one part can be safe, but put one foot on a weak area, and you'll go straight through into the water.' He grimaced. 'It isn't the first time I've rescued someone from falling through ice, and it won't be the last.'

Flora looked at him. 'They're fine, but are you OK? You had to crawl out on the ice.'

'On a ladder. I'm fine. I'm wearing a drysuit and several layers underneath—and Rob got me that coffee, so that's warmed me up.' His eyes crinkled at the corners as he looked at her. 'I'd better get back to work. See you later.'

'See you,' she said, smiling back.

* * *

After school, Joey spent the afternoon racing round with Banjo, and he was asleep when Tom arrived to pick him up. Banjo stood next to Joey, on guard duty, and Tom ruffled the dog's fur. 'You're a good boy,' he said softly. Then he turned to Flora and handed her the flowers.

'They're lovely, Tom, but you really don't need to bring me flowers.'

'I do, today.'

She looked puzzled. 'Why?'

'Last night.' He took a deep breath. 'About that...I owe you an apology. I didn't mean to come on so strong.'

She didn't meet his eyes. 'It's not a problem. I know you didn't mean it that way.'

Something in her voice alerted Tom: Flora obviously thought she wasn't attractive enough for any man to want to kiss her. How on earth had she got that idea? He cupped her face in one hand and gently moved her chin so she was looking him straight in the eye. 'Flora, you do know you're beautiful, don't you?'

'Me? *Beautiful*?' Her face was filled with astonishment. 'You must be joking. I'm nothing like a WAG.'

Was that her definition of beauty? It wasn't his. 'I'm glad you're not. You're not caked in make-up, and you don't spend hours doing your nails and dyeing your hair. Yours is a natural beauty. And very, very real.'

She went bright pink.

'And then you have depths. You're not one of these shallow, boring women. You're kind and you're sweet and...' And he wanted her very, very badly. Too much to be able to resist. 'Flora.' He breathed her name, dipped his head and kissed her again. This time with intent. His mouth moved over hers, teasing and coaxing, until she gave a tiny sigh, slid her free arm round his neck and kissed him back.

'I'm not going to apologise for that one,' he said when he broke the kiss. 'Just so you know, I meant it.'

She blushed again and her lips parted, as if inviting him to kiss her some more.

'You taste of vanilla,' he said softly.

'It's lip salve.'

He smiled. 'Keep wearing it. I like it.'

She flushed again. 'Tom, you can't— I mean, I'm not your type.'

'No? So what do you think is my type?'

'Someone glamorous. Someone tall.' She swallowed hard. 'Someone *thin*.'

He'd begun to be bored with glamour. Height didn't matter. And he loathed dating women who nibbled on a stick of celery and refused pudding in case it made them put on a few grams; he much preferred the company of women who actually enjoyed eating out with him.

'Wrong on all counts,' he told her softly. 'And why are you putting yourself down? You have delicious curves, Flora. Curves that make me want to...' He slid both hands down her sides, moulding her curves. 'You're lovely. Luscious.'

He took the flowers from her hand, put them on the table, then scooped her up and sat down on the sofa, pulling her onto his lap. 'I know I probably shouldn't be doing this. I don't have the right to ask to start seeing you—my life is complicated, and I'm already taking way too much advantage of your good nature.' He stole a kiss. 'But I've been thinking about you all day. All week, really,' he admitted ruefully. 'I haven't been able to get you out of my head since the day I met you.'

She shook her head. 'But that's not possible.'

'Why's it so hard to believe? Flora, you're a pocket Venus. You have the most gorgeous mouth. And you taste...' he brushed his mouth against hers again '...like heaven.'

* * *

Self-consciousness washed through her. He'd just called her a pocket Venus. She knew she was just frumpy and overweight. And right now she was probably crushing his legs, and he was doing the macho firefighter thing and pretending she wasn't.

'Flora.' He kissed the tip of her nose. 'You look worried. Do you want me to back off?'

'No-o.'

'You don't sound very sure.' He twined the end of her ponytail round his finger. 'OK, let me ask you a different question. Will you go out with me?'

'I...' Heat flooded into her face. 'Look, I, um, haven't dated much.' And she certainly hadn't ever had a serious boyfriend. 'I'm not very good at this.' She bit her lip. 'And you're...'

'I'm what?' he prompted gently.

Sex on legs. Not that anything would drag that admission from her. 'You must have women falling at your feet all the time,' she said unhappily. Gorgeous women. Glamorous women who were used to dating and had all the right social skills.

'I admit, I get teased at work for having a fan club. There are a few women who insist on baking me cakes.'

She'd just bet there were.

'And some of them are in their eighties,' Tom said.

Maybe, but she was pretty sure that a good deal more of them would be around her own age.

'Some of them think of me as a surrogate grandson who rescues their cat and checks that their smoke alarms are working properly. I'm polite to everyone who makes me cakes, I thank them for their kindness but I don't make a habit of going around kissing women.'

Which wasn't the same thing as saying that they didn't kiss him.

He kissed her again. 'I guess I'm trying to say that there's something about you. I can't get you out of my head. And I really, really like kissing you.' He caught her bottom lip between his, just to prove it.

And this time she couldn't help kissing him back.

When he broke the kiss, he settled her against him, wrapping his arms round her. 'You know, this is the first time my world's felt right this year,' he said softly. 'So can I see you?'

'Tom.' She stroked his face. 'I wasn't expecting this to happen.'

'Do you mind?'

'It scares me a bit,' she admitted. 'I'm not used to this.'

'I'm not going to hurt you, Flora. I like you. A lot.'

'Are you sure this isn't—well, just gratitude?'

'Because you're helping me with Joey? Given that I was dreaming about you last night,' Tom said, 'and you'd really be blushing if I told you exactly what was happening in that dream…No. It's definitely not just gratitude.'

She blushed anyway. Tom had been having raunchy dreams about her?

'You're adorable,' he said softly. 'Actually, I love it when you go all pink and flustered. It makes me want to kiss you and fluster you some more. And your eyes are amazing. They have these little amber flecks in them. Like gold.'

That was what people always said when they knew you weren't drop-dead gorgeous and they tried to compliment you: they said you had nice eyes.

'And your ears.'

Now, that she hadn't expected. She stared at him in surprise. 'My ears?'

'Uh-huh.' He nibbled one lobe, very gently, then kissed his way down the sensitive spots at the side of her neck, making her shiver. 'And your mouth. It's a perfect rosebud. It's beautiful. Tempting. Irresistible.' He kissed her again, to make the point. 'And your curves are delicious.' He kept his arms very firmly round her. 'I like you, Flora. Very much. As a person, because you're warm and sweet and kind and you make the world seem a better place.' He paused, making eye contact. 'And as a woman. I really, *really* like you as a woman.'

'I like you, too,' she admitted shyly. 'As a— As a man.'

'So how about we see where this takes us?'

She took a deep breath. 'OK. But, as far as Jocy's concerned, you and I are just friends—which keeps things stable in his world and he isn't going to worry that suddenly neither of us will have time for him.'

'That's another thing,' Tom said softly. 'You think about other people. How things affect them. You're incredibly empathetic.'

'It's my job. I'm a nurse.'

'No, Flora, it's who you are,' he corrected. 'And it's yet another thing that draws me to you.'

She still found it hard to believe that Tom was serious—how could he possibly want her, when he could have his pick of the most gorgeous women in this part of Cornwall?—and yet his dark eyes were sincere. He wasn't spinning her a line.

Joey stirred and she wriggled off Tom's lap. 'Joey,' she said softly.

Tom stole a last kiss, then went to scoop his nephew off the beanbag. 'Come on, sweetheart. You're sleepy. Let's get you home.'

To Flora's surprise and pleasure, Joey didn't wriggle out of his arms and actually let Tom carry him to the car.

'See you tomorrow, Flora,' he said softly. 'And thank you.'

Flora still couldn't quite believe what had just happened: that Tom had actually sat with her on his lap, had kissed her and told her he thought she was gorgeous.

She pinched herself. It hurt. So she wasn't dreaming, then.

And the flowers he'd brought her were still on the table. She hadn't even put them in water yet; she'd been too caught up in the way Tom had cradled her on his lap and kissed her. She smiled and put the flowers in a vase—and she was still smiling when she fell asleep that night.

On Friday evening, Tom had news. 'I'm going to do the show-and-tell at Joey's class next week.'

'That's great—he'll enjoy that.'

'And there's something else—I play football in the local emergency services league. Our team's having a "dads and sons" match on Sunday morning, when I'm off duty. I'm going to take Joey; will you come with us?'

'I've never been to a football match.'

'Because you hate football?'

She wrinkled her nose. 'Well, it's not really my sort of thing.' And she'd been utterly hopeless at sport at school— always the last to be picked for any team.

'Ah, but this is different. And Joey and I could do with someone standing on the sidelines cheering for us,' Tom said.

Put like that, how could she refuse?

Then she thought of something. 'So you're working tomorrow?' Being Saturday, Joey wouldn't have school.

'Yes.'

'Do you want to bring Joey over?'

'I can't impose on you like that.' Before she could protest that it was fine and she didn't mind, he added softly, 'Kevin's parents are coming down to see him for the day. Actually, they're coming this evening and staying overnight, so I'd better get back and sort my place out, because it's a tip.' He smiled at her. 'The match on Sunday starts at ten so we'll pick you up at half past nine, OK?'

'Half-nine it is,' she agreed.

He kissed her swiftly but very, very sweetly. 'Sorry I have to go so soon—I would rather stay with you, but Joey needs to see his grandparents.'

'Of course he does. I understand, Tom.'

'I can't believe how lucky I am to have found you.' He stole a last kiss. 'We'll see you on Sunday morning.'

CHAPTER SEVEN

ON SUNDAY, Tom picked Flora up at half past nine on the dot and drove her to the playing field. She felt ridiculously shy as she climbed out of his car. Tom seemed to know everyone; people were coming up all the time to talk to him or clap him on the back and ask how many goals he thought he'd score in the match. And she didn't know a single one of them. Nobody from Penhally was here; this was a completely different crowd to what she'd been expecting. The only person she could see that she recognised was Megan Phillips—and Megan was standing on the sidelines, shoulders hunched and hands in her pockets, her body language making it very clear that she didn't want to talk to anyone.

This was awful. Just like one or two of her mums had confided to her about the baby and toddler group, the first time they'd been—everyone else knew each other and had bonded into a little group, and they weren't part of it. Flora wasn't part of this group, either.

Her advice to her mums had been to take a deep breath and start talking to someone, and they'd soon find something in common.

What a hypocrite she was—she couldn't even follow her own advice. She didn't have a clue what to say. What did she have in common with these glamorous women in their tight jeans, fashionable boots and waxed jackets? She couldn't even go over and talk to them about children, because Joey wasn't really hers. Besides, she only recognised a couple of the children on the pitch from Penhally, and a swift scan of the sidelines told her that their mums weren't at the match—they were obviously at home looking after the younger children.

In the end, she simply stood on the sidelines, watching Tom and Joey, thinking miserably that she was never going to fit in with Tom's crowd. Maybe they ought to stop this disaster of a relationship before it had really begun.

Megan shoved her hands deeper into her pockets. What an idiot she was, turning up to the father-and-son football match. And all to catch a glimpse of Josh. Stupid, really. Josh was only there because one of the emergency department doctors had got flu and had had to drop out. He didn't even have a child with him.

Though if things had been different, he would've done. A seven-year-old boy. A boy with Josh's indigo-blue eyes and ready smile, perhaps. A boy who adored his father and had grown up knowing how much he was loved by both his parents...

The back of her throat felt tight. There was no point in wishing things were different, because they weren't. She'd lost the baby. And more. She never would have a child of her own. The nearest she could get to it was through her work, saving the lives of other people's precious babies.

And that had to be enough.

She swallowed hard. She really shouldn't have come today. Better to leave now—before Josh saw her and started asking questions.

To her surprise, Flora discovered that she enjoyed watching the game and cheering as Tom scored a goal. She had a flask of hot chocolate in her basket ready for half-time, and had also spent the Saturday afternoon making a batch of brownies and cookies. She poured a small mug of hot chocolate for Joey; Tom simply stole her mug, deliberately sipped from exactly the same spot that she had, and gave her a smile that made her knees go weak. And suddenly it didn't matter that she was on her own on the sidelines; Tom and Joey wanted her there, and that was the main thing.

'Enjoying it?' Tom asked.

She smiled. 'Yes.' It wasn't a complete fib; now he and Joey were here with her, she was definitely enjoying it.

Josh spotted Megan on the sidelines. On her own. But why would she come to a football match? Unless…

'Pay attention, Josh! That was an easy pass. You should've scored.'

'Sorry, mate.' Josh held his hands up in acknowledgement of the fault. But all the same he couldn't help looking for Megan during the match, trying to catch her eye. When the whistle blew for half-time, he caught one of the others. 'Can you substitute me for a bit? Something I really need to do.'

'What, *now*?'

'Yes, now,' Josh said, clapping his team-mate's shoulder. If Megan was here, unless she was here as the medical support— which he very much doubted—it was to see him. And he couldn't pass up the chance that she might be ready to talk to him. To start sorting things out between them.

Except, when he reached the place he'd seen her, she wasn't there. He scanned the sidelines and couldn't see her there, either. Maybe she was in the car park.

But a swift search of the car park told him that Megan had gone.

Needing a moment to himself, he leaned against the bonnet of his own car. Why had she come here in the first place? He didn't have a clue what was going on in her head. But one thing he did know: they needed to talk. Properly.

Five minutes into the second half, one of the players fell to the ground and rolled onto his back, clutching his leg. The referee stopped the match. Automatically, Flora went over; her skills were needed, and that was enough to push her shyness and feelings of awkwardness into the background. 'I'm a nurse,' she explained. 'Can I do anything to help?'

The referee gave her a grateful look. 'Yes, please. This is Ian.'

'What happened, Ian?' she asked.

'My ankle's killing me,' he groaned.

'Can I take a look?'

He nodded, his face white with pain.

'I'll need to take your boot off. Is that OK?' When he gave his consent, she crouched down, removed his football boot and drew the sock down so she could see his ankle properly, then probed his ankle gently.

'Ow. That hurts,' Ian said.

'It's a pretty nasty sprain,' Flora said. 'Looks like you've landed awkwardly—you've twisted the joint and it's damaged your ligaments. I'm afraid you're not going to be able to play for the rest of the match. Did you hear a "pop" in your ankle when it happened?'

'Yes—and then it started hurting like crazy.'

'I'm pretty sure it's not a fracture, just a simple sprain, but it's going to hurt for a couple of weeks,' she warned him. 'You'll need to rest it for the next couple of days with ice to reduce the swelling, wrapped in some kind of cloth so it doesn't burn your skin. I'd suggest fifteen minutes of ice treatment per hour, but no more than three hours in total over the next twenty-four. You also need to use an elastic bandage from your toes to the middle of your lower leg, to support the sprain. And if you can put a couple of pillows on a chair and prop your ankle up so it's higher than your heart, it'll help it heal more quickly. If you've got some ibuprofen at home, that'd be best painkiller to use because it'll help reduce the swelling.' She smiled at him. 'If it's still giving you a lot of gyp tomorrow it might be worth going to the emergency department at St Piran's and ask them to take a look, but I'm pretty sure it's only a sprain rather than a fracture.'

'I know you from somewhere, don't I?' he asked.

'I'm a nurse at the Penhally Bay Surgery,' she said. 'And I'm the school liaison nurse.'

He nodded. 'That's where I've seen you—my boy's in Year Six. He's been nagging me lately about my lunchbox not being healthy enough and telling me to swap the cake for another piece of fruit.'

She laughed. 'Glad to hear the message is getting through.'

He moved, and gritted his teeth as pain clearly shot through him. 'Thanks for looking after me. You're here with Tom, aren't you?'

'I…um…' Flora couldn't help blushing. 'Yes.'

Ian smiled. 'He's a top bloke, our Tom.'

'Absolutely,' she agreed. 'Ian, I don't have an ice pack with me, but I do have an elastic bandage. I can at least strap up your ankle and get you to elevate it until you can get a lift home.'

A couple of the other football players helped him up and supported him over to his car; Ian called his wife on his mobile phone and asked her to get a taxi to the football ground and rescue him. Flora strapped up his ankle, made sure that he was comfortable, and then went back to watch the end of the match.

'What happened to Ian?' Tom asked when he came over to her at the end of the match.

'He sprained his ankle.'

'Poor guy. It's going to make things difficult for him at work—he's a police officer.'

'He's going to be on desk duty for a few days, then,' Flora said.

'Did you enjoy the match, Joey?' Tom asked.

Joey nodded but his eyes were very dark. Tom and Flora exchanged a glance, guessing that the little boy was thinking of his dad. Tom crouched down. 'Hey. You played really well. And I bet your dad would have been really proud of you.'

Joey's bottom lip wobbled for a second, then he turned away.

Tom bit his lip, clearly thinking he'd made a mess of it.

Flora squeezed his hand and mouthed, 'You said the right thing. Don't blame yourself—just give him a moment.'

'We'd better go home and have a shower, because we're both covered in mud,' Tom said. 'And we have to be home for one, because Grandma said that's when lunch is going to be ready. She's cooking chicken, your favourite.'

'Is Flora coming?' Joey asked.

Flora hadn't been invited and had no intention of muscling in. After all, she was really just Tom's friend—acquaintance, really. She had no real connection to Kevin or to Susie.

Tom glanced at her, and she shook her head silently.

'No, we've already taken up her morning with the football. She has things to do round the farm. Come on, we'll drop her home and you can say hello to Banjo, and then we have to get going,' Tom said.

Before Flora knew it, she was home again, just her and the dog. Funny, a week ago that had been fine with her. Right now, it felt…empty.

Which was totally ridiculous.

She couldn't be falling for Tom—and Joey—that fast. Cross with herself, she made sure that she was busy for the rest of the day. Even so, the time dragged; the next morning dragged, too, because Tom was off duty and was taking Joey to school himself.

But at lunchtime she was catching up with paperwork in the surgery when her mobile phone rang.

'Hi. Are you busy tonight?' Tom asked.

'Not particularly,' Flora said. 'Why?'

'Because I'd like to invite you to dinner at my place. Joey tells me that he's enjoying cooking with you in the mornings, so he and I are going to be chefs. Is there anything you don't eat or you're allergic to?'

'No.'

'Great.' He gave her his address and directions. 'See you at six?'

'OK. Six it is.'

Flora felt ridiculously shy as she ended the call. This felt like a proper date—especially as it was Valentine's Day.

Valentine's Day.

Should she get Tom a card, or was that being a bit pushy? Was it too early in their relationship?

Oh, help. She was no good at this dating stuff. But on the way to Tom's flat, she dropped into the supermarket to buy a box of chocolates for Tom and Joey as a host gift and a huge display of cards caught her eye. She spent a while choosing one: nothing mushy, just a photograph of a simple heart-shaped box filled with chocolates. Sitting in her car, she simply wrote Tom's name inside it and signed it with two kisses; then she slipped the card into the envelope and put it in her handbag. She'd give it to him later, if she felt the moment was right.

Tom's flat was in a modern block on the first floor. She rang the doorbell, feeling ridiculously nervous.

He answered the door. 'Come in. Joey's just watching some cartoons. Can I take your coat?' He gave her a brief kiss hello as he took her coat, and her knees went weak. 'You look gorgeous,' he whispered. 'I love that colour on you.' She was wearing a black calf-length skirt and a teal-coloured top.

Colour seeped into her face. 'Thank you.' She strove for lightness. 'You don't look so bad yourself.' In dark trousers and a white shirt, he looked absolutely edible; she wanted to kiss him again, but at the same time she didn't want to seem pushy.

'Jojo, Flora's here,' he called.

Joey appeared from the living room. 'We made you dinner.'

'Thank you. And I brought you these as a gift.' She handed him the chocolates. 'Though they're for after dinner, OK?'

'Thank you.' Joey smiled at her. 'I made this at school.' He handed her an envelope.

'For me?'

He nodded.

When she opened it, there was a huge lump in her throat. The envelope contained a simple card with a heart shape cut out from red tissue paper. Inside, it said, *'To Flora from Joey'*, in very careful handwriting, and there were two kisses.

'That's lovely, Joey, and what beautiful handwriting.'

'We made cards at school.' He bit his lip, and she knew what he wasn't saying—that the children had all made them for their parents. 'I made one for Uncle Tom, too.'

She glanced at Tom and saw the sheen in his eyes; clearly the card had had a real emotional impact on him, too. She crouched down to Joey's level. 'This is the nicest card I've ever had. Can I give you a thank-you hug?'

Joey deliberated and she thought he was going to say no—then he nodded.

She hugged him. 'Thank you. And I'm going to put this on my fridge when I get home.'

'Can I watch cartoons again now?'

'Sure you can,' Tom said. 'I'm going to give Flora a guided

tour.' He showed her around the flat. 'Living room, obviously.'
There were lots of photographs on the mantelpiece: an older
couple that she assumed were his parents; a wedding picture
that she guessed was Susie and Kevin, as there was another
of the same couple with a baby; a picture of Tom with a much
smaller Joey on his shoulders. There was one large bookcase
crammed with books, and another crammed with films; she
wasn't surprised to see a state-of-the-art games console next
to his TV.

'Kitchen diner.' The kitchen was at one end and there was
a table at the far end, by the window.

'Something smells nice,' she said.

'Bathroom, if you need it.' Plain, masculine and gleamingly
clean, she noticed.

'And those two...' he gestured to the final two closed doors
'...are my room and Joey's.'

'So where did you put Kevin's parents when they stayed?'

'My room, and I slept on the couch. It wasn't a big deal.'
He glanced at his watch. 'Dinner's about ready. Would you
like to go and sit down? Joey—time for dinner, sweetheart.'

Joey and Flora sat down at the kitchen table, and Tom
brought in the meal.

'Chicken with cream and asparagus sauce. I'm impressed.'

'The sauce is from a packet,' Tom admitted with a smile.
'Joey, I take it you want ketchup with yours rather than my
sauce?'

The little boy nodded.

Pudding turned out to be ice cream, out-of-season rasp-
berries, and choc-chip cookies. 'Shop-bought, I'm afraid,'
Tom confessed. 'I know they're not up to your standard.'

'They're still lovely, though—thank you. And I insist on
doing the washing-up.'

Tom made them both a coffee, then ran a bath for Joey

while Flora made a start on the washing-up. She could hear a 'Hang on, I need to check it's not too hot before you get in—OK, safe now. Are there enough bubbles in there?' There was the sound of splashing, and then Tom reappeared, looking a bit damp.

'Joey's sense of humour,' he said.

She just laughed.

He came to stand behind her, wrapped his arms round her waist, and kissed the skin at the edge of the neckline of her top. 'You're adorable.'

'You're not so bad yourself, Tom Nicholson.' She twisted round slightly so she could kiss him. 'And that was a gorgeous meal.'

'Chicken, baked potatoes and vegetables? It wasn't exactly posh. Cooking isn't my strong point, but I'm trying.'

'It tasted good and it was a balanced meal,' she said. 'You're doing just fine.'

He kissed her again, then released her and picked up a tea-towel so he could start drying up. By the time they'd finished, Joey was ready to come out of the bath.

'Can I read you a bedtime story?' Flora asked.

Joey smiled, looking pleased, and found a story about a dog.

Tom joined them, sitting on the end of Joey's bed while Flora read. When it came to the part in the story where the dog talked, Tom did the voices and Joey's face lit up.

Flora kissed the little boy when she'd finished. 'Goodnight, sweetheart. Sleep well.'

Tom tucked his nephew in, and kissed him too. 'Goodnight, Jojo. See you in the morning.' Quietly, they left the room; she noticed that Tom left the door ajar and the landing light on.

'He gets bad dreams if it's dark,' Tom said. 'I put a night-light on when he's asleep, but he likes the light on in the landing while he's falling asleep.'

'Bless him.'

'Do you have to go yet, or will you come and sit with me for a while?' he asked.

'I'll stay,' she said.

He smiled, switched the light over from the main overhead lamp to an uplighter, and put some very quiet music on the stereo.

'I like this,' she said.

'It's good stuff to chill out to,' Tom told her. He scooped her onto his lap and kissed her; Flora, instead of worrying that she was squashing him, nestled closer, enjoying the closeness.

'I was touched that Joey made that card for me,' she said.

'He made the same one for me,' Tom said. 'When I opened it, I was so choked, I could hardly speak. And he actually let me hug him to say thank you.'

'It sounds as if he's made a decision to let you close.'

'I hope so. And he held my hand on the way to school today.' He paused. 'He said you told him he had to hold your hand between the car and school so you knew he was safe.' He swallowed hard. 'He said he wanted to know I was safe, too.'

'Oh, Tom—that's great.'

'If it hadn't been for you and Banjo I'd still be struggling. It's your warmth that's helped him open up to me,' he said. 'So I owe you.'

'You don't owe me anything.'

'Are you sure about that? I was kind of hoping to pay you in kisses.'

She smiled. 'Tom, you don't have to pay me.'

'Spoilsport,' he teased. 'Let me ask you another question.' He pulled her slightly closer and whispered in her ear, 'Will you be my Valentine, Flora Loveday?'

There was a huge lump in her throat; it was the kind of

question she'd never thought anyone would ask her, much less a man as beautiful as Tom Nicholas. 'Yes,' she whispered.

In answer, he kissed her. The kiss deepened, became more demanding, and, the next thing she knew, they were lying full length on the sofa, his body pressed against hers and leaving her in no doubt that he was aroused.

'I'm not going to push you into anything,' he said softly, his hand gliding along the curve of her bottom. 'I just wanted to lie with you in my arms.' He nudged the neckline of her top aside and rested his cheek against her shoulder. 'You smell of roses and vanilla. It makes me hungry.'

'What, after all the ice cream you ate tonight?' she teased.

He laughed. 'You make me hungry, Flora. And being with you…I don't know. You make me feel different. In a good way.'

They lay there quietly together, just holding each other and listening to the music. When the album finished, Tom went to check on Joey. 'He's asleep, bless him. I've just put his nightlight on.'

Shyness washed over Flora. 'I guess I ought to be going. Banjo needs his walk.'

'OK. Ring me when you get home, so I know you're home safely?'

It felt strange that someone was concerned about her; she was so used to just getting on and doing things by herself. It warmed her, too. 'Sure.'

'Before you go.' He handed her an envelope. 'Open it later.'

A Valentine's card? she wondered. She fished the card from her bag and handed it to him. 'For you,' she said shyly.

'Great minds think alike, hmm?' He kissed her lightly. 'Thank you, honey.'

'Open it later,' she said, not wanting him to open it in front of her.

'OK.' He paused. 'I'm doing show-and-tell with Joey tomorrow.'

'I thought you had a day off?' she asked, surprised.

'I am, but I'm still going to be there with the crew. I wouldn't miss it for the world. And I was wondering if you might be free for lunch tomorrow?'

It was a busy day, with surgery in the morning and then a postnatal class in the afternoon. 'It'd have to be a really quick one,' she said.

'Great—how about a picnic on the beach if it isn't raining?' He smiled. 'And we'll eat the picnic in my car if it's wet.'

'That'd be lovely.'

He kissed her goodbye at the door, his mouth sweet and soft and tempting. Desire and need flowed through her, and she kissed him back lingeringly.

When she got home, unable to resist any longer, she opened the envelope. The front of the card had a cartoon of a bee that had obviously flown in a heart shape, with the words 'bee my honey' written in the heart. Inside, Tom had written 'My adorable Flora' and signed it with two kisses. That was Tom all over, she thought: jokey and charming on the outside and keeping all the deep emotion inside.

She called him. 'I'm home.'

'Good. Did you open the card?'

'Yes.'

'Was it OK?'

'It was lovely, Tom.' She bit her lip. 'Sorry mine was a bit, well, drippy.'

'No. It was sweet. Like you.' His voice grew husky. 'Next time I eat a chocolate, I'm going to think about kissing you.' Heat spread through her at his words. 'See you tomorrow, honey.'

* * *

Her surgery the next morning was as she'd expected, apart from her ten-o'clock appointment, fifteen-year-old Emmy Kingston, who really should've been at school. 'Can Shelley stay with me?' Emmy asked, gesturing to her friend.

Emmy was guarding her stomach and the way she was standing made Flora think the worst. It wasn't her place to judge, but if her suspicion was right then the poor child would need all the support she could get. 'If you want her to stay with you, then that's fine.'

Emmy looked relieved, and accepted Flora's invitation to sit down.

'Tell me about it,' Flora said. 'How can I help you?'

'I've done something really stupid, and my parents are going to kill me.' Emmy bit her lip and a tear rolled down her face. 'I should've said no but I... It's so hard. And you're going to think...'

Flora reached out and squeezed her hand. 'I'm not going to think *anything*, sweetheart. I'm a nurse, and my job is to help you.'

'And you won't tell my mum and dad?'

'Your appointment is absolutely confidential,' Flora reassured her. 'It's between you and me, unless I think you're at risk of being hurt or abused. The important thing is that you're protected, OK?'

Another tear rolled down Emmy's cheek.

'Show her, Em,' Shelley said, patting her shoulder.

Gingerly, Emmy lifted up her top to reveal—not quite what Flora had expected. The girl had a pierced navel and the area around the piercing was bright red and swollen; there was a yellowish discharge from her belly button.

'That looks really painful,' Flora said. 'How long has it been like that?'

'I had it done on Saturday. Mum and Dad said I wasn't allowed to, so I didn't tell them I was doing it. I had a sleepover at Shelley's so they wouldn't see.' Emmy's voice wobbled. 'I wish I hadn't done it now.'

'It looks to me as if it's infected. It's quite common to get a bacterial infection with a piercing—have you managed to keep it dry over the last three days?'

Emmy nodded. 'That's what the piercer said, don't wash it even with salt water or it might get infected. I did everything he said.'

'You've just been a bit unlucky,' Flora said. 'I want to take your temperature—sometimes these infections can turn really nasty, and I want to be sure you're not developing septicaemia or something really scary. Is that OK?'

Emmy gave her consent, and Flora checked the girl's temperature. 'The good news is that we've caught the infection in time—your temperature's fine. You'll need some antibiotic cream to clear up the infection and stop it hurting, and if it doesn't start getting better by Friday you'll need to come back and see the doctor to get some antibiotic tablets.' She quickly tapped information into the computer. 'Try not to touch your belly button or pick at it, in the meantime.'

'It hurts too much to touch it,' Emmy said ruefully.

'Antibiotics will help with that,' Flora reassured her. 'It might be worth taking some paracetamol as well. Dr Lovak will sign the prescription for you when he's seen his next patient, if you don't mind waiting in the reception area for a few minutes?'

Emmy exhaled sharply. 'So it's going to be all right?'

'Yes.'

'See? I told you,' Shelley said, hugging her shoulders.

'And you're not going to tell my mum?'

'No,' Flora said, 'but I think you should.'

Emmy shook her head. 'I can't. Mum will go *mad*.'

'When you came in,' Flora told her gently, 'the way you were standing and holding your tummy, I thought you might be pregnant. I wouldn't mind betting your mum's thinking the same thing and she's worried sick about you—especially as my guess is that you've been avoiding her since Saturday.'

'I have,' Emmy admitted, biting her lip.

'Then talk to her tonight,' Flora advised quietly. 'Yes, she might shout at you for going against her wishes, but she'll want to know that you're all right.'

'She'll make me take it out.'

'That's not a good idea until the infection's cleared up—it needs to be able to drain and make sure that an abscess doesn't form. You can always tell her to ring me if she wants some reassurance,' Flora said.

Emmy's lower lip wobbled. 'Thank you so much.'

Flora patted her shoulder. 'A couple more days and you'll feel a lot better, I promise. But if you don't, come back and see Dr Lovak. We're here to help you, not shout at you or judge you, OK?'

'OK.' Emmy rubbed the tears away with the back of her hand, and let her friend shepherd her out to the reception area.

Flora had just seen her last patient and was finishing typing up her notes when her phone beeped. It was a text from Tom: *'Am in the car park whenever you're ready.'*

'On my way', Flora texted back, and went out to meet him.

He greeted her with a kiss.

'How did show-and-tell go?' she asked.

'Unbelievable.' Tom's eyes glittered. 'I actually saw Joey nudge the boy next to him and say, "That's my Uncle Tom." He sounded really proud.'

'That's because he *is* proud of you, Tom.' She hugged him. 'Well done, you.'

'How was your morning?' he asked.

'Busy, but good.'

He kissed her again. 'When do you need to be back?'

She glanced at her watch. 'In forty-five minutes.'

'Right—beach it is.' He drove them down to the car park by the beach; he had a picnic rug in the back of the car, along with a flask of hot chocolate and a bag from the deli containing sandwiches and fruit.

Flora enjoyed just being with him, having a leisurely lunch and then sitting on the rug with his arms wrapped round her, listening to the sea and the shrieks of the gulls.

'This is a perfect day,' he said softly, resting his cheek against her hair. 'Being with Joey this morning, and being with you right now. And you're definitely the silver lining in the school fire—I wouldn't have met you, if it hadn't happened.' He drew her closer. 'And I'm really glad I've met you, Flora.'

'I'm glad I've met you, too.' With Tom in her world, everything seemed so much brighter. Crazy—and no way would she admit that to him, not yet—but it was true. Tom made her feel special. As if she mattered.

'So when am I going to see you again?' he asked when he'd driven her back to the surgery.

'I have tomorrow off, if you want to do something.'

He looked sombre. 'Could I ask you something?'

'Sure.'

'The other day, you said you'd help if I wanted to go through Susie's things…'

'And I meant what I said. Of course I'll help.' She stroked his face. 'Are you sure you're ready for it, Tom?'

'No, and I'm not sure I'll ever be ready,' he admitted, 'but it has to be done.'

'It's better to do it with someone else,' she said softly. 'I had help and it got me through one of the hardest days ever.'

He hugged her. 'Thank you. Can I pick you up when I've taken Joey to school?'

'Absolutely.' She kissed him. 'And, Tom?'

'Yes?'

'Try not to brood about it. Yes, it'll be tough, but you won't be on your own. See you tomorrow.'

CHAPTER EIGHT

ON WEDNESDAY morning, Tom picked Flora up after he'd taken Joey to school, looking very sombre. For once, his car stereo was silent, and the grim set of his jaw told Flora that he wasn't in the mood for conversation, either.

He parked outside one of the cottages near the cliffs, and she noticed his hand was shaking as he opened the front door. He took a deep breath when he stepped inside, then leaned his head back against the wall and closed his eyes. 'I hate this. It feels so wrong.'

'I know.' She took his hand and held it, willing him to take strength from her nearness.

'Clearing out their house makes everything seem so final.' He swallowed hard. 'I suppose I was leaving it in the hope that it was all a bad dream and they'd come back—but they're not coming back, are they?'

'No, Tom, they're not,' she said, as gently as she could.

'It's such a waste. Such a bloody waste. There are people out there who hurt others, who lie and cheat and make people miserable, and they seem to swan through life without any worries. And people like my sister and her husband, people who were kind and always helped others...' He shook his head in anguish. 'It's not fair. Why did they have to die?'

There was no answer to that. All she could do was hold his hand.

A muscle worked in his jaw. 'OK. I'm pulling myself together. Let's do this.' Then he looked completely lost. 'How do you go about packing up someone's life?'

This was something she could help with. Something she'd been through herself. 'You think of the good times,' she told him. 'You keep the nice memories as you go. And you have boxes. One for things to go to the charity shop, one for things you want to keep—even if you're not up to dealing with them yet, like photo albums—and one for things you're going to throw out.' She paused. 'You don't have to do it all at once, Tom. We can do just one room at a time, if it makes it easier on you.'

He shook his head. 'It needs to be done, and I've organised for the council to come and take the furniture to help families that need rehoming.' He took a deep breath. 'Part of me thinks I ought to move in here and give Joey some continuity. But I just *can't*, Flora. I can't live here with all these memories. They'll suffocate me.'

'Joey will understand when he's older,' she reassured him. 'He has a new life now and it'll be easier for him to get used to that if he lives with you away from here.'

He nodded. 'We'll do the hard stuff first. Bedroom.'

Flora helped him take the clothes out of the wardrobe and pack them into bags he was planning to take to the charity shop. 'Maybe you could to keep something for Joey—his dad's favourite sweater or his mum's favourite dress,' she suggested. 'Something personal for him, for the future.'

'Yeah, you're right.'

Tom's face was set. Grim. She knew this was ripping him to shreds inside, and yet he was trying so hard not to show any emotion.

The kitchen was next; it was easy to pack up, because there was nothing really personal there. Except for the outside of the fridge, photographs and postcards and little notes held on with magnets. Tom stripped those and put them in the 'deal with later' pile.

When they started to pack up the living room, the strain was really etched on his face. Books, music, photograph albums... She could practically see the tension radiating from his body.

And then he picked up a photograph from the mantelpiece. His hand shook, and he dropped it; she heard a crack as the glass smashed. Reaching down to deal with it, Tom sucked in a breath, and she saw red blooming over his hand.

'Kitchen. Now.' She made him stand under the light so she could check the cut for fragments of glass, then cleaned the wound and put a pad on it. 'Press on it. It'll staunch the flow,' she said. 'And I'll get rid of the broken glass.'

'I'll do it.'

'Tom, I want you to sit there for three minutes, and that's a medical order,' she said, taking an old newspaper into the living room. She wrapped the broken glass in some newspaper, then turned the frame over. She could see why he'd dropped the frame; the photograph was of Tom himself, with his sister and Joey, looking incredibly happy.

Memories.

Sometimes the good ones were the ones that hurt you most. She'd found it hard to look at her parents' photographs for the first couple of months, feeling the loss ripping through her again every time she saw them.

Gently, she removed the photograph from the broken frame and slid it inside one of the photograph albums to keep it safe. Then she wrapped up the broken frame and took the two parcels into the kitchen. 'All done,' she said quietly.

'Sorry. It just...' His voice caught.

She held him close. 'I know. I've been there myself. Come on. I think it's time we took a break. Let's go back to mine for lunch.'

Back at the farmhouse, she took a jug of home-made vegetable soup from the fridge and heated it, then set it on the table along with cheese, butter and some rolls she'd bought at the bakery the day before.

Tom pushed his plate away untouched. 'Flora, I'm sorry to be rude—I don't think I can possibly eat.'

'Yes, you can; and, yes, you will.'

'I feel too choked.'

Remembering how Kate Tremayne had chivvied her, and how she'd appreciated it later, she refused to let him give in. 'You need to keep up your strength, for Joey's sake. Listen, Tom, I didn't really know your sister, so I can't imagine what she'd say in this situation—but if she loved you as much as you loved her, I'm pretty sure she would've wanted you to remember the good times and celebrate her, not mourn her.'

Tom dragged in a breath. 'Yes, she loved me—even though I drove her crazy when I was a teenager. And I loved her. I would've done anything to spare her what happened, Flora. And Kevin—he wasn't just an in-law I had to tolerate for Susie's sake. I really liked him. You know they say you can't choose your family? Well, he was the kind of bloke I would've chosen to have as my family.'

'I know what you mean. But you still have Joey, and they'll both live on in him,' she said softly. 'You'll see them in his face as they grow up—and there will come a day, Tom, when you can talk to him about them without it hurting. You'll be able to tell him how much they loved him and how proud they'd be of how he's growing up.'

He closed his eyes. 'Right now, it doesn't feel like it.'

'Of course not, because you're not there yet. Trust me, it'll come—you'll still get days when you wake up and you know there's a big empty space in your life and you want to howl, but it gets easier to deal with as time passes.'

He opened his eyes again and looked at her. 'Is it like that for you?'

She nodded. 'Sometimes one of my dad's favourite records will come on the radio, or I'll smell my mum's perfume in a department store, and it still chokes me inside—but it's getting easier. It just takes time and you need to be a bit less hard on yourself. Let people close to you, Tom, and they'll help you.'

'I do let people close to me.'

She said nothing, just stroked his face and gave him a sad little smile.

Tom thought about it later that evening. Was Flora right? Did he let people close to him? Or did he use all the terrible jokes and puns that were his stock-in-trade at work to keep people at bay?

The more he thought about it, the more he started to realise that Flora had a point. He *didn't* let people that close. And, if he thought about it, he could trace it right back to when Ben had died. The first person he'd really lost, his best friend, and yet he'd never even visited Ben's grave. He'd withdrawn a bit after Ben had died, until his mum had talked about taking him to see the doctor; and then he'd realised that if he didn't start smiling and laughing, she really would take him to see someone. He hadn't wanted that kind of fuss. So he'd started telling silly jokes, smiled all the time, and driven Susie to distraction with practical jokes. But he'd never really let anyone close again. He'd kept everything on the surface.

Which was one of the reasons he was struggling to be a stand-in dad to his nephew, because he didn't have a clue what he was meant to do, how he was meant to feel.

And the more he thought about it, the more it worried him. Because he was starting to let Flora and Joey a lot closer than he was really comfortable with—and it scared him. Not because he was scared of being close to them, as such, more because he was scared of letting them down in the worst possible way. His job was dangerous—and he knew firefighters who hadn't made it. People who'd left grieving families behind.

Was that why he'd never let his relationships get too serious? And why he was struggling so hard to be a stand-in dad to Joey? Because he didn't want to leave a gaping hole in people's lives, and Joey had already lost so much?

He lay awake for a long, long time—and right at that moment he really could do with Flora in his arms. He needed her quiet strength, her warmth to comfort him. And that scared him even more. He'd never felt as if he'd needed a girlfriend before. He'd enjoyed female company, had fun with a carefree bachelor lifestyle…but this was different. Flora was nothing like the women he usually dated. She was quieter, more serious. She had depth.

And that made her incredibly dangerous. With her shy smile and her beautiful soft brown eyes and the sheer warmth she exuded—there was a real possibility that she could steal his heart. And break it.

Tom was still brooding about it on Thursday morning, when he dropped Joey at Flora's for breakfast. And he brooded all morning through inspection and cleaning the equipment, until the Tannoy warbled.

'Turnout, vehicle 54. Person fallen in river, Penhally Bay.'

This could be nasty, Tom thought. The cold snap had lasted a while now, so the water would be very cold and there was a real risk of the victim developing hypothermia. If the river was running swiftly, even if they managed to cling on to a branch or a rock, the current might pull them away and send them downstream,

He headed to the engine with the rest of the crew. Bazza

was in the driving seat and Steve was checking the computer. 'It was called in by mobile phone,' he said. 'So details are a bit sketchy—hopefully they'll call back with more information.'

Halfway to the village, Steve's mobile rang. 'Yup—uh-huh. Thanks.' He ended the call. 'It turns out it isn't a person in the river, it's a dog.'

Tom had come across this kind of thing before. 'Please tell me the owner hasn't tried to jump in and save the dog,' he said.

'No, the owner's an elderly man. He was walking by the river when he slipped on the ice and fell. Apparently he might have broken his hip—the ambulance is on its way. When he fell, the dog plunged down the bank and ended up in the river. The poor guy's frantic, but in too much pain to move.'

'Hopefully we can rescue the dog before the paramedics whisk him off to St Piran's,' Tom said. 'Walkway, ladder or rope, do you think?'

'We'll know as soon as we see it,' Steve said.

Even without the co-ordinates, they would've been able to see the site straight away, as the ambulance was already there. As Tom got out of the fire engine, he could see the paramedics gently lifting an elderly man onto a stretcher. The man was clearly distressed, calling, 'No, no! I can't go until Goldie's safe.'

Tom walked over to him. 'I'm Tom Nicholson—and I'm going to rescue your dog,' he said. 'Her name's Goldie?'

The elderly man was in tears. 'She fell down the bank. It's my fault. I slipped, and I caught her as I fell. She's like me, not so steady on her pins.' He choked on a sob. 'She's been in the water for ages. She's too old to cope with it. I've killed her.'

'No, you haven't,' Tom reassured him. 'Dogs are far more

resilient than you'd believe. Hang on in there, and I'll get her back for you.'

As soon he looked over the river bank, he could see that the elderly yellow Labrador was stuck against a branch and was clearly getting tired.

'Has anyone called the local vet ready to treat Goldie when I get her out?' he asked the crowd of bystanders.

'I'll go—they're just round the corner,' one man said.

'Thanks. And if someone could get a towel or a blanket to wrap her in?' He turned back to the crew. 'I'll go. It's going to be quickest if you rope me. The dog's too big for a tube—' the crew had tubes they could scoop smaller animals into and lift to safety '—so we'll get a rope round her, too, and I'll lift her.'

Slowly, knowing that his crew had the rope and could stop him falling if he slipped, he made his way down the bank to the dog.

'Goldie,' he called softly, 'hang on in there. I'll get you back to your family.' He knew the dog couldn't understand what he was saying, but he hoped the tone of his voice would reassure her and calm her.

'There's a good girl. Not long now. I'm just going to put the rope round you.' He'd just got the rope round her when there was a loud crack and the branch broke. The sound terrified the already frightened dog, who reacted by sinking her teeth into Tom's arm.

It hurt like mad, but he swallowed the yell, knowing it would panic the dog even more and earn him a second bite. 'OK, Goldie,' he said through gritted teeth. 'There's a good girl. Nearly there.'

The dog struggled in his arms, but he had her roped safely.

But, with his arms full of wet, tired, heavy dog, there was

no way he was going to be able to make it up the slippery bank on his own. 'I've got her. Haul me up,' Tom called up.

Slowly, slowly, the team hauled him up.

A flash popped in his face as he reached the top, the dog in his arms.

'Oh, for pity's sake,' he said, frowning. 'You can have your story in a minute. We need to get this dog treated, first.'

'Absolutely right,' Melinda Lovak, the local vet, said crisply. She crouched down and wrapped a towel round the shivering dog. 'Well done for bringing her out,' she said to Tom. Tenderly, she dried the dog. 'Hello, Goldie. Not the best time of year to go for a swim, is it?' she asked.

The dog looked slightly less frightened, clearly knowing the vet.

'There's a good girl,' Melinda said softly. Swiftly, she checked the animal over. 'Looks like you're going to be fine after your dip. Let's go and tell Bob, shall we?'

There was a faint wag of the tail.

'Bob, she's absolutely fine,' Melinda told the elderly man in the ambulance. 'Look, you can see her. The fireman got her out and she's wagging her tail.'

'The dog can't come in the ambulance, love,' the paramedic told her.

'What's going to happen to her?' Bob asked. 'I live on my own. I can't go to the hospital, I need to stay with Goldie.'

'Yes, you can, because you need to be treated,' Melinda said. 'Don't worry about her. I'll take her back to the surgery with me. Dragan and the boys won't mind if we have another dog for a few days—or, if Goldie decides she doesn't like it with Bramble at our place, Lizzie Chamberlain at the kennels will take her in until you're back on your feet.'

Bob was almost in tears. 'Thank you—I don't know what I'd do without her.' He looked at Tom. 'And thank you. You saved her life.'

'That's what I'm here for,' Tom said simply. 'I'm glad she's all right.'

'She'll be absolutely fine,' Melinda reassured Bob. 'Now go and get yourself fixed, OK? I'll ring the hospital later to let you know how Goldie's doing.'

The paramedic closed the door and the ambulance headed off to St Piran's.

Tom's arm was throbbing; wincing, he rolled up his sleeve to look at it.

'You need to get that looked at,' Melinda said.

Tom shrugged. 'It's not that bad. I'm fine.'

'Trust me,' she said with a smile, 'I've been bitten enough in my time. That's a puncture wound, so it could get infected—and you probably need a tetanus jab.'

He grimaced. 'Oh, great.'

She laughed, 'A big fireman like you, scared of a little needle? Don't be such a baby!' she teased. 'The doctor's surgery is just over there and it'll take ten minutes, tops.' She made a fuss of the dog. 'And I'd better get this one in the warm. Come on, girl.'

'You've had your orders,' Steve said with a grin. 'And she's a vet. She knows what she's talking about.'

'And can I interview you now?' the reporter asked.

'Look, it was just a routine rescue. No big deal,' Tom said.

The reporter smiled at him. 'But our readers love this sort of story. It's a feel-good story, perfect to lift people's spirits at a miserable time of year.'

'I...' He sighed. 'OK. As long as you put something in there about keeping your dog on a lead when you're walking by an icy river, and calling the emergency services rather than risking your own safety—in this kind of weather, you can get into difficulties really quickly and it means the emergency services have to do twice the amount of work, rescuing you as well as your pet.'

'I'll make sure I put that in,' the reporter said. She glanced down at his left hand and clearly saw that he wasn't wearing a wedding ring. 'Actually, maybe I can take you for a coffee? You must be freezing.'

'He's going to the doctor's to get his arm seen to, love,' Steve put in.

'I can interview you while you're waiting to be seen,' the reporter said with a smile, 'and then maybe we can go for a coffee afterwards.'

Tom didn't want to go for coffee with anyone except Flora; though they were keeping things to themselves, right now, and he wasn't going to make life awkward for her by giving a declaration in front of half of Penhally. 'Mmm,' he said noncommittally.

He had no idea if Flora was in surgery this morning or if she was working at one of the schools, and suppressed the hope that she might be the one to patch him up. And he still had to give the reporter a story. Feeling embarrassed, he went up to the reception desk, explained what had happened, and asked if someone could fit him in.

'Sit down, and we'll call you as soon as the nurse is free,' the receptionist said with a smile.

The reporter wasn't budging. 'So how did you feel when you saw the dog?'

'The same as the rest of the crew—we wanted to get her back safely on dry land, and reassure her owner so that he'd let the paramedics treat him,' Tom said. 'Look, there isn't much of a story. We simply responded to an emergency call.'

'But the dog was heavy. And it bit you.'

'The dog was cold, tired and frightened. She didn't mean to hurt me.'

'And the bite won't put you off rescuing the next dog?'

'Of course not. It's my job,' Tom said firmly.

'OK.' She finished scribbling notes on her pad. 'Shall we go for that coffee anyway?'

'Sorry, I have to get back to work,' Tom said.

She took a business card from her handbag. 'If you think of anything else, give me a call. Actually, it'd be nice to run a few features on the local emergency services. Maybe I can come and shadow you for a day.'

Something in her eyes told Tom that she didn't have just business in mind. And his suspicion was confirmed when she added, 'And, since you can't make that coffee, maybe I can take you out for a drink to say thanks for your help.'

The reporter was pretty; three months ago, Tom might've accepted the invitation. But things were very different now. 'That'd be nice. I'll have to check when my partner's free,' he said.

'Your partner?'

Three months ago, those words might've made him run a mile. But now...now, it was different. 'I assume the invitation extends to her, too?' Tom said, knowing full well that it wouldn't.

'I, um, sure. Of course.'

His name flashed up on the board above the reception desk. 'Sorry, I need to go.'

'Sure. Catch you later,' she said, and Tom had a pretty fair idea that she wouldn't call him at all.

To his mingled pleasure and embarrassment, it turned out that the nurse on duty was Flora.

She looked worried when he walked into her treatment room. 'What's happened? Are you all right?'

'I rescued a dog from the river, and she bit me.'

'Right, let me take a look—whose dog was it?'

'I didn't catch his last name. His first name's Bob. He's quite elderly, and the dog's a yellow Labrador called Goldie.'

'I know who you mean. Bob Thurston. Is he all right?'

'He slipped on the ice—the paramedics were worried enough to take him to St Piran's, so my guess is that he's probably broken something. Goldie slid down the bank and into the river. Luckily she was swept against a branch and stuck there, otherwise who knows how far she could've ended up downstream.'

'And she bit you? But Goldie's really gentle.'

'She was scared. It's not a big deal.'

'Does it hurt?'

'A bit,' he admitted. 'It throbs more than anything.'

'OK. Let me take a look—I want to make sure there isn't any damage to the structures beneath the bite, tendons and what have you. Is Goldie OK?'

'The vet's taken her back to the surgery. She says she'll look after her.'

Flora smiled. 'That's Melinda all over—she's lovely like that. She helped me find some homes when one of the feral farm cats had a litter. Jess Carmichael at the hospital—well, Jess Corezzi now she's married—took a couple, too.' She finished examining his arm. 'That looks fine,' she said. 'Tom, is your tetanus up to date?'

'I think so.'

'Mind if I check?' She looked up his record. 'It is. So you're safe from having a big fat needle in your arm.'

'Pity,' Tom said. 'I could've asked you to kiss it better.'

'You wish.'

'So how about it?' he asked.

'That depends on how brave you are while I sort this out.' She gave him a local anaesthetic, cleaned the wound, making sure there were no foreign bodies in it, and debrided some of tissue. 'I'm not going to stitch this,' she said, 'because it's a puncture wound, and you're more likely to get an infection if

I close it. And you do need antibiotics to be on the safe side, so I'll ask the doctor to write you a prescription.'

'OK. Do I get my kiss for being brave now?'

'Tom, I'm at work and so are you. I have patients waiting,' she protested. But she gave him a swift kiss.

'Would that be on account?' he asked hopefully.

She rolled her eyes. 'Yes. Go and rescue someone.'

'I'd rather scoop you up in a fireman's lift and take you somewhere quiet,' Tom said. He stole another kiss. 'But I'll do that later. Thanks for patching me up.'

'It's what I do,' she said with a smile.

When Tom had finished his shift, he drove to Flora's farmhouse to pick up Joey.

'How's your arm?' she asked.

'Sore,' he admitted, 'but it's OK.'

Joey looked worried. 'What's wrong with your arm?'

'I rescued a dog today—she fell in the river and got stuck. She was a bit worried when I rescued her,' Tom explained, 'and dogs can't tell you in words that they're scared, so she bit me. She didn't mean to hurt me, she was just frightened.'

'I know the dog,' Flora said. 'She's really quiet and soft, normally—she's quite old, too. She's a yellow Labrador called Goldie.'

'And she's doing absolutely fine,' Tom added. 'I rang the vet before the surgery closed, to see how she was. I'm fine, too, Jojo. Flora cleaned me up and put a dressing on, and I've got some special tablets so I don't get an infection in the wound.'

'So you rescued Uncle Tom,' Joey said to Flora.

'I was just doing my job—like he was doing his,' Flora said with a smile. 'Actually, I had to do a rescue myself today. This cold snap really seems to be knocking everyone for six. Young Jane Hallet in Year Four fell over in the playground at lunchtime and broke her arm, poor thing. I was there so

I could give her a painkiller and put her arm in a sling to make her more comfortable, but her mum had to take her to the emergency department in St Piran's. Luckily it happened just after her mum Marina finished her shift in the kitchen, so Marina was able to take her. I'll drop in to see them tomorrow on my way back from lunch and see how she is.'

'So what were you doing today?' Tom asked.

'Healthy eating with the Year Sixes—one of the girls has just been diagnosed as a diabetic, so we were talking about sugar and how the body processes it. I have a quiz so they can guess how many teaspoons of sugar are in each item.' She smiled at him. 'Guess how many teaspoons of sugar there are in a can of fizzy drink?'

'The non-diet sort, I assume?' Tom asked.

'Uh-huh.'

He thought about it. 'Five?' he guessed.

'Too low. Joey?' she prompted.

'Seven?' the little boy suggested.

'Closer—but still too low. Believe it or not, it's nine,' she told them. 'That's why they're really bad for teeth. We did some experiments with eggshells in different sorts of drink so the children could see what effect the drinks would have on their teeth.'

'Eggshells being made of the same sort of stuff as teeth?' Tom asked.

'Exactly. Anyway, when they saw which ones dissolved, it's made a few of them think that maybe water's the best drink you can have.' She smiled at Joey. 'I'll do that with your class when you're in Year Six. But I'm going to be doing germs and super-soap with your class after half-term. And we might do the eggshell thing too, if you think it sounds like fun.'

Joey nodded enthusiastically.

'Ah, so you like science? Excellent. We can do some kitchen experiments,' Flora said. 'I know how to make a volcano.'

Joey beamed. 'That's cool.'

'Hey, can I be in on this?' Tom asked. 'And I know an experiment about how to make a plastic bottle into a rocket.'

'This sounds like a very half-term kind of thing to do,' Flora said. 'And I've heard the mums at school talking about that new science museum just up the coast. They say it's really good.'

'I think we need to go,' Tom said. 'What do you think, Joey?'

The little boy nodded.

'Then it's a date. Flora, is there any chance you can have a day off, next week, and come with us?' Tom asked.

'I'll check at work tomorrow to see if I can swap a shift with someone,' Flora said. 'Given that I won't be doing my usual school sessions, I should be able to get a day off.'

'Cool,' Joey said, smiling at both of them.

CHAPTER NINE

ON FRIDAY, Flora dropped Joey at school and spent the morning working at the high school, doing a couple of talks about healthy eating and one about sexual health. During her lunch break, she drove out to Chyandour Farm on the outskirts of Penhally to see how Lizzie was doing.

As she reached the end of the drive, she saw the fire engines there; water was being sprayed onto one of the barns.

Tom came over to her as she climbed out of the car. 'Just the woman we could do with.'

'What's happened?'

'The lower barn caught fire. John rang us, then tried to beat out the flames, but he burned his arm. Can you take a look?'

'Sure.' She grabbed her medical kit from the car, then followed Tom to where John Hallet was standing. She persuaded him to go and sit down in the kitchen so she could take a look at his injuries properly and treat him.

'I only popped in to see how Lizzie was doing—I wasn't expecting to treat you, too,' she said wryly.

'They say things come in threes,' John said. 'Let's just hope they don't!'

She looked at his arm. 'I'm relieved to say the burns are pretty superficial. If it had been your hands, I would have sent you to St Piran's, but I can dress this for you. Have you taken anything for the pain?'

'Not yet.'

She gave him a painkiller, then cleaned and dressed the burn. 'So how's Lizzie doing?'

'She wants to be back at school, but Marina had to take her to St Piran's to have her cast on today. She'll be fine,' John said. 'Nicola's home with a headache. I'll get her to come down and put the kettle on and make tea for everyone.'

Nicola Hallet was the quiet one in the family, Flora remembered, the only one who wasn't sporty or glamorous. Her older sisters Stacey and Keeley were both model-thin and stunning, popular with all the girls in the village and drooled over by the boys; young Lizzie was into tap-dancing and gymnastics and athletics, and was always talking about how her older brother Jonathan was the captain of the football team at the primary school last year and had a purple belt in kick-boxing. And she had a feeling that Nicola had a pretty hard time fitting in.

'If she's got a headache, she's probably better resting. I can make the tea,' she offered.

'No, she'll do it. She's been that mardy, lately.' John called up to her, and a minute or so later Nicola came downstairs into the kitchen.

'We need some tea for the firefighters, love,' John said.

Nicola nodded and filled the kettle with water.

'How's your headache?' Flora asked.

Nicola shrugged. 'It'll go.'

'Have you taken anything for it?'

Nicola shrugged again. 'I will in a bit.'

Flora looked at the girl, wondering. Nicola had always been a bit on the plump side, but she'd definitely put on weight since Flora had last seen her—and she was trying to hide it with baggy clothes. Remembering her own teenage years, how she'd felt she didn't fit in and had cheered herself up with chocolate biscuits, Flora wondered if Nicola might be worried about something and comfort-eating as a way of dealing with it. Not that she'd ask the girl in front of her dad.

'Let me give you a hand with the tea, Nicola,' she offered. 'John, if you can do us a favour and find out who takes sugar?'

'Will do,' he said.

As soon as he'd closed the door, Flora asked gently, 'Is everything all right, Nicola?'

'I'm fine. Just fine,' Nicola said. 'It's only a headache.'

Flora was pretty sure it was more than just a headache making the girl miserable. 'You're not having any problems at school?'

'Why should I be?'

'No reason,' Flora said quietly. 'I just remember that it's hard being a teenager, that's all. And sometimes people make it harder for you.'

Nicola just shrugged, and concentrated on putting tea leaves in the pot.

'If you ever need anyone to talk to, you know you can always come and see me at the drop-in clinic at school. Or at the surgery. Anything you say will be just between you and me, OK?'

For a moment, Flora thought that the girl was going to say something—but then the kitchen door opened and John walked back in. Any chance that Nicola would confide in her vanished instantly.

She didn't get a chance to talk to Nicola when the tea had been handed round, either, because the girl had disappeared back to her room. And Flora was due back in the surgery for the afternoon, so she had to get on. 'If you're in pain or you see any sign of infection, John, don't be stubborn about it—come and see us at the surgery.'

'I'll be fine.'

John was of the old school—and that meant he'd only see the doctor if he was in so much pain that he couldn't sleep. 'As long as you know that the sooner we look at a problem, the quicker it is to fix it,' she said gently. 'Don't be too proud or too stubborn.'

'All right, love,' he said.

After surgery that afternoon, Flora picked Joey up from school as usual, and made dinner with him. When Tom arrived after his shift, he gave her a hello hug and ruffled Joey's hair; Flora was pleased that the little boy didn't pull away.

While Joey played with Banjo, Flora made coffee for herself and Tom.

'Flora, are you busy next weekend?' Tom asked.

She was never busy. Not that she wanted him to think she was completely desperate. 'I'm not doing anything important. Why?'

'It's the football league dinner—kind of a late Valentine's ball sort of thing. We have it every year. It's the local emergency services league, so all the teams have a table—fire crews, the police and the medics—and we take our partners with us. The fire crew team has a huge rivalry thing going on with the medics, but it's all in good fun and—well, I know it's a bit late notice, but I wasn't even sure if I was going to go this year, the way things were. But my parents are going to be here next weekend and they're more than happy to babysit for us, if you'd like to come to the dinner with me?'

He wanted her to go to a posh do with him? Help. She never got invited to posh dos like this. She didn't have a thing to wear, or a clue where to find something suitable. And if it was the same crowd as the football lot, who were incredibly cliquey, she wasn't sure she wanted to be there. 'Um, can I think about it?'

He looked slightly hurt, but shrugged. 'Sure. Can I ask you something else?'

She spread her hands. 'Of course.'

'My parents are coming over from France for a week or so. They're staying for a long weekend, then visiting Mum's brother, and then they're coming back next weekend. So I was wondering…will you come to dinner at my place tomorrow night to meet them?'

Asking her to a formal dinner as his date was one thing, but now he was asking her to meet his parents. As his friend—or as his girlfriend?

'I…um…' Oh, help. This situation was way outside what she was used to.

'They're nice, my parents. And they said they'd like to meet you.'

His parents knew about her? What had he said? Had he told them that she was Joey's babysitter, or that he was seeing her?

'Please?' he added.

How could she resist the appeal in his gorgeous dark eyes? 'All right.'

'Great. It'll be a proper home-cooked dinner. About six?'

Which meant it'd be early enough for Joey to be eating with them, she guessed. 'Sure. I'll be there.'

'I'd better get back,' he said. 'They'll be here in an hour or so.' He looked at Joey. 'Want a fireman's lift to the car?'

Joey's eyes brightened. 'Cool,' he said.

Tom looked delighted that Joey was finally opening up to him again, returning to their old rough-and-tumble relationship, and hoisted his nephew over his shoulder. But Flora noticed his wince of pain. She slipped her coat on and followed them out to the car. When Tom had strapped Joey into the car seat and closed the door, she said, 'Is your arm hurting you?'

'No.' But he didn't meet her eye.

'Tom?'

He shook his head. 'It's nothing. Just a bruise.'

Not his arm, then. And the fact he wasn't telling her straight made her suspicious. 'Where?'

'My back.'

'And you did that rescuing Goldie?'

He flapped a dismissive hand. 'Look, I'm fine.'

'Tom,' she said warningly.

He rolled his eyes. 'OK. There was another fire this afternoon. A little girl was stuck in her bedroom. Just as I got her out, the roof collapsed and a beam caught my shoulder. I'm fine.'

Flora's eyes narrowed. 'The roof collapsed.'

'Yes, but it missed me. Well, most of it missed me. And the little girl's absolutely fine.'

There was something he wasn't telling her. He was an experienced firefighter. He would've known if the structure was dangerous and the roof was likely to cave in—and yet he'd gone in anyway. And she remembered what he'd told her when he'd spoken about Ben. *I almost never lose anyone. I remember how it was for his parents...I don't want anyone else to go through that.*

And so he took risks. More risks, she thought, than anyone else on his crew would take. Reckless, even, because he didn't think of his own safety.

'Was anyone else with you?' she asked.

'No, they were putting out the fire.'

'So you went into a burning building, on your own, to rescue someone. You could've been killed.'

He frowned. 'Flora, it's my job. What was I meant to do, let her burn?'

'She was stuck in her bedroom. You could've put a ladder at the window or something, so you didn't have to go through the dangerous bit of the building to rescue her.'

'What I did was quicker.'

Maybe—but it was also something else. Something that really worried her. And it had to be said. 'And r-reckless.'

Tom lifted his chin. 'It's my job, Flora. I rescue people from fires.'

'I know, but you go above and beyond. You don't protect yourself enough.' She dragged in a breath. 'You could've been killed. And what would've happened to Joey, then?'

Tom stared at her. 'So what are you saying? That I should give up being a firefighter? It's who I *am*.'

'I know that.' It was like that for her, too, with her job. 'I'm not saying this right.' And she'd started to stumble over her words. 'I just don't want you to take stupid risks, Tom. It's not going to bring Ben back. It's not going to b-bring your sister back. And if you die, what about Joey?' She was shaking now, so worried and angry when she thought about what could have happened that the words spilled out before she could stop them. 'What about me?'

Tom looked utterly shocked. 'Flora, I...'

She shook her head. 'You could've been really badly hurt. If you'd been trapped under that beam, you could've been killed, or so badly burned that...' She choked the words back. 'That little girl could've died.'

'She's fine. And so am I. It's just a bit of a bruise.'

A huge bruise, she'd bet, though she couldn't make him show her. Not outside, on a chilly February night, while Joey was sitting in the car, his face white with anxiety as he looked at them.

'Joey's waiting. You'd better go.'

Tom took a step towards her, as if he was going to kiss her, and she took a step back. Not now. She was still so angry with him for taking a stupid risk, for not thinking before he acted, that she didn't want to kiss him. She wanted to shake him—shake some sense into him.

'Flora—'

'Joey's waiting,' she said again, taking another step back.

Tom's face tightened, and he got into the car without another word.

She waved as he drove off—more for Joey's sake than for Tom's—and then headed back inside.

It was the first time she could ever remember shouting at anyone. The first time she'd ever had a real fight with anyone. And it felt horrible. But what else could she have done? If Tom was taking risks like that at work…

She was miserable for the rest of the evening. When the phone rang, much later that night, she didn't answer it. The answering machine clicked in, and she heard Tom's deep voice leaving a message.

'Flora, it's me. I've been thinking about what you said, and…well, you have a point. It never occurred to me. When I'm at work, everything else is excluded. I don't think of anything except my job. And you're right, I do need to think about other things. About Joey.' He paused. 'About *you*. I'll call you tomorrow morning, OK? Bye, honey. And I'm s—'

The answering machine beeped and cut him off.

Had he just been about to apologise?

But words were easy. Actions were harder. If he wasn't prepared to put Joey first and take more care of himself, this wasn't going to work.

At practically the crack of dawn, the phone rang again. Flora answered it automatically.

'Sorry, did I wake you?' Tom asked.

'Sort of.' She hadn't slept too well.

'I apologise. But I needed to talk to you. About last night.'

'I'm sorry I shouted at you.'

'You were right,' he said softly. 'My life's different now—if

I take risks, it impacts on more than just me. I need to think about that. Properly.' He paused. 'I'm sorry for worrying you.'

'OK.' Flora had no idea what to say next. Never having had a huge row with someone, she didn't have a clue how to make up, either.

'Will you still come for dinner tonight?' he asked.

He still wanted to see her? Or—a nasty thought crept in—was it that he was worried about losing a babysitter?

'Please? And then I can apologise properly, in person.' He sighed. 'I don't want to fight with you, Flora.'

'I don't want to fight with you, either.'

'Then will you still come for dinner? Please?'

'I... OK.'

'Good. See you tonight. And I am sorry.'

'Me, too.'

She thought about it all day. What did you wear when you met your partner's parents for the first time? In the end, she decided to wear the black skirt and teal top she knew Tom liked. She left her hair loose, but put an Alice band in it to keep it off her face. She'd forgotten to ask him if she should bring red or white wine, so she played it safe and bought a decent bottle of each, plus chocolates and a magnetic fishing game for Joey. If it all went pear-shaped, she could play a game or two with Joey, then claim a headache and leave early.

Tom answered the door to her. 'Hi. You look lovely.'

'Thanks.' She felt the betraying colour seep into her face and wished she'd worn make-up, except she was hopeless at anything other than lipstick; her parents had always told her she didn't need to wear it, so she'd never joined the other girls at school in experimenting with eye-shadow and blusher. Ha. Blusher. She blushed way too much as it was.

He drew her into his arms and rested his cheek against her

hair. 'I really am sorry, honey. And you've given me a lot to think about.'

'I'm sorry, too. I was pushy.'

'You,' he said softly, 'were absolutely right.' He kissed her lightly. 'Come in.'

She handed the wine over.

'You really didn't need to bring anything,' he said, 'but thank you. That's really sweet of you.'

Joey rushed over to greet her and gave her a hug. 'For me?' he asked when she handed him the bag.

'For you,' she said with a smile.

He peeked inside. 'Oh, wow! Will you play with me, Flora?'

'If Uncle Tom says there's time before tea, of course I will. Otherwise we'll have a game afterwards,' she promised.

'Cool.' He beamed at her.

'Flora, these are my parents, Thomas and Lisa—Mum and Dad, this is Flora.' Tom introduced them swiftly.

Tom looked very like his father, Flora thought, and Thomas Nicholson was just as tall as his son; though he had hazel eyes, like Joey's. Tom had clearly inherited Lisa's eyes. 'I'm pleased to meet you both,' Flora said shyly, shaking their hands.

'I hope you like roast chicken,' Lisa said. 'It's Joey's favourite.'

'I promised you a proper home-cooked dinner tonight, so you knew I wasn't going to have anything to do with it,' Tom said with a grin, resting his hand on Flora's shoulder.

She smiled, and his parents laughed.

'Can I do anything to help?' Flora asked.

'No, love, you're fine,' Lisa said. 'Go and sit down. You've got time to play that game with Joey if you want to.'

Within five minutes, Flora had Tom and his father sitting on the floor with her and Joey, and Joey was clearly thrilled to have everyone playing with him. As well as pleasing the little boy, the game broke the ice for her, so she found it easy to answer Tom's parents' questions about herself over dinner, about her job and where she lived.

'Flora's got a farm but she used to be scared of the chickens,' Joey said. 'And she's got a way cool dog. He's called Banjo and he's a springer spaniel.'

Tom stared at his nephew, clearly dumbstruck by the fact that he was talking so much.

'She's got a picture of him on her phone,' Joey added. 'Can I show Nanna Lisa, Flora?'

'Sure.' Flora delved into her handbag, retrieved her phone and let Joey show the photo of the dog to his grandmother.

'Very cute,' Lisa said.

'He's an old softie,' Flora said with a smile.

After she'd told Joey a bedtime story and promised him another game of fishing later in the week, Flora helped Lisa wash up.

'You've been really good for Joey,' Lisa said quietly. 'And for Tom. I was so worried about the pair of them. Thomas and I were going to come back from France and help out, but Tom said it wouldn't be fair to any of us. Thomas's arthritis is bad and I'm not as young as I was; I just can't do all the things that a young lad needs people to do with him.' She sighed. 'And Joey went so quiet after the accident. He'd hardly speak; and I can see you've made a huge difference to him. You've really helped bring him back out of his shell.'

'He's a lovely boy,' Flora said, 'a real pleasure to have around.'

'And Tom—you've changed him, too,' Lisa said thoughtfully. 'He's less guarded. He doesn't use those awful jokes as a wall as much as he did.'

'He told me about Ben,' Flora said softly.

Lisa nodded. 'It changed him, when Ben died. He'd never show any emotion after that; he turned everything into a big joke and never let anyone talk to him about serious things.' She bit her lip. 'And he adored his big sister. Losing Susie hit him hard, but he just wouldn't talk about it to anyone—he clammed up or changed the subject.' She paused, looking hopeful. 'Has he talked to you about her?' Lisa looked worried sick about her son.

'He has,' Flora reassured her gently. 'It was probably easier for him to talk to me because he knew I'd been there myself— I lost both my parents last year.'

'Oh, my dear, I'm so sorry.'

'I don't have any regrets about the past,' Flora said. 'My parents knew I loved them and I knew they loved me. I would've liked a bit more time with them, but it just wasn't to be.' She shrugged. 'I miss them but, the way I see it, I'm really lucky that I had them for twenty-three years.'

Lisa hugged her. 'Tom's right, you're special.'

Tom—who, on his own mother's admission, wouldn't talk about serious things—had told his parents that she was special... There was a lump in Flora's throat as she hugged Lisa back.

She enjoyed the rest of the evening, chatting to Tom's parents over coffee and chocolates, and then realised with a shock that it was almost ten o'clock. 'I'd better get back,' she said.

'It was lovely to meet you,' Lisa said. 'And Thomas and I were thinking, you both deserve a night out, so we've booked a table for you both for tomorrow night at a little place down the road that's meant to do excellent food. It's our treat, and we've already paid the bill, so don't argue.' She smiled. 'We're going to take Joey to the pictures in St Piran's in the afternoon and have something to eat out afterwards, so you don't have to worry—we'll have a wonderful time.'

'Thank you,' Tom said, looking stunned. 'That's really nice of you, Mum.'

'I don't know what to say,' Flora said, 'except thank you. That's so kind.'

'Just enjoy it,' Lisa said, hugging them both.

CHAPTER TEN

THE meal was perfect. Beautifully cooked, beautifully presented…and Flora, for once, found it hard to eat. Because this was the first time that she and Tom had been out on a proper date, on their own. It wasn't like their fun impromptu lunches on the beach or playing in the park with Joey; this suddenly felt very serious and very grown-up. And her shyness was back to hobble her.

Then she caught Tom's eye and realised that he was as nervous as she was.

'You've gone shy on me again, and I don't have a clue why I'm so nervous,' Tom said. 'This is crazy. We talk for hours over lunch and when we're with Joey.'

'But this is different.' She swallowed hard. 'It's a proper date.'

'Our other dates were proper dates,' Tom said. 'But I know what you mean. This feels…' He paused. 'Different.'

With each course, Flora felt more and more awkward.

And then a band started playing.

'Dance with me?' Tom asked.

This was where she really ought to tell him she wasn't good at dancing. She'd never been one for the school discos, and her parents had never played the kind of music that her schoolfriends' parents had played.

'I have two left feet,' she said quietly as he led her onto

the dance floor. 'So I apologise in advance if I tread on your toes.'

'You won't,' Tom said confidently. 'My parents made Susie and I have lessons when we were teenagers. Follow my lead, and this is going to be just fine.'

To her surprise, he was right. Instead of feeling clumsy and gawky, she found herself actually dancing with him—it felt effortless, and as if she were floating. She'd never, ever experienced this before, and she loved it.

'OK?' he asked.

'Much better than OK,' she said. 'I've never been able to do this sort of thing before.'

'All you need is confidence,' Tom said softly. 'And I didn't tell you, you look lovely tonight. Your hair looks amazing.'

Flora felt as if she was glowing.

And when the music slowed down, Tom kissed her.

In public.

And although her knees had gone weak, he was holding her, supporting her, and she didn't fall flat on her face.

The evening went by way too quickly, and Flora wasn't quite ready for it to end when Tom dropped her at home.

'Would you like to come in for a coffee?' she asked.

'I'd like that. Very much.' He smiled at her.

When she switched the kettle on, he stood behind her and wrapped his arms round her waist, drawing her back against him. His mouth traced a path down the sensitive cord at the side of her neck, and she sighed with pleasure.

'Flora.'

She wriggled round in his arms and reached up to touch his cheek, rubbed her thumb along his lower lip.

Tom sighed and drew her thumb into his mouth, sucking hard; a wave of heat slid through her. When he released her thumb, he kept his hand curved round hers; he kissed the centre of her palm and folded her fingers over it, and then traced a path down to where a pulse beat rapidly in her wrist. He touched the tip of his tongue to it, and she shivered. 'Tom.'

Everything seemed to blur, and then she was in his arms, and he was kissing her properly, his mouth demanding and yet enticing at the same time, making her want more. Her arms were wrapped round his neck; his fingertips slipped under the hem of her top and he stroked her skin, the pads of his fingers moving in tiny circles.

His hands settled for a moment at the curve of her waist, then moved round to her midriff. Her heart began to beat faster as his hand moved upwards, so very slowly; she could feel her breasts tightening and her nipples hardening.

And then she panicked.

He sensed it and pulled back. 'What's wrong?'

'I...' She bit her lip, feeling a fool. How could she tell him? 'I'm not good at—at *this*,' she whispered miserably.

'Usually, when a man says that to a woman, he's the one at fault and he's trying to boost his ego at her expense,' Tom said drily. 'Just so you know, I don't think you're bad at this at all.' He stole a kiss. 'You make me feel..., I don't know. I'm not good at the verbal stuff. Wonderful.' He took her hand and placed it against his chest. 'Feel that?'

His heart. Beating. Hard. Fast.

'Yes,' she whispered.

'That's what you do to me, my adorable Flora.'

She swallowed hard. He was under a real misapprehension here, and she was going to have to tell him the truth. 'Nobody actually said I was bad at it.'

'You just assumed it?' he guessed.

She shook her head. 'I...um...' Oh, why was it so hard to say?

'Tell me,' he said softly.

She felt colour shoot into her face. 'Did I just say that out loud?'

"Fraid so.' He squeezed her hand. 'What is it? Am I pushing you too fast?'

'It's not that,' she said miserably. She wanted him, all right. He made her feel the way that nobody else had ever done. 'I've always had a quiet life. I never did all the partying as a student. I was too busy studying.' Unable to face the scorn she knew she'd see in his face when he learned the truth, she closed her eyes. 'I'm still a virgin.'

Tom said nothing, and she knew she'd blown it.

'I know. It's pathetic. Twenty-four and never been touched.'

'It's not pathetic in the slightest.' To her surprise, she found herself lifted off her feet and carried over to the sofa. Tom sat down and settled her on his lap. 'You're not pathetic at all,' he said fiercely. 'You're a lot of things, but you're definitely not pathetic.' He traced her lower lip with the pad of his thumb. 'You're beautiful. You're sweet. You make me feel as if I could conquer the world.'

'But?' She could see it in his eyes. A huge, enormous, horrible *but*.

'But,' he said, 'I want to behave honourably towards you.' He grimaced. 'Actually, no, I don't. I want to carry you upstairs and kiss you and touch you until you feel as if you're dissolving. I want to make you feel as amazing as you make me feel.'

She swallowed hard. 'But my virginity's in the way.'

'It's something precious,' he said. 'Not something you should throw away. You should hold out for the right person.'

'So I'll be a virgin on my wedding night? That's...' She shook her head. 'That's so old-fashioned, Tom. I'm twenty-four years old and this is the twenty-first century.' She bit her lip.

'When I was at school, all the cool girls used to laugh at me. Fat, frumpy Flora, they called me. They always said I was so old-fashioned. And I hated it, Tom. I wanted to be cool, just like them.'

'No.' He wrapped his arms round her, pulling her closer. 'You're better than cool. You're real. Genuine. And, just for the record, you're not fat. You're deliciously curvy. And you're not frumpy—you're natural, rather than being caked in gunk.'

'But you're going to leave and go home now. And you're not going to touch me again.' And the knowledge made her feel as if her heart had cracked right down the middle.

'Because I'm trying very hard to do the right thing,' Tom said. 'To be honourable.'

'What if,' she said slowly, 'I don't want you to be honourable?'

His eyes darkened. 'What are you saying?'

'What if…?' she said. 'What if I want to go to bed with you? It's not as if I don't know the theory—I'm a nurse. I just…haven't done the practical side of things before, that's all.'

Colour slashed along his cheekbones. 'Are you sure about this, Flora?'

She was as nervous as hell, and her voice was shaking, but she said the words and meant them. 'I'm sure.'

'Absolutely sure?' he checked.

In answer, she kissed him. Hard.

'No pressure,' he said softly, and kissed her again. 'My beautiful, adorable Flora. Do you have any idea how precious the gift you're giving me is?'

'I want you, Tom,' she whispered.

'I'm with you all the way, honey,' he said, his voice husky. He scooped her up in his arms again and carried her up the stairs.

'What about your back? You were hurt on Friday.'

'I'm fine. Nothing that a hot bath couldn't sort out. And, right now, all I can think of is how much I want to make love with you.' He kissed her, his mouth hot and arousing. 'Which one's your bedroom?'

'On the left.'

He opened the door, then gradually let her down until her feet were touching the floor, keeping her body pressed close to his all the way so that she was left in no doubt of his arousal.

Doubts flickered through her again. A man as gorgeous as Tom had no doubt dated plenty of girls. Girls who knew what they were doing.

'What's the matter?' he asked softly.

'Just...I don't want to disappoint you.'

He switched on the bedside light, then got her to sit down on the edge of the bed and knelt down in front of her. He took both her hands in his. 'Look me in the eye, Flora Loveday.'

She did so.

'Now listen to what I'm telling you. You're not going to disappoint me. *Ever*,' he emphasised. 'And I'm going to do my best to make sure this is good for you. If I do anything that makes you feel uncomfortable, just tell me and I'll stop.' He drew her hands to his mouth. 'You have no idea how much self-control I'm having to use, right now. But I'm going to take this slowly, because I want to enjoy every single second of this. And I want you to enjoy it even more.'

Excitement rippled through her.

'Flora,' he said, his voice low and sensual, 'I'd like to see you.'

She felt incredibly self-conscious, but lifted her arms and let him peel her top up and over her head.

Then she remembered that she was wearing a very plain, functional bra. How she wished she'd bought something frivolous and lacy. She crossed her hands automatically over her breasts, not wanting him to see the boring, frumpy garment.

'You want me to stop?' he asked.

She bit her lip and shook her head. 'It's not that.'

'What, then?' His voice was very, very gentle.

'My bra's horrible. It's embarrassing.'

He smiled at her. 'I have an idea. Let's get it out of the way, so it doesn't spoil this for you. How about I close my eyes and undo your bra without looking?' His smile went all the way up into his eyes and she knew that he was laughing with her, not at her.

'I'm being silly, aren't I?'

'No, you're not—and I want the first time to be good for you,' he said. 'You're beautiful.' He kissed her lightly. 'And now I'm closing my eyes.' He deftly removed her bra and dropped it on the floor.

And then he opened his eyes and sucked in a breath. 'Wow. *Flora*. I don't know what I want to do first—touch you or taste you or just look at you. You're *gorgeous*.'

The expression on his face told her that he was completely sincere; Flora blushed again, but this time from pleasure rather than embarrassment.

He was still kneeling in front of her; he cupped her breasts in his hands, lifting them up and together and teasing her nipples with the pads of his thumbs. 'Seriously, seriously gorgeous. And your skin's so soft.' He swallowed hard. 'Flora, I really need to…'

'Yes,' she whispered, and he dipped his head, closing his mouth round one nipple.

She knew the theory.

But she hadn't been prepared at all for the way Tom made her feel. The surge of desire that ran through her entire body; the hot, wet, tight feeling between her thighs; the need for *more*. More of what, exactly, she wasn't sure, but she needed it. She slid her hands into his hair and drew him closer.

He paid attention to her other nipple, and she arched against him. 'Tom,' she whispered.

He stopped and looked up at her; and she noticed just how wide his pupils were. Huge with desire. 'Yes, honey?'

'I want to see you, too.'

He smiled. 'OK.' He removed his tie and dropped it on the floor, then undid the top button of his shirt and spread his arms. 'I'm in your hands. Do what you want with me.'

All hers.

Wow.

She unbuttoned his shirt, revealing strong pectoral muscles and a sprinkling of hair on his chest. 'You're beautiful, Tom.'

She slid the soft cotton from his shoulders and enjoyed stroking his bare skin, feeling his musculature tightening under her touch.

'My turn now?' he asked. At her nod, he said, 'Stand up.' He unzipped her skirt and let it slide to the floor; her slip went the same way, and then he slowly peeled her tights down, stroking her skin as he moved lower. 'Gorgeous. And all mine,' he said, pressing a kiss against her navel.

Flora sucked in her stomach, feeling self-conscious, and he stood up, too.

'We need to even this up a bit.'

She knew what he meant. Her hands were shaking as she undid the button of his trousers and then lowered his zip; she eased the material down over his hips and he stepped out of his trousers, heeling off his shoes and his socks as he did so. His underpants outlined his arousal, and he was bigger than she'd expected. Help. This was going to be the very first time; she wasn't sure whether she felt more nervous or excited.

Maybe it showed in her face, she thought, when Tom said

softly, 'Let me tell you how this is going to be. I'm going to touch you, and kiss you, all over. You can do whatever you like to me. And then...' his breath hitched '...then I'm going to make you completely mine.'

Gently, he lifted her up and laid her against the pillows, then climbed onto the bed beside her. He kissed and stroked his way down her body, clearly taking notice of what made her react more strongly because he lingered in some places and skated over others. He took his time exploring her with his mouth and hands, from the hollows of her collarbones down to the soft undersides of her breasts, her navel, her hipbones.

And then, just when she thought he was going to cup her sex with his hand and deal with the ache inside her, he shifted and started from her feet, stroking her insteps and kissing the hollows of her ankles. She discovered that the backs of her knees was definitely an erogenous zone; her sex felt hot and wet and tight, and it was as if her body was slowly being wound up to a pitch.

Finally, he slid his fingertips under the waistband of her knickers and drew the material down.

'You're so beautiful,' he whispered, 'absolutely gorgeous— and I need to touch you, Flora. I really, really need to touch you.'

'Yes.' She barely recognised her voice, it was so low and husky.

He kept his eyes locked with hers as he stroked her inner thigh. Anticipation made her breath hitch; she had no idea how this was going to be, how it was going to make her feel.

And then, at last, he let one finger glide across her sex, and she found out.

Like nothing on earth.

A shiver of pure desire went through her. 'Oh, Tom,' she whispered.

He wasn't going to...?

Her cheeks flamed as he knelt between her thighs.

And then she stopped thinking at all as his tongue flicked lightly over her clitoris. She slid her hands into his hair, sighing his name—not really knowing what she was asking for, but knowing that he was driving her crazy.

He teased her with his mouth and his fingers. Her body tensed even further, to the point where she didn't think she was going to be able to handle any more, and then suddenly the pressure peaked and released, shocking her with the depths of pleasure. She cried out his name.

He shifted up to hold her close. 'OK?'

'I think so.' She felt the colour in her face deepen. 'I didn't realise it would be like that. It was incredible, Tom.'

He stroked her face. 'Do you know how it makes me feel, knowing I'm the first person who's been able to make you feel like this? As if I'm king of the world,' he said softly.

'I feel pretty good myself,' she said, her voice shaking.

'This is just the start, honey,' he promised.

She wasn't sure when he'd removed his underpants, but when he climbed off the bed she was left in no doubt of just how big and how strong Tom Nicholson was. Though she knew he'd be gentle with her; he'd already given her pleasure she'd never dreamed existed, and he was planning more.

He found his wallet in his pocket and removed a condom.

'OK?' he asked. 'If you want to wait, that's fine.'

'No—I want you, Tom.' I want you to love me, she thought—and realised in that moment that she loved him, absolutely. It didn't matter that she hadn't known him that long; he was kind, gorgeous and strong, and she trusted him to keep her safe.

He rolled the condom on and knelt between her thighs, nudging them apart, then bent to kiss her. 'You're beautiful,

Flora. You take my breath away. And I've wanted this almost since the first moment I met you.'

A thrill went through her at his words. 'You're beautiful, too.'

Slowly, slowly, he eased into her. She felt a sharp twinge and he must've realised it too, because he paused, giving her time to get used to his weight and the feel of him.

'OK, honey?' he asked.

She nodded. 'Very OK.'

'You're sure I'm not hurting you?'

'Not any more.'

He kissed her, then lifted her hips so he could push deeper into her. And then Flora discovered that he'd been telling the truth, that the first climax was just the start. Pleasure started to build and build again; warmth spread through her, coiling and pulling tight, and then the release hit her.

She felt his body tighten inside hers; she looked into his eyes and saw them go wide with pleasure as his own climax hit.

He held her tightly afterwards. 'My adorable Flora,' he said softly.

Finally, he gently withdrew from her. 'I'll be back in a moment, honey.' He was completely unselfconscious as he left the bed, but Flora wriggled in embarrassment. She couldn't just lie there, naked, waiting for him to come back. Should she get dressed, or would he expect her to stay in bed? Unsure, and feeling ridiculously shy, she grabbed the duvet to cover herself.

When Tom came back, he was smiling. 'You, Flora Loveday, are a wonderful woman, and I feel incredibly privileged.'

He climbed into bed beside her and pulled her into his arms. 'Right now, I just want to hold you; it feels wonderful to have you in my arms, your skin against mine.' He brushed a kiss over her temples. 'What I'd really like to do is fall asleep with you in my arms and wake up with you in the morning, but I can't do that—it's not fair to Mum and Dad.'

'What's the time?' She glanced at her bedside clock. 'They'll already be worried about you.'

'It's almost midnight. They won't be expecting me back just yet—they knew when they booked the table that there was a band as well, and they'll guess that I'll have coffee with you.'

She bit her lip. 'I didn't actually make you any coffee.'

He smiled. 'You can remedy that some other time. I'm not going anywhere and you sure as hell aren't moving from my arms right now.'

Gradually her tension eased, and it felt good to lie in his arms like this, with her head against his shoulder. Little by little, her eyes closed, and Flora finally fell asleep, warm and comfortable.

CHAPTER ELEVEN

TOM wished he could stay in bed beside Flora all night—but he couldn't. His carefree bachelor life was gone now; and, even though he knew that his nephew would be perfectly safe with his grandparents, he also knew that it wouldn't be fair to them if he stayed here with Flora. They'd worry that something had happened to him, and the car crash that had taken Susie and Kevin from them would be uppermost in their minds. He couldn't put them through that kind of torment. And it wouldn't be fair to Joey, either; the little boy needed security, and seeing Tom there in the morning would help.

Reluctantly, and careful not to wake Flora as he did so, Tom wriggled out of the bed and dressed swiftly. She looked so peaceful that he couldn't bear to wake her. But he also wasn't just going to walk out and abandon her. Not when she'd given him something so very precious.

He tiptoed downstairs, and Banjo was instantly alert.

'Shh, she's asleep. Don't bark,' Tom said softly.

He went over to the memo pad by her phone and scribbled a quick note.

You look adorable, asleep—couldn't bring myself to wake you! Have to get back to Joey, but will call you in the morning. T x

He left the note propped against the kettle, where she'd be bound to find it in the morning, made a brief fuss of Banjo and persuaded the dog back to his basket, then quietly let himself out of the house.

Driving back to his flat, he thought about Flora. The way she'd responded to him. The wonder in her eyes.

And then it hit him.

He'd felt that exact same sense of wonder. And not just because he'd known that this was a big deal for her—it had been a big deal for him, too. He'd never really let himself connect with anyone in the past: but tonight he'd connected with Flora. Heart and soul. It was like nothing he'd ever experienced before.

Oh, hell.

He'd always promised himself that he'd never let his relationships get serious. It wasn't fair to expect someone else to face the burden of the risks he took every day in his job.

And yet he'd done it. Fallen for her completely. Her warmth, her kindness, the sweetness in her smile—everything about her drew him. And, at some point over the last couple of weeks, he'd stopped guarding his heart. More than that, he'd actually given his heart to her. Freely and completely.

Oh, double hell.

What did he do now?

Because now the whole world was different. Two months ago, he'd been a carefree bachelor, enjoying life as a single man. Now he was a stand-in father to someone who'd lost almost his whole world—and he couldn't risk letting Joey lose the bits he had left. And he wasn't a carefree bachelor any more: he was involved with Flora. Really involved with her, from the centre of his heart.

Letting Joey down wasn't an option.

Un-falling in love with Flora also wasn't an option; being with her had shown him that, before, he'd only been living part of a life. There was much more to it than working hard, and playing just as hard. Football was fun, but teaching Joey how to dribble and score goals was even better. And as for parties with loud music…maybe he'd suddenly grown up overnight, but he discovered that he'd rather have a walk on the beach and a soundtrack of laughter.

With Flora and Joey, he could have a real family. The same kind of love his parents had. The same kind of happiness his sister had had.

But Flora had made him think, the other night, and now he knew that the happiness and love were bitter-sweet: at any time a fire could turn rogue and take him from them. He'd be forced to let them down in the most fundamental way, unable to fight his way back to them.

On paper, it was easy. All he had to do was take the danger out of his life so they wouldn't have to shoulder the risk of losing him.

Change his job.

In real life it wasn't quite as simple as that. As he'd told her the other night, fighting fires and rescuing people wasn't just his job, it was who he *was*. He'd joined the fire brigade at eighteen, straight after his A levels, and had never looked back. How could he walk away from the job he loved, from what'd he'd done for almost half his life and the whole of his adult life?

Without that, he didn't have a clue what he'd do.

But maybe the small hours of the morning wasn't the best time to make decisions. He needed to sit down and work out what all his options were. Make a rational decision. Do the right thing.

When he let himself quietly into the flat, he discovered that his mother was waiting up for him. 'Did you have a nice time?'

'Wonderful, thanks,' he said as he sat next to her on the sofa.

'Sure? You look a bit worried,' Lisa said.

'I'm fine. I just realised I'm a bit late back,' he fibbed, 'and I didn't want you to be worrying about me.'

'It doesn't matter that you're six feet four and thirty-two years old. You're still my baby and always will be, so I'll always worry about you,' Lisa said with a smile, ruffling his hair.

'Is Joey all right?'

'Yes, and we all ate far too much ice cream, was lovely— just like taking you and Susie to the cinema when you were little.'

'Mmm, I remember.' He gave her a wistful smile. 'I had a really happy childhood, Mum.'

'Good. That's what we wanted.'

'That's what I want for Joey, too.' He sighed. 'And I'm not making a very good job of it. Flora's helped a huge amount, but...I'm never going to be good enough, Mum.'

'Don't do yourself down, love. Joey's been through a lot. But he knows you're there for him and he knows you love him, and that's going to help him through,' Lisa said. 'Don't worry. It's all going to be fine. You're doing your best, and that's all anyone can ask.' She kissed the top of his head. 'I'd better let you get some sleep. See you in the morning.'

Tom lay awake for much of the night, trying to work out what he ought to do. But he still hadn't come to a decent compromise the next morning. He showered, dressed and made himself a mug of tea, then Joey appeared.

'I hear you ate lots of ice cream yesterday,' Tom said as he poured his nephew a glass of milk.

Joey nodded.

'How was the film?'

'Good. Can we play fishing?'

Tom smiled. 'Sure we can.'

They were in the middle of their third game when his mother emerged from the bedroom, wrapped in a towelling robe and yawning.'

'The kettle's hot, Mum. Do you want some tea?' Tom asked.

'Thank you, darling.'

When Joey went to get dressed, Tom asked quietly, 'Mum, would you mind very much if I sneaked over and had breakfast with Flora this morning?'

Lisa raised an eyebrow. 'She's really important to you, isn't she?'

He smiled. 'I'm not answering that one.'

'Well, she's the first girl you've actually let us meet—and that tells me a lot. She's lovely,' Lisa said. 'I like her very much, and I think she'll make you happy.'

'Mmm, but it's whether I'll be able to make her happy.' He bit his lip. 'I'm a firefighter.'

'And she's a nurse, so she's going to understand the demands of your job a lot more than someone who doesn't work in the emergency services.'

'Maybe.'

'Are you thinking about giving it up, love?'

'I don't know.' He sighed. 'Mum, being a firefighter. It's who I am. I can't see myself as anything else—the world wouldn't feel right. But...I've got Joey to think of now, and Flora, and... It's a lot for them to have to put up with. All that worry.' He shook his head. 'I can't work this out.'

'And I'm not the person you should be talking it over with,' Lisa said softly. 'Find out what Flora thinks.'

He already knew what she thought. That his job was dangerous and he took reckless risks that could mean Joey was left alone.

'Talk it over with her. But don't rush into anything.'

He smiled wryly. 'Yes, you're right. It's too fast. I've only known her for a few days.'

'That's not what I meant—when you meet the right one, you'll know.' Lisa smiled. 'And I think you might just have met your "the one", in Flora. I've never seen you like this about anyone else. No, I meant you need to talk things through and weigh up all your options, not just rush in and do what you think is the right thing. Now go and have breakfast with your girl. We'll see you later.'

'Where are you going?' Joey asked when he came back from his room, fully dressed and wearing odd socks.

'To see Flora,' Tom told him.

'Can I come?'

'Another time,' Lisa said, 'because I want you to teach me how to make that lovely French toast you say Flora makes. How about being Chef Joey and taking Grandpa some breakfast in bed?'

Tom gave his mother a grateful look, and kissed both her and Joey goodbye. 'I'll be back soon. Flora has to be at work at half past eight.'

He called in at the out-of-town supermarket on the way to the farm and bought flowers and croissants. When he rang the doorbell, Flora took a while to answer, and she was wearing her dressing gown, so he'd clearly woken her.

'Perfect timing,' he said with a grin. 'This means I can have breakfast with you and then I can have a shower with you.'

'Tom Nicholson, that's shocking!' But she was smiling. 'I wasn't expecting to see you this morning.'

'Mum and Dad are with Joey and I wanted to see you for breakfast.' He handed her the flowers. 'These, because you're beautiful.'

She sniffed them. 'Thank you, they're lovely.'

'And these, because... Oh, wait. Forget about the healthy

eating stuff you do with your classes. These, because they're the nicest breakfast ever.'

She peered into the bag and laughed. 'I love croissants, too. And I have posh strawberry jam from the farm shop.'

'Brilliant.' He paused. 'Did you find my note this morning?'

She smiled. 'Yes. I have to admit, I felt a bit strange when I woke up and you weren't there, but I knew you had to get back for Joey.'

'I wish I'd woken with you.' He stroked her face. 'You look so cute when you're asleep. Like a little dormouse.'

'A dormouse?' She raised an eyebrow. 'Thanks. I think.' But her eyes were sparkling.

She made them both coffee, put the flowers in water, and Tom thoroughly enjoyed feeding her croissants and licking jam from her fingers. Not to mention having a shower with her after breakfast.

'Tom, I'm going to be late!' she said, sounding shocked, when they finally made it back to her bedroom and she glanced at her clock.

'No, you won't. I'll drop you at the surgery. Do you need your car this afternoon?'

'Only to get home.'

'That's easy, then. I'll pick you up,' Tom said. 'I thought maybe we could take Joey out ten-pin bowling and then eat out at that new burger place.'

'That'd be lovely. Provided you let it be my treat,' she added. 'And I insist on that.'

Flora made it to the surgery with three minutes to spare. Kate Tremayne smiled at Flora as she walked in. 'I'm not going to ask,' Kate said, 'but it's lovely to see you sparkling like this.'

Was what she'd just done with Tom so obvious? Flora felt herself blush to the roots of her hair. 'Um...'

Kate laughed. 'It couldn't happen to a nicer couple. And Tom's a sweetie.'

Flora was gobsmacked. 'How did you know?'

Kate raised an eyebrow. 'Penhally's not exactly a huge place—and when you're holding hands on the beach with someone, you can expect someone to spot you.' She paused. 'And Nick took me out to dinner last night. The food's good at The Mackerel, isn't it?'

'You were there?' Flora looked at her, aghast. 'I'm so sorry I was rude and didn't say anything to you. I just didn't see you.'

Kate smiled. 'I know, love. You two only had eyes for each other.'

Flora felt her blush deepen. 'I guess so.'

She discovered during her surgery that morning, while doing a blood-pressure check for one of her patients, that Kate hadn't been the only person to see her and Tom at the restaurant.

Worse still, Mrs Evans, whose venous ulcer she was dressing, had seen Tom kissing her goodbye in the surgery car park that morning.

'Your young man's a lovely boy. He rescued my neighbour's dog from the river last week, and he never made a fuss when Goldie bit him—he's a smashing young lad,' Mrs Evans said. 'He's a keeper, you mark my words.'

By lunchtime, Flora realised that quite a few people in Penhally had already got her and Tom married off, and her protests that it was still very early days were just ignored.

'You make a lovely couple, dear,' was the standard response.

She just hoped that Tom wasn't getting the same kind of comments, or he might start avoiding her.

But he was there with Joey to meet her from work, and Joey greeted her with a hug. They made a quick stop back at the farmhouse to let Banjo out and feed him, then went off ten-pin bowling. Tom put the bumper bars up on their lane and got Joey to use the ramp, and Joey was thrilled to get a strike.

This, Flora thought, was what it felt like to be a family. *And she loved it.*

Josh scanned the hospital canteen as he walked in: force of habit. Most of the time, Megan wasn't there. It was as if she had some kind of radar system that told her when he was having a break so she could avoid him.

But then he saw her at a table in a quiet corner. On her own.

It was too good a chance to miss. He headed straight over to her table. 'Megan.'

Her eyes widened. 'I'm about to go.'

'Don't go,' he said softly. 'Stay and talk to me. I'm just going to get myself a sandwich. Can I get you a coffee?'

'I...'

She was wavering; hope bloomed within him. 'I saw you at the football match, the other week.' And she'd avoided him at the hospital ever since.

'I was just passing.'

That might've been true, because the football pitch was halfway between St Piran's and Penhally, where Megan lived. But she wouldn't be 'just passing' after her shift at that time of the morning. Not that he was going to call her on it. He didn't want her to bolt. 'Stay and have coffee with me?'

Hell, she was beautiful. Even with her hair pulled back for work, she was beautiful. And he knew exactly what her hair looked like when it was tumbled over her shoulders. Tumbled over his pillow. Soft and silky and...

He dragged in a breath. Not now. He needed to take this slowly. Get her to talk to him again. 'Please, Megan?'

She looked wary, but she nodded. 'OK.'

Josh wanted to punch the air. 'Back in a second, OK?'

Even though he grabbed the first sandwich he could see from the chiller, by the time he'd paid for them and two coffees, he could see that Megan had changed her mind.

'Sorry. My bleep just went.'

She might've been using it as an excuse; then again, it might not be. Her department was busy.

But this felt just a little too convenient.

'Sorry,' she said again, and fled.

Tom and Joey met Flora at the surgery on Tuesday with a picnic basket; although it was cold, it was dry and for once not windy. They ate sandwiches on the beach, then went for a walk to collect shells.

'So have you thought any more about going to the football dinner with me?' Tom asked.

'I'm still thinking about it,' she admitted.

'Sure. I don't want to rush you.'

Which made her feel even worse, because he was being so patient with her. The dinner was less than a week away, and there would be a cut-off point for getting tickets.

But she still couldn't help thinking that someone as popular as Tom could have absolutely anyone he wanted. Was he only spending time with her for Joey's sake? And besides, despite what they'd shared on Sunday night, he hadn't actually said he loved her—just that she made him feel amazing.

Was she expecting too much? All she'd ever wanted was someone who loved her for herself. Could Tom be that man?

And why couldn't she shake the feeling that this was all going to go horribly wrong?

Flora was miserable all evening; and, at the surgery the next morning, Kate Tremayne came in to the treatment room and closed the door behind her.

'Are you OK, Flora?'

Flora summoned a smile. 'Of course I am,' she lied.

'Don't fib.' Kate put her hands on her hips. 'You've got five minutes before your first patient. Now talk.'

Flora opened her mouth to say that nothing was wrong—but ended up spilling all her doubts. She finished miserably, 'He's asked me to go to the football league dinner with him, and I don't have a clue what to wear—I don't exactly go to posh dinners. And, if I do go, he's going to be surrounded with people all night and I won't know anyone there.'

Kate squeezed her hand. 'Love, first of all, Tom sees you exactly as you are—and you're lovely. You probably will know people there, because there are a few medics who play in the league. So I think you should say yes. Go to St Piran on Saturday morning, buy yourself a fabulous dress, and knock his socks off.'

Flora was none too sure that she'd be able to do that, but she knew that Kate meant well. 'Thanks, Kate. I will,' she said.

On Thursday, Flora went to the science museum with Tom and Joey. Not having children of her own, she'd never visited it before, and she loved it as much as Joey did.

Tom and Joey insisted on trying every single one of the interactive exhibits—from Joey standing inside a giant bubble, through to doing a duet on the giant keyboard where you pressed the notes with your feet, and making a tornado inside a bottle. The bubble show—where the woman on stage actually managed to set bubbles on fire—and the planetarium shows were also a huge hit with Joey. And Flora discovered a whole heap of leaflets they could take home to make their own experiments. 'We're definitely going to have to try making our own slime—what colour d'you reckon, Joey?'

'Green,' Joey said enthusiastically.

She laughed. 'Good call.'

She took photographs of Tom and his nephew together, having fun.

'Excuse me, love.' A middle-aged woman smiled at her. 'Would you like me to take a picture of the three of you? I know how it is when you're always the one behind the camera.'

The three of them.

Like a family.

'That'd be wonderful,' Flora said warmly, and returned the compliment by taking a picture of the woman with her grandchildren.

Tom had reverted completely to being a child, and Flora found his enthusiasm adorable. Over lunch, he looked through Flora's leaflets.

'Making a plastic out of milk? Oh, now, we have to do that. Hey, Joey, did you know this is how they used to make windows for aeroplanes in the Second World War?'

'Really?' Joey asked, wide-eyed.

'That's what it says here.'

'Wow.' Then Joey smiled. 'This is the best day ever.'

Flora, seeing the look of relief mingled with delight on Tom's face, had a lump in her throat.

Tom hugged his nephew, and then Flora. 'I'm having a brilliant day here, too, and I wouldn't have wanted to share this with anyone else except you two.'

'Snap,' Flora said. 'I never knew this sort of place could be so much fun.'

'It's just the best,' Joey said.

* * *

That evening, when Joey was in bed, Tom said, 'So what do you want to do on Saturday?'

She frowned. 'I thought you were going to the football dinner?'

'Not without you,' he said. 'And you've been avoiding the subject, so I know you don't really want to go.'

She sighed. 'Tom, they're your friends and it's something you all look forward to at the end of the season, isn't it?'

'Absolutely,' he agreed, 'but if it's the choice of going to the dinner or spending time with you, it's a no-brainer.'

He'd really give up something he was looking forward to, for her? She remembered what Kate had said. *Tom sees you exactly as you are...I think you should say yes.*

She stroked his face. 'Tom, I'm not going to stop you going.'

'I don't want to go without you. Come with me, honey.' He stole a kiss. 'I know you're probably worrying that you won't know anyone there, but they're a nice bunch and they won't shut you out.'

They had at the football match, Flora thought.

Although she didn't say it aloud, her reservations must have shown on her face because Tom said softly, 'You'll be part of the crowd because you're with me—you're my girl.'

And this time he'd be with her instead of running around on a pitch, so it might be different. She took a deep breath. It was time to be brave about this. 'What's the dress code?'

'Black tie.'

Which meant a cocktail dress—and she didn't possess one. 'I'd better go shopping, then.'

'You'll really come with me?'

She nodded.

He hugged her. 'I'm so glad. I'll go shopping with you, if you like.'

'No. Joey would hate being dragged round dress shops.' She

smiled. 'And anyway, I'd like to surprise you.' She thought again about what Kate said. *Knock his socks off.* Maybe, just maybe, it was time to stop being shy, frumpy Flora and show Tom that she was a woman who was worthy of him.

CHAPTER TWELVE

ON SATURDAY afternoon, Flora drove to St Piran. She couldn't
see any dresses that would suit her in the first three shops
she went into, and the assistants in the fourth turned out to
be really snooty; she didn't even approach them, because she
could see them mentally sizing her and wondering what on
earth she thought she was doing in their shop when they were
so clearly in the market for people five dress sizes smaller.

But then she saw a beautiful floaty dress in the window of
a little boutique. It probably wasn't right for her, but maybe
there was something else that would catch her eye.

'Can I help you?' the assistant asked.

'I'm just looking,' Flora said.

'For anything special?'

The assistant looked genuinely interested and didn't give
the impression that she would only be interested in selling
size-eight clothes. 'I'm going to a black-tie dinner. I need a
cocktail dress, and I don't have a clue what will suit me.'

The assistant's eyes lit up. 'Would you trust me to pick
something for you?'

'I… Well, sure.'

To her surprise, the assistant didn't even ask her size. She
looked through the racks and picked out several dresses in very
bright colours—the kind of colours that Flora never wore.

'Should I have a black dress?' Flora asked.

The assistant smiled. 'Your colouring's gorgeous, so don't hide yourself in black.'

Help, Flora thought. I don't want to stand out from the crowd.

The assistant put a gentle hand on her shoulder. 'Is he special?'

'Yes.'

'Then you'll stand out from the crowd for him anyway, so you might as well do it properly.'

Flora was beginning to agree until the assistant handed her a bright turquoise dress. It had a wrap front with a V-neck and wide shoulder straps, plus layers of silk georgette in the skirt, and it was much shorter than the kind of thing she normally wore, finishing just at the knee. She looked dubiously at it. 'I don't think I'm thin enough to wear this.'

'This shape will look fantastic on you. Just try it on and see what you think,' the assistant coaxed. 'If you hate it we'll try something else.'

Flora looked at a dress with a much higher neck. 'Something like that.'

'That's absolutely wrong for you—you need to be tall and a stick insect to suit that style,' the assistant said. 'You're much better off with something that flatters you, like this, or maybe an Empire-line dress.'

Flora knew when she was beaten and tried the dress on. To her surprise, it looked amazing.

'Just what I thought. Hang on, you need accessories.' A couple of moments later, the assistant returned with a turquoise and silver pendant, and a pair of silver strappy shoes with medium kitten heels. 'Try these. And if you wear your hair up with just a couple of curls tumbling down to soften your face…' She demonstrated, and Flora stared at herself in the mirror, barely recognising herself.

'And you're so lucky—you have fabulous skin. All you need

is a touch of eyeliner, mascara and lipstick—you're going to look amazing, and he's going to think he's the luckiest man on earth,' the assistant finished with a smile.

'Thank you—you've been really kind.'

The assistant smiled. 'My pleasure. It's lovely to be asked for advice instead of having someone come in with set ideas who refuses to try something that'd really suit them.' She paused. 'Forgive me for being rude, but you know the other way of giving yourself loads of confidence?'

'No.' Flora knew she needed all the help she could get on that front.

'Really, *really* nice underwear.'

Flora loved the silk and lace confections that the assistant showed her, and couldn't resist a buying matching set. The whole outfit came to quite a bit more than she'd intended to pay, but she didn't care. In this underwear and this dress, she was going to feel fantastic—and she was going to knock Tom's socks off.

On impulse, she texted Kate when she got home. *'Thanks for your advice. Found really lovely dress.'*

Two minutes later, her phone rang. 'That's great. What about your hair and make-up?' Kate asked.

'The shop assistant said I should wear my hair up. I was going to see if Maureen could fit me in this afternoon at the salon.'

'On a Saturday afternoon in half-term, you'll be lucky.' Kate paused. 'Let me come over and do your hair and make-up, then I can see the dress as well.'

'Kate, I can't ask you to do that.'

'You're not asking, I'm telling you,' Kate retorted.

It was the work of only a few minutes. When Flora looked in the mirror, she could hardly believe it was her. Kate hadn't caked her with make-up, and yet her eyes looked huge and luminous, and her mouth was a perfect rosebud.

'You're going to have an amazing time.' Kate hugged her.
'Let yourself be happy with Tom, Flora. You deserve each
other.'

Tom arrived at seven to pick her up. When she opened the
door, he didn't say a word, and Flora's heart plummeted. She'd
thought she looked good. Had she got it so wrong? And then
Tom blew out a breath. 'Flora. You— I— You…' He shook
his head. 'I'm gibbering. Sorry. You look so fantastic, I can't
remember how to speak. That dress… God, I want to carry
you upstairs to bed right now and forget about the dinner
dance.'

Flora was lost for words.

'But I'm not going to,' Tom continued, 'because I want to
show you off.' He smiled at her. 'You always look lovely to
me, but tonight…tonight, you're *glowing*.'

Confidence, she thought. Confidence that Tom had given
her.

When they arrived at the dance, as Flora expected, Tom
was in demand; but he kept his arm round her the whole
time and introduced her to everyone on his table. A couple of
them knew her anyway from the village, but to her pleasure
everyone seemed to accept her.

'Weren't you at the football match, the other week?' one
of them asked.

Flora bit her lip. 'Um, yes.'

'I didn't realise you were with Tom or I'd have asked you
to come over and join us,' she said. 'You must've thought we
were all so snooty.'

'I did feel a bit out of place,' Flora admitted.

'I'm so sorry. Tom never brings his girlfriends to anything,
so I just assumed you were with another crowd. Well, I'm
Cindy, and it's lovely to meet you.' She beamed at Flora. 'And
it's especially lovely seeing our Tom so happy.'

Over the next few minutes, Flora discovered that, actually,

she *was* a part of Tom's crowd. She was included in the general teasing about how the wives forced the men to hold the league dinner to make up for all those weekend afternoons spent freezing on the sidelines of a football pitch and the amount of scrubbing they had to do to get the mud out of their kit. She discovered that people were interested in what she did, and interested in her opinion. It wasn't just the champagne that made her feel heady: it was Tom, because he made sure that he was sitting next to her with his arm round her shoulders, more or less telling the whole world that she was his.

Megan was really beginning to regret accepting the invitation to the football league dinner. If she'd known that Josh would be there, she wouldn't have come.

Oh, who was she kidding? Seeing him was torture—and yet not seeing him was just as bad.

This whole thing was a mess. No way was she a home wrecker, the sort of woman who destroyed someone else's marriage on a whim. Her feelings for Josh—despite the fact she'd tried to bury them for all those years—were still the same. But she knew it wasn't going to lead anywhere. How could it? Too much had happened.

And there was Rebecca.

Beautiful, fragile Rebecca.

No, she couldn't be the one to destroy Josh's marriage. To hurt another woman the way that she'd been hurt.

When Tom was dancing with Flora, a tall, glamorous, slinky blonde came up to them. 'Tom. Make sure you save a dance for me, yes?'

Tom simply smiled. 'Sorry. Tonight I'm dancing with my girl, and only my girl—and anyone who wants to dance with her is just going to be disappointed, too.'

'Tom, I'm not that insecure,' Flora said. Not any more. 'If you want to dance with your friends, that's fine.'

'That's the point.' Tom stole a kiss and drew her closer. 'There's only one person I want to dance with tonight. She's in my arms, right now—and that's how it's staying.'

'Dance with me?'

No. Tell him no. Tell him you don't dance.

And yet Megan found herself on the dance floor with Josh.

And he *would* choose to show off with a waltz. Typical Josh.

'I've missed you,' he said. 'You've been avoiding me.'

'You know why.'

'How would I know, when you never talk to me, Megan?'

A muscle flickered in her jaw. 'There's nothing to talk about, Josh.'

Josh's eyes became pleading. 'Megan.'

'You have a wife,' she said crisply, taking a step back that forced him to drop his hands from the dance hold. 'Maybe you should be talking to her. Go home, Josh.' And, just to make sure that he couldn't follow her, she headed for the ladies' toilets.

Josh stared after her. Hell, he hadn't meant to upset her. He just wanted to… No, he wanted *her*. And he realised yet again what a huge mistake he'd made, all those years back. He should never have married Rebecca; he'd tried to anaesthetise his feelings and in the end he'd been unfair to all of them. Himself included.

So what now? He and Rebecca didn't want the same things any more. They'd agreed before they'd married that there would be no children; and now Rebecca had changed her mind, was desperate for a baby; but Josh knew that having a baby wouldn't repair their broken marriage. If anything, their marriage would crack even further under the strain. And Josh had lived in a family fractured by the pressure of children. He'd been forced to take the place of his excuse of a father—of course he couldn't have stood by and watched his mother struggle on her own—and no way did he want to go back to that. One generation of that was enough.

Frustrated, hurt and completely confused, Josh headed for the bar.

'Are you all right?'

Megan didn't even look at the woman who had just walked into the toilets. 'Yes,' she fibbed.

'You don't look it. Can I get you a glass of water or something?'

'No, but thanks for offering.' She looked up, this time, and recognised the concerned-looking woman in front of her. Flora Loveday, the school nurse. 'I'll be fine. Just a bit of a headache.' And a whole lot of heartache, otherwise known as Dr Josh O'Hara. Megan forced a smile to her face. 'Are you having a nice time tonight?'

Flora simply glowed. 'Yes. Tom's danced with me all night.'

'Tom the firefighter? He's lovely.' Megan had worked with him a couple of times. He reminded her of Josh—everybody's friend, full of good humour and charm—except she didn't think that Tom was the type to lie, the way Josh had lied to her.

'Yes. I still can't believe how lucky I am. I never expected to find...' Flora paused, looking dismayed. 'Megan? What's wrong?'

Megan scrubbed the tear away. 'I'm fine.' There wasn't a cure for heartache. Unless she could excise Josh from her heart—and she hadn't managed to do that in eight years of trying. 'I think I'll get a taxi home.'

'Let me call it for you, and I'll sit with you while you're waiting,' Flora offered. 'Have you taken anything for your headache yet?' She rummaged in her handbag. 'I've got some paracetamol, if you need it.'

'No, I just need some fresh air and some sleep. You know how busy things get at a hospital.'

'True,' Flora agreed.

Megan splashed water on her face, then called a taxi on her mobile phone.

Flora went out to the reception area with her; on the way, she caught Tom's eye and gestured that she'd be a few minutes. She saw Megan into the taxi, then went back to Tom, who was sitting back at their table, chatting to his friends.

'Everything all right?' he asked as she joined him.

'Megan—you know, the paediatrician from St Piran's?— had a bit of a headache. I waited with her until her taxi arrived.'

'That's my Flora,' Tom said softly, stealing a kiss. 'Looking after everyone.'

'Do you mind?'

'It's one of the things I adore about you,' Tom said, stroking her face. 'My adorable Flora.'

They danced together for the rest of the evening; and Flora found herself disappointed when the band finally stopped playing.

'Come on. I'll drive you home,' Tom said.

Flora was still high on dancing with him all evening. Enough to take a risk when she'd unlocked the front door. She hadn't quite finished knocking his socks off, yet. 'Tom, your parents are with Joey tonight, aren't they?'

'Yes.'

'Are they expecting you home?'

He went very still. 'What are you asking, Flora?'

'I'm asking you to stay the night with me.' She lifted her chin. 'To sleep with me. And wake up with me.'

He moistened his lower lip. 'Are you sure about that?'

'Very sure.'

He smiled. 'Give me two minutes to make a phone call.'

'And I'll let Banjo out while you're doing that.'

By the time she'd called the dog back in and locked the front door, Tom had finished his call.

'OK?' she asked.

He nodded.

She smiled. 'Good. And now I'm taking you to bed.' She took his hand and led him up the stairs to her room. The curtains were already drawn but she didn't put the overhead light on; instead, she switched on a string of fairy lights that she'd draped above the bed earlier.

'Wow. This is like a princess's boudoir,' Tom said.

'Which makes you Prince Charming, yes?'

'Me, I'm just a humble firefighter,' he said with a grin.

'No, you're gorgeous. And you're all mine.'

He laughed. 'If this is what champagne does to you, remind me to keep a bottle in the fridge at all times.'

'It's not the champagne,' she said. 'It's you.' He'd given her the confidence that made her feel as if she could do anything.

Slowly, she undressed him; she untied his bow-tie first, then removed his jacket.

Tom tried to undo the zip at the back of her dress but she wagged a finger at him. 'Uh-uh. I'm in charge.'

Her face was very serious; Tom hid his amusement, not wanting to hurt her. Flora couldn't be bossy if she tried. But he liked the surge of confidence; tonight, she simply sparkled. 'In that case, honey, I'm completely in your hands—do what you want with me.'

'Good.' She plugged her MP3 player into a set of speakers by her bed, and soft jazz filled the room. She stood on tiptoe and kissed him, then finished undoing the buttons of his shirt, sliding the material off his shoulders.

He waited for her to hang it over the back of a chair, knowing that she was the tidy sort.

As if she'd guessed what he was thinking, she gave a grin and tossed it over her shoulder, just to prove that she didn't always run to type. She explored his chest with her fingertips, moving in tiny circles across his skin; he caught his breath as her hands moved lower, to his abdomen.

'Nice six-pack, Mr Nicholson,' she said.

And then his mouth went dry as she undid the button and zip of his formal trousers.

'Gorgeous,' she breathed.

'Flora.' He had to stop himself grabbing her; he knew she wanted to be in charge and he had to be patient—even though right then he really wanted to pick her up and lay her back against the pillows before easing into her.

Slowly, slowly, she eased the material of his trousers over his hips.

He helped her then, kicking his shoes off and stepping out of his trousers, pulling his socks off at the same time.

'Turn round,' she said.

He did so, in a slow pirouette.

'Just gorgeous,' she said. 'Tom, you're perfect.'

'That's pretty much what I think about you,' he said. 'And, pretty as your dress is, I really want to take it off.'

She shook her head. 'You'll have to wait. I have other plans.'

He had no idea what she had in mind, but he was definitely playing by her rules tonight. 'I'm in your hands,' he told her.

She pulled the duvet aside and patted the pillows. 'Lie down.'

He did so, and she stood at the end of the bed, swaying to the music. His mouth went dry as she slowly, slowly peeled off her dress.

'Oh, wow. That lace stuff…it's gorgeous.' And he was desperate to take it off her.

She gave him a shy smile. 'You like it?'

'Very much. You're beautiful, Flora.'

She finished peeling off everything except her knickers, then sashayed over towards him.

'I need to touch you, Flora.' His voice was hoarse with need.

She glanced down at his underpants, which were hiding absolutely nothing. 'Mmm. I can see that.'

His breath hissed. 'Flora.'

She held up a finger. 'Wait.' She went to the drawer of the cabinet by her bed, opened it, and withdrew a condom. 'I think we might need this.'

Flora had bought condoms?

He must have spoken aloud, because she looked hurt. 'I'm not that staid and boring, Tom.'

'No, of course you're not.' He leaned forward and kissed her lightly. 'Just that it's my job to take care of you.'

'This is the twenty-first century. And I'm not fat, frumpy Flora any more.'

'You're gorgeous, curvy, incredibly sensual Flora,' he said. 'And I really, really need to touch you.' He dragged in a breath. 'I really, really need you to touch me. Before I implode.' He took her hand and tugged her towards him.

To his pleasure, she climbed onto the bed and straddled him. She manoeuvred him so she could remove his underpants, and then the only thing between them was the lace of her incredibly pretty knickers. He could feel the heat of her sex against his skin, and it sent him dizzy. 'Flora. I'm begging. Please?'

She ripped open the foil packet and slid the condom over his penis. Her hand was shaking slightly, but she was completely in control—and he was happy to let her take the lead, loving the new confidence she was showing.

She lifted herself slightly, drew the material of her knickers to one side, positioned him at her entrance and then slowly, slowly lowered herself onto him.

She leaned forward and touched her mouth to his before rising and lowering herself back on to him. As her arousal grew, she tipped her head back; Tom shifted so he could kiss her throat. He could feel the pulse beating hard there, just like his own heart was racing with desire and need and...*love*.

He felt her start to ripple round him, and he was lost.

'My adorable Flora. I love you,' he whispered, and kissed her hard as his climax shuddered through him.

She looked completely stunned.

'Are you OK?' he asked, wrapping his arms round her and holding her close.

'Yes.' She frowned. 'Did you just say what I think you said?'

He nodded. 'I'm sorry. I know it's fast. I know it's crazy. But my mum said something last weekend, something I know now is just so true. She said when you meet the right one, you *know*. And I do.'

'You love me,' she said in wonder.

'I love all of you, from those beautiful soft curls down to your pearl-pink toenails and everything in between. All that you are, I love,' he said softly.

Her eyes filled with tears. 'Oh, Tom. I love you, too.'

'Good.' He smiled. 'I was hoping you'd say that.'

Tom dealt with the condom, then switched off the music and the lights. Flora cuddled into him, resting her head on his shoulder; and he drifted off to sleep with his arms wrapped round her, feeling warmer and more at peace than he could ever remember.

CHAPTER THIRTEEN

FLORA woke the next morning in Tom's arms. He was already awake, and smiled down at her. 'Good morning, sleepyhead. How's the hangover?'

'What hangover?'

'The champagne you drank, last night,' he reminded her.

'I didn't drink that much,' she said with a smile. 'It wasn't champagne that made me all giddy. That was you.'

'I know the feeling—that's what you do to me.' He stole a kiss. 'I love you, Flora.'

She'd never get tired of hearing this. Never. 'I love you, too,' she said softly.

'So what are we doing today?'

'Much as I'd like to stay here with you all day, that's not an option.' She paused. 'Aren't your parents going back to France this evening?'

'Yes.'

'Then how about I cook us all Sunday lunch,' she said, 'and we spend the afternoon on the beach making sandcastles with Joey until they have to go?'

Tom held her close. A day with all the people he loved. *His family.* 'That,' he said, 'sounds absolutely perfect.'

'Turnout, vehicles 54 and 55. RTC.' There was a pause. 'Cutting gear needed.'

Road traffic collision.

Given the cold snaps they'd had over the winter, Tom had had to face several car accidents since he'd lost his sister to one. But this was the first time since then that they'd been told up front that they'd need cutting gear.

Please, God, let them be able to free the trapped and get everyone safely to hospital. Don't let another family have to go what his had gone through.

It turned out to be only one vehicle involved, wrapped round a tree. It looked as if the driver had hit black ice and spun off the road.

'The ambulance is on its way but we need to check out the driver now. Tom, you've got the ALS training,' Steve said.

'OK, Guv. I'm on it.' The passenger's side of the car was bent round the tree; Tom tried the driver's door, but it was jammed. He tried the rear passenger door, and to his relief it opened.

There wasn't a huge amount he could do before the ambulance arrived, but he could do the basics. ABCDE—airway, breathing, circulation, disability, exposure.

'I'm Tom, one of the fire crew,' he said, leaning in through the back door. 'The ambulance is on its way and we're going to get you out, mate. What's your name?'

'Ethan.'

The driver could speak, which meant his airway was clear. His breathing seemed a bit shallow, but Tom couldn't get a proper look to see if Ethan was losing any blood. ABC. D: disability. There were no immediate neurological problems, he thought, because Ethan had been able to answer a question. But as for exposure, checking the extent of his injuries—that would have to wait until they'd cut him out.

'Do you have any pain anywhere, Ethan?' Tom asked.

'My neck,' Ethan said.

Could be whiplash; could be a spinal injury. 'As soon as

the ambulance is here, we'll get a collar on you and get you out. Anywhere else?'

'My legs. My foot's stuck.'

The front of the car had crumpled, so Ethan's foot was probably caught between the pedals. They'd need the cutters to get him out—and they'd have to take the roof off the car to move him.

'We'll get you out of here soon. Can you remember what happened?'

'I was late for a meeting—then the car fishtailed and I was heading straight for the tree.'

Which sounded like a classic case of black ice. Given that he was running late, Ethan probably hadn't been giving his full concentration to the road; black ice was tough to spot at the best of times, but when you weren't looking for it you didn't stand a chance. Tom glanced into the car's interior. He couldn't see any passengers, but he needed to check. 'Were you on your own in the car?' he asked.

'Yes,' Ethan said.

'OK. I'm going to talk to my station manager about the best way to get you out. I'll be back in two minutes.' Steve was already assessing the car when Tom went to talk to him. 'Possible spinal injury, and his foot's stuck.'

'We're going to have to open the car for the ambo crew so they can get a board in, then,' Steve said. 'And probably cut the pedals to free him. Right. Let's stabilise the car.'

'I'll tell him what we're doing.' Tom leaned into the back of the car again. 'Ethan, we're going to make the car safe so it won't move, and then the paramedics are going to get you out, OK?'

'Uh-huh.'

The first emergency vehicle to arrive wasn't the ambulance, as Tom had expected, but the rapid response unit car. Josh O'Hara climbed out of the front seat.

'Hey, Tom. Looks nasty. What have we got?'

'Just the driver—his name's Ethan. He's talking, but the front's jammed so I can't tell if he's bleeding or how badly he's injured. His neck hurts and his foot's trapped.'

'If I get a collar on him, can you cut him out?'

'Sure.'

While Josh sorted out the collar, Tom and the rest of the fire crew sorted the rams and spreaders.

'Can you sit with him while we cut him out?' Tom asked.

'Course I will.'

Tom handed him the blue tear-shaped plastic shield and leaned into the back. 'Ethan, we're going to cut you out so the doctor can take a proper look at you. It's going to be noisy in here, but don't worry—Josh is going to stay with you. We have to cut through the windscreen, so Josh is going to hold a shield in front of you to make sure you don't get any glass in your face.'

'Uh-hmm.' Ethan's voice sounded slurred and Tom exchanged a concerned glance with Josh.

'Ten minutes and you'll be out of here,' Tom said.

By the time they'd cut him out, the ambulance crew had the trolley next to the car, ready to take Ethan in, and Josh had got a line into him so the all-essential fluids could go in. Tom put a shield over Ethan's legs to protect him, then used the cutter to snap the pedal trapping his legs. After that, the paramedics took over, getting a spinal board on Ethan, then taking him off to St Piran's.

Josh looked at Tom. 'You OK?'

'Yeah.' Just. And he knew why Josh had asked. 'I admit, it's making me think of my sister. And I just wish…' But wishing couldn't make things right. Couldn't bring her back.

Josh laid a hand on Tom's shoulder. 'I'm sorry, mate. There's nothing anyone can do or say to fix it.'

'No.' Tom looked at Josh. 'You don't look so good yourself. Is this bringing back memories for you, too?'

'No. It's just that life can be so... Have you ever done something you really, really regret later?'

Josh was usually the life and soul of the football match, joking and laughing afterwards. And Tom had the strongest feeling that his friend was doing exactly the same as Tom himself had always done: using laughter as a shield to hide his emotions. It looked to him as if Josh needed to talk to someone. And it might as well be him. 'Look, it's practically lunchtime,' he said. 'You must be due a break, too.'

'Well, yeah.'

'Fancy grabbing a sandwich?'

Josh shook his head. 'A sandwich won't do. Even if it comes with chunky fries.'

'If it's a serious carb fix you need, how about pizza?'

'That,' Josh said, 'would definitely work for me.'

'OK. See you at Luigi's in twenty minutes?'

'You're on.'

Twenty minutes later Josh walked into the pizza parlour to see Josh already there. Josh ordered a pizza loaded with absolutely everything, and wisecracked his way through the whole meal. Tom waited until their coffees had arrived, then said gently, 'OK. You do the same as I do—tell enough jokes and it'll all go away. Except it doesn't.' He paused. 'So what's happened?'

Josh sighed. 'It's messy.'

'I'm not going to spill to anyone. Tell me,' Tom encouraged him.

'Years ago, I fell for someone. It went wrong—and it was my fault.' A muscle flickered in Josh's jaw. 'I never forgot her, but there was no way we were going to be together.'

'And you got married on the rebound?' Tom asked. He'd heard the rumours that Josh's marriage was in trouble, and his wife never appeared at the football matches nowadays. Tom had met Rebecca a couple of times; she was nice enough, but maybe a little too picture-perfect.

Josh sighed. 'No. I loved Rebecca, thought I did, but if I'm honest I know I never felt the same connection with her as I did with my ex. We've been drifting apart for years.' He looked grim. 'I don't think our marriage can be saved and I don't think either of us really wants to try saving it.'

'So you're looking at divorce?'

'I guess so. We want different things out of life. She wants a baby above all else.'

'And I take it you don't?'

Josh grimaced. 'I've never wanted kids—never—and she knows that. We had a deal.' He blew out a breath. 'And now I've done something really stupid. I got drunk at the dinner on Saturday night. And…you know how it is. You're tired, you're not thinking about what you're doing. She was warm, she was there—and, God help me.' He raked a hand through his hair. 'I shouldn't have done it. It wasn't fair to her. I didn't use a condom—and she didn't stop me.'

Tom looked at him in sympathy. 'Have you talked to her about it since?'

'No. She's pretending it never happened, but we both know it did. And we both know why it happened, too.' Josh sighed. 'This is crazy. I don't love her any more, and she doesn't love me. I ought to let her go, find someone who'll give her what she wants.'

'And you're still thinking about the girl you lost?' Tom guessed.

'It would help,' Josh said drily, 'if I didn't have to work with her.'

Tom blew out a breath. 'Tricky one. Does she know you still have feelings for her?'

'I'm not sure. She won't discuss it with me. On Saturday,

she told me to go home to my wife. And, like an idiot, I did. And…' He sighed. 'Rebecca knew I was drunk, that I wasn't thinking straight. And I'll never forgive myself if we've made a baby.'

'She's not on the Pill?'

'She was,' Josh said, but his tone made it clear he didn't think she was any more.

'It doesn't always happen first time,' Tom said. 'You're a doctor. You know the odds.'

'Yeah.' Josh drained his coffee. 'Well, enough of my problems. How are things with Joey?'

'He's really started to open up to me,' Tom said. 'Funny, I used to be like you. I never thought I wanted kids. But now I'm Joey's stand-in dad…and I'm getting used to it. More than that, I'm actually enjoying it.'

'And you have Flora. She's a sweetheart.'

'A definite keeper,' Tom said.

'I hope it works out for you,' Josh said. He glanced at his watch. 'And we'd better get back on shift. See you at the game on Sunday?'

'Absolutely. And we're going to beat you four-nil,' Tom said with a grin.

'In your dreams.' Josh clapped him on the shoulder. 'Thanks, mate.'

'I didn't do a lot.'

'You listened. It helped.'

Though, seeing the shadows in his friend's eyes, Tom wasn't so sure.

'Good day?' Flora asked as Tom walked in.

'Sort of.' He ruffled Joey's hair, made a fuss of Banjo, then came to steal a kiss from Flora. 'I had to cut someone out of a car today.'

Joey went very still.

'He skidded on the ice,' Tom said gently, 'but he was all right. He wasn't very well when he got to hospital, but they made him better. He's got a sore shoulder and a broken ankle, but the doctors told me he's going to be fine.'

'That's good.' Flora put a mug of tea in front of him.

'I've been thinking,' he said. 'I'm going to resign from the fire service.'

'What?' She stared at him. 'Why? You love your job. It's who you are.'

'I know.' He wrinkled his nose. 'But I think it's the only way.'

'The only way to do what, Tom?'

'I know what I want out of life. I want to be a family with you both,' Tom said. 'And my job's dangerous. It's not fair to make you take on that burden.'

'Tom, we love you for who you are—and you've always been a firefighter. It's what you've always wanted to do. You'd be miserable doing anything else.'

'Maybe.' He looked at Flora and Joey. 'But you're worth it.'

'Don't we get a say in this?' Flora asked.

Tom frowned. 'How do you mean?'

'We know what you do is dangerous but it's an important job. Provided you don't take stupid risks—and you know exactly what I mean by that—I can handle it,' she told him. 'Joey?'

Joey frowned. Then he said, 'I love you, Tom.'

Tom stared at him, completely unable to speak. A month ago, Joey had barely been stringing two words together and had hated being touched; he never, but never spoke about anything emotional. And now, unless his hearing had suddenly gone skewy...

He glanced at Flora, and knew that he'd definitely heard Joey say it.

I love you.

'I love you too, sweetheart,' he whispered.

'If your fire engine had gone to rescue my mum and dad, they'd still be here instead of going to heaven,' Joey said.

Tom felt as if his soul had just been flayed. The little boy had that much confidence in him? And yet, even though Tom knew he was incredibly committed to his job, he wasn't sure that he could've saved Susie and Kevin. Nobody could've been pulled out of a collision like that. 'Joey, sweetheart, I don't know if anyone could've saved them,' he said softly.

'But if anyone could, you could,' Joey said. 'And I don't want someone else to lose their mum and dad because you're not on the team any more.'

'Out of the mouths of babes,' Flora said. 'He's got a point. You're good at what you do. No, you're amazing at what you do.'

'But wouldn't you both be happier if I had a less dangerous job—something that didn't risk my life?' he asked.

Flora and Joey looked at each other, clearly considering it, then shook their heads in unison.

'I'd still be worrying about you,' Flora said, 'but I'd be worrying that you were unhappy, not that you were in danger.'

'So you'd be OK if I stayed as a firefighter?' He could really have it all—a family *and* his career? It was really that easy? He'd spent days and days trying to work out what he should do, ever since Flora had made him realise that he had to consider Joey before he took the more dangerous risks. And he'd come to the conclusion that there wasn't a middle way—that he'd have to give up who he was.

And now, it seemed, he didn't.

Joey nodded. 'You're really cool, Uncle Tom.'

'I second that,' Flora said.

Banjo barked, as if to third it, and Flora and Joey laughed.

'If we're a family,' Joey said, 'does that mean we'll all live here with Banjo?'

'Would you like that?' Tom asked.

Joey nodded. 'You'd be like my dad and Flora would be like my mum. That'd be cool. And then you'd have a baby.'

'A baby?' Flora asked, looking surprised.

'Because that's what people do when they get married. Have babies. And I'd be a big brother.' He beamed. 'That'd be cool, too.'

Tom thought of Flora, pregnant with his child, and sheer desire surged through him. 'Sounds good to me. Flora?'

She coughed. 'Is that a proposal, Tom Nicholson?'

He smacked his forehead. 'I'm meant to be down on one knee, and there should be champagne and diamonds and—'

'And none of that's important,' Flora interrupted. 'What's important is exactly what Joey said.'

'So how about it? Would you marry us and be a family with us?'

'Would you?' Joey said. 'And can we live here?'

Flora smiled at them. 'I can't think of anything in the world I'd rather do. Yes.'

Tom picked her up and swung her round, Joey whooped with glee, and Banjo barked madly. And when he set her back down on her feet, he enfolded Joey in a hug along with Flora. 'My family,' he said. 'My perfect dream come true.'

ST. PIRAN'S:
TINY MIRACLE
TWINS

MAGGIE KINGSLEY

I often wonder how my sister Elizabeth puts up with my many crises of confidence when I'm writing, without ever saying to me, 'Maggie, get a grip!' or strangling me, but she does. So thank you, little sister, and this book is dedicated to you, for your patience, forbearance, and all the times you've listened to me when I've said, 'OK, do you think *this* would be better?' without running screaming from the room.

CHAPTER ONE

People say time heals everything but it doesn't, not completely, never totally. Sometimes all it takes is the overheard fragment of a song, a whispered comment, or an unexpected meeting, and the scab that time has so carefully placed over the old wound begins to come apart, leaving the pain just as acute as it ever was, just as raw.

'So, the rumours are true, then,' Sister Brianna Flannigan observed as she sipped her coffee in the canteen of St Piran's. 'A troubleshooter really is coming to the hospital to see which departments should be closed?'

'And not just coming, I'm afraid.' Megan Phillips sighed. 'He's actually arriving some time today if the grapevine is correct.'

'But this is a good hospital,' Brianna protested. 'The staff are dedicated, the quality of surgery is second to none, and it provides a much-needed medical resource for the people who live in this part of Cornwall.'

'Agreed.' Jess Corezzi nodded glumly. 'But, according to the board, we're leaking money like a sieve, and...' She held up her hands and made pretend speech marks. '"Something Has to be Done".'

'But surely that doesn't have to mean ward or—heaven

forbid—complete department closures?' Brianna demanded. 'There must be some other way to save money.'

'Canning my job will probably be the first thing on this auditor's list,' Jess said ruefully. 'Counselling patients, and their families, as I do...' She shook her head. 'I can't see him regarding that as necessary.'

'But your job is vitally important,' Brianna protested, her large brown eyes troubled. 'The parents of my babies in NICU need you—'

'As do the parents, and kids in Paeds,' Megan chipped in, but Jess didn't look convinced, and Brianna could understand why.

If the auditor had been drafted in to make economies he was bound to look at the non-nursing staff first, and though she and Megan might think Jess's counselling role essential she had a horrible suspicion this money man would not.

'What does Gio think?' Brianna asked, thinking of Jess's handsome Italian husband, a neurosurgeon who had arrived at St Piran's the previous autumn and swept her friend off her feet.

'He thinks like you, that the auditor will recognise how valuable my work is and recommend shelving the new specialist paediatric burns unit instead, but frankly...' Jess shrugged. 'I can't see that happening. There is a need for that unit, plus the building is almost complete, and Admin have already asked that foreign prince to perform the grand opening in a couple of months.'

Brianna didn't think Gio's suggestion likely, either, and neither did Megan, judging by her expression.

'At least both your departments will be safe,' Jess continued bracingly. 'No one in their right mind would shut down a neonatal intensive care unit or a paediatric ward.'

Brianna could think of one man who would. One man

to whom statistics and efficiency had always been more important than people, and she shivered involuntarily.

'You OK?' Megan asked with a slight frown, and Brianna forced a smile.

'I just don't like all this talk of department closures. This hospital has been my...' She came to a halt. She had been about to say 'refuge', but though she, Jess and Megan had become friends during the two years she'd been at St Piran's there were areas of her life that were strictly off limits, and her past was one of them. 'I've been so very happy here,' she said instead.

'Me, too,' Jess replied, and Megan nodded in agreement.

'Look, do we know anything about this man?' Brianna asked. 'Where he's from, what other hospitals he's been to?'

'All we know is he's from London,' Jess replied, and the shiver Brianna had felt earlier became more pronounced.

'London?' she echoed. 'Jess—'

The insistent bleep of a pager brought her to a halt. All three women instantly reached for theirs, but it was Megan who got to her feet with a groan.

'Nothing wrong in Paeds, I hope?' Brianna said, and Megan shook her head.

'It's Admin. They've got themselves in a real flap about this visitation. Yesterday they wanted everything in duplicate. Now they've decided they want everything in triplicate.'

With a rueful smile the paediatric specialist registrar headed off towards the canteen exit but, as Brianna and Jess watched her, the door suddenly opened and Josh O'Hara, the consultant from A and E, appeared. He clearly said something to Megan, actually put out his hand to stay her, but she pushed past him without a word, and Brianna and Jess exchanged glances.

'The atmosphere's not getting any better between those two, is it?' Brianna said, and Jess sighed.

'I guess it can't. Not when Josh is married to Rebecca, and Megan's most certainly not a home-wrecker.'

'Has…?' Brianna cleared her throat awkwardly. 'Has she said anything to you about him?'

'I only know there's a past history there, not what it is, and I wouldn't dream of asking,' Jess replied. 'My guess is they were an item years ago, before Josh got married, but as to what happened or why they split up…' The hospital counsellor lifted her shoulders helplessly. 'I just wish he hadn't taken the consultant's job in A and E. OK, so he didn't know Megan would be working at St Piran's, but can you imagine how awful it must be, having someone you once loved reappear in your life like this?'

Brianna could. She didn't want to imagine it, but she could, all too vividly.

Secrets, she thought as she watched Josh walk slowly across the canteen then stare unenthusiastically at the lunch menu. She, Jess and Megan, all of them had secrets. Maybe that's what had drawn them together, made them friends. That, and the fact they never pried into one another's private lives so she'd had no idea until a few months ago that Jess had HIV, or that Megan was nursing a badly broken heart, while neither of them knew she…

Don't go there, Brianna, she told herself. *Don't go there, not ever.*

'The annoying thing is, I like him,' Jess continued as Josh picked up a doughnut and coffee, then morosely went to sit at an empty table near the back of the canteen. 'Whatever happened between him and Megan in the past, I still think he's one of the good guys.'

'And does your husband know you consider Josh "one of the good guys"?' Brianna asked, her brown eyes dancing, and the counsellor laughed.

'Gio knows I only have eyes for him,' she replied. 'I just wish…this situation between Megan and Josh… I just wish there was something I could do to help.'

Brianna wished she could, too, as she and Jess left the canteen and went their separate ways. She'd liked Josh O'Hara from the very first minute she'd met him. For sure he'd teased her when he'd discovered she was from Ireland as he was, had said that with her long, auburn hair she reminded him of the 1940s Hollywood actress, Maureen O'Hara, but she knew he hadn't been hitting on her. He was just a natural-born charmer, adept at making people feel at ease. Unless, of course, that person was Megan Phillips, she thought with a deep sigh.

And she could have done with Josh at her side, dispensing a whole bucketload of his charm, she decided as she swiped her ID card to gain entry to NICU, only to walk straight into Rita, NICU's ward clerk, and her least favourite member of staff in the hospital.

'I'm not late back from lunch, Rita,' Brianna said, consulting her watch pointedly, 'the unit doesn't appear to be on fire, I'm sure you would have paged me if any of the babies was giving cause for concern, so can I assume you want to report one of the nursing staff for some petty infringement?'

'He's here,' the NICU ward clerk hissed. 'The auditor. He arrived half an hour ago, and I've got him in my office, looking at some files, but I don't know how long I can keep him there.'

'Have you considered chains, manacles, possibly a straitjacket?'

'This is not a laughing matter, Sister Flannigan,' Rita retorted. 'Mr Brooke is still in Theatre—'

'Which is probably just as well,' Brianna interrupted. 'Letting Babbling loose amongst walking, healthy people...' She shook her head. 'Not a good idea.'

'Neither is referring to our head of department by that stupid nickname,' Rita protested, apparently conveniently forgetting that she called their consultant Mr Brooke 'Babbling' just as often as the rest of the staff in NICU did.

'Rita—'

'First impressions count, Sister, and we've already got off to a bad one with Mr Brooke not being here to meet the VIP.'

'Yes, it really was *very* inconsiderate of little Amy Renwick to get so sick, wasn't it?' Brianna said dryly, but her sarcasm was lost on the ward clerk.

'It certainly couldn't have happened at a worse time,' Rita agreed. 'I only have two years left to work before I retire and the last thing I want is the unit closing down before I'm ready to go.'

Yeah, and you're all heart, Rita, Brianna thought, but she didn't say that.

'I very much doubt anyone would ever contemplate shutting down a neonatal intensive care unit,' she said, deliberately echoing Jess's optimistic words, but Rita wasn't placated.

'We're grossly understaffed,' the ward clerk declared, her tightly permed grey curls practically bristling with indignation, 'and this auditor is bound to notice. Lord knows, I'm not one to complain—'

You never do anything but, Brianna thought irritably. In fact, it would be a red-letter, stop-press, post-it-to-the-world-on-Twitter day if Rita managed to get through one day without complaining.

'And no-one can say I'm not doing my best,' Rita continued, 'but, without a nurse unit manager, I'm fighting an uphill battle.'

Brianna was sorely tempted to tell the woman she might find her job considerably easier if she didn't spend half her time prying into everyone else's business and the other half spreading gossip, but the trouble was the ward clerk was right. They *were* finding it tough without a nurse unit manager, and though Admin had promised to advertise the post after Diego Ramirez returned to Spain, there had been no sign yet of them doing anything.

'I'm sure the auditor will make allowances for us,' she declared, 'and now, if you'll excuse me—'

'Selfish, that's what I call it,' Rita continued. 'Mr Ramirez leaving us all in the lurch. In my day people had a sense of duty, a sense of responsibility, but nobody cares about standards nowadays. Look at all the unmarried mothers we get in NICU. Feckless, the lot of them. In my day—'

'I'm sure every family behaved like the Waltons, and nothing bad ever happened,' Brianna interrupted tersely, 'but right now, if you're so anxious about making a good impression, wouldn't it be better if you simply got on with your job?'

Rita's mouth fell open, she looked as though she'd dearly like to say something extremely cutting, then she strode away with a very audible sniff, and Brianna gritted her teeth.

She would undoubtedly pay later for what she'd said—Rita would make sure of that—but the ward clerk had caught her on the raw today. Actually, if she was honest,

Rita always caught her on the raw with her 'holier than thou' attitude to life.

'Walk a mile in my moccasins.'

It was one of her mother's favourite sayings, and her mother was right, Brianna thought as she washed her hands thoroughly then applied some antiseptic gel to ensure she didn't carry any bacteria into the unit, except…

She bit her lip as she caught sight of her reflection in the small mirror over the sink. 'The country mouse'. That was what her colleagues had called her when she'd been a student nurse, but that had been fourteen years ago. She wasn't a country mouse any more. She was thirty-two years old, the senior sister in a neonatal intensive care unit, and time and life had changed her. Especially the last two years.

Don't, Brianna, she told herself as she felt her heart twist inside her. *Don't start looking back, you can't, you mustn't, not now, not ever.*

And normally she didn't, she thought as she took a steadying breath before tucking a stray strand of her auburn hair back into its neat plait, only to realise her hand was shaking. Normally she lived in the now, determinedly refusing to look back, or forward, and it was all the fault of this damned auditor. His arrival was upsetting everyone, turning what had been her refuge into a place of uncertainty, and she didn't want uncertainty. She wanted the hospital to stay exactly as it was. Her haven, her sanctuary, her escape from all that had happened.

'Blasted number-cruncher,' she muttered as she used her elbow to push open the door leading into the NICU ward. 'Why can't he just go away and play on a motorway?'

'You wouldn't be talking about our esteemed visitor, would you?' Chris, her senior staff nurse, chuckled, clearly overhearing her.

'Got it in one,' Brianna replied, feeling herself beginning

to relax as the familiar heat in the unit enveloped her, and she heard the comforting, steady sound of beeping monitors and ventilators. 'Anything happen over lunch I should know about?'

'Mr Brooke's not back from Theatre yet and neither is Amy Renwick.'

'So Rita told me,' Brianna replied. 'It looks as though he's had to remove part of Amy's intestine after all.'

It was what they'd all been hoping the consultant wouldn't have to do. Amy Renwick had been born twelve weeks premature, and scarcely a month later she'd been diagnosed with necrotising enterocolitis. The condition wasn't uncommon in premature babies—their intestines were frequently insufficiently developed to handle digestion—but generally it could be controlled with antibiotics. In Amy's case, however, the antibiotics hadn't worked. Mr Brooke had thought he might only have to drain the infected fluid from her stomach, but, from the length of time he'd been in Theatre, it looked very much as though that solution hadn't proved to be an option.

'Is Mrs Renwick here?' Brianna asked, and the staff nurse nodded.

'She's in the parents' restroom—very upset, of course—but her family's with her.'

And they'd been a tower of strength over the past few weeks for Naomi and her husband, Brianna thought as she lifted a file from the nurses' station. Not all of their parents were so lucky. Some families lived too far away to provide emotional support, while other families simply couldn't deal with the constant up-and-down pressures of having a very premature baby.

And sometimes the people, the person, you were so sure you could depend on let you down, she thought with a sudden, unwanted, shaft of pain.

'You OK, Brianna?'

The staff nurse was gazing uncertainly at her, and Brianna manufactured a smile.

'You're the second person to ask me that today, and I'm fine,' she replied. 'I've just got a bad attack of Monday blues, not helped by the imminent arrival of this blasted auditor—'

'Who, if I'm not very much mistaken, has just arrived with Babbling and Rita,' the staff nurse warned in an undertone. 'And, if that *is* him, he looks scary. Good looking in a designer-suited, high-powered sort of way, but most definitely scary.'

Quickly, Brianna glanced over her shoulder, and in that split second her world stood still. Dimly, she heard their NICU consultant introduce the man at his side as Connor Monahan, but she didn't need the introduction. The six-foot-one rangy frame, the thick black hair and startling blue eyes, the expensive city suit and equally top-of-the-range laptop that he was carrying… It was the man she hadn't thought about—had refused to allow herself think about—for the past two years, and the file she'd been holding slipped from her nerveless fingers and landed on the floor with a clatter.

From beside her she heard Chris's small gasp of surprise at her unusual clumsiness, saw Mr Brooke's glare of irritation, but what pierced her to the core as she quickly retrieved the file then straightened up was the way the familiar blue eyes had flashed instantly from recognition to anger. How those same blue eyes were now boring deep into her, tearing her heart apart just as it had been torn apart two years ago.

'I can assure you my staff are not normally so clumsy, Mr Monahan,' she heard Mr Brooke declare, and saw Connor shake his head dismissively.

'Accidents happen,' he replied, 'and, please, everyone, call me Connor. I'm not here to judge anyone. My visit to this hospital is merely as an observer, to find out how a hospital like this serves its local community.'

'Yeah, right,' Chris muttered. 'And like we don't all know that he's been sent in to find out which department should be closed, so he can give up on the "let's all be friends" routine. And, oh, Lord, Mr Brooke is now insisting on introducing everyone,' the staff nurse continued, rolling her eyes heavenwards. 'What's the bet he won't remember half our names?'

Brianna didn't care if the middle-aged consultant did or not. She was too busy keeping her eyes fixed firmly on the file in her hand, wishing she was anywhere but here, but, out of the corner of her eye, she could see the inexorable approach of a pair of mirror-bright black shoes, could smell an all-too-distinctive sandalwood aftershave, and she sucked in an uneven breath, willing this moment to be over.

'And this is Sister Flannigan,' Mr Brooke announced when he drew level with her.

'Sister Flannigan,' Connor repeated slowly, and Brianna winced as she reluctantly raised her head to look up at him.

Never would she have imagined anyone could put quite so much sarcasm into her surname, but Connor just had.

'She's only been with us for two years,' Mr Brooke continued, clearly completely oblivious to the atmosphere, 'but since then she's become an indispensable member of the team.'

At any other time Brianna would have savoured the praise from the portly consultant, who never gave anyone any, but not today, not when she saw Connor's left eyebrow rise.

'So, you've been living here in Cornwall for the last two years, have you, Sister Flannigan?' he said with deliberate emphasis, and Brianna clasped the file in her hands even tighter.

Don't, she wanted to say. *Please, don't. Not here, not in front of everyone.* But she couldn't say anything, not with her boss listening, not with Rita's eyes darting avidly between her and Connor, her mind clearly already whirring away with speculation.

'Yes, I've been here for two years,' she muttered, 'and now if you'll excuse me…'

'Oh, absolutely not,' Connor declared, his voice ice-cold and implacable. 'In fact, I *insist* you stay.'

Had he always been quite so tall, so intimidating? she wondered as she involuntarily took a step back. Of course he had. He couldn't possibly have grown since she'd last seen him, and he'd always possessed an air of authority and power, and yet she felt transported back in time to the little country mouse she'd once been, and she hated feeling that way.

'I'm afraid you really will have to excuse me,' she said, putting as much defiance into her voice as she could muster. 'I have babies to attend to, and I also need to talk to the mother of one of our patients. Her daughter has just undergone major surgery—'

'From which we are hopeful she will make a full recovery,' Mr Brooke interrupted. 'Of course, the next few days will be critical, as I will explain to Mrs Renwick myself.'

Which is exactly what I *don't* want you to do, Brianna thought unhappily. Of course, all operations carried risks, but not for nothing had the nursing staff in NICU nicknamed their consultant 'Babbling' Brooke. Brilliant surgeon though he might be, he would persist in constantly—and at great length—giving parents the worst-case scenario

possible, terrifying them witless in the process. Megan
would have handled Naomi Renwick so much better, but
Megan wasn't here.

'It would be no trouble for me to talk to Mrs Renwick,
Mr Brooke,' she said desperately. 'I could go now—'

'Not running away from me, are you, Sister Flannigan?'
Connor said, and she bit her lip savagely.

Had she been the only one in the unit who had heard
the unspoken word *again* in his comment? She hoped she
was, she prayed she was.

'Of course not,' she replied. 'I just... I know Mrs Renwick
very well... I'm her daughter's primary carer—'

'And I'm her daughter's surgeon, and head of this department, so I will speak to her,' Mr Brooke interrupted with
a finality that told Brianna there was no point in arguing.
'Now, Connor, I'm sure our ward clerk will be only too
happy to let you examine more of our files—'

'Which I'm sure would be absolutely fascinating,'
Connor interrupted, 'but I'm only going to be in St Piran's
for the next six weeks so what I'd like to do in NICU, over
the next few days, is interview all of your staff individually.
Form an idea from them of how they think they fit into
this unit, what their duties are, gain the bigger picture, if
you like.'

Six weeks? Brianna thought, glancing from Connor to
Mr Brooke with ill-disguised horror. Connor was going
to be in the hospital for *six weeks*? Even if he only spent a
few days in NICU, it was going to be a few days too many
and Mr Brooke clearly thought the same.

'I really don't see why there's any need for you to interview my staff when I can give you the bigger picture immediately,' he said. 'Sick babies come in here, my nursing
staff and I attempt to make them better. End of story.'

Brianna could have kissed the consultant, but Connor

merely smiled the smile of a man who had no intention of having his intentions thwarted.

'I still want to speak to your staff,' he insisted evenly. 'My interviews will take no longer than half an hour, and after that I will simply be a silent observer. In fact, I doubt you'll even notice I'm here.'

I'll notice, Brianna thought, desperately praying their consultant would feel the same but, to her dismay, he had clearly become bored with the conversation and simply shrugged.

'Fine—whatever,' he said. 'Just don't get in my way, or the way of my staff. So, who do you want to interview first?'

Connor made a show of glancing over the assembled nurses, but Brianna knew who he was going to choose, just as she knew Connor knew it, too.

'I'm sure Sister Flannigan and I will find a lot to talk about,' he declared with a smile that didn't even remotely suggest it would ever reach his eyes. 'Mr Brooke, do you have an office or room I could use as a base while I'm here at the hospital?'

He wanted to use NICU as his base? Even when he was assessing other departments he would keep returning to NICU as his base? *No*, Brianna thought desperately, dear heavens, *no*.

'I'll get Maintenance to clear out the nurse unit manager's office for you,' the consultant replied vaguely. 'It's not in use at the moment, but there are confidential files in it that will have to be secured, so in the meantime you could use the nurses' staffroom if you want.'

Connor nodded.

'Sounds good to me,' he said.

It didn't sound good to Brianna, and neither did the way Connor shadowed her all the way out of the ward and

down the corridor as though he was convinced she might
bolt. And she would have bolted, she thought, if she hadn't
known that a pair of five-foot-two-inch legs could never
have outrun the six-foot-one-inch legs of the man at her
side.

'Would you like some tea, coffee?' she said, walking
quickly over to the kettle as soon as they entered the staffroom, desperate to delay the inevitable for as long as possible. 'There's some herbal tea here, too, though I can't
vouch for it being drinkable, and hot chocolate—'

'So, is it still *Brianna* Flannigan,' he interrupted, 'or
did you change your Christian name as well as your
surname?'

She stared at the cork board which one of the nurses
had affixed to the wall above the kettle and cups. Postcards
from far-away places were pinned to it, along with old
birthday cards and congratulation cards, and there was also
a whole array of cartoons that should have been funny but
she had never felt less like laughing.

'I…I kept my Christian name,' she muttered, mechani-
cally switching on the kettle and spooning some coffee into
a cup, though she didn't really want anything. 'Flannigan
was my mother's maiden name.'

'But not yours,' he said. 'You do realise I could get you
fired for working at this hospital under a false name?'

He could, she knew he could, but suddenly she didn't
care. Suddenly she felt cornered, and defeated, and wearily
she turned to face him.

'OK, get me fired,' she said. 'If that's what you want to
do, then go ahead and do it.'

'Of course that's not what I want!' he exclaimed, tossing his laptop onto the nearest seat. 'What do you take me
for?'

I don't know, she thought as she gazed up into his cold,

rigid face. *I don't know because I feel like I don't know you any more, and I'm wondering now if I ever did.*

'Look, can we sit down?' she said. 'You standing there—looming over me like some spectre of doom—isn't helping.'

With a muttered oath he sat down, and, after a moment's hesitation she abandoned the kettle and took the seat opposite him.

'You really were determined I wouldn't find you, weren't you?' he said, his blue eyes fixed on her, daring her to contradict him. 'Changing your surname, moving to a one-horse town in the back of beyond in Cornwall.'

'Connor, it wasn't like that—'

'Wasn't it?' he interrupted, his voice dripping sarcasm. 'So how—exactly—would you interpret it?'

'I wanted…' Oh, but this was so hard to explain, and she wanted to explain, for him to understand. 'I just wanted…' Her voice broke slightly despite her best efforts to keep it level. 'Some peace. All I wanted was some peace.'

'And to get that you had to walk out on me?' he said incredulously. 'Walk out without a word?'

'I left you a letter,' she protested, and saw his lip curl with derision.

'"I need to be on my own for a while,"' he quoted. '"I need some space, some time to get myself together". That's hardly an "I'm leaving you, and I'm never coming back", dear-John letter, is it?'

'Connor—'

'You applied for this job without telling me, didn't you?' he said. 'You applied for it, and got it, and yet you never said a word to me about what you were planning to do.'

She swallowed hard. 'Yes.'

'So that's why you only ever took three hundred pounds out of our joint bank account,' he declared, fury deepening his voice. 'You didn't need any more money because you had this job to come to.'

'Yes,' she whispered.

'Why, Brianna, *why*?' he demanded, thrusting his fingers through his black hair, anger, hurt and bewilderment plain on his face. 'I thought we were happy, I thought you loved me.'

'Things…things haven't been right between us for a long time, Connor,' she replied, 'you know they haven't—'

'That's nonsense,' he retorted, and she clasped her hands together tightly, desperately trying to find the words that would make him understand.

'I was going under, Connor,' she cried. 'After what happened—you wouldn't talk to me, you wouldn't let me talk, and I knew—if I didn't get away—I was going to slide further and further into the black pit I'd fallen into, and if I kept on falling…' She took an uneven breath. 'I was scared—so scared—that I would never be able to get myself out again.'

'And me—what about me?' he exclaimed, his blue eyes blazing. '*Two years*, Brianna, it's been *two years* since you left and in all that time you never once lifted the phone to tell me you were OK, never once even sent me a scribbled postcard to say you were alive.'

'I was going to write, to tell you where I was,' she declared defensively, but had she really been going to? It wasn't something she wanted to think about, far less face. It was enough of a shock to see him sitting there in front of her. 'Connor—'

'You left your phone behind, the house keys, the police wouldn't help me—'

'You went to the police?' She gasped, her eyes large with dismay, and he threw her a look that made her shrink back into her seat.

'What the hell did you expect me to do? Did you think I'd simply stay home in our flat, night after night, watching TV, thinking, Well, I expect Brianna will come back eventually? *Of course* I went to the police. I thought…' He closed his eyes for a second, and when he spoke again his voice was rough. 'I thought you might have done something…stupid, but they said as you'd left a note, and your parents knew you were safe, it wasn't a police matter but a domestic one.'

'I'm sorry,' she murmured. 'I didn't realise—I never imagined you'd go to the police—'

'Can you imagine how that made me feel?' he said, his lips curving into a bitter travesty of a smile. 'When the police told me your parents knew where you were, but I didn't? I went back to Ireland, to your parents' farm in Killarney, thinking you might have gone there, and, when I discovered you hadn't, I begged them to give me your address, even your phone number, so I could at least hear your voice, know you truly were safe, but they wouldn't give me either. They said you'd made them promise not to tell me anything, that you would contact me when you were ready.'

'I'm sorry, so sorry,' she repeated, willing him to believe her. 'I didn't…' She shook her head blindly. 'I wasn't thinking clearly, not then. I just…'

'Had to get away from me,' he finished for her bitterly, and she bit her lip hard.

'Connor, listen to me—'

'Every time I heard on the news that a body had been found in some secluded spot I feared it was you,' he continued as though she hadn't spoken. 'Every time someone was pulled out of the Thames I thought, Please, don't let it be Brianna, but, as time went on, God help me, I sometimes…' He took a breath. 'Sometimes I hoped it *was* you because at least then the waiting would be over. All I needed…all I wanted…was to know you really were safe, and yet you denied me even that, Brianna.'

'I would have called you, I would have talked to you,' she said, her voice trembling, 'but I knew talking to you wouldn't help, that you wouldn't listen.'

'How can you say that?' he demanded angrily. 'Of course I would have talked, of course I would have listened!'

'You didn't before when I needed you to,' she said before she could stop herself. 'All you ever did was cut me off, change the subject, or you'd ask me…' She swallowed convulsively, hearing the tears in her voice, and she didn't want to cry…she so didn't want to cry. 'You kept asking me what was wrong, and I thought I'd go mad if you asked me that one more time because it was so obvious to me that everything was always going to be wrong, that it was never going to be right.'

'You're not making any sense—'

'Because you're not *listening*, just like you always don't,' she flared. 'Whenever I try to talk to you, you never ever *listen*.'

'Well, I want to talk now,' he countered. 'To talk properly with no lies, deception or half-truths, only honesty.'

She knew he was right, but talking honestly meant resurrecting everything that had happened, meant having to face it again. She hadn't forgotten, she never would, but over the past two years she'd managed to come to a kind of acceptance, and to talk about it now… She didn't think her heart could take that, and she shook her head.

'Connor, this isn't the time, or the place.'

'Then *when*, Brianna?' he exclaimed, and there was such a lacerating fury in his blue eyes that she winced. 'When will be the time, or the place?'

She wanted to say, *Never—nowhere*. She wanted even

more to say she wished he had never come, had never found her, but she didn't have the courage.

'I don't know,' she said wretchedly. 'I don't—'

She bit off the rest of what she had been about to say. The door of the nurses' staffroom had opened, and Megan's head had appeared hesitantly round it.

'I'm really sorry,' the paediatric specialist registrar began, glancing from Brianna to Connor, then back again, 'but I'm afraid Brianna is needed in the unit.'

Brianna was hurrying towards Megan before she had even finished speaking, but when she reached the door she heard Connor clear his throat.

'We have to talk, Brianna, and talk soon,' he said.

She thought she nodded, but she couldn't be sure. All she knew was she had to get away from him, and she was halfway down the corridor before Megan caught up with her.

'Brianna—'

'Is it Amy Renwick? Is she back from Recovery, and there's a problem, or—?'

'Actually, I'm afraid I lied, and you're not needed in the unit at all,' Megan interrupted, looking shamefaced. 'It's just…I was passing the nurses' staffroom and I heard the auditor yelling at you. I wasn't eavesdropping, honestly I wasn't,' she continued as Brianna stared at her in alarm. 'It's just the walls in this place are so thin, and you sounded… Well, you sounded really upset, and in need of rescue.'

'I did—I was,' Brianna said with a small smile.

'I think you should make a formal complaint,' Megan declared angrily. 'It's one thing to inspect a unit, to ask the staff questions about how it's run, but harassing someone…' She shook her head. 'That's completely out of order.'

'Megan, I don't want to make a complaint,' Brianna

replied. 'My interview is over, done with, so let's just leave it, OK?'

'Not on your life,' the paediatric registrar insisted. 'If this Connor whatever his name is—'

'Monahan. His name's Connor Monahan.'

'Thinks he can ride roughshod over the nursing staff, upset them, then he can think again. I can understand why you might be reluctant to make a complaint, but I'm not. I'm more than willing to march up to Admin right now, and tell them they'd better warn him to back off or they'll have the nurses' union on their doorstep.'

Megan would do it, too, Brianna thought, seeing the fury in her friend's face, and it was the last thing she wanted. It was hard enough for her to deal with Connor's reappearance in her life without having the staff in Admin gossiping about it after they'd been told all the facts, and she would have to tell them all the facts.

'Megan, it's got nothing to do with the nursing staff, or the unit,' she said unhappily. 'It's me. It's to do with me. You see, Connor Monahan and I... We know one another.'

Her friend gazed at her blankly for a second, then a look of horrified realisation appeared on her face.

'Oh, lord, he's not an ex-boyfriend of yours, is he?' she exclaimed. 'Oh, Brianna, I'm so sorry, what a nightmare for you.'

'A nightmare, for sure.' Brianna nodded. 'But you see...' She took a deep breath. 'The trouble is, Connor isn't an ex-boyfriend. He...he's my husband.'

CHAPTER TWO

'BUT Mr Brooke said yesterday—after Amy's operation—that she might need another operation,' Naomi Renwick said, her eyes dark with fear. 'He said he wouldn't know for the next seventy-two hours whether he'd successfully removed all of the infection, so you'd be keeping a very careful eye on her.'

'Which I would be doing whether Amy had been operated on or not,' Brianna replied, wishing the ever-pessimistic consultant to the darkest reaches of hell. 'Naomi, your daughter is doing very well. We have no reason to think she will require another operation—'

'But if she does... She's so little, Sister, so very little, and if she needs another operation...'

'We'll deal with it just as we've dealt with all the other problems Amy has faced since she was born a month ago. Naomi, listen to me,' Brianna continued, as Amy's mother made to interrupt. 'I can't give you any guarantees—no one can, but, please, *please*, don't go looking for bridges to cross. Amy's temperature's normal, her colour's good. In fact,' she added, 'just look at her.'

Naomi Renwick gazed down into the incubator where her daughter was vigorously kicking her little legs despite the fine line of sutures across her stomach, and her lips curved into a shaky smile.

'She's beautiful, isn't she?' she said, and Brianna nodded.

'She is, and right now she's in the best possible place, getting the best possible care, so hold onto that, OK?'

Brianna hoped Naomi Renwick would, but she wished even more, as she turned to discover Connor standing behind her, that her husband would dog some other nurse's footsteps, if only for a little while.

Twenty-four hours, she thought as she began walking down the ward, all too conscious he was following her. Just twenty-four hours ago her life might not exactly have been perfect, but at least she hadn't felt permanently besieged. Now she felt cornered, under attack, and it wasn't just by his presence, or his continual questions about the unit. It was the way he managed to somehow incorporate so many barbed comments into what he was saying that was wearing her down, little by little, bit by bit.

'How many incubators does the NICU at Plymouth have?' he asked, and she came to a weary halt.

'Twelve,' she replied, 'which is double our capacity, but their hospital covers a far greater area and population than St Piran's, so it's bound to be bigger.'

'I also notice from your ward clerk's files that every baby has a primary carer,' he continued. 'That doesn't seem to be a very efficient system in terms of time or personnel.'

'Not everything can be measured in terms of time management, or personnel distribution,' she said acidly. 'Especially the care of very vulnerable babies.'

'I see,' he said, but she doubted whether he did as she watched him type something into his state-of-the-art phone, which could probably have made him a cup of coffee if he'd asked it to.

Figures, statistics had always been his passion, not people, and he didn't seem to have changed.

'Connor—'

'Does this unit normally have quite so many unused incubators?' he asked, gesturing towards the two empty ones at the end of the ward.

'There's no such thing as "normal" in NICU,' she protested. 'We've had occasions when only three of our incubators have been in use, times when we were at full capacity, and last Christmas we were so busy we had to send babies to Plymouth because we just couldn't accommodate them. It was tough for everyone, especially the families.'

'It would be.' He nodded. 'Christmas being the time when most families like to be together.'

And you've missed two with me. He didn't say those words—he didn't need to—but she heard them loud and clear.

'Things don't always work out the way we planned,' she muttered, 'and babies can't be expected to arrive exactly when you want them to.'

'Not babies, no. Grown-ups, on the other hand,' he added, his eyes catching and holding hers, 'have a choice.'

And you chose to walk away from me. That was what he was really saying, and she swallowed painfully.

'Connor, please,' she said with difficulty. 'This is a good unit, an efficient unit. Please don't make this personal.'

His eyebrows rose. 'You think that's what I'm doing?'

'I *know* it is,' she cried. 'Look, I can understand you being angry—'

'I'm sorry to interrupt,' Rita interrupted, looking anything but as she joined them, 'but I'm afraid we've had a complaint about your car, Sister Flannigan.'

'A complaint?' Brianna echoed in confusion, and Rita smiled.

A smile that was every bit as false as the sympathetic sigh with which she followed it.

'You've parked it in the consultants' side of the car park today instead of the nurses'. Easily done, of course, when you're stressed—'

'I'm not stressed—'

'Of course you are, my dear,' Rita declared, her face all solicitous concern, but her eyes, Brianna noticed, were speculative, calculating. 'How can you possibly not be when you're doing two jobs?'

'Sister Flannigan has two jobs?' Connor frowned, and Rita nodded.

'Our nurse unit manager returned to Spain a few months back, and, as Admin haven't yet appointed his replacement, Sister Flannigan has had to temporarily step into the breach, which is probably why we're not as efficient as we should be.'

'I can't say I've noticed any inefficiency on Sister Flannigan's part,' Connor replied, attempting to walk on, but Rita was not about to be rebuffed.

'Oh, please don't think I'm suggesting Sister Flannigan is inefficient—'

Yeah, right, Rita, Brianna thought angrily, and this is clearly payback time because I chewed your head off yesterday.

'But when you're as much of a perfectionist as I am,' the ward clerk continued, all honeyed sweetness, 'I do like everything to be just so.'

'Which makes me wonder why you're still standing here,' Connor declared, 'and not back in your office, dotting some i's and crossing some t's.'

The ward clerk's mouth opened and closed soundlessly for a second, then she clamped her lips together tightly.

'Well, no one can ever accuse me of remaining where

I'm not wanted,' she said, before stomping away, and Brianna sighed.

'Which, unfortunately, isn't true.' She glanced up at Connor hesitantly. 'Thanks for saying what you did, for backing me up.'

For a moment he said nothing, then his lips twisted into something like a smile. 'I thought I always did. I thought we were a team.'

They had been once, she remembered. There had been a time when she couldn't have imagined her life without him, and then, little by little, things had changed, and two years ago...

'I'm sorry, Connor,' she murmured, 'so sorry.'

'Sorry you left, or sorry I found you?'

His eyes were fixed on her, and the awful truth was she couldn't give him an answer, not without hurting him, and she backed away from him, afraid he would realise it.

'The car,' she said haltingly. 'I have to...I need to move my car.'

She was gone before he could stop her and, when the ward door clattered shut behind her, Connor clenched his fists until his knuckles showed white.

She hadn't answered him. He'd asked her a simple, easy-to-answer question, and yet she hadn't answered him, and he needed—wanted—answers.

Dammit, she owed him that at least, he thought furiously. When he'd first seen her yesterday, his initial reaction had been to thank God she was safe, his Brianna was safe, but then anger had consumed him. A blazing, blinding, irrational anger that she could be standing in front of him looking better than he'd seen her look in a long time, had been living happily in Cornwall for the last two years, when he'd been to hell and back, fearing the worst. And she'd disappear out of his life again in an instant given half a chance. He'd seen it in her dark brown eyes, in the way she looked at him.

Well, she wasn't going to walk away from him a second time, he decided. This time he wanted answers, proper answers, and not some nonsense about him never talking to her, never listening, and he headed for the ward door to follow her.

'I'm really very sorry about this, Sister Flannigan,' Sid, the hospital handyman, said uncomfortably after she'd moved her car out of the consultants' bay and into the nurses' part of the car park. 'To be honest, I don't think there should be any divisions in the car park, but some consultants...' He shook his head. 'It's a status thing for them, you see.'

'It's all right, Sid, truly it is,' Brianna said quickly. 'I don't know where my brain was this morning...' Well, she did know—it was on Connor, she'd been thinking about Connor, and how she didn't want to meet him again, but she wasn't about to share that even with someone as nice as their handyman. 'So could you please tell whoever it was who complained that it won't happen again?'

The middle-aged handyman didn't look any happier. In fact, she could hear him muttering under his breath, 'Officious twit...that's what he is,' as he walked away, and she smiled, but, as she closed her car door, her smile vanished.

It would be so easy to simply get back into her car, and drive away. No one would miss her for a while, and if she kept on driving, and driving, she might eventually reach a place where Connor would never find her. She could start again, change her name again, and—

'Don't, Brianna,' a feminine voice said gently. 'I know what you're thinking, and it won't solve anything.'

'It might,' Brianna muttered, as she turned to see Jess watching her.

'Megan told me about Connor being your husband. She wouldn't normally break a confidence—you know she wouldn't,' the counsellor added quickly as Brianna stared at her in alarm, 'but she's worried about you.'

'I know, but…' Brianna shook her head. 'Jess, have you ever wanted to run away? To just run away, leave everything behind, and start all over?'

'I did—I have,' the counsellor replied. 'When the staff at the hospital I worked in before I came to St Piran's found out about me having HIV…a lot of them cut me dead, crossed the street to avoid me—'

'Oh, Jess!'

'And I couldn't bear it so I ran, and then…' She sighed, a low, sad sigh. 'Well, you know what happened. That reporter from the *Penhally Gazette* broadcast my condition all over his newspaper, and I wanted to run again, but I knew if I did, I would be leaving behind the people, the hospital I felt I'd become such a part of.'

'And Gio,' Brianna murmured. 'You would have been leaving him behind, too.'

'I had no guarantees he would stand by me when he found out the truth, Brianna. He could have walked away and, if he had, then I…' Jess managed a watery smile. 'I would just have to have lived with it.'

Brianna stared down at the car keys in her hand.

'I don't know if I'm as strong as you are.'

'I think you are,' Jess said softly, 'but it's your choice, Brianna. You can stay and confront your fear, or you can run, but if you do run don't forget that whatever you're scared of won't go away. It will always be there, like a dark shadow hanging over you.'

Her friend was right, she knew she was. Running wasn't

the answer, but to stay and try to get Connor to talk to her, to really talk…

'Jess…' she began, only to look sharply round with a frown. 'Did you hear that?'

'Hear what?' Jess said in confusion. 'I can hear the traffic, the birds in the trees—'

'It's a baby. A baby in distress, and it's close by.'

Jess stared at her as though she was suddenly having grave doubts about her mental stability but, having worked with babies for most of her adult life, Brianna could recognise a baby's cry from five hundred paces, and this baby was in trouble. Big trouble.

'Maybe it's a cat,' Jess observed, following Brianna as she headed back to the consultants' part of the car park. 'Cats and kittens often make a sound like a baby.'

But it wasn't a kitten or a cat. It was a baby who hadn't been there when Brianna had moved her car just a few minutes ago. A baby lying wrapped in a white shawl beside Jess's husband's glossy Aston Martin. A baby whose face was blue, and who was breathing in tiny, rasping gasps.

'Oh, my God!' Jess exclaimed, as Brianna swiftly lifted the tiny bundle into her arms and cradled its head against her breast. 'Who on earth would leave a baby here?'

'It doesn't matter who,' Brianna replied. 'This baby needs attention, and it needs it now.'

She was off and running before Jess could reply. Running so single-mindedly she didn't see the tall figure walking towards her until she almost collided with him.

'Brianna, we need to…' Connor looked down, then up at her incredulously. 'That's a baby.'

'Ten out of ten for observation,' she replied, 'and now can you please get out of my way because it needs help.'

NICU was the obvious place to go, she realised as she ran on with Jess and Connor following her, but she didn't know if the bundle in her arms would make it that far, so she sighed with relief when she saw Josh walking across the entrance foyer of the hospital.

'Hello, gorgeous, where's the fire?' He grinned as she raced towards him.

'No fire,' she replied breathlessly. 'It's a newborn, I found it in the car park, and it's floppy, blue and breathing oddly.'

All Josh's amusement disappeared in a second.

'Jess, can you page Mr Brooke and tell him to come down to A and E immediately? And, if you can't get him,' he added as the counsellor turned to go, 'page Megan. Brianna—you and the baby—A and E—now.'

'My guess is respiratory distress syndrome,' Brianna said as she hurried into A and E and placed the baby on one of the examination tables. 'See how his skin and muscles are being pulled in every time he takes a breath?' she added, carefully unwrapping the shawl. 'How tight his abdomen is?'

'It's a boy?' Connor said, his voice sounding slightly constricted, and Josh frowned at him.

'Who are you?' he demanded. 'The baby's father?'

'I'm Connor Monahan, the hospital auditor.'

'Which doesn't explain why you're here, so I suggest you go and audit something. OK, I wants sats, a ventilator, an umbilical line and a cardio-respiratory monitor,' Josh told his staff. 'And a face mask—the tiniest we've got.'

'BP low, heart rate too high,' one of the A and E nurses declared. 'This baby is going to go into shock if we're not careful.'

'Not on my watch, he won't,' Josh said grimly. 'Where's that umbilical line?'

'Josh, can't you hurry up and stabilise him?' Brianna

said, her eyes fixed anxiously on the baby boy. 'He needs the resources we have in NICU.'

'Agreed, my beautiful colleen,' Josh replied as he began to insert the umbilical line, 'but, as you know very well, stabilising can't be rushed. Poor little mite,' he continued as he checked the cardio-respiratory monitor. 'He can't be more than a couple of days old, which means his mother must need medical attention, too.'

'Yes—yes—whatever,' Brianna said quickly, 'but hurry, Josh, please, hurry.'

'This respiratory distress thing,' Connor said, 'can it be cured?'

Josh looked round at him with irritation.

'Why the hell are you still here? Run out of departments to audit already?'

'I asked a question, and I'd like an answer,' Connor declared, his voice every bit as hard as Josh's, and a small smile curved the A and E consultant's lips.

'Are you quite sure you're not the baby's father? OK—OK,' Josh continued as Brianna threw him an impatient look. 'Yes, Mr Monahan, RDS can be cured. Premature, and very underweight, babies often don't produce enough surfactant in their lungs to help them breathe, but we can give it to them artificially through a breathing tube.'

'But only in NICU,' Megan declared as she swept into A and E, pushing an incubator, 'so can we have a little less chat and a lot more action?'

'I'm simply answering Mr Monahan's question, Megan,' Josh answered mildly, but the paediatric specialist registrar was clearly not about to be placated.

'A question we don't have time for,' she retorted.

'Oh, I always have time for questions,' he countered. 'I don't always give the right answers—'

'Now, there's a surprise—*not*,' Megan replied, her voice cold. 'Perhaps if you spent less time—'

'Look, could the two of you park whatever problem you have with one another and concentrate on this baby?' Brianna exclaimed, then flushed scarlet when she saw Megan's hurt expression and Josh's eyebrows shoot up. 'I'm sorry—I shouldn't have said that—I'm just…'

'Worried.' Josh nodded. 'Understood. OK,' he added as he carefully lifted the baby boy and placed him gently into the incubator, 'this tiny tot is good to go.'

Brianna instantly began pushing the incubator out of A and E towards NICU but it didn't make her feel any better. She'd hurt Megan, she knew she had, and it wasn't as though she hadn't known Megan and Josh had some sort of history so to say what she had…

'Megan, I'm sorry,' she murmured when they reached the unit and Chris began hooking the baby to their monitors. 'What I said—'

'Forget it,' Megan interrupted tightly. 'OK, I want an ultrasound scan, more X-rays and the ophthalmologist.'

'Do you want me to check the sats again?' Brianna said uncertainly. 'Josh's staff did them in A and E, but…'

'Double-check them. Josh's staff aren't specialists, we are.'

'He is going to be all right, isn't he?' Connor asked as he hovered beside them. 'That doctor in A and E—the one who was flirting with Brianna—seemed to think he would be.'

'The doctor's name is Josh O'Hara, and he wasn't flirting with me,' Brianna said swiftly, seeing Megan's head snap up. 'He was just being pleasant.'

'Was he indeed,' Connor murmured dryly, and Brianna could have kicked him for the dark shadow that suddenly appeared in Megan's eyes.

'Look, Connor, why don't you wait outside?' she said abruptly. 'All you're doing is getting in the way.'

'I'll stay,' he said firmly, and, when she turned back to the baby with a shrug, he took a shallow breath.

He couldn't leave, and it wasn't just because he was genuinely concerned about the baby Brianna had found. When she'd almost collided with him outside the hospital he'd been unable to believe what she'd been carrying. The little form so motionless, the shock of thick black hair… For a moment it was as though the last two years had never happened, and then he'd blinked, had seen Brianna's blue uniform, and the two years had rolled back again, bringing with them all the old pain and heartbreak.

He'd told himself that all he wanted from her was answers. He'd told himself she deserved to be punished for what she'd put him through, but he'd seen the pain in her eyes when that A and E consultant had been examining the baby. She was still in her own private hell, just as he was, and lashing out at her wasn't the solution, not if he wanted her back. And he did want her back, he realised, feeling his heart twist inside him as he saw her gently touch the little boy's cheek, because without her… Without her he had nothing.

'Shouldn't the police be alerted?' he said. 'If this baby is only days old, won't his mother need help, too?'

'Good point,' Megan declared. 'Did you see anyone hanging about the car park, Brianna?'

'To be honest, I wasn't looking,' she replied.

In fact, Brianna thought with dawning horror, if Jess hadn't turned up when she had, she would probably have been halfway up the motorway by now, and God knows when this baby would have been found.

'Damn,' Megan muttered. 'Chris, could you try paging Mr Brooke again, see if we can track him down?'

'There's something wrong?' Brianna said, her eyes flying to the baby in the incubator, and Megan shook her head.

'"Wrong" is too strong a word. I'd just be a lot happier if this little chap wasn't quite so inactive. Jess said he was crying when you found him, and yet now…'

'Maybe he's just cold?' Brianna suggested hopefully, and Megan frowned.

'Maybe, but I'd really like Mr Brooke to take a look at this little one. Which reminds me,' she continued, 'we can't keep calling him "little chap" or "little one", until his mother comes forward.'

'How about Patrick?' Chris suggested. 'It's March the seventeenth soon, St Patrick's Day, and you're Irish, Brianna, so I vote we call him Patrick.'

Brianna stared down at the baby boy in the incubator. He was so small, so very small, scarcely 5 pounds in weight, and, gently, she adjusted the pulse oximeter taped to his little foot.

'Harry,' she said softly. 'I'd like…I want to call him Harry.'

She heard Connor's sharp intake of breath, knew what he was thinking, but she didn't turn round, didn't acknowledge him, and Chris shrugged.

'Personally, I still like Patrick, but, as you found him, Brianna, if you want to call him Harry, then Harry he is.'

Just until his mother comes forward, Brianna told herself as she carefully slipped a hat over the baby's head to make sure he didn't lose any more heat. He would only be Harry until his mother claimed him, she knew that, and the mother would come forward, she was sure she would, but until then... Until then she would make sure this little Harry always had someone to care for him, to watch out for him.

It was a very long afternoon. Mr Brooke might eventually have arrived, and announced that in his opinion little Harry was most definitely suffering from respiratory distress syndrome, but he departed again with the observation that he also couldn't rule out the possibility of bronchopulmonary dysplasia.

'Remind me never to be on a sinking ship with that man,' Brianna observed with feeling, and Megan laughed.

'Yeah, he's a regular little ray of sunshine, isn't he?' She glanced down at her watch, and gasped. 'Hey, shouldn't you have been off duty hours ago?'

'I know, I just wanted...' Brianna shrugged helplessly. 'I wanted to stay until I was sure little Harry was OK.'

'Well, in the time-honoured hospital jargon,' Megan replied, 'he's doing as well as can be expected, and to be honest that's about as much as we can expect in the circumstances.'

'How old do you think he is?' Brianna asked, and Megan frowned.

'I'd say a day—two days at most. We're still waiting for the results of the scans to confirm his gestational age, but I don't think he's premature, just very small, which would suggest his mother probably wasn't eating properly.'

'And she's out there somewhere, needing help.' Brianna sighed. 'And I don't have the faintest idea what she looks like. If I'd only kept my wits about me, looked about before I rushed her son into the hospital...'

'Hey, don't beat yourself up over it—Jess didn't see anyone either,' Megan replied, then glanced over her shoulder and lowered her voice. 'How's it going with Connor?'

Brianna grimaced. 'What do you think?'

'At least he seems to have finally left for the day,' Megan observed, 'or maybe he's just annoying the hell out of the staff in some other department. Whichever it is, I'd cut and run if I were you. And, yes, I'll phone you at home if there's any change in Harry,' she continued as Brianna made to interrupt, 'so go, will you?'

Brianna laughed and nodded, but, as she turned to leave, she paused.

'Megan, what I said this afternoon in A and E… If I could take it back, I would. If I could reverse the clock, I'd do it in a minute. What I said was so thoughtless—'

'But correct,' the paediatric specialist registrar interrupted. 'Josh and I should have been concentrating on little Harry. It's just… I'm afraid the two of us only have to be in the same room together now and…' She smiled a little unevenly. 'Let's just say it's not good.'

Brianna knew exactly what Megan meant as she left the unit and drove home, but the trouble was she didn't even have to be in the same room with Connor for her nerves to be on edge. Even when she got home to her cottage in the small fishing village of Penhally, and had changed into a pair of jeans and a sweatshirt, she couldn't relax, couldn't stop thinking about him.

Diversion, she thought as she picked up a book, only to just as quickly discard it. If she'd reached home at her normal time she would have gone for a walk on the beach to try to calm herself, but it was too dark for that now. What she needed was something—or someone—to channel her thoughts elsewhere, so, when her doorbell rang, a little after nine o'clock, she hastened to answer it. With luck it might be Jess who sometimes stopped by to discuss how the parents of a baby in NICU were—or weren't—coping, and they could have a cup of coffee, and chat, but it wasn't Jess on her doorstep, it was Connor.

'If you're here to talk to me about the unit,' she said quickly, 'it's late, it's been a long day, and I'm tired.'

'I haven't come to talk to you about the unit,' he replied, putting out his hand to stop her as she began to close the door on him. 'I've come to see you.'

And he had a suitcase with him, she noticed with dawning dismay. A suitcase that could only mean one thing.

'Connor, you can't think…' She dragged her gaze away from the suitcase, and back to him. 'You're not expecting to move in here with me, are you?'

'I figured it was stupid to keep staying in a hotel when you have a house within easy driving distance of St Piran, so I checked out of my hotel this evening.'

'But you can't,' she protested. 'People will talk. They'll say—'

'That a husband is living with his wife?' he suggested, and she flushed, and regrouped hurriedly.

'But won't your impartiality be compromised if you stay with me?' she exclaimed. 'I know you would never shut down an NICU but people could think—might suggest—I had exerted undue influence upon your report.'

'Then people would be wrong, wouldn't they?' he replied smoothly. 'So, are you going to leave me standing on the doorstep, or let me in?'

He'd backed her into a corner. Her only way out would be to tell him the truth, that she didn't want him in her home, prodding and poking at old wounds, but though he had asked her for honesty she knew she couldn't be quite that honest with him.

'You'd better come in,' she said in defeat.

'Nice house,' he observed as he followed her down the

narrow hallway into her sitting room, having to duck to avoid hitting his head on the old oak beams across the ceiling. 'Very…compact.'

'Tiny, you mean,' she said. 'I suppose it is, but I like it.'

'And this is where you've been living for the last two years?' he said, putting his suitcase down by the coffee table, and she nodded.

'I lived in nurses' accommodation at the hospital for a few weeks when I first came to Cornwall, but I wanted somewhere to call home so I rented this.'

'You have a home,' he reminded her, 'in London. Our flat.'

But it isn't mine, she thought. It never was mine, but I don't think I'll ever get you to understand that.

'Would you like something to eat?' she said, deliberately changing the subject. 'I was just about to raid my kitchen.'

'That would be nice.'

She didn't know if it would be nice, but eating something would certainly be preferable to them simply staring at one another in awkward silence for the rest of the evening, or, even worse, talking about things she didn't want to talk about.

'Chilli, lasagne or beef casserole?' she asked as she went into the kitchen and opened the freezer.

'Lasagne was always my favourite.'

It had been. She couldn't recall how many times she'd made it for him in the past but that had been then, this was now.

'Lasagne it is,' she said, and, as she placed it in the microwave, she prayed he would eat it quickly so she could retreat to the safety of her bedroom.

But he didn't eat quickly. In fact, he seemed to be in no hurry at all.

'This is lovely,' he declared as he forked some lasagne into his mouth. 'Every bit as good as I remember.'

'I'm glad,' she said, pushing her own lasagne around the plate without enthusiasm. 'Would you like some wine to go with your meal?' she continued, half rising to her feet, only to sit down again as he shook his head. 'Connor...' *Get it out,* she thought, *just say it.* 'Why have you really come?'

'Because we need to talk, and there's never any opportunity at the hospital.'

Which was fair enough, but that didn't mean she had to like it.

'That doctor at the hospital,' he continued, 'the A and E one who was flirting with you—'

'How many times do I have to tell you he wasn't flirting with me?' she interrupted with a huff of impatience. 'Josh is from Ireland, as you and I are, and the way he talks... It's just his style. He does it with every woman he meets, whether she's nine or ninety. And anyway,' she added for good measure, 'he's married.'

'So are you,' Connor observed, staring pointedly at her left hand, 'and yet you're not wearing your wedding ring.'

Damn, she'd forgotten about that, and she felt a warm flush of colour creep across her cheeks.

'I took it off when I came here,' she said uncomfortably. 'I thought...I felt it would be easier, would mean I wouldn't have to explain anything, or answer any awkward questions.'

'And is that what I am for you now—an awkwardness?' he said, putting down his knife and fork. 'Someone it's better not to think about, someone who can be jettisoned as easily as pulling off a ring?'

She could see the hurt in his blue eyes, but what could she say? Wasn't that exactly how she regarded his reappearance in her life? As something she'd far rather not deal with, someone she wished hadn't reappeared? And yet the man sitting in front of her was her husband, the man she had once pledged to love for the rest of her life.

'Connor, I know you want answers—and you're entitled to them,' she said unhappily, 'but I can't deal with this right now. I'm sorry—'

'You keep saying that as though it somehow makes everything all right,' he retorted, and she bit her lip.

'I know it doesn't make everything all right. I know it's not enough, but...' She took a breath, and it sounded unsteady even to her own ears. 'Can't you see this is hard for me?'

'And you think it's easy for me?' he exclaimed. 'Easy for me to sit at a table with my wife, knowing she doesn't want me here? Easy for me, today in the unit, when you named that baby Harry? You should never have done that, Brianna, *never.*'

She stretched out her hand to him, half in apology, half in a plea for understanding, but he pulled away from her.

'Connor, he hasn't got anyone, not right now,' she said with difficulty. 'He's all alone, and he...he's so very little, so fragile, and he reminded me so much of our son.'

'But he isn't our son,' he retorted, pain clear in his eyes. 'He isn't our Harry, Brianna.'

'I know,' she said. 'I know he has a mother, that she'll come back for him eventually, but until then—'

'You can pretend he's Harry?' he finished for her, his eyes fixed on her, daring her to contradict him. 'You can pretend we didn't lose our son—is that what you're saying?'

'No— Yes—' She shook her head. 'I don't know. All I know is this baby needs me right now, Connor.'

'*I* need you!' he exclaimed. 'I'm here, and *I* need you.'

'But when I needed you, you weren't there for me,' she blurted out, and saw his face contort with disbelief.

'How can you say that?' he demanded. 'I was always there for you, and our son. *Always!*'

'Not enough to let me cry for him after he died,' she threw back at him. 'Whenever I cried you'd say, "Don't cry, Brianna. You mustn't cry."'

'You were making yourself ill—'

'And whenever I tried to talk about him you changed the subject. My parents—my friends—because Harry died twelve hours after he was born—they never saw him, so he wasn't…' She swallowed hard. 'He wasn't real to them. They had no memories of him, only you and I did, but you… You just seemed to want to airbrush him out of our lives.'

'That is an unforgivable thing to say,' he replied, his voice raw. 'He was my son, too.'

'A son you would never talk about—a son you never cried over!'

'Brianna, if talking would have brought Harry back, I would have talked myself hoarse,' he protested, 'but talking wouldn't have changed anything, you know it wouldn't.'

'It would have kept him alive for me,' she said, tears thickening her voice. 'It would have kept him alive, and with us, but you… It was like you'd decided it was better to pretend he'd never lived, had never been.'

'Brianna—'

'All through the funeral you just sat there as though what was happening…what the priest was saying…was nothing to do with you while I... I kept thinking he'll wake up, Harry's going to wake up, and cry, and they'll realise they've made a mistake, and then I can take him home, and I so...' She let out a small sob. 'I so wanted to take him home.'

'Brianna, please—'

'You want to know how I really felt before I left you?' she continued, dashing a hand across her eyes. 'I wanted to die, Connor. All I wanted was to die, so I could be with Harry, and then he...' Her voice broke. 'He wouldn't be alone, and I couldn't bear the thought of him being alone, in the dark, with no one to hold him.'

'Brianna, *don't*,' he said, his voice cracking. 'Please, *don't*.'

'See—you're doing it again,' she cried. 'You say you want us to talk, but every time I try, you cut me off.'

'Because I can't bear to see you upset,' he said hoarsely. 'I can't bear to see you suffer like this.'

'Connor—'

'You're right,' he said, abruptly getting to his feet. 'It's been a long day, and we're both tired, and I still need to unpack.'

His face was closed and tight. It was the expression she'd grown used to seeing before she'd left him. The one that told her he didn't want to listen to her, didn't want to hear what she was saying, and she stood up, too, in defeat.

'What about the dishes?' he continued as she walked past him towards the kitchen door. 'You could wash, and I could dry, just like we used to.'

'Leave them,' she muttered. 'I'll do them later.'

'But—'

But nothing, she thought, walking determinedly into the sitting room, then up the narrow staircase to the first floor, leaving him with nothing to do but follow her. She didn't want to play happy couples with him in the kitchen, pretending that everything was all right over the washing-up. They weren't a happy couple. They hadn't been one for a very long time.

'The bathroom's in here,' she said as she opened the first door on the landing. 'It has both a bath and a shower so you can have whichever you want.'

'Looks good,' he replied with a smile, which she didn't return.

'I hope you'll be comfortable in here,' she said, walking into the next room. 'There's a double bed so you shouldn't feel cramped, and plenty of hanging space for your clothes—'

'But it's not your room.'

It was a statement, not a question, and she smoothed down the duvet, which didn't need smoothing, and deliberately avoided his eyes.

'The room faces south so you'll get the sun in the morning,' she continued, 'and there's a lovely view of Penhally bay and the harbour—'

'Brianna, when I said I needed you, I meant every word.'

His voice was soft, entreating, and she forced herself to look up at him. He was the man she had married, the man she'd fallen in love with all those years ago, and yet now... She knew she should feel something, ought to feel something, but it was as though her heart was frozen, and where there should have been love for him there was nothing but pain.

'Connor, I can't just go back to the way we were before Harry died,' she said haltingly. 'I can't pretend everything's all right between us, or forget, or—'

'Share my bed.'

She shook her head, unable to speak.

'Would…?' He took a deep breath. 'Would you rather I just left?'

'Yes' would have been her honest answer, but she knew she couldn't say that. She'd accused him of never talking, of never telling her what he was thinking and maybe, if he stayed, maybe he might talk, maybe he might listen, and she had to at least give him that opportunity.

'You have every right to be here,' she said.

Which wasn't what he wanted to hear, he thought as she left the room. He didn't want to hear he had a 'right' to be there by virtue of being her husband. He wanted her to say she wanted him there, but she hadn't.

Why had he come? he wondered as he sat down heavily on the bed. He should never have come, except…

He'd told himself he wanted answers. He still wanted them, but he wanted more than that. He didn't want to lose her, not again. He didn't want her to just slip away from him, and she was slipping away, he knew she was.

With a sigh he stood up and walked over to the window and gazed out. It was too cloudy tonight for stars, but he could see a light in the distance. A light that went on and off rhythmically. A lighthouse, his brain registered. A lighthouse, which gave hope to sailors lost at sea, and hope was all he had right now. A hope that was much fainter than the lighthouse's bright beam, but he would hold onto it because there was nothing else he could do.

CHAPTER THREE

'I JUST wish I could have been more help to the police yesterday,' Brianna said as she checked the cardio monitor above Amy Renwick's incubator. 'They were so kind, so patient—even offered to bring in their face-imaging expert, to see if I could re-create an image of Harry's mother—but I honestly and truly don't remember seeing anyone in the car park.'

'Neither did Sid, or Jess, so you're not the only one,' Megan said soothingly. 'Have the police had any luck identifying where Harry's shawl might have been bought?'

Brianna shook her head.

'Apparently it can be bought in lots of high-street shops, which means the mother could have come from anywhere.'

'She'll be some local, unmarried teenager.' Rita sniffed as she appeared, clutching a sheaf of forms. 'You know the sort—the airhead kind who think having a baby will be fun until they're presented with the reality. I'd wager my next pay cheque we'll never see her again.'

'Of course we'll see her,' Brianna said, hearing Megan's sharp intake of breath. 'She'll realise she's made a mistake, and come forward to claim her son. What mother wouldn't?'

'The irresponsible sort,' Rita declared. 'The sort whose

families have never given them any proper values, or a
decent upbringing. *My* daughters waited until they had a
wedding ring on their finger before they hopped into bed
with the first man who paid them any attention.'

'Girls—women—become pregnant for all sorts of
reasons,' Brianna said stiffly, 'and I don't think we—as
medical staff—should set ourselves up as either judge or
jury.'

'Too right,' Megan said, her voice ice-cold. 'Are those
forms for me?' she continued, gazing pointedly at the
papers in Rita's hand.

'They're admission slips for the babies who came in last
night,' the ward clerk replied. 'You have to sign them in
triplicate.'

'Bureaucracy gone mad,' Megan muttered. 'What's the
stats for the new admissions?'

'Both full term,' Brianna replied. 'One has severe jaundice, the other congenital hypothyroidism. Mr Brooke
started the jaundiced baby on phototherapy last night, and
the CH baby is being given oral thyroid hormone.'

'Good.' Megan nodded, then frowned as she gazed out
over the ward. 'Unfortunately that means we're now at full
capacity, so let's hope we don't get hit by another emergency admission.'

'And that would be a problem?'

Connor had joined them, his phone poised and ready
in his hand, and Brianna gritted her teeth at the sight of it,
and him.

'We have six incubators, which now have six babies in
them,' she replied. 'Do the maths, Connor.'

'I can count as well as you can,' he replied mildly, 'but
I understood you had an arrangement with the hospital in
Plymouth to take any babies you were unable to admit?'

Out of the corner of her eye, Brianna could see Megan

determinedly shepherding Rita towards the ward door, but she didn't give a damn whether Rita stayed and eavesdropped or not.

'We do,' she declared, 'but, as I explained to you yesterday—though you clearly weren't listening—sending babies so far from their homes is upsetting for everyone.'

'I hardly think a thirty—or thirty-five—minute drive could be considered particularly stressful,' Connor observed, and Brianna gritted her teeth until they hurt.

'I wonder how stress-free you'd find that journey if you received a phone call in the middle of the night telling you your baby's condition had deteriorated?' she demanded. 'Or how stress-free you'd be if you arrived to discover your son, or daughter, had died? Not all babies leave NICU alive, Connor.' She met his gaze. 'You should know that.'

It had been a low blow, and she knew it, as she saw all colour drain from his face, but she'd had enough of him today. If she was going to be honest, she'd had more than enough of him by the time they'd shared an excruciatingly awkward breakfast in her home this morning, and the last thing she needed was him dogging her every step, making stupid comments.

'Sister Flannigan?'

Brianna glanced over her shoulder to see Naomi Renwick hovering uncertainly by the ward door, clearly unsure as to whether she should approach or not, and hitched a smile to her lips.

'What can I do for you, Naomi?'

'Nothing, really. It's just…' Amy's mother flushed. 'Experience has taught me that if more than one person is clustered round my daughter's incubator, something's wrong.'

'Far from it,' Brianna insisted. 'I completed Amy's obs about half an hour ago, and there was no sign of any post-op infection, and her sats are perfect. Of course, we're going to have to wait and see what happens when we start feeding her orally instead of through an IV line, but at the moment I'd say everything's looking pretty good.'

'Thank you, Sister, thank you so much,' Naomi said, letting out the breath Brianna knew she'd been holding. 'I know it's silly to always suspect the worst, but sometimes—'

'It seems as though all you've done, since Amy was born, is take one step forward and two steps back,' Brianna finished for her. 'I do understand, but try not to worry, OK?'

'I'll try,' Naomi promised, and, when Brianna hurried across the ward in answer to Megan's beckoning wave, she smiled up at Connor. 'Sister Flannigan is always so encouraging, isn't she?'

'She would appear to be,' he replied noncommittally.

'Are you a doctor, Mr...Mr...?'

'Monahan. Connor Monahan,' he said, 'and, no, I'm not a doctor. I'm...' His lips curved a little ruefully. 'I guess you could call me a glorified accountant.'

'Right.' Naomi nodded, clearly none the wiser. 'This is my daughter, Amy,' she continued, gently touching the incubator. 'She was born two months premature.'

And I don't want to know this, Connor thought, half turning to go, but Mrs Renwick wasn't finished.

'All the nursing staff here are really wonderful,' she continued, 'but Sister Flannigan... She's something special, you know?'

He did know, he thought as he noticed Brianna's brow begin to furrow at whatever Megan was saying. He'd known it from the very first moment they'd met, when he'd been twenty-two, and Brianna had been twenty-one. All it had taken was one shy smile from her, across the dance floor in her home town of Killarney, and he'd fallen for her completely.

'It's like she somehow knows how all we parents feel,' Naomi observed. 'That she's not simply mouthing words of sympathy, but really understands what it's like to worry, and to fear.'

They had both known worry, and fear, Connor thought, feeling his stomach clench as memories surfaced in his mind, memories which were as bitter as they were unwanted. When Harry had been born, one month early, he'd known so little, been so naive. What's a month? he had asked himself. Babies of less than twenty-eight weeks survived, so a one-month-early baby was nothing, but then the hospital consultant had dropped his bombshell.

'Everyone says Mr Brooke is an excellent surgeon,' Naomi continued, 'and I'm sure he is, but he is a little…a little…'

'Brusque?' Connor suggested, and Naomi chuckled.

'Downright depressing would be closer to the truth. I know he has to be honest, but…'

'You'd prefer a little less honesty, and a bit more hope?'

Naomi nodded. 'Dr Phillips is always very upbeat—she's nice, too. In fact, I'm surprised a pretty woman like her isn't married, but then neither is Sister Flannigan, and I think she's just lovely.'

She was, Connor thought, glancing across the ward at Brianna. With hair the colour of burnished autumn leaves, large brown eyes and a smile that had always made his heart beat faster, she looked again like the girl he had married ten years ago rather than the skeletally thin woman who had left him. Over and over again he had begged and pleaded with her to eat, but she'd simply stared back at him with eyes that seemed to have grown too big for her small face. Now she'd regained some of the weight she'd lost, and he could not help but wonder what—or who—had finally persuaded her to eat.

'I understand… Sister Flannigan…I believe she's quite close to that A and E doctor—Josh O'Hara?' Connor commented, despising himself for asking, but needing to know nevertheless.

'Oh, no,' Naomi replied. 'He does come into the unit occasionally, and he certainly makes her laugh, but he's married, and, even if he wasn't, I wouldn't say he was Sister Flannigan's type.'

'You wouldn't?' Connor said hopefully, and Naomi shook her head.

'If you want my opinion, I'd say Dr O'Hara and Dr Phillips would be better suited. They just sort of look right together, if you know what I mean, though, of course, people do say it's often opposites who attract.'

Everyone in Killarney had wondered what Brianna had seen in him, Connor recalled wryly—she with her gift of always being able to talk to anyone, and he so very reserved unless he was discussing a balance sheet—but they'd been happy, they'd loved one another, and then Harry had been born.

'It's so sad about Harry.'

Connor's eyes shot to Mrs Renwick, wondering for one awful moment if she could possibly have read his mind, but she wasn't talking about his son. She was gazing at the incubator nearest the wall, and his forehead creased with foreboding.

'His condition has worsened?'

'Oh, no—at least, I don't think it has,' Mrs Renwick said quickly. 'I meant it's very sad that his mother abandoned him like that, but at least he's got Sister Flannigan.'

And Connor wished the child hadn't as he watched

Brianna walk away from Megan to the little boy's incubator. God knows, he meant the child no harm but, after just one day of looking after him, he knew Brianna was getting too close, and if this child died…

He closed his eyes tightly, but it didn't help. Nothing would ever erase the memory of that day when they'd come home from the hospital, after it was all over. Never had he heard anyone cry the way Brianna had cried, like an animal racked with pain, and he never wanted to hear that sound again, but the longer this baby's mother didn't come forward the more involved Brianna would become, and all he could see was heartbreak ahead for her no matter what happened.

'Are you all right, Mr Monahan?'

He opened his eyes to see Naomi gazing up at him with concern, and manufactured a smile.

'I'm fine. It's just…wards like this… You never know what's going to happen next, and I find that…unsettling.'

'My husband's the same.' Naomi nodded. 'He likes certainty, too, but I keep telling him, think positive, it's the only thing you can do.'

And Connor was positive something had just gone very wrong as he saw Megan join Brianna at Harry's incubator, and his wife begin to shake her head angrily.

'I'm afraid you'll have to excuse me, Mrs Renwick…'

He was vaguely aware that Amy's mother said something in reply, but he couldn't have said what. His eyes were fixed on Brianna. She looked upset now as well as angry, and whether she wanted him at her side was immaterial. He was going to be there.

'Problem?' he said as he approached her, and saw Megan bite her lip.

'There's a reporter outside in the corridor from the *Penhally Gazette*,' the paediatric specialist registrar replied.

'He wants to interview Brianna for his newspaper, and Admin think it would be an excellent way to give Harry more exposure, and perhaps encourage his mother to come forward.'

'And Admin can whistle Dixie as far as I'm concerned because I know damn fine that the only exposure Vermin would give Harry is the muckraking kind,' Brianna said tartly.

'Vermin?' Connor echoed, his eyebrows rising.

'His actual name is Kennie Vernon,' Megan replied, 'but he's known as Vermin for a very good reason. Not only does he work on the principle of never letting the truth get in the way of a good story, he's also the man who told the world—or at least the St Piran and Penhally part of it—that Jess has—'

The paediatric specialist registrar came to a sudden, red-cheeked halt, clearly deeply mortified by what she had almost said, and Connor glanced from her to Brianna, his eyebrows raised.

'Jess Corezzi has what?' he asked, and saw Brianna grimace.

'She has HIV, Connor,' she said in a low undertone. 'And before you say anything—'

'All I was going to say was, so what?' he replied, and Brianna sighed.

'Unfortunately that wasn't most people's reaction when Vernon splashed her condition all over the front page of the *Penhally Gazette*. I will never, ever forgive him for the way he crucified her, Connor, and for Admin to think I'd be willing to even be in the same room as that man, far less give him an interview...'

'Look, would it help if I sat in with you?' he said. 'I wouldn't interfere, I promise I wouldn't,' he added as Brianna began to shake her head, 'but I do have a lot of experience in dealing with the press through my work, and, whether you like it or not, Admin is right. The more press exposure the hospital can generate about this baby, the better.'

Megan caught Brianna's gaze.

'He's right,' she said reluctantly. 'I know you don't want to do it—I wouldn't want to either—but if Connor is there as back-up...?'

'I don't need back-up,' Brianna said, annoyance plain in her voice. 'I'm a big girl. I don't need my hand held.'

'No one is suggesting you do,' Connor said gently. 'But don't ever underestimate the press, Brianna, and sometimes two heads are better than one when it comes to dealing with the enemy.'

For a moment Brianna said nothing, then she let out a small, grudging sigh.

'OK. All right. I'll do it. Where is the little toad?'

Megan grinned.

'I told him to wait outside in the corridor. I also made him thoroughly scrub and disinfect his hands. He wasn't very happy about either.'

'Good,' Brianna declared. 'OK, Connor, let's you and I go and slaughter the little jumped-up slimeball.'

Wrong, Brianna, Connor thought as he followed her out of the ward and he saw the man waiting for them at the end of the corridor. Kennie Vernon might look like a refugee from a very bad eighties pop video, with his goatee beard and ponytail, but the muddy brown eyes that watched them walking towards him were calculating and shrewd. This was not a man to underestimate. This was a man who would use anyone, and anything, to get himself out of the *Penhally Gazette* and into one of the big London newspapers, and Connor instinctively moved closed to his wife.

'Sister Flannigan,' Kennie declared with a smile that

was every bit as false as the replica Rolex on his wrist. 'How very pleasant to meet you.'

'I'm afraid I can't the say the same,' she replied. 'I'm not that big a hypocrite.'

Kennie's smile didn't slip at all as he transferred his gaze to Connor.

'And you are…?'

'He's…' Brianna came to a dead halt. How on earth was she supposed to introduce Connor? If she said he was her husband, Vermin would dig deeper, and if she said Connor was an auditor, that would give the reporter an even bigger story for the *Penhally Gazette*. 'He's—'

'Connor Monahan. Sister Flannigan's PR adviser,' Connor announced, and it wasn't only Brianna's jaw that dropped.

'You have a public relations adviser?' Kennie said to Brianna, but again it was Connor who answered.

'Naturally,' he said, in a tone that suggested only complete losers didn't. 'Now, I'm sure you don't want to conduct this interview in a corridor,' he continued, 'so shall we adjourn to my office?'

He opened the door of the nurse unit manager's office pointedly, and Kennie Vernon walked into it without a word, but as Connor made to follow him, Brianna caught hold of his arm.

'Why the hell did you say that?' she hissed. 'About you being my PR adviser?'

Connor shrugged. 'I had a sort of flash of inspiration.'

'Yeah, right,' she replied. 'Well, try not to have too many more of them, OK?'

And he smiled. A smile that made her heart clench because it suddenly transported her right back to that night in Killarney when her eyes had met his over the crowded dance floor. She'd known immediately that he wasn't local, and so had all the other girls.

'He's here on holiday,' someone had whispered. 'From Dublin.'

And her friends had all giggled, and nudged one another, because, to them, Dublin was somewhere exotic, somewhere exciting. He'd looked so out of place in the village hall, dressed in his crisp white shirt, blue tie and smart black trousers, while all the other young men had been wearing jeans and T-shirts, but when he hadn't reacted to her friends' giggles, or their fluttering eyelashes, they'd all muttered, 'Stuck-up prat,' and dismissed him, but she'd hadn't.

She'd kept sneaking curious glances at him, and his eyes had eventually met hers, and he'd smiled. The same half crooked, half self-deprecating, smile he was smiling now, and she hadn't seen that smile in such a long time.

'What?' he asked as she stared up at him, and she shook her head.

'Nothing. It's…nothing.'

But it was, she thought as she went into the nurse unit manager's office. It was a painful reminder of how she'd once felt about the man at her side. A bitter-sweet reminder that she'd once loved him more than life, and had thought nothing would ever separate them.

'I understand Jessica Corezzi was with you when you found this baby?' Kennie declared, sitting down and instantly flipping open his notebook, pen poised.

'Yes, she was,' Brianna replied, deliberately remaining standing.

'She married a consultant at the hospital recently, didn't she?' Kennie murmured. 'Which is somewhat surprising given the circumstances.'

Because Jess has HIV, Brianna thought angrily. That's

what you're saying, you horrible little man. That you're
amazed she could actually find someone willing to marry
her, and she wasn't about to let him get away with that.

'Now, just one minute,' she began, only to pause when
Connor shook his head warningly at her.

'Both Jess Corezzi and Sister Flannigan found the baby
together,' Connor said smoothly, 'but, unfortunately, neither
of them saw the mother. Or the father, come to that,' he
added with a smile. 'After all, why be sexist, why assume
it was the mother who left the baby there?'

'Right.' Kennie Vernon nodded, looking slightly bemused, but he wasn't finished. Not by a long shot. 'It's
strange, don't you think, Sister Flannigan, that the baby
should be found in the consultants' car park?'

'Strange?' she repeated, puzzled. 'I'm sorry, but I don't
understand what you mean.'

'I was just wondering whether the unfortunate mother
might perhaps have had a relationship with one of the consultants in the hospital,' Kennie said, 'and she left the baby
where he would find it because he'd dumped her.'

And you know exactly whose car little Harry was found
next to, Brianna thought furiously. It was Gio Corezzi's car.
Jess's husband.

'Mr Vernon,' she began, but Connor cut across her
again.

'I fear you may have been reading far too many trashy
novelettes, Mr Vernon,' he drawled. 'Surely the most plausible explanation is that the mother left her baby in that
particular car park because it was the furthest from the
road and she wanted to ensure her child didn't become…'
He frowned in apparent concentration. 'Now, what's the
word I'm looking for… Ah, yes. Road kill.'

Road kill? Brianna thought, shooting her husband an

appalled glance, and could almost have sworn she saw him wink back at her.

'I think the term you were searching for, Mr Monahan, is road fatality,' Kennie Vernon said stiffly, then flipped over a page of his notebook. 'Colour of hair and eyes of this child, and does he have any distinguishing features like a birthmark or a mole?'

'Harry has black hair, and blue eyes,' Brianna replied, 'but no birthmarks or moles.'

'Harry?'

'We didn't want to keep calling him Baby X,' Brianna replied uncomfortably, 'so we decided to name him Harry until his mother comes forward.'

'I'd like to take a photograph—'

'No, absolutely not,' Brianna interrupted. 'I can take a photograph of him for your newspaper if you want one, but I cannot allow you into the ward because of the risk of infection.'

Kennie leant back in his seat, and smiled at her with a smile she did not care for.

'Are you always this obstructive, Sister Flannigan?' he asked, and she saw Connor move forward a step.

'Sister Flannigan is merely stating hospital policy,' her husband replied in a tone that suggested arguing would be most unwise, but that did not prevent the reporter from trying.

'I'd like to remind both of you of the rights of the press—'

'Which I do not think would ever include endangering the life of a very vulnerable baby,' Connor declared.

'But—'

'You could, of course, apply for a court order,' Connor continued smoothly, 'but I think that would be...unwise.

Unless you wish to be front-page news yourself for harassing a minor?'

Kennie shot Connor a look that was positively venomous, then snapped his notebook shut.

'Thank you for your time,' he said as he stood up. 'That will be all.'

'No, it won't.' Brianna sighed as the reporter strode out the office without a backward glance. 'He'll be back.'

'Undoubtedly,' Connor agreed. 'But round one to us, I think.'

'I'm just very glad you were on my side,' Brianna said with feeling, and Connor smiled, a slightly lopsided smile.

'I always was, I always will be,' he said simply.

There was no answer to that except one, which she knew would hurt him immeasurably, so she opted to change the subject.

'Road kill, Connor?' she said as she led the way into the corridor. *'Road kill?'*

'I had a momentary memory lapse, couldn't remember the correct phrase.' He grinned, and she shook her head at him and chuckled.

'Yeah, right,' she said. 'And like I would ever believe that. You never forget anything.'

'Except, it seems, the things that really matter,' he murmured.

His eyes were troubled, but what could she say to him when she knew he'd spoken the truth?

'Have you seen our graduation board?' she asked, trying to change the subject.

'Your what?' he said with an effort, and she pointed to the board on the corridor wall, which was covered with baby pictures.

'It started shortly after the unit was opened,' she said.

'Parents of babies who had left the unit, gone home, began putting up pictures of their children to give other parents encouragement, to let them see there was light at the end of the tunnel, and it sort of snowballed.'

He grimaced slightly. 'I see. Brianna—'

'Hands,' she said. 'If you're going back into the ward you need to thoroughly scrub and disinfect your hands.'

'Oh. Right. Sorry,' he replied, but after he'd thoroughly scrubbed his hands, and she had, too, he turned to her uncertainly. 'How can you bear to work here after losing Harry? Don't you find it incredibly stressful to be constantly surrounded by very ill babies?'

'It can certainly be challenging, and upsetting at times,' she agreed as she pushed open the ward door, 'but…you see…with Harry…' She took a steadying breath. 'There was nothing I could do, nothing anyone would let me do, but working as a nurse in here, I know there are times when I can make a difference, times when my skills matter, and I can help.'

'Yes, but even so, don't you—?'

'Oh, *hell*.'

For a second, Connor was completely bewildered by her exclamation, but as he looked past her, into the ward, he saw what she had. Megan was standing at the top of the ward, her eyes fixed firmly on one of the monitors, while Josh was ostensibly deeply in conversation with Mr Brooke, but only a fool wouldn't have noticed that the A and E consultant's eyes kept darting in the direction of the paediatric specialist registrar.

'What gives between those two?' Connor asked in an undertone. 'Every time they meet I swear Megan's back couldn't get any stiffer if she had a poker strapped to it, and yet Josh constantly seems to be trying to gain her attention.'

'It's none of my business,' Brianna replied firmly, 'or yours.'

'Fair point,' Connor conceded, 'but it's odd.'

It *was* odd, Brianna thought as Mr Brooke bore Connor off to interview some of the nurses in Gynae, and she saw Josh make an attempt to talk to Megan, an attempt she very quickly rebuffed. Normally, Josh didn't seek Megan out. They might occasionally meet because of their work, but he had never actively attempted to get her to talk to him so this was different, and puzzling.

'You OK?' she said to Megan when Josh finally left.

The paediatric specialist registrar faked a smile.

'Shouldn't that be my question?' she said. 'After all, you were the one who was being interviewed by horrible Vermin, so how did it go?'

Which was as neat a way as any of avoiding answering, Brianna thought, but who was she to point the finger?

'He was his usual obnoxious self,' she said, 'but Connor took no prisoners.'

Megan nodded.

'Connor…' she began carefully '…he seems…nice. Maybe a bit of a statistic obsessive—'

'A bit?'

'OK, a lot,' Megan agreed with a small chuckle, then her face grew serious. 'Look, Brianna, I guess, what I'm trying to say—very badly—is, if you want to—you know—talk at any time, I'm a good listener.'

'Me, too, if you ever want to talk—you know—about Josh,' Brianna replied.

'Yeah, well, Josh and I…' Megan gave a dismissive smile that didn't fool Brianna for a second. 'That ship sailed a long time ago.'

Had Connor and her ship sailed, too? Brianna wondered as the rest of the day sped by in a round of obs, X-rays and scans. She didn't know, but neither did she want to answer the other question of whether she actually wanted to still be on board.

But it was a question that wasn't going to go away, she realised when her shift ended, and she drove home to find Connor's Range Rover already parked outside her house. It was a question she was ultimately going to have to face, but not now, she decided as she got out of her car, grabbed her jacket, and determinedly took the rocky path that led down to the beach.

Except the walk had been a very bad idea, she realised when she reached the shore and recognised a familiar figure standing there, gazing out to sea. A figure who saw her just as soon as she saw him, giving her no chance to slip away.

'I thought I'd get some air,' he said as she slowly walked towards him.

'Me, too,' she replied. 'I often walk here after work. I find it helps if...' She had been going to say, 'If I'm stressed,' but that didn't seem the kindest thing to say in the circumstances. 'I find it clears away the cobwebs.'

A bracing March wind was blowing across the beach, whipping the slate-grey sea into frothy white breakers, and sending dark clouds scudding across the sky, and Connor smiled wryly.

'I can believe that,' he said, and an involuntary chuckle broke from her.

'You hate it here, don't you?'

'Not hate, exactly,' he replied as she began walking along the beach, and he fell into step beside her, 'but...' He waved his hand towards the small cottages dotted along the hillside, the rows of houses nestling further down around the bay that made up the town of Penhally. 'Don't you find it incredibly claustrophobic? All those net curtains constantly twitching, the way everyone knows everyone else's business, and what they don't know they make up?'

'People can only know what you choose to tell them,' she replied. 'For sure they can speculate, gossip, but you'll find gossips everywhere.'

'But Penhally—and St Piran—they're both so far from civilisation,' he insisted, and she smiled.

'When I first came here I heard a holidaymaker say that to one of the old fishermen, and he said, "It all depends on what you mean by 'civilisation'". Of course we don't have big shops, and there's no cinema, or any sort of nightclub, but if you need help it's always given. Actually, it reminds me a lot of home.'

'But it's nothing like London,' he protested, and she blinked.

'I meant Killarney. London was never my home.'

'Brianna, we lived in London for nine years,' he replied with ill-disguised irritation. 'It was most definitely our home.'

'Maybe for you,' she muttered, but he heard her, and came to a halt, forcing her to stop, too.

'All right, explain,' he demanded, and she opened her mouth, then closed it again to marshal her thoughts.

'Do you remember the flat we rented in Killarney when we first got married?' she said, and he groaned.

'Do I ever? It was so small, and dingy, and whenever I had a bath every damn pipe in the place rattled.'

'OK,' she conceded, with a small gurgle of laughter, 'so the plumbing wasn't the greatest—'

'And the mice...' He rolled his eyes heavenwards. 'Brianna, the place was overrun with mice, and you'd never let me kill any of them so I was constantly catching them in those humane boxes, and taking them outside, until Mr Fitzgerald told us that unless I took them at least six miles away they'd find their own way back.'

'So you used to load up the car every weekend, and drive them out to the country,' she chuckled, remembering, and he shook his head ruefully.

'A proper eejit I looked, too, emptying all of those boxes into a field like some sort of Pied Piper.'

And his Irish accent was coming back, she noticed, the accent he had so carefully excised from his voice because he didn't want to be thought provincial by all the big shots in London.

'And don't forget Mrs O'Leary in the flat next door,' he continued. 'Always wanting to tell us how much the flats had gone downhill since her husband died, and that bright red wig she wore—'

'Oh, I'd forgotten all about her wig,' Brianna declared, starting to laugh, 'and her hats—do you remember the hats she used to wear—all those feathers, and ribbons, and bows?'

'Brianna, I swear those hats will remain scarred on my psyche for ever,' Connor said with a shudder.

And she laughed out loud, and it was so good to hear her laugh, had been so long since he'd heard her laugh, and her cheeks were flushed with the wind, and her eyes were sparkling with a life and a vibrancy he hadn't seen in them since they'd lost Harry, and, without thinking, he reached out and touched her cheek, only to see her step back and the light in her face instantly disappear.

'It's beginning to get dark,' she said, half turning. 'We ought to start heading back.'

'Oh, I'm sure we can risk a few more minutes,' he said quickly, wanting so much to recapture her laughter, not wanting to return to her cottage where he knew she would shut him out again. 'What made you think of our flat in Killarney?'

'I guess…' She looked out to sea. The breakers were much higher now, the clouds more louring. 'I guess it's because even though it wasn't the greatest flat in the world, it was our home, and I was so happy there.'

'You never objected when I started applying for jobs in England,' he said, pointedly, and she sighed.

'I was so young when we got married, Connor, and my mother said a wife should always follow her husband wherever he wanted to go, and I didn't question that. I know different now. I know it should have been a joint decision.'

'But why did you never tell me you were unhappy?' he demanded. 'Why did you never say, "Connor, this isn't the life I want"?'

'I wasn't unhappy. Unhappy…' She shook her head help-lessly. 'Unhappy makes it sound as though I was crying in secret, miserable all the time, and I wasn't. I just felt… detached. As though my life was on hold while I was in London, but eventually I'd start living again.'

He gazed at her uncomprehendingly.

'But, every time I went for a promotion, you were always solidly behind me, saying, "Go for it." Every time I found us a nicer flat, a bigger flat, you seemed so happy, and when I decided to go it alone, to set up my own business, you were thrilled to bits.'

'Because you were,' she admitted. 'I shouldn't have pretended—I see that now—but you were so determined to make it big in England, and money—status—they always mattered much more to you than they did to me. All I ever wanted was enough money for us to get by, a nice place to live in, and…and a family. I would have been more than happy to stay in Killarney, with you working at the local accountant's office, and me in the hospital there.'

'But my career…my own business…' He dragged his fingers through his hair, his eyes bewildered. 'Brianna, I did it all for you, so you wouldn't ever end up like my mother.'

'Your mother?' she echoed in confusion. 'There was nothing wrong with your mother. She was a lovely lady—'

'Who I watched grow old before her time, trying to put enough food on the table to feed myself and my dad, and my three brothers,' Connor said bitterly. 'All her married life she had to scrimp and save, and she never…' He shook his head. 'Brianna, she never got anything pretty, or silly, or frivolous, and I vowed when I watched her, sitting up to all hours of the night, trying to find enough money to pay for the food, and rent, and electricity, that my wife would never have to do that.'

'Connor, it wasn't your father's fault that the only work he could get was occasional because he had emphysema—'

'I know that,' he said impatiently. 'I don't blame him.'

'And your mother *loved* your father,' she insisted. 'Even though they never had much money, there was always laughter in your house, and your mother wanted your father, not the things he could buy her, just as I only ever wanted you and not the fancy flats, or the posh London address.'

'That's easy for you to say when you never had to go without when you were growing up,' he retorted. 'Your parents had their own farm, their own animals, and chickens. They weren't dirt poor like my parents.'

His parents had been poor, she remembered. The tenement flat they'd lived in, in Dublin, had seemed so dark to her when she'd first visited, but it wasn't the darkness she remembered. It was Connor's mother beaming at her, clearly delighted with her son's choice, and his father enveloping her in a hug even though he could barely walk by then.

'I know my parents were more comfortably off than yours,' she said awkwardly, wishing she could somehow make him understand, 'but there was never any shortage of love in your home.'

'You can't live on love, Brianna,' he said, annoyance tingeing his voice, 'not in the real world.'

She opened her mouth, then closed it again.

'Maybe the truth is I'm just a country girl at heart,' she said with an effort, 'and London was just too big, too impersonal for me. Maybe…maybe if we'd had children it would have made a difference. I don't know, I honestly don't.'

For a long moment he said nothing, and when he did speak his voice was low, bleak.

'We both took the decision to turn off Harry's life-support system, Brianna.'

'I know,' she said unevenly. 'I know we did. I'm not… I don't blame you for that.' She took a deep breath. There was something she had to say to him. Something that had revolved round and round in her mind like a canker for the past two years, and, even if his answer broke her, she still had to ask. 'You never really wanted children, did you?'

He swung round to her, his hair streaming back in the wind, appalled horror plain on his face.

'How can you say that?' he exclaimed. 'How can you even *think* it? Harry was my son, my baby, too. We tried for so many years to have him, and when we lost him… How can you say I didn't want him?'

'Then why, when I was pregnant, did you never seemed as excited as I was?' she pressed. 'I couldn't wait for Harry to be born, and yet you… You never went shopping with me for baby clothes, or helped me choose a cot, or—'

'God dammit, Brianna, I was working flat out, twenty-four seven,' he protested. 'I didn't know whether you would want to go back to work after the baby was born so I wanted to make sure we were financially secure. Just because I didn't go shopping with you, or race around our flat doing high fives all the time, doesn't mean I didn't want him.'

And he was holding something back, she knew he was from the way he wasn't quite meeting her eyes.

'Connor—'

'You seem better now than when I last saw you,' he said.

Better. Was she better? She certainly no longer cried herself to sleep every night, no longer woke up in the dark thinking Harry was somewhere in the house, lost, distressed, needing her, but better now…?

'I don't think you ever get over the death of a child,' she said with difficulty. 'You just somehow get through it, one day at a time. At the beginning, after Harry died, there were days when I wondered if I would even make it to the next day, and days when I honestly didn't care if I didn't. I felt so alone, you see, so very much alone, but now… The pain's still there, the ache and the longing for him is still there, but it's…duller.'

'Why do you keep saying you were alone?' he exclaimed. 'You weren't alone. *I* was there, *I* was with you.'

'But I couldn't talk to you, and you…' She pulled her coat closer to her. It was getting colder, so much colder, but he'd asked her a question, and he deserved an answer. 'You didn't seem to…to care the way I did. When we got home from the hospital, you'd taken everything away. His cot, his clothes, his toys—'

'I was trying to make things easier for you,' he protested.

'I thought…if you saw them…it would only make you more upset.'

'And you thought, if they weren't there, I'd *forget*?' she said incredulously, and he flinched.

'I was trying to help, Brianna, to protect you—'

'What you did was take all the decisions away from me,' she declared. 'I might have wanted Harry's room to stay exactly as it was. I might have wanted to burn every single thing in his room, or pack it all away, or give it to charity, but you didn't give me that choice.'

'I'm sorry, but when we lost Harry—'

'Will you stop saying that?' She flared. 'We didn't lose Harry. He wasn't a…a parcel we inadvertently left behind on a train and never got back. He *died*, Connor.'

His face twisted. 'I know.'

'Then why do you never say it?' she demanded. 'Why do you always say we lost him?'

'Lost…died…' A muscle in his jaw clenched. 'What difference does it make? It means the same thing.'

'No, it doesn't. Connor—'

'Has it all gone, Brianna?' he said, holding out his hand to her hesitantly. 'The love we once shared. Has it all gone?'

She stared back at him silently. She didn't want to hurt him. He looked so suddenly vulnerable, so completely unlike the utterly self-confident Connor she had always known, but he had told her he wanted no lies, no half-truths, only honesty.

'I don't know,' she replied. 'I honestly and truly don't know.'

And she turned and walked away from him, leaving him gazing bleakly after her.

CHAPTER FOUR

'HAVE you seen this?' Connor exclaimed, tossing a copy of the *Penhally Gazette* down onto the coffee table in the staffroom.

Brianna glanced dismissively at the front page, and shook her head.

'I don't read the *Gazette*—haven't ever since they printed that disgusting article about Jess. If Vermin has included some snotty comment about the poor quality of my photograph—'

'Read the article.'

Something about Connor's tone had Brianna putting down her mug of coffee, and picking up the newspaper.

'"Abandoned baby found in St Piran Hospital car park",' she read out loud. '"Sister Flannigan of the neonatal intensive care unit…" blah, blah, blah "…baby has been named Harry…"' She frowned up at Connor. 'OK, so it's not the greatest prose style in the world, but I don't see—'

'Read the last paragraph.'

Obediently, she continued reading.

'"The mother has as yet not come forward,"' she murmured, '"but this newspaper can also exclusively reveal that Sister Flannigan is currently…"' Her eyes flew to Connor's then back to the newspaper, '"is currently living with Connor Monahan, an external auditor brought in by the St Piran Hospital board to determine cost-saving measures which could include ward closures."' Slowly she lowered the newspaper. 'How the hell did he find that out, Connor? How, on God's green earth, was Vermin able to find that out?'

'I was going to ask you the same thing.'

'You think I *want* people to know you're my husband?' she said without thinking, then flushed scarlet when she saw the pain in Connor's eyes. 'I didn't mean that—it came out all wrong—'

'I don't give a damn about him knowing I'm staying at your cottage,' he interrupted angrily. 'To be honest, he wouldn't be much of a reporter if he hadn't done some snooping, and he was bound to notice my car sitting outside your home all night. What I want to know is how he discovered why I'm here, in the hospital?'

'Oh, come on, Connor, it's hardly a state secret,' she protested. 'Rumours about why you were coming to St Piran's started filtering out of Admin over a month ago. The only things we didn't know were who you were, and the actual day of your arrival.'

'Brilliant.' He groaned. 'Just brilliant. My assessment is supposed to be hush-hush. *Nobody* was supposed to know anything about it until I'd made my report—the board were quite specific about that.'

'But it's hardly your fault if St Piran's is a hotbed of gossip,' she replied. 'It's a hospital, Connor. Gossip and rumour go with the territory.'

He sighed, and rubbed his fingers wearily over his face. 'I can only hope the board see it that way.'

'You mean, they could fire you?' She gasped, and he grimaced.

'Breach of confidentiality, going public with something

they wanted to keep private… Let's just say they're not going to be very happy with me.'

'But *you* didn't tell anyone,' she protested. 'It was the gossiping staff in Admin. They're the ones who should be torn to shreds, not you.'

'And you'd care if I was?' he said, unable to hide his surprise, and she rolled her eyes in exasperation.

'Of course I'd care,' she replied. 'I know how much your work means to you.'

He'd far rather she knew just how much *she* meant to him. Far rather he could somehow find the right words, instead of always saying the wrong ones. She'd hardly spoken at all this morning over breakfast, and he hadn't dared to. All he'd been able to think, as he'd stared at her lowered head, was how had they come to this, how had they grown so far apart, that they couldn't even make any kind of conversation any more?

'Connor…?'

She was gazing up at him with concern, and he managed to smile. She'd said things hadn't been right between them even before Harry, and maybe she was right. Maybe he'd somehow lost sight of what she wanted in his determination to achieve what he'd believed they both did, but there had to be a way back for them, a way of reaching her.

'What's done is done,' he said. 'All I can do now is try to achieve some damage limitation.'

And not just in this job, he thought as he followed Brianna back to the ward, and the minute she appeared the entire staff fell awkwardly, and all too guiltily, silent.

'I take it you've all seen this morning's edition of the *Penhally Gazette*?' Brianna said, her back ramrod-stiff, but her cheeks, Connor noticed, were pink. 'So, to satisfy your curiosity, I am not conducting an illicit affair with Mr Monahan. He's my husband.'

Megan threw her an 'I'm so sorry about this' look, Chris's mouth fell open, as did the mouths of the other nurses, but Rita was clearly not going to be quite so easily satisfied.

'But I don't understand,' she said, all innocent confusion, as the nurses around her scattered, clearly not wanting to get involved. 'How can Mr Monahan be your husband when you never said you were married, far less to the man who's auditing this hospital?'

'I fail to see why Sister Flannigan needed to tell anyone anything about her private life,' Connor replied before Brianna could reply. 'And she, of course, understands the need for complete confidentiality regarding the nature of my job.'

'Even so,' Rita said, 'I still think—'

'Oh, I wouldn't,' Connor interjected, his voice soft, and velvet, and deadly. 'I really would seriously recommend you don't. But in the meantime,' he added with a smile that would have had Brianna backing off fast, 'why don't you run away and make sure the rest of the hospital staff knows the latest, stop-press new? I'm sure you must be just itching to spread the word, and it will save Sister Flannigan the trouble of having to post a bulletin on the notice board.'

The ward clerk needed no second bidding, and, when she'd gone, Brianna sucked in a shaky breath.

'Remind me never, ever to cross swords with you,' she murmured, 'but thanks. Again.'

'Any time,' he replied, then caught her gaze. 'And I mean that.'

He did, too, she thought. Connor would have thrown himself in front of a runaway horse to protect her, would have gone fearlessly into battle on her behalf at the merest hint of a threat, but sharing his feelings with her... That was something else entirely.

'Yikes, but that was impressive, Connor.' Megan grinned as she joined them. 'But how in the world did Vermin ever find out you were staying at Brianna's cottage?'

'I'm afraid my car's not exactly forgettable,' Connor replied ruefully, 'plus leaving it outside Brianna's house all night... I guess that was just asking for trouble.'

'I suppose so.' Megan sighed. 'But maybe it's better if everyone knows the two of you are married. Some things... it's not always wise to keep them under wraps. When the truth comes out, as it always does, the repercussions can be worse.'

And she was talking about herself, Brianna realised from the dark shadows she could see in Megan's eyes. Not about Connor and her, but about herself, and Connor knew it, too, judging by his slight frown, and she glanced helplessly across at him and, to her relief, he came to her rescue.

'How are all your little patients this morning?' he asked, and Megan grabbed his question with clear relief.

'Our jaundiced baby seems to be making good progress, as is our congenital hypothyroidism little boy,' she replied. 'Amy Renwick's beautifully stable, and all the other babies are doing very well, though I have to say little Harry's a bit too quiet for my peace of mind.'

'How can a baby be too quiet?' Connor asked, clearly puzzled, as Megan walked over to the little boy's incubator and he and Brianna followed her. 'I would have thought quiet meant content, happy?'

'It can,' Megan agreed. 'And he certainly seems to be responding to the surfactant, but...' She shook her head. 'He just seems a bit lethargic, to me.'

'Just because he isn't constantly moving around in his incubator, as some of our babies do, doesn't mean there's anything wrong with him,' Brianna said swiftly. 'As Connor said, he's probably just a very contented baby.'

Megan nodded, but she didn't look convinced, and a chill of foreboding crept up the back of Connor's neck as he stared down at the baby who was lying, unmoving, in his incubator. As Megan had said, there was quiet, and there was quiet, and he had never once heard this baby cry. Brianna might not think there was anything wrong, but he wondered how much of that was denial on her part because the baby did look like their son. Not strikingly so, but enough to make him feel slightly sick inside.

'My gut feeling is we're missing something,' Megan declared, 'so I want those blood results chased up, more X-rays, a spinal tap, a CT-scan—'

'You think he could be brain-damaged?' Connor gasped, and could have bitten off his tongue when he saw Brianna's face whiten.

'I'm not into guessing games, Connor,' Megan replied firmly, 'and I'm probably simply overreacting, and he's actually one contented little boy, but I want to cover all bases.'

'Right,' he murmured, backing up a step. 'OK, I have notes I want to transfer from my phone to my laptop, so I'll…I'll head off to my office and let you get on with it.'

Megan smiled slightly as Connor strode quickly out of the ward.

'He's getting quite attached to our Harry, isn't he?'

'Who wouldn't when this little one is such a cutesy?' Brianna replied, then took a deep breath. 'The spinal tap… Are you thinking sepsis?'

'Hell, Brianna, I'm not thinking anything,' Megan insisted. 'I just…'

'Have a gut feeling.' Brianna nodded.

She'd had them, too, in the past. A nurse's sixth sense

warning that, despite what their monitors and hi-tech machines indicated, there was something not quite right.

'Do you want me to page Babbling?' she asked, and Megan shook her head.

'Let's wait for those blood results, and while we're waiting we'll do a spinal tap before we pull in our resident Cassandra. And speaking of prophets of doom,' she added dryly, 'I think Rita wants a word with you.'

'Oh, joy,' Brianna muttered with feeling, glancing over her shoulder to see the ward clerk clearly attempting to catch her attention, and Megan laughed.

'Just don't kill her, OK?' she said. 'Removing all that splattered blood from the unit...' She grinned. 'Nightmare.'

But it wasn't Rita who wanted to speak to Brianna outside in the corridor. It was Jess, her face alight with excitement.

'I think I might know who the mother of your abandoned baby might be!' she exclaimed without preamble.

Which was good news, Brianna told herself, as she felt her heart give an uncomfortable, and unexpected, dip. It was tremendous news, the very best of news, and yet she found herself having to struggle to return Jess's smile.

'That's...that's brilliant,' she replied, all too conscious that Connor had come out of the nurse unit manager's office, and was listening intently. 'Who is it?'

'Do you remember me telling you some months ago about the girl I saw who gave me a false name?' Jess replied.

'A false name?' Brianna repeated in confusion, and Jess shook her head at her.

'You *must* remember. She came in the day that poor young car mechanic, Colin Maddern, was killed in a car crash. She told me her name was Marcia Johns, and I thought it sounded odd, and it wasn't until she'd gone I realised why. She'd clearly picked the name from one of the pharmaceutical posters on my wall.'

'I can sort of vaguely remember that.' Brianna frowned. 'But what makes you think she could be Harry's mother?'

The counsellor held up three fingers and counted them off.

'Number one, it was very clear to me she'd been deeply in love with this Colin even though she couldn't have been much older than sixteen. Number two, she gave me a false name, and why would she do that unless she was afraid I might make enquiries and find out who she really was and where she lives?'

'Jess—'

'And number three,' the counsellor continued triumphantly, 'even when I spoke to her I felt she was hiding something, that there was something else she wasn't telling me.'

'Did she look pregnant?' Brianna asked, and for a second Jess looked downcast. Then she brightened.

'She wouldn't have if she was only two, or three, months gone, and this must have been…six…seven months ago.'

'Would you be able to give the police a description of this girl?' Connor asked, to Brianna's acute annoyance, and Jess frowned.

'She was blonde—well, more corn-coloured, really—and her eyes were grey, but the trouble is I only saw her twice. Once when she came to the hospital, and once when I was out with Gio in his car.'

'Nevertheless, I think you should tell the police what you know,' Connor declared, and Brianna bit her lip.

What right did he have to interfere, to put in his

pennyworth? The baby's mother's identity had nothing to do with him.

'Jess, you can certainly go to the police if you want,' she said, 'but let's look at the facts here. You don't know the girl's real name, and you don't even know if she was actually pregnant. All you know for certain is she had blonde hair, and grey eyes, and there must be dozens of girls out there who would fit that description.'

'My own granddaughter, Nicola, for a start,' Rita observed as she came out of her office, clearly having been hovering behind her door, listening to every word, 'and I'm telling you this. If the police start stopping every sixteen-year-old girl in the street and asking if she's recently given birth, there'll be hell to pay from the parents.'

Jess flushed.

'Damn, but I hadn't thought of that. I'm so sorry, folks,' she added. 'It just all seemed to fit, but you're right—I don't have enough information, only guesswork.'

'I still think you should speak to the police,' Connor declared, but the counsellor shook her head.

'If I remember anything else, I will, but right now... For all I know I've just put two and two together and come up with five, and that's not going to help anyone.'

'What will happen to Harry if his mother doesn't come forward?' Brianna asked, and Jess sighed.

'When he's well enough, Social Services will arrange for him to go into care or be fostered, until he can be adopted. Look, I know that sounds awful,' she continued quickly, seeing Brianna's expression, 'but there are some really good foster-parents out there.'

'I suppose so,' Brianna said unhappily, 'but it seems a pretty wretched start in life for a little baby.'

'Brianna...'

She could hear the caution in Connor's voice, the concern, but she didn't turn round—couldn't.

'I wouldn't give up hope yet of his mother coming forward,' Jess observed bracingly. 'It's only been two days since you found him, and there could be dozens of reasons for her not coming back to claim him.'

'Yeah, like her thanking her lucky stars she's got rid of him,' Rita declared, and Jess rolled her eyes at Brianna.

'I have to go,' she said. 'I have wall-to-wall clients today—'

'Which reminds me,' Brianna declared. 'When you've a minute, could you have a word with Naomi Renwick? She's been doing marvellously, managing to keep most of her anxieties pretty much under control since her daughter was born, but I get the feeling things are starting to get on top of her, and...'

'You think she needs someone not directly involved with her daughter's medical care to talk to her?' Jess nodded. 'Not a problem. I can't see her today, but I'll definitely drop by tomorrow.'

'Nice woman,' Connor said as Jess hurried away. 'Seems very caring, as well as capable.'

And if he thought that, then maybe Jess's job would be safe, Brianna realised, letting out a silent whoop of joy.

'Her husband's very nice too,' she replied, just in case Connor was eying up the neurology department for cutbacks. 'Gio Corezzi, the neurosurgeon?'

'I'm sure Mr Corezzi is very nice,' Rita chipped in, before Connor could reply, 'but, when you think about it, what do any of us really know about him?'

'What's there to know?' Brianna said in confusion. 'He's a brilliant surgeon, he's Italian, and he's happily married to Jess.'

'He is *now*,' Rita replied, 'but he wasn't nine months

ago, and don't you think it's odd this baby should be found next to his car?'

Brianna turned slowly to face the ward clerk. 'I'd watch what you were saying, if I was you, Rita.'

'I'm only making an observation—'

'No, you're not,' Brianna interrupted, more angry than she'd been in a long time. 'You're saying that Gio—Gio who loves Jess more than he loves his own life—could have had some…some sort of sordid liaison the minute he arrived in St Piran, and then dumped the woman.'

'I'm only pointing out that it's strange—'

'Have you been talking to Kennie Vernon?' Brianna demanded. 'Because if you have, and I hear this repeated anywhere in the hospital, I'm going to tell Gio what you said, and, believe me, the courts take a very dim—and expensive—view of slander. Understood?'

From Rita's scarlet face it seemed she did, and, as she strode into her office, and slammed the door behind her, Connor shook his head.

'What an absolutely appalling woman. Why on earth does the hospital employ her?'

'Because, despite the fact that she's a nosy, interfering gossip,' Brianna replied, 'she is also, unfortunately, very good at her job.'

'Which is a great pity,' he observed, 'because I would have relished the opportunity of recommending she be given her marching orders.'

'At least she only has two more years to work here before she retires.' Brianna sighed. 'Of course, there's every chance I'll probably have killed her before then, but…'

Connor tilted his head at her. 'You've changed, haven't you?'

'In what way?' she asked, puzzled.

'The Brianna I knew would never have chewed Rita's

head off. She might have wanted to, but she would have been far too afraid of hurting someone's feelings.'

'Yeah, well, maybe I don't care so much about other people's feelings now,' she replied. 'Maybe I care more about what is right.'

He smiled, an odd, almost self-mocking smile.

'You don't need me any more, do you?'

Her eyes flew to his. 'Don't need…?'

'When we first got married, I thought—I sort of expected—that I'd always be…' He shrugged a little awkwardly. 'Your protector, I guess. My role was to be Tarzan—'

'And I was Jane?' she said, and try as she might she couldn't stop the corners of her mouth from lifting. 'Um, Connor, I think maybe you should pick a different comparison because somehow I don't ever see you swinging through the trees wearing only a loincloth.'

'You know what I mean,' he said, his cheeks slightly flushed, 'but look at you now. You have your own home—'

'It's rented.'

'A career you've made all by yourself, a circle of friends, and you didn't need my help to get any of those things. In fact, you probably didn't even need me against Vermin.'

'Oh, yes, I did,' she said with feeling. 'Connor—'

'I'm just thinking, you see,' he said, his face suddenly sad, 'if I'm not your protector, your defender, then there really isn't any place in your life for me now, is there?'

He meant it, she realised. For him, there was only one role that a husband should play in a marriage, and because he believed he was now an irrelevance to her, he was giving her the opportunity to say, 'No, you're right, there is no place for you,' and he would leave, and she'd never see him again.

But was that really and truly what she wanted? She'd

thought it was, when he had first come to St Piran's but, now, staring up at him, seeing his face under the fluorescent lighting, she found herself thinking how very tired he looked, how unexpectedly vulnerable, and how his shirt was ever so slightly crumpled. Which was a stupid thing to think, an inconsequential thing, and she knew it was, but she'd never seen him looking anything but perfectly groomed, and she tentatively put out her hand to him.

'Connor, a man needs to be a whole lot more than simply a protector in a marriage, otherwise we women would only ever marry bodyguards or boxers.'

His lips curved into an uneven smile, and he captured her hand in his.

'Then there's still hope for me—for us?'

She wanted to say, yes, she did so want to say, yes, but there were so many unresolved issues between them, and too many questions still unanswered.

'I can't answer that, not yet. I'm sorry,' she added gently, hearing him sigh, 'but you said you wanted me to be honest, and right now, that's all I can say.'

He nodded. 'I guess...' His shoulders lifted, and he forced a laugh. 'I guess it's better than "Goodbye".'

And before she realised what he was going to do, he'd raised her hand and planted a kiss in the centre of her palm. A kiss so gentle that his lips scarcely brushed her skin, and yet she felt a faint flutter of warmth curl and wrap itself around her frozen heart. A faint flutter that deepened and grew when he held her hand close to his own heart and she could feel it beating.

'Bree...?'

He hadn't called her that for such a long time, not for such a very long time, and tentatively she raised her own hand to touch his cheek, saw him close his eyes, and turn his head so his lips almost touched her fingers, and then he let out a muttered oath when the unit door opened and Josh appeared, looking grimly determined.

'No prizes for guessing who he's come to see,' Connor muttered as he released her hand. 'For a bright man, it's sure taking him a long time to get the message that Megan's not interested.'

'Shush,' Brianna whispered warningly. 'What can we do for you, Josh?'

'I didn't realise you guys were married,' he said, and Brianna rolled her eyes.

'Now, that *was* fast, even for Rita,' she observed dryly, and Josh grinned.

'I want to talk to Megan.'

'Josh, do you really think this is wise?' Brianna said uncertainly. 'She clearly doesn't want to talk to you—'

'But I *have* to talk to her,' the A and E consultant insisted. 'Brianna, please, tell her that.'

'OK, I'll tell her, but don't be surprised if she says she's too busy,' she replied, but, as she turned to go back into the ward, she saw Mr Brooke beckoning imperiously to her from outside his office. 'Oh, damn. Look I'm sorry, Josh, Mr Brooke wants me. Connor, could you find Megan, and tell her Josh really needs to speak to her?'

'I'll try,' he replied.

Which was about as much as anyone could do, Brianna thought as she hurried down the corridor towards Mr Brooke.

'This had better be good, Josh,' Megan declared as she came out of the ward, looking both flustered and irritated. 'Unlike you, who seem to have unlimited free time at your disposal, I am really busy.'

'You're always busy, always avoiding me,' he replied, 'but this is important.'

'It always is, according to you,' she said. 'OK, all right. Spit it out, but make it fast. I have a hundred and one things to do.'

'Rebecca's left me.'

For a second there was no expression at all on Megan's face, then, to Josh's dismay, her face whitened with shock.

'Is this because of me?' she said hoarsely. 'Has she heard rumours about me? Josh, I'll speak to her, tell her that what happened between you and I happened years before she married you, and we didn't even have a proper relationship back then, just...' She bit her lip. 'Just one night of madness that should never have happened.'

'Megan—'

'You haven't told her about Stephen, have you?' she exclaimed, horror tingeing her voice. 'You haven't been insensitive enough to tell her that we had a baby, and he died? Oh, Josh, she must be so hurt—so upset—'

'I haven't told her we had a child. I...' He swallowed convulsively. 'Only you and I know that, and only you and I ever will. Look, Megan, I thought... Rebecca leaving me... I thought...I hoped...you'd be pleased.'

'*Pleased?*' she echoed faintly. 'You thought I'd be *pleased* to have been the cause of someone's marriage ending?'

'I shouldn't have said "pleased"—"pleased" was the wrong thing to say,' he declared desperately, 'and you haven't ended my marriage. Rebecca and I... Our marriage has been slowly dying, bit by bit, for years. It was one of the reasons we moved to St Piran, both of us hoping we might be able to salvage it, but I think we always knew it wasn't salvageable.'

'I'm sorry,' she said, sincerity plain in her face. 'Sorry

for Rebecca, sorry for you. Nobody wants a marriage to fail.'

'I think, perhaps, looking back, that I should never have married her,' he replied. 'That it was a mistake.'

She opened her mouth, then closed it again, and backed up a step, her eyes narrowing.

'A mistake,' she repeated slowly. 'It must be really comforting for Rebecca to know she was a mistake.'

'Megan—'

'But, then, I was a mistake, too, wasn't I, Josh?' Megan continued icily. 'You and I making love when we were students—that was another of your mistakes. Oh, and Stephen. I guess he was *a mistake*, too.'

'Megan, listen to me—'

'You *married* Rebecca, Josh, so presumably you felt something for her at one time?'

He had, he remembered, but the feelings he'd felt for his wife had been nothing like the feelings he'd experienced towards the white-faced, angry woman standing in front of him. With Rebecca he'd felt comfortable, at ease, had thought they wanted the same things from life, while with Megan... His feelings had been so terrifying in their intensity that he'd run from them rather than face them. Run because he'd sensed that Megan embodied everything he'd always feared. Commitment, honesty, family, ties.

'I married Rebecca because I thought...' He let out a long, shuddering breath. 'I thought we wanted the same things, but I don't think we ever really understood one another, whereas you and I...'

'You and I *what*, Josh?' Megan said her voice tight.

'I'm sorry, I'm not explaining this very well—'

'You think you can just take up where you left off, don't you?' she interrupted, disbelief plain in her voice. 'You think that because your wife has walked out on you, I'll be only too ready and willing to leap back into your bed again despite what you did, despite…' Her voice broke slightly. 'Despite you taking everything of any value from me.'

'No, of course I didn't think that,' he protested.

'Then why is it so all-fired important to you that I should know?' she demanded. 'Why do you think it would matter a damn to me whether your wife has left you, or if you're still happily married to her?'

He took a step towards her, and saw her back away still further.

'Look, I'm saying this all wrong,' he faltered. 'It's coming out all wrong.'

'Oh, I think it's coming out just right, Josh,' she retorted. 'Thanks for the update on your private life, but there was no need for you to hurry up here to tell me. I could have waited like everyone else until Rita spread the word.'

And she walked away from him, leaving him gazing in despair after her.

'You want *me* to be the new nurse unit manager?' Brianna gasped as Mr Brooke beamed benignly at her. 'But… why?'

'Because you're not only my most qualified member of staff, you're also the best,' he replied as she gazed at him, open-mouthed. 'And—believe me—those two things don't always necessarily go together.'

'But…'

'I know it's going to mean getting to grips with a whole lot of unfamiliar paperwork, but the job's yours, if you want it. You do want it, don't you?' he added as Brianna stared at him uncertainly.

Nurse Unit Manager. It was her dream job, the job she'd always wanted. Of course she knew it wouldn't be easy. The post carried a huge amount of responsibility, and she'd seen how many hours Diego Ramirez had needed to put in just to keep on top of all the paperwork, but she wanted it, she really did, except… If she accepted the post it would mean there was no possibility of her going back to Connor. He was a city man, with a high-powered city job. He'd never move to Cornwall in a million years, which meant, if she accepted the job, she would be accepting that her marriage was over.

Well, it is, isn't it? her mind whispered, and she took an unsteady breath.

'Mr Brooke, I'm flattered—immensely flattered—you think I can do this—' she began, and Richard Brooke put up his hands quickly.

'I can hear a "but" coming and I don't want to hear a "but". Look, I've put my neck on the line here by telling Admin I want it to be an in-house appointment, so will you at least think about it? I can't give you too long to make up your mind, because we desperately need a replacement for Nurse Ramirez, but—frankly—I can't see why you're hesitating.'

Neither could Brianna as she walked slowly out of Mr Brooke's office. It was what she'd always wanted, to be in charge of the nursing staff in a unit, and if the consultant had only asked her last week she wouldn't have hesitated for an instant, but now… Now she didn't know what to do, and the last person she could talk to it about was Connor.

At least she was able to avoid his far-too-acute gaze for the rest of the day. When she got back to the ward, Megan told her he'd gone to Men's Surgical to interview the staff there and, for a moment, Brianna considered confiding in the paediatric specialist registrar, but one look at Megan was enough to tell her that her friend was struggling with her own private demons. Whatever Josh had so desperately wanted to talk to Megan about, it had obviously upset her greatly, but her closed face did not invite conversation and, for once, Brianna was relieved when her shift was finally over.

'He's still going to be here tomorrow, you know,' one of the night nurses said with a chuckle when Brianna made her customary stop at Harry's incubator to check on him before she left.

'I know,' Brianna replied, 'but I just like to say good-night to him. He doesn't have a mother so...' She shrugged awkwardly. 'Silly of me, I guess.'

The night nurse said nothing, but Brianna knew what the woman was thinking. That she was breaking the cardinal nursing rule of 'Never get too close, never become too involved, with a patient' but she wasn't getting too close. She was simply doing her job, doing the best she could for little Harry, and if a small voice in the back of her head was whispering its own warning, that small voice was just overreacting.

Exactly as Connor was, she thought ruefully when she eventually got home, and found him pacing up and down in front of her cottage.

'I was beginning to think your car had broken down,' he said. 'That I was going to have to come out and rescue you before the storm breaks.'

Actually, he was right about the storm, Brianna realised as she squinted up at the sky. Ominous black clouds were rolling in from the west, the wind was picking up, and small drops of rain were already beginning to fall.

'I thought you might be tired when you got back,' he continued, hovering behind her as she trudged wearily into her cottage, 'so I tossed a coin, and put some chilli in your microwave when I heard your car.' He glanced anxiously at her. 'I hope that's OK?'

'Sounds good,' she said with an effort. 'Have I time to

shower and change? I always think I smell so overpower-
ingly of disinfectant when I get back from the hospital.'

'Sure.' He nodded. 'You've plenty of time. In fact, take
all the time you need. I've already set the table, and put on
the fire, so there's nothing for you to do.'

She wished there was as she went upstairs, and showered, and changed into a pair of jeans and a sweater. She
wished even more that he would stop being so helpful, so
thoughtful, when she didn't want him to be any of those
things. It just made everything so much harder.

'You seem a bit preoccupied tonight,' he observed after
they'd eaten a largely silent meal. 'Nothing wrong at the
hospital, I hope?'

'Everything seemed pretty quiet when I left,' she murmured. 'Megan's going to chase up little Harry's blood tests
results. They generally take seventy-two hours, so they're
not late, but I know she'll be a lot happier when she sees
they're normal.'

And if they're not?

The unspoken words hung between them, and neither
of them voiced them.

'What did Mr Brooke want to see you about?' Connor
asked as he began to collect their dirty dishes.

'Oh, nothing important,' she said evasively. 'Just boring
stuff like paperwork.' He didn't believe her, she knew he
didn't, and quickly she went over to the sink, and turned on
the tap. 'I'd better get these dishes done. It's getting wilder
out there, and we might get a power cut.'

And it was getting wilder, she thought as she stared out
of her kitchen window into the darkness. The wind was
now buffeting the house, and squally rain was battering
against the windows. She loved it when it was like this, so
wild and tempestuous. It always made her feel like a small

bird in its nest, listening to the elements raging around her, but Connor clearly didn't share her feelings.

'Not very seasonal weather, is it?' he observed with a grimace as he picked up a tea towel. 'March... You think of daffodils, and crocuses, and spring approaching, not howling gales and rain.'

'You can get wild weather at any time of year,' she replied, and he nodded.

'It rained a little on our wedding day, didn't it? Your mother said June would be a lovely month to get married in, and it rained.'

'*Rained?*' she exclaimed. 'Connor, it poured solidly all day, and we had hailstones, and a gale-force wind.'

'Oh, come on,' he argued. 'There might have been the odd shower or two—'

'I don't know whose wedding you're remembering, but it certainly isn't ours.' She chuckled as she added some washing-up liquid to the water in the sink. 'The train at the back of my dress got completely soaked when my father and I had to make a mad dash from the car to the church, we had to have all the wedding photographs taken in the reception hall instead of outside the church because nobody could stand upright, and Ellie Warburton, my flower girl, fell in a puddle, and cried for the duration of the reception.'

'Lord, so she did.' He grinned. 'Why was Ellie one of your flower girls anyway? She didn't seem to know you from a bar of soap.'

'She didn't, but my mother insisted because she's some sort of cousin of mine, twenty zillion times removed, and her family would have been deeply offended if she hadn't been asked.'

'Right,' he said, clearly none the wiser as he began

drying their plates. 'OK, so the weather was bad, but everything else was perfect.'

'You corrected Father Driscoll during the ceremony.'

'I did not!'

'You did too,' she declared. 'When he said, "Do you, Connor, take Brianna Kathleen to be your lawfully wedded wife?" you said, "I, Connor, take Brianna Kathleen O'Donnell to be my lawfully wedded wife." You're not supposed to say the bride's surname.'

'I didn't want there to be any mistake,' he protested. 'I thought there might be dozens of Brianna Kathleens in the world and I wanted to make sure I was marrying the right one—my one.'

'My mother was mortified.' Brianna smiled as she remembered. 'She said she'd never be able to look Father Driscoll in the face again when he told her afterwards that he'd never been corrected in church before.'

'Well, like I said,' Connor declared defensively, 'I wanted to be sure I was marrying my Brianna Kathleen.'

'And then my Uncle Joe sang his party piece at the reception,' Brianna continued with a shudder. 'My father promised faithfully not to let him, but halfway through the evening he said, "Sure, Brianna, a wedding's not a wedding unless Joe sings *Delilah*."'

'Does your Uncle Joe ever remember the right words?' Connor asked, and Brianna shook her head.

'Never.' She laughed.

Laughed with such genuine amusement and happiness that he put down the tea towel and caught her soapy hands in his.

'Do you know what I remember most about our wedding day?' he said softly. 'It was turning round when I heard the wedding march and seeing you coming down the aisle towards me. You looked… Oh, you looked so beautiful it took my breath away, and I thought, Connor, lad, how in the world did you ever get so lucky to win this angel?'

'Flatterer,' she said shakily, trying to pull her hands free without success.

'Gospel truth,' he said huskily. 'All I could think was, Please let her reach my side quickly, before the gods or the fairies snatch her away and keep her all to themselves.'

'Connor, I'm getting soap suds all over the floor,' she protested, completely unnerved by the intensity of his gaze, but he ignored her.

Instead, he reached behind her, and, before she could stop him, he'd unplaited her hair and spread it out over her shoulders.

'Your hair was loose,' he murmured, 'just like it is now, and you had flowers threaded through it. Flowers that matched your bouquet, all the colours of the rainbow they were, but paler, and the scent...'

'Freesias...' she whispered, feeling her heart rate pick up. 'They were freesias.'

'And when I said I would honour and keep you, in sickness and in health, until death us do part, I meant every single word.'

She had meant those words, too, but it hadn't been his death, or hers, that had parted them, it had been Harry's.

'Connor...'

'You never told me you were going,' he said, sliding his hands down her back. She could feel his hands trembling— or perhaps she was. She couldn't be sure. 'How could you do that, Brianna? How could you just disappear, never telling me where you were, whether you were safe?'

'I was wrong,' she said unevenly. 'I see that now, but all I could think was if...if I could just get away from you, from London, from everything that reminded me of Harry, I'd be all right.'

'But why Cornwall—why here?'

'Because…' She closed her eyes, and took a shuddering breath. 'Nobody would know me. Nobody would be able to point their finger and say, "She's the one whose baby died. She's the mother whose baby died," and because they couldn't I thought—not that I would forget—I won't ever forget—that it might be…easier.'

'Bree, I have missed you so much,' he whispered, his voice constricted. 'Missed seeing you, missed hearing your voice, and I have so missed holding you.'

He was holding her now. He'd wrapped his arms around her, and then, gently, oh, so tenderly, he kissed her, and when she sighed against his mouth she heard him groan. A groan that seemed to come from deep down inside him, and it felt so good to be held, so good to be kissed, that she kissed him back, and felt him shudder, but as his kiss became more insistent, and he pulled her even closer to him, she suddenly felt the patent evidence of his arousal, and she flinched. She didn't intend to, didn't mean to, but she flinched, and she knew he felt it because she could see the pain of rejection in his eyes as he drew back from her.

'Connor, I'm sorry,' she said unevenly, 'so sorry, I don't know why I—'

'I understand,' he interrupted bleakly.

How could he, she wondered, when she didn't understand her reaction herself? That she'd wanted to be held by him, she'd wanted his arms around her, but, the moment she'd realised that just holding her wasn't enough for him, something inside her had frozen, something within her had screamed, No.

'It isn't you,' she said. 'It's me.'

'It's all right, *a chuisle mo chroí*,' he said with an effort. 'You've had a long day and you're tired. You should get some sleep. I'll finish clearing up in here,' he continued when she tried to interrupt. 'You get yourself away to your bed.'

'But—'

'Goodnight, Bree.'

He had turned back to the sink, and slowly she walked away from him but, when she reached the kitchen door, she half turned.

A chuisle mo chroí.

Pulse of my heart.

It was what he'd called her on their wedding night, when they'd made love for the very first time, and she wanted to say something, knew she should say something, but no words would come. No words that would explain what she couldn't explain, and, as a tear trickled down her cheek, she slipped away, leaving him gazing out of her kitchen window, his face in shadow.

CHAPTER FIVE

RITA was smiling. It was never a good sign when Rita smiled. Either the ward clerk had discovered a new and particularly juicy piece of gossip, or she was about to dump someone in a very large pile of manure, and, whichever it was, Brianna knew she wasn't up for it today—she really wasn't.

'Something I can help you with, Rita?' she said with an effort as the ward clerk sidled up to her, her face distinctly conspiratorial.

'It's about your husband, Sister Flannigan...'

Don't go there, Rita, Brianna thought. If you value your life, don't ask me why I've been living alone in Cornwall for the last two years while I have a husband in London, because, if you do, you're dog meat.

'What about my husband?' she said coolly.

'Just that it's such very good news that he *is* your husband.' Rita beamed. 'I mean, I think we can now safely say my job is completely secure because he'd never shut down any department you worked in.'

Incredible, Brianna thought as she stared at the ward clerk. The woman was completely incredible, but she wasn't about to let her get away with it.

'I don't think we can say that at all,' she replied. 'In

fact, I can assure you my husband would never allow any personal bias to influence him.'

Rita tapped the side of her nose, and winked.

'Of course you *would* have to say that, wouldn't you, Sister, but enough said, message understood, and I won't say another word.'

Which will be a first, Brianna thought grimly, but as Rita bustled away, her anger swiftly faded.

She had such a headache this morning, such a blinding, thumping headache. She'd scarcely slept last night, had spent every hour tossing and turning, reliving what had happened in her kitchen. At least Connor hadn't appeared in the unit yet, and she wondered if his absence was deliberate. She wouldn't have blamed him. She'd allowed him to kiss her, allowed him to hold her, and then she'd rejected him. Rejected him for no reason she could fathom except, perhaps, her body had been telling her that she no longer wanted him, that there was nothing left of their marriage.

'You OK?'

She half turned to see her staff nurse, Chris, regarding her with concern, and grimaced slightly.

'I have a thudding headache this morning,' she replied. 'And before you ask,' she added, 'I've taken something for it, so I can't take anything else.'

It had been Connor who had pressed the aspirin into her hand, she remembered. He'd taken one look at her face this morning, made her breakfast, pressed the pills into her hand, then suggested she should consider taking the day off, but his solicitude had only made her feel worse.

'I'm afraid I'm going to add to your headache,' Chris declared. 'Vermin's here.'

Brianna swore under her breath.

'If that low-life thinks he can get another interview with me—'

'Actually, he wants to speak to Mr Brooke, though why he thinks our consultant will be able to give him any more information than you did is anyone's guess.'

'Where is he—Vermin, I mean?' Brianna asked.

'I've left him cooling his heels in the corridor.'

'The hospital sewer would have been better,' Brianna replied, then frowned slightly. 'You did tell him Mr Brooke has a clinic later on this morning, after his ward rounds, so he's not going to be able to see him any time soon?'

A look of mock dismay appeared on the staff nurse's face.

'Oops, but would you believe I completely forgot to tell him that?'

'Not for one second.' Brianna laughed. 'But it will do Vermin no harm to kick his heels for a couple of hours.'

'That's what I thought,' Chris declared smugly, then her eyes lit up. 'Your husband's here.'

'Is he?' Brianna said dully, without turning round, and Chris dug her gently in the ribs.

'Talk about dark horses. I don't know how you managed to keep quiet about him. He's quite something, isn't he?'

'You said he was scary,' Brianna reminded her, and the staff nurse's smile widened.

'I still think he is, but in a *very* sexy sort of a way.'

Chris thought her husband was sexy. So, too, she remembered, had the wives and girlfriends she'd sat next to at the dinner parties Connor had taken her to in London. Dinner parties whose sole purpose seemed to be for the businessmen there to boast about the deals they'd struck. Networking, Connor had called it, as she'd sat in silence throughout these meals, feeling completely out of place and uncomfortable. Nobody had ever been interested in her when they'd discovered she was a nurse. Zero networking opportunities, the men had clearly thought, while their wives and girlfriends had eyed Connor up, and tried to flirt with him.

'Couldn't you at least *try* to make conversation?' Connor had said impatiently after one of the dinners. 'The other wives, and girlfriends… They always seem to be able to find something to say, but you just sit there like a little frightened mouse.'

And she'd wanted to say that most of the wives and girlfriends' conversations seemed to involve flirting with him, but she hadn't.

'Your head's still sore, isn't it?' Connor declared as he walked across to her and Chris bustled away.

'It's better now,' she lied, and saw his left eyebrow lift.

'Yeah, right. How's everyone doing?' he continued, glancing at the incubators around them. 'How's the baby who was abandoned?'

'His name is Harry, Connor,' she said irritably. 'He seems quite content.'

Quiet, you mean, Connor thought, and quiet doesn't mean the same as content, you know it doesn't, but you won't accept that.

'Brianna—'

'The little girl with jaundice is progressing well,' she said.

She was deliberately changing the subject, he knew she was, but he knew better now than to push.

'Should the soles of her feet, and the palms of her hands, be quite so yellow?' he asked, and saw Brianna smile.

'They're that colour because she had pretty severe jaundice. Every newborn has elevated bilirubin—it's a by-product of haemoglobin, which is usually eliminated from the body as waste—and it's that excess bilirubin which makes so many babies' skin look yellow. Normally, the baby's liver will start functioning at full speed within a few days, but sometimes they need a little help, which is what we're giving her.'

'And the baby who has congenital hypo…hyper…'

'Congenital hypothyroidism,' she finished for him. 'It occurs when a baby's thyroid gland is absent or under-developed at birth.'

'That sounds serious.'

'It used to be. In the past, a baby could end up with permanent mental retardation, and development delay, but we can now give a synthetic thyroid orally.'

'Fascinating,' he said, meaning it, and she laughed.

'There have been an amazing number of medical advances in recent years, and what is even more marvellous is scientists keep on discovering more and more treatments, more and more cures. Although…' The light in her eyes suddenly dimmed. 'Not for everything.'

He knew what she was thinking, and he didn't want her to be thinking of their son, and this time it was he who changed the subject.

'Little Amy. Mrs Renton's daughter—'

'Mrs Renwick,' Brianna corrected him. 'She's progress-ing well, too. Naomi isn't doing quite so well but I'm hoping Jess will be able to help her.'

'Maybe we should have seen someone like Jess,' he murmured. 'After Harry…you know…'

'Died,' she prompted. 'Just say it, Connor. Nothing awful is going to happen if you say that word.'

But he didn't.

'Maybe we shouldn't have thought we could go it alone, cope alone,' he continued, his face bleak. 'Maybe if we had accepted the help the hospital offered, things might have been…easier.'

'Maybe,' she murmured, and she looked so suddenly lost that he longed to reach for her, to put his arms around her, but he'd tried that last night and she clearly hadn't wanted his touch.

Was it too late for them? he wondered as he saw her smile past him, and he turned to see Mrs Renwick had arrived. He didn't want to believe it was, but he never seemed able to say the right thing, never seemed able to do the right thing, to give her what she wanted, needed, but that didn't mean he wasn't going to try. It wasn't in him to give in without a fight, and this fight involved the highest stakes he'd ever played for. This was one he simply couldn't lose.

'I'll leave you to it,' he said in a low undertone as Mrs Renwick walked towards them. 'I have notes to copy over to my laptop, and I think Amy's mother looks as though she needs you.'

Naomi did, Brianna thought. There were dark shadows under her eyes, and her face was white, and pinched.

'I think you should go home to bed, Naomi,' she said as Connor slipped away. 'Forgo your visit today.'

'I'm fine,' Mrs Renwick replied. 'I just had a very bad migraine yesterday, the third this week, and they tend to wipe me out.'

Stress, Brianna thought. Mega-, mega-stress.

'Your daughter had an excellent night, and is currently moving all over the place inside her incubator,' Brianna declared with a smile. 'Every time I put her to the top, she manages to make her way to the bottom. In fact, I reckon you've got a future long-distance walker there.'

Naomi didn't even attempt to raise a smile.

'You're very kind, Sister, and I know I must seem like the most negative person in the world to you—'

'Of course you're not.'

'But sometimes it's so hard to keep on being positive. My daughter is the most wonderful, precious, joy to me, but...' Naomi bit her lip. 'I told my husband last night she's going to be our only child. I can't go through this again—I just can't.'

'And statistically you won't have to if you decide to give Amy a little brother or sister,' Brianna said gently. 'Though having had one premature baby does put you at a twenty to forty per cent risk of having another one, look at it another way. It also means there's a sixty to eighty per cent chance you won't.'

Naomi nodded, but Brianna could tell she hadn't convinced her, and she wasn't surprised. Having a premature baby was so emotionally draining for parents. All too often, every day seemed to bring with it a new challenge, a new worry, but if anyone could reassure Naomi it would be Jess.

And the counsellor was as good as her word. She arrived midafternoon, and bore Mrs Renwick off to the parents' room, smoothing over Amy's mother's protestations of not having time by insisting she needed a cup of coffee but hated drinking it alone.

'She's good, isn't she?' Megan observed when Jess and Mrs Renwick had gone. 'I wish we had the time to do what Jess does, but we're so constantly snowed under with all the medical procedures we need to perform on the babies that the emotional needs of the parents far too often get overlooked.'

'She's one of a kind, that's for sure,' Brianna agreed. 'And...' She looked over her shoulder to make sure there was no one near, least of all Rita. 'I *think* her job is safe.

Connor hasn't said so—not in so many words—but he *did* say she was very capable so...'

'It's looking good.' Megan breathed with a sigh of relief. 'He didn't...' She grimaced. 'Look, I know I shouldn't be asking you this, but he hasn't given you any indication of which department he might be recommending for the chop, has he?'

'I'm afraid Connor doesn't talk about his work,' Brianna said ruefully. 'Actually, Connor's not big on talking, full stop.'

'One of the strong, silent types, eh?' Megan smiled, but Brianna didn't.

'You could say that,' she murmured, then cleared her throat. 'I've not seen Josh today.'

'Hopefully he's finally remembered which department he's actually supposed to work in,' Megan replied tersely.

Which pretty well ended that conversation, Brianna thought, but she couldn't leave it there even though she knew she probably should. The specialist paediatric registrar looked as ragged as she felt.

'Megan, I know this is none of my business—'

'His wife's left him, Brianna.'

'Josh's wife?' Brianna said faintly. 'But...'

'Yes, I know,' Megan said, her lips twisting slightly. 'Rita must be really beginning to lose her touch if she hasn't managed to pick up that juicy bombshell yet.'

The specialist registrar's voice was hard, brittle, but if ever a woman was close to tears Megan was.

'I think I saw his wife once at a hospital reception,' Brianna said carefully, 'but I've never met her.'

'She was—is—very beautiful,' Megan said. 'But not happy. I don't...' She took a shallow breath. 'I don't think she was very happy.'

'Was...?' Oh, lord, but this was so very hard to say, but

Brianna knew she had to say it. 'Was that what Josh wanted to talk to you about yesterday?'

Megan nodded.

'Not that it's of the least interest, or consequence to me, of course,' she said. 'I mean, whether he's married or single. It's not like he and I...' Her voice trembled slightly. 'It's not like we mean anything to one another.'

'Oh, Megan—'

'*Don't*,' the specialist paediatric registrar said quickly. 'Please, don't give me any sympathy, or I'm going to embarrass myself, and you.'

'You could never embarrass me,' Brianna said softly. 'Not ever. Josh's wife leaving him… Do you think…are you hoping…?'

'I don't know what I'm thinking, or hoping,' Megan replied with difficulty. 'I just wish…oh, how I wish…he'd never come to St Piran's, that I'd never had to meet him again.'

Because now I have to think about things I don't want to think about, remember things that might have been better kept buried. That was what Megan was saying, and Brianna understood exactly how she felt.

'Megan, listen to me—'

The specialist paediatric registrar shook her head warningly, and Brianna glanced over her shoulder to see Connor approaching.

'Great timing, Connor.' She sighed as Megan hurried away, and her husband's eyebrows rose.

'I can always go away again,' he offered, and she shook her head.

'Too late, I'm afraid.'

And for more than one thing, she thought with dismay when she saw Mr Brooke sweeping into the ward, all smiles. If Vermin had convinced the consultant that she would be willing to give him another interview she was going to throw a hissy fit. A big one.

'Ah, Sister Flannigan,' Mr Brooke declared. 'The very person I was hoping to see.'

'Mr Brooke, if this is about Vermin—I mean Kennie Vernon,' she began, 'he's had all he's ever going to get out of me.'

'Who's Kennie Vernon?' the consultant said with a frown.

'The reporter who wanted to talk to you. The man who's been hanging about in the corridor for the last couple of hours?' she added helpfully. 'Looks like a very bad eighties rock star, dressed all in black, goatee beard?'

'I haven't seen anyone like that this morning,' Mr Brooke replied in confusion. 'No, this is about you, my dear, and my offer,' he continued, ushering her away from Connor to the side of the ward. 'I really need your decision soon. Time and tide, remember, Sister Flannigan, time and tide.'

'Yes. Absolutely,' she muttered, wishing—oh, wishing so much—that the consultant would simply shut up.

He had such a very carrying voice even when he was trying to talk in an undertone, and though Connor was apparently deep in conversation with Chris he'd always been able to listen to two conversations at once.

'As I told you, I can't wait long,' Mr Brooke continued. 'You know how short-staffed we are, and, if you decide to step up to the plate and accept the nurse unit manager's job, we'll need to advertise for a replacement for your job.'

'I appreciate that,' Brianna said. *Please shut up*, she thought. *Please just shut the hell up.* 'And I'll give you my decision by the beginning of next week.'

'Good. Good.' Mr Brooke beamed, then turned on his heel. 'Ah, Connor. A word with you, if I may? I've had a talk with ENT, and they say you can interview their staff next week if that suits you.'

Brianna didn't wait to hear her husband's reply. She was too busy heading for the ward door. She was due a break, and she intended taking it right now. Not in the canteen—with her luck, she'd probably run into Josh—but the nurses' staffroom sounded good. A coffee, and more aspirin for her head sounded even better.

But her hoped-for peace and quiet didn't last long. Within minutes, Connor had appeared and seemed hell-bent on tearing the staffroom apart.

'Can I assume you've lost something?' she said as he turned his attention to the waste paper bin after riffling through the magazines on the coffee table.

'A memory card.' He frowned. 'I've been transferring my notes on the various departments I've been assessing from my phone to my laptop via a memory card, and I can't find it.'

'That'll teach you to be so damned hi-tech.' She could not help but chuckle. 'Use a clipboard and pen next time like the rest of us ordinary mortals.'

'Oh, very funny,' he said irritably, and she took pity on him.

'What does this memory card look like?'

'About the size of a small matchbox, but wafer thin.'

Brianna stared at the abandoned magazines, the un-washed coffee cups and discarded biscuit packets that littered the nurses' staffroom, and shook her head.

'Yeah, well, good luck with finding something that small in this place.'

'Maybe I left it at your cottage,' he murmured. 'I've already searched the nurse unit manager's office, and it's definitely not in there.'

'Don't you have a back-up memory card?'

He nodded. 'I do, but I'd still like to find the original. It has a lot of sensitive data on it.'

'Should MI5 be worried?' She grinned. 'Maybe we should—'

The rest of what she'd been about to say died in her throat when the staffroom door opened, and Jess appeared, her face shining.

'You look as though you've just won the lottery,' Brianna declared, and Jess's smile widened even further.

'It's something much, *much* better,' the counsellor said excitedly. 'I've remembered something else about the girl who I think could be Harry's mother. It came to me when I was talking to Mrs Renwick.'

'When you were talking to Naomi?' Brianna said, and Jess nodded.

'Naomi was wearing an initial necklace, and I suddenly remembered that the girl I met was wearing one, too. In fact, the second she saw me looking at it, she pushed it down into her blouse.'

'Can you remember what the initial was?' Connor asked when Brianna said nothing.

'M— no, N— Or was it M?' Jess shook her head with frustration. 'It was one or the other, I'm positive.'

'So what you're saying is we should be looking for a teenager, with blonde hair, and grey eyes, who may—or may not—have been pregnant when you saw her, and whose first name could start with the initial N or M?' Brianna declared. 'Jess, apart from the fact that this girl could be a complete red herring, think of all the girls' names that start with those initials. It would be like looking for a needle in a haystack.'

'Not that big a haystack,' Connor observed thoughtfully. 'Knowing it's either N or M would cut out a lot of teenagers in the area.'

'And what use is that?' Brianna said irritably. 'Even if we made a list of all the girls in the area whose Christian names begin with the letter N or M, we can hardly phone them up and say, "Have you been pregnant recently?"'

'Flora,' Jess declared. 'Flora Loveday's the health visitor for Penhally. I could phone her—ask if she's noticed any girl who fits my description. A girl who might suddenly have become rather plump recently.'

'And Flora will give you a complete roasting if you ask her that, you know she will,' Brianna protested. 'She'll cite patient confidentiality, and she'd be right.'

Jess grimaced.

'I know.' She sighed. 'It's just… Oh, this is so frustrating. I feel I'm so close, so very close to finding this girl. All I need is one extra piece of the jigsaw.'

'Jess—'

'I wonder if I could get a list of all the families in the area?' the counsellor continued. 'The electoral roll only gives the names of those old enough to vote—but…'

'And what then?' Brianna said, trying and failing to hide her irritation. 'I don't want to rain on your parade, but maybe you should just give up on this amateur sleuthing, and leave it to the police to track down Harry's mother. Personally, I think she's most likely to be someone from outside the county, rather than a local girl.'

'No, she's local,' Jess declared emphatically, 'and I still think it's the girl I met.'

'Oh, for heaven's sake, why can't you just accept it's not?' Brianna said tartly, and Jess blinked.

'Brianna…' Connor cautioned, and she rounded on him.

'It's true, Connor! This whole scenario of the girl who Jess happened to meet, who may, or may not, have given her a false name, and who may, or may not, be Harry's mother, is crazy, you know it is. I understand that Jess wants to help, but enough is enough!'

'Right,' Jess murmured, beginning to back away, her cheeks darkening. 'I'm sorry—you know—for bothering you like this, and I won't do it again.'

And before either Connor or Brianna could say anything she'd left the staffroom, and Connor shook his head at Brianna.

'That wasn't very kind.'

'Maybe I don't feel kind,' Brianna retorted. 'Maybe I've just heard enough of Jess's half-baked theories to last me a lifetime.'

'And maybe you don't want this baby's mother to come forward at all,' he said, and Brianna got to her feet impatiently.

'Of course I do. I just think—'

She never did complete what she'd been about to say. The emergency alarm sounded, and she was out of the staffroom in a second.

'What's wrong—what's happened?' Connor asked, hurrying after her.

'It's one of the babies,' Brianna replied, frantically washing her hands. 'Something's badly wrong with one of the babies!'

And it was Harry. Harry's monitors which were sounding the alarm, and Megan and Mr Brooke were already at his incubator.

'Pulmonary haemorrhage, Brianna,' Megan murmured, as she hurried round the incubator to insert another IV line. 'Looks like patent ductus arteriosus.'

'What does that mean?' Connor asked, trying not to get in the way, and wishing the monitors would stop making their shrill noise.

'Left heart failure,' Brianna replied tightly, and

Connor closed his eyes, feeling as though someone had punched him.

Heart failure. Their son had died because of an inherited heart defect, which meant it wasn't the same, but it felt like it.

'Why didn't that show up before?' he demanded. 'He's had enough X-rays and scans. Shouldn't it have shown up then?'

'It can sometimes happen to babies who have respiratory distress syndrome,' Megan explained. 'We don't know why, but when it happens it happens fast.'

'I want an echocardiogram, and I want it now,' Mr Brooke ordered.

Chris was gone in a flash, and somewhere in the ward Connor could hear one of the babies crying as though it somehow knew that…

Don't go there, his mind warned. *Don't even think that.*

'Is there anything I can do?' he asked as he saw Brianna flipping switches, changing lines, completely in control, though both her face and lips were white.

'Just keep out of the way,' she replied. 'Are we looking at thoracoscopic surgery?' she continued, glancing across at Mr Brooke.

'There's a strong risk of laryngeal nerve damage if I do that,' he declared as Chris appeared with the echocardiography machine. 'Plus I could end up with a ligation of the pulmonary artery if I make even the tiniest mistake.'

'There's also the mortality rate to consider,' Megan pointed out.

'Which is currently one per cent,' Brianna replied, as she applied some gel to Harry's chest. 'Pretty good odds, I'd say, plus you don't make mistakes, Mr Brooke.'

The consultant shook his head.

'Nice compliment, Sister, but all surgeons can make mistakes, and, with a baby as little as this, we could be also looking at damage to the thoracic duct.'

'Yes, but thoracoscospic surgery is much less risky than a thoracotomy,' Brianna argued, 'and we're running out of time here.'

'Agreed.' He nodded as Chris placed the transducer on Harry's chest. 'OK, let's see what we've got.'

To Connor, the echocardiogram seemed to take an eternity. The pictures on the screen meant nothing to him, but they clearly meant something to Brianna, Megan, Chris and Mr Brooke, because there was a lot of muttering and a lot of pointing.

'What have you decided?' he asked when Chris removed the transducer, and both Megan and Brianna looked at Mr Brooke.

The portly consultant chewed his lip, then nodded.

'Thoracoscospic surgery. Dr Phillips, Sister Flannigan, you'll assist.'

Chris was already pushing Harry's incubator out of the ward, and as Brianna made to follow her Connor put out his hand to stay her.

'He is going to be all right, isn't he?' he said.

'I don't know,' she replied, her bottom lip trembling slightly. 'I honestly don't know. Mr Brooke's a brilliant surgeon. He has lousy people skills, but when it comes to operating, he's the best, but... Look, why don't you go back to my cottage?' she continued. 'I don't know how long the op will take—'

'I'm going nowhere,' he said, but as Brianna turned to leave he added, 'Would it be wrong of me to wish you all luck? I know on the stage it's considered very bad luck to say that, so they say break a leg, but—'

'We'll take your good wishes,' Brianna declared. 'With this one we're going to need all the luck we can get.'

And she was gone, and Connor stood in the centre of the ward, knowing he had never felt quite so alone, while the other nurses bustled about, a kind of normality returned for them.

It had been so different with their own son, he thought as he walked slowly out of the ward and down to the nurses' staffroom. He and Brianna had sat together in the consultant's room, holding one another's hands in a vice-like grip as though that might somehow keep Harry with them, while the consultant had explained very gently, and very kindly, that there was nothing he could do. The damage to Harry's heart was too severe, he'd said, and the kindest thing would be to switch off his life-support system.

The kindest thing.

Connor gritted his teeth. He'd wanted to hit the consultant when he'd said that. Kind shouldn't have meant simply allowing their child to die. Kind should have meant the medical staff doing everything they could, never giving up, not them recommending they switch off the only thing that was keeping their son alive.

With an effort, he pushed open the door of the staffroom and went in. Were there any more depressing places than empty staffrooms and waiting rooms? he wondered as he sat down and let his head fall back against the seat. Brianna had been right when she'd said being able to do something was infinitely preferable to having nothing to do but wait, but wait he would, for as long as it took.

Wearily, Brianna walked down the corridor towards the staffroom. Chris had told her Connor was there, had been there ever since they'd taken Harry to Theatre, and she was grateful, so very grateful, that he'd stayed.

Gently, she opened the door in case he'd fallen asleep, but his head snapped round immediately, and she could see the hesitation in his eyes, the desire to know, and yet the fear of knowing, too.

'He's fine,' she said. 'The op was textbook perfect, and he's back in his incubator, breathing well.'

She saw him exhale, then his eyes scanned her face.

'How are you?'

'Shattered,' she admitted. 'Relieved. Happy.'

'Then, let's go home, Bree,' he said, getting to his feet. 'You're just about out on your feet, and you said yourself he's out of the woods, so let's go home.'

To his surprise, she didn't even attempt to argue, which proved how exhausted she was, and she didn't protest either when he put some food into the microwave when they got home, then pulled out a chair for her.

'I know you probably feel too tired to eat,' he said when the lasagne was ready, 'but you really should try.'

And obediently she picked up a fork. And she did eat, though he very much doubted if she knew what she was eating, but at least she ate.

'You're not still worrying about him, are you?' he said when she finally pushed her plate away, and she shook her head.

'When I was in Theatre,' she murmured, 'all I could think was how fleeting life can be. How, in the blink of an eye, everything can suddenly change, and you never get to do the things you want, or say the things you should, and then it's too late.' She raised her eyes to his. 'Do you remember asking me whether I was sorry I had left, or sorry you'd found me?'

He gazed back at her, clearly confused, obviously wondering why she was saying this now, and then he nodded.

'I remember.'

Say it, Brianna, she told herself. *Tell him everything because you might not ever have this moment again.*

'I was sorry you'd found me because I didn't want you to find me.'

His face twisted. 'I see.'

'No, you don't, because I haven't finished yet,' she said swiftly. 'I left you because I knew I had to get away from everything. From our flat, my memories and, yes, from you because every time I looked at you I saw Harry. Harry dying in my arms, Harry's life slipping away from him, and you…' She took a breath. 'You were slipping away from me, too, and I didn't want to face the fact that not only had my son died, but my marriage was over, so it was better to hide, better not to have to face that truth.'

'But our marriage wasn't over,' he declared, bewilderment plain in his blue eyes. 'Why in the world did you think it was?'

'Connor, even before Harry was born, we might have shared the same flat, but we barely talked, hardly ever saw one another—'

'I was *working,*' he protested. 'You know what working in the city is like. If you rest on your laurels, you don't get considered for the big deals, and I had to keep on working hard if I wanted to stay in the game.'

'But even when you came home, you used to shut yourself away in your study,' she said, 'and I'd wait, and wait, and maybe, if I got lucky, you'd share a few words with me, and I'd go to bed and fall asleep alone, not knowing what you were thinking, or…' Her eyes skittered away from his. 'If you still loved me, or you'd found someone else.'

'You thought I was *cheating* on you?' he exclaimed, plainly dumbfounded. 'Bree, I have *always* loved you, and I always will.'

'Then why did you increasingly shut me out?' she cried.

'And don't tell me you didn't, because you did, you know you did. You hardly ever held me, or kissed me, and...' A faint tinge of colour crept over her cheeks, but she was going to say this come what may. 'We only ever made love if I asked you to.'

He bit his lip savagely, and, at first, she didn't think he was going to answer her, and then he met her gaze, and she saw pain and heartache in his eyes.

'I know we did, and I am sorry, so sorry, but...' He shook his head blindly. 'Oh, hell, but this is so hard for me to say because I don't want to hurt you. You've been hurt so much already.'

'Say it, Connor,' she urged. 'Whatever it is, just say it.'

'I knew...' He took an uneven breath. 'I knew how much you wanted a child—I wanted a son or a daughter, too— but as the years went by, and you didn't become pregnant, I felt...' His eyes tightened. 'You didn't want to make love to me any more—not to me. That all I'd become for you was a sperm donor. Someone you needed to go through the motions with to get yourself pregnant, not someone you wanted to be there for you, not someone you wanted to give you pleasure.'

'You thought that?' she said, horror-stricken by his revelation. 'Oh, Connor, why didn't you tell me, why didn't you say something?'

He clenched his jaw. 'It's hardly the sort of thing you can say to your wife, is it?'

'But it would have explained so much,' she declared. 'I thought you didn't want me any more, that you'd fallen out of love with me, and I was so scared to ask you outright because I thought, If he's found somebody else, I won't be able to bear it.'

'There's never been anyone but you, Bree,' he said simply. 'There never will be.'

'I'm so sorry,' she said with a sob. 'Sorry I made you feel…redundant. I never meant to. I just… I wanted a baby so badly, but my desire for one shouldn't have made you feel you meant less to me than achieving that. Can you ever forgive me?'

To her surprise, he half turned from her, his face pain-racked.

'Don't, Bree, please, don't apologise to me. It only makes me feel worse.'

'Worse?' she echoed. 'What do you have to feel so badly about? I was the one at fault, not you.'

'You've no idea how I wish to God that was true, but it isn't, it isn't,' he said, his voice ragged.

'Connor—'

'You asked me before whether I wanted Harry, and the truth is…' He lowered his head for a second, and, when he looked up again, his eyes were agonised. 'Bree, when you were pregnant, you were so ill all the time. I used to listen to the other men at work, the ones whose wives were pregnant, saying how well their wives looked, how happy and blooming, and every night…' He balled his hands into fists. 'Every night I would go home and find you with your head down the toilet, being sick again. Nothing you ate seemed to stay down, and instead of looking blooming you just seemed to get thinner and thinner.'

'It was a difficult pregnancy,' she said, gently putting her hand on his arm. 'Some just are, and I didn't care about being sick. I just wanted our son.'

'I know you did, but…' He drew in an anguished breath. 'I hated him before he was born, Bree. I knew it was wrong,' he said quickly when she drew back from him, appalled. 'I knew I shouldn't feel that way, but seeing you so ill, knowing he was the one doing it to you… I was frightened. So frightened I was going to lose you, and no baby was worth losing you for, so, yes, you were right, I didn't want him.'

'Not even when he was born?' she said, her eyes dark, her voice barely audible. 'Didn't you want him even then?'

'When he was born…' Pain twisted across his face. 'Oh, Bree, when I saw him I suddenly knew why you hadn't given a damn about being so sick all the time. He was so beautiful, wasn't he, and I thought…' His voice shook. 'I thought, This is my son. This beautiful, tiny, little person is *my son*. And I thought my heart was going to burst with joy, and then…all hell broke loose. The doctors and nurses were running everywhere, and they took him out of your arms, and there were all these tubes and wires, and I thought, Stop it, stop what you're doing, you're hurting him, and you mustn't hurt him.'

'I remember,' she said, her voice suspended.

'And when the doctors said he wouldn't live…' Connor shook his head, and something like a sob broke from him. 'All I could think was, It's my fault. God has listened to me, and decided, OK, if you don't want him, I'll take him away from you.'

'No, Connor, oh, no!' she exclaimed, instinctively reaching for him, but he lurched to his feet, evading her. 'It wasn't like that, you mustn't think like that. No words, or thoughts, of yours could have caused Harry's heart condition. It was an inherited heart defect. A horribly, cruel, inherited defect.'

'I still blame myself,' he said raggedly, screwing his eyes shut. 'Every time I go to bed at night, and close my eyes, I still see him, so small, so fragile, and looking so much like you.'

'I always thought he looked like you,' she said unsteadily, and Connor shook his head.

'You, he was all you, and when he died… Bree, half of me died with him because I'd failed him, I'd failed you.'

'You didn't—you didn't,' she cried, getting to her feet and clasping his hands tightly in hers. 'Connor—'

'All my life I've set myself goals, Bree,' he said hoarsely, 'and I've ticked them off one by one, but the one thing I knew you wanted above everything else was a child, and when they said we should turn off his life support…' A shudder ran through him. 'I wanted to fight with them, to tell them to go to hell, to tell them *I* would save our son if they couldn't, but I couldn't save him, I knew I couldn't, and to feel I had no control, no power to alter anything… that broke me, Bree.'

She stared at him blindly, so wanting to help him, to somehow find the right words to say to help him, because she had never seen him like this before, a man in torment.

'Why didn't you tell me any of this?' she exclaimed. 'Oh, Connor, you should have told me this.'

'You were going through hell, and I…' He bit his lip. 'I didn't want to burden you with how I felt.'

'But we could have shared it,' she protested. 'All I could see was that you didn't seem to care—not like I cared. You wouldn't talk about him—'

'Because I always seemed to say the wrong thing,' he said. 'If I didn't talk about Harry you got so angry, and if I did talk about him you cried, and I couldn't…I couldn't bear to see you cry when there was nothing I could do to make it any better.'

'All I ever needed was for you to let me cry, Connor,' she said, her voice breaking. 'Just for you to let me cry and for you to…to talk about Harry, so I could feel you understood, that you felt the same way I did.'

'I did, Bree. Oh, God, how I did,' he said. 'I wanted him back, too. I wanted to be able to hold him again, and keep him safe, but I couldn't keep him safe, and…' A tear trickled down his cheek, and he pulled his hands out of hers. 'I'm sorry… I have to… I have to…'

He was walking swiftly towards the staircase and she ran after him.

'Connor, wait,' she begged, trying to catch hold of his arm, but he shrugged her off, and began climbing the stairs.

'Leave me be, Bree,' he said over his shoulder, his voice choked. 'I don't…I don't want you to see me like this.'

'Like what?' she cried. 'Showing me you care, showing you feel? Connor, it's not shameful to cry, it's not a sign of weakness.'

He came to a halt at the top of the stairs, his face averted.

'It is,' he said, his voice cracked. 'I should be supporting you, not the other way round.'

'Can't…can't we support one another?' she exclaimed. 'Comfort one another?'

'Bree, enough, please,' he entreated, and she walked round him, and caught his face in her hands.

'Don't, Connor, oh, please…don't shut me out,' she said, 'not this time.'

He screwed his eyes tight shut again, but it didn't help. She could see tears trickling down his cheeks, running into his nose and mouth, and for a moment he stood rigidly still and then suddenly he reached for her, and she caught him and, when he buried his face in her neck, he broke down completely.

Broke down and cried in great shuddering, gasping sobs

that tore at her heart, making her cry, too, but she didn't try to stop his tears, knew how much she'd hated it when he'd tried to stop hers, and knew, too, how much he needed to finally cry.

'I'm sorry, so sorry,' he said eventually, his voice raw, his eyes red-rimmed. 'You shouldn't have had to witness that.'

'Yes, I should,' she insisted, cupping his face with her hand. 'You loved Harry, just as I did.'

'Would…?' She saw him swallow hard. 'Would you stay with me tonight, Bree? I just want to hold you,' he added quickly. 'Nothing else—I just want to hold you, and not… not be alone any more.'

And she nodded, and took him to her bed, and held him close, and eventually they fell asleep, wrapped in one another's arms. And some time in the middle of the night, he woke her, and reached for her, and she knew what he wanted, and this time she wanted it, too. This time she wanted to make love to him, and, as she touched him, and he touched her, they both cried again. Not the racking, heart-rending tears they'd shed in the past, but tears that were healing tears, tears for a past they could not change, that left them clinging to one another, neither of them ever wanting to let go.

CHAPTER SIX

CONNOR smiled slightly as he rolled over onto his back, and heard the small, protesting sigh that Brianna made as she followed him and nestled up again against his side.

It was going to be all right. Everything was finally going to be all right. When he and Brianna had made love last night it had been both a wonderful and also a cathartic experience for them both, and this morning he felt new, reborn, as though the world was yet again full of endless possibilities, instead of the dark and empty place it had been for the last two years.

Today is the first day of the rest of your life.

Who had said that? He couldn't remember, but today was most definitely the start of a new life for both of them and he wasn't going to screw it up this time round. This time he would get it right.

Gently, he put his arm round her, not wanting to wake her, but, when he rested his chin on the top of her head, he heard her yawn.

'What time is it?' she murmured.

He squinted at the bedside clock. 'A little after seven.'

'I have to get up,' she said regretfully. 'Auditors might be able to lie in bed for as long as they like, but nurses don't have that luxury.'

He tightened his grip on her, not wanting to let her go,

and knowing he wanted her all over again as she stretched against him.

'Pity about that,' he said, tracing the length of her spine with his finger and feeling her shiver. 'I was kind of hoping...'

'I'm sure you were,' she said, as she raised her head and looked up at him, her brown eyes dancing, before rolling over onto her back, 'but I need a shower, and some breakfast.'

He propped himself up on his elbow and gazed down at her.

'We could shower together. Very eco, that. Saving water, heating, and think how much faster we'd get clean if we washed each other.'

'Yeah, right.' She chuckled. 'And like I don't know that the state of the planet would be the very last thing on your mind if we got into the shower together. Connor, I don't have time.'

'But I can be real fast when it comes to showering,' he insisted. 'See, what I'd do first would be to put some soap on my hands, and then I'd do this...'

Slowly he smoothed his hands over her shoulders, tracing the length of her collarbone.

'Connor, I really don't—'

'And then,' he interrupted, his voice becoming a little huskier as his palms slid down onto her breasts. 'I'd wash you here. Very carefully, of course,' he continued, hearing her suck in her breath sharply as he began sliding his hands up and down and over each breast, circling and circling them until the nipples peaked, 'because I know how very sensitive your breasts are.'

'Connor, I...I think you should stop now,' she said faintly, and he shook his head at her.

'You see, that's the beauty of us showering together.

You wouldn't have to think,' he murmured. 'And after I'd washed your breasts—because I'm a really thorough sort of a man—I'd cover you with plenty of soap down here,' he continued, sliding his palm down her stomach, slowly, oh, so very slowly, until he cupped her. 'And then,' he added, as he began to stroke and stroke her, easing her thighs further and further apart, 'I'd do this, though of course you'll just have to try to imagine the soap. How very wet it would be, how very warm, how…liquid.'

'I'm…I'm trying not to.' She gasped, biting her lip when his finger slipped inside her and he continued to stroke her, and she felt the heat beginning to build. 'Connor…please… *please stop*!'

'Hey, but it sure does take a lot of effort to get you really clean, doesn't it?' He chuckled as he increased the pressure of his fingers, and she began to writhe beneath him. 'Maybe I'd also need to do this…'

And he bent down and replaced his fingers with his tongue. Gently at first, licking into her so gently, and then his tongue began to probe further, and further inside her, and she put her hands on his head, and arched up against him, as she felt the throbbing begin, the pulsing begin.

'Connor, oh…oh, my…oh, my *God*!'

And suddenly she jerked and convulsed, shaking and trembling, her heartbeat drumming in her ears as the heat went everywhere.

'Good?' he whispered in her ear, and she nodded breathlessly.

'Very good, amazingly good, stupendously good.'

'And there was you thinking it would take me for ever to get you clean if we shared a shower,' he said with a wicked grin.

She stared back at him for a heartbeat, then, before

he knew what she was doing, she had pinned him onto his back.

'My turn now,' she said, her eyes gleaming. 'My turn to play torturer.'

'Really?' he said huskily, exhaling sharply when she began tracing her fingers down his chest.

'Oh, absolutely.' She nodded as she bent her head, and licked one of his nipples, and then the other, and heard him gasp. 'It's only fair, after all. In fact…' she continued, as she slid her hand down his stomach, and he tensed with anticipation. 'In fact…'

'In fact, what?' he whispered as she suddenly sat up.

'Sorry,' she said, her eyes dancing with devilment. 'I'm afraid this is going to have to be put on hold, because I've just noticed the time, and if I don't hurry up and have a proper shower I'm going to be late.'

'*Brianna!*'

'Yes?' she said, her lips curving, as she slipped out of bed and headed for the door.

'I take back what I said about you being an angel,' he protested. 'You're a witch!'

'Probably.' She grinned.

And he laughed. Witch or angel, he honestly didn't care. She was his again, and that was all that mattered.

Except it wasn't, he realised when he grabbed a quick shower after she'd had hers, and hurried down to the kitchen. Normally, the percolator would be on, and the table would be laid, but this morning none of those things had been done. She was standing by the kitchen window instead, gazing out, and, when she heard him come in, the smile that greeted him was tentative in the extreme. Something had clearly happened between the shower and the kitchen, and that something was making her think, and he didn't want her to think, to have any doubts.

'Fruit juice and cereal for breakfast as usual?' he said brightly.

'Fine,' she replied, retrieving two bowls from the cupboard and putting them on the table.

'Coffee or tea? It will have to be instant if you want coffee,' he added. 'It will take too long if we wait for the percolator.'

'Instant coffee,' she murmured. 'And plenty of it. I find I need lots of caffeine in the morning nowadays.'

'Me, too, or I'm hell to live with.' He grinned. 'Or hellier than I would be.' He frowned. 'Is there such a word as hellier?'

'I expect so,' she said. 'Or if there isn't, there should be.'

Something was most definitely wrong, he thought as he switched on the kettle, then took some orange juice out of the fridge and filled two glasses. Everything had been perfect, just perfect, and now she looked nervous, unsure, as though there was something she wanted to say but wasn't quite sure how to phrase it.

The job, he suddenly realised. It would be that damn job Brooke had offered her. He'd overheard the consultant asking her about it, and she clearly wanted to take it, but she'd realised he wouldn't want to move here, and she was right. Penhally and St Piran were probably very nice for holidaymakers who weren't big on excitement, but what sort of work would he get here? Hell, he'd be reduced to making spreadsheets, and advising the local butcher and baker on their tax returns. Well, it wasn't a problem. There must be dozens of nurse unit managers' jobs in London, and he'd help her scour the nursing magazines for them, and then she could have what she wanted, and he could, too.

'Something wrong?' he said, deliberately giving her an opening, but she shook her head.

'No, no problem,' she replied with a smile he didn't buy for a second.

OK, he thought. Give her time, give her space, don't crowd her, she'll mention the job when she's ready.

'Cream or milk on your cereal?' he asked. 'Actually, scrub the cream,' he added with a frown as he noticed the use-by date. 'You know, you really will have to go shopping.'

'I'll do it before I come home tonight,' she murmured, then he saw her take a deep breath.

Here it comes, he thought. Here comes the 'Mr Brooke has offered me the job I've always wanted, and I don't know what to do about it', so say the right thing this time, Connor, or you're toast.

'I was just thinking about Harry,' she said, taking him completely by surprise. 'The baby I found, not our son,' she added quickly, 'and I was wondering…if his mother doesn't ever come forward…how would you feel…?' She rearranged the salt and pepper cruet on the kitchen table. 'How would you feel about us adopting him?'

Oh, *hell*. He'd known she was getting far too close to this child, much too involved, but he'd never imagined anything like this, hadn't for one second seen this coming.

'Bree—'

'If his mother never claims him,' she said quickly, 'he'll be sent to a foster-home, and though I'm sure they're wonderful places—nothing like the orphanages of the past— they're not like a real home, are they? Connor, we could give him a home, be his parents,' she continued, eagerness plain in her eyes. 'I know he wouldn't be ours in the sense of us being his real mother and father, but we could give him so much.'

'I understand that,' he began carefully, 'but, sweetheart, we're both still young, and though I know it took us a long time to conceive Harry, that doesn't mean we couldn't try for a child of our own again.'

'*No!*' she said vehemently. 'The heart defect Harry was born with, it's an inherited condition, so it could happen again, and to wait for nine months, feeling him—or her—growing inside me—always wondering, always fearing, never knowing… I can't do that, I *can't.*'

'But—'

'The little Harry in the hospital…he *needs* me, Connor, and we have so much love we could give him.'

Slowly he walked over to her, and put his hands on her shoulders, forcing her to look up at him.

'I know we do, but, Brianna, are you sure you want this child for the right reasons?'

She shook her head impatiently.

'What better reasons could there be than me wanting to give him a home, parents, love?'

'You could do that for our own child—'

'I've explained to you why I won't risk that,' she declared. 'Weren't you listening—didn't you hear what I said?'

He *had* heard, he thought. Much more than she probably wanted him to hear.

'Bree, what you're saying is, you want a baby, but you want a no-risk baby,' he said gently. 'You want the baby in the hospital because, though he has health problems, they're health problems that can be cured, and you'll be able to take him home. You're scared, Bree,' he continued as she tried to interrupt. 'You're scared of the unknown, of what might happen if we try for another child—and I can understand that, I feel the same way—but that isn't the right reason to adopt this child.'

'I want him because I can give him what he doesn't

have,' she protested, shrugging herself free from his hands. 'A mother, a father, a home. Why is that so very wrong?'

'It isn't, if it was the whole truth, but it isn't, you know it isn't. Bree, after Harry died, I read up on heart defects. They can be detected now by antenatal screening at eighteen weeks—'

'And then what?' she interrupted. 'If the scan discovered there was something wrong, do you honestly think I would opt for an abortion? I'd have to carry on with the pregnancy, knowing…' She took a ragged breath. 'Knowing that the baby inside me was going to die, just like Harry died, and I don't think I'd be able to survive that.'

He wanted to argue with her. He wanted to tell her that perhaps it wouldn't happen, that maybe the odds would fall on their side this time, but she looked so stricken, and the Harry in the hospital did need a home. Would it be so very wrong to agree to what she wanted even though he knew, instinctively, that it was for all the wrong reasons?

'Connor?'

She was waiting anxiously for his reply, and he sighed.

'Even if I agree to this, it's only been four days since you found him. His mother could still come forward.'

'A normal mother wouldn't have left her child for four hours, far less four days,' she argued back. 'And much as I don't want to agree with Rita, maybe she's right, maybe Harry's mother doesn't want him, which gives us all the more reason to give him a home, where he'd be wanted.'

'And then there's the actual adoption process,' he continued. 'There are couples who have been on waiting lists for years, and just because he's in your ward doesn't mean you can jump the queue.'

'I know that—I understand that,' she insisted, 'but we could try. Will you at least agree that we could try?'

Her eyes were large, pleading, and he wished he could

think of something to say that would dissuade her. He didn't want her to be hurt again, he so desperately didn't want her to be hurt, but he knew how high the odds were against any adoption agency fast-tracking them to the top of their list, and those odds were too high.

'Connor. Please,' she continued softly, and he sighed, then nodded reluctantly.

'If the baby's mother doesn't come forward, we'll see if adopting him is possible,' he said, and saw her face light up with a smile that tore at his heart.

'Thank you,' she said fervently. 'You won't regret it, I know you won't.'

He hoped to heaven he wouldn't, as he watched her hurry across the kitchen to take the cereal packet out of the cupboard, her step light, her lips still curved into a happy smile. He could only hope to heaven that everything would turn out all right.

'You're looking very happy this morning, Sister,' Naomi Renwick declared.

'I feel happy.' Brianna smiled. 'It's a lovely spring morning, all of the babies had an excellent night, including your daughter, so what more could I wish for?'

'My wish would be to take my daughter home,' Naomi replied. 'I know, I know,' she continued as Brianna opened her mouth to interrupt, 'she's doing really well, and in a couple of weeks you're going to try feeding her orally, but…'

'You want to take her home now,' Brianna finished for her, and when Mrs Renwick nodded, she put her arm round her. 'It *will* happen, honestly it will. Good grief, even Mr Brooke is happy with her, and you won't often hear me putting the words "Mr Brooke" and "happy" in the same sentence.'

Naomi chuckled. 'That's what Mrs Corezzi said yesterday. She's very nice, isn't she?'

'She's one of the best.'

'And so are you, Sister Flannigan,' Mrs Renwick declared, and, before Brianna realised what she was about to do, Naomi had leant forward and kissed her cheek. 'In fact, if there was an award for nurse of the year, you'd get my vote.'

'And now you've got Sister Flannigan completely speechless.' Megan laughed as she joined them. 'And that takes some doing, I'm telling you.'

Naomi laughed, and Brianna laughed, too, but her cheeks were burning when she accompanied Megan across the ward.

'That was very nice of her to say,' she murmured. 'Not that I am—or could be—nurse of the year, but—'

'Brianna, you're damn good at your job so no more of this false modesty,' Megan insisted. 'And talking about jobs,' she continued, lowering her voice, 'a little bird in the shape of our portly consultant tells me you're going to be our new nurse unit manager?'

'I haven't accepted the job yet, Megan,' Brianna replied quickly. 'I'd like to, but it's…complicated.'

'One of the complications wouldn't happen to be a certain man who has a very definite spring in his step this morning, would it?' Megan said, her eyes twinkling, and Brianna smiled.

'Connor, and I… We had a long talk last night—'

'I'd say you did a lot more than talk, judging by how you both look today,' Megan said shrewdly, and, when Brianna crimsoned, she chuckled. 'Knew it. So, what's the problem?'

'I do love him, Megan,' Brianna replied. 'I loved him when I married him, and the love's still there. A bit bruised, a little bit battered, perhaps, but it's still there, and this time I think we could make our marriage work, make it a partnership of equals, but...'

'Not here in St Piran.'

It was a statement, not a question, and Brianna bit her lip.

'What would he do here, Megan? His whole career is centred around London. Coming to hospitals like St Piran's... It's a one-off commission, not a permanent job.'

'He could change his life, his career,' the paediatric specialist registrar pointed out. 'People downsize all the time, throw up their high-powered jobs and move to the country to keep chickens or pigs.'

Brianna let out a giggle. 'Can you honestly see Connor keeping chickens or pigs?'

'Well, no,' Megan conceded, 'but I'm sure there's lots of other things he could do if he put his mind to it.'

'How can I ask him to do that?' Brianna protested. 'He's happy where he is.'

'So, in this partnership of equals,' Megan said slowly, 'you're going to be the one who has to give up everything, and return to London?'

Return to London. Just the thought made Brianna's heart plummet. Return to their modern flat, the anonymous streets, to feeling as though her life was on hold again.

Except it wouldn't be like that, she thought as her eyes drifted past Megan to little Harry's incubator. If everything went well, she would have Harry, she would have a child, and that would make everything different. It would.

'It will work this time,' she said firmly. 'I'll make it work.'

'If you say so,' Megan replied. 'Just...'

'Just what?' Brianna asked, seeing her friend's face grow suddenly serious.

'Don't tell Mr Brooke you don't want the job, at least not yet. Connor will be here for another four or five weeks, so take that time to make sure you've both resolved everything between you.'

'I will.' Brianna smiled. 'But you worry too much.'

'Probably,' Megan admitted, 'but just be careful, OK?'

There was nothing to be careful about, Brianna thought as she walked over to little Harry's incubator, and smiled down at him. Everything was going to be fine. She just knew it, could feel it. Harry had come through the operation with flying colours, and already she could see he was brighter, more alert, and Connor had just been trying to protect her when he'd talked about the difficulties of adoption. The authorities were bound to see they were an ideal couple. They were both still young, were comfortably off, had been married for ten years, and she'd give up work, be a stay-at-home mum, so Harry would never have to come home from school to an empty house. And there were so many parks in London, it would almost be like being in the country. And her parents would love him, she knew they would, and—

'Brianna.'

'Are you trying to give me a seizure?' she protested, whirling round to see Connor standing behind her. 'Please don't creep up on me like that, not when I'm miles away.'

'I saw that.'

Something was wrong, she realised. His face was carefully blank, his eyes even more so, and, when she smiled encouragingly up at him, he didn't smile back.

'Hey, whatever it is can't be that bad,' she declared, and saw him flinch.

'There's someone outside you need to see,' he said.

Even his voice sounded strange, as though it was being forced out of him.

'Look, if it's Vermin again,' she began, 'you can tell him—'

'It's not Vermin. It's…' He shook his head. 'I think you should come.'

'Connor, you know I don't like surprises,' she protested. 'Can't you just tell me who it is?'

He didn't answer. He simply walked over to the ward door and opened it, and she sighed.

'This is crazy,' she grumbled. 'I'm really busy right now, so I'm warning you, whoever it is had better want me for a very good reason.'

He still didn't say anything and, when she first went out into the corridor, she was none the wiser. Rita was standing there with a face like stone. No big surprise there, she thought wryly. Jess was beaming broadly at her, but, then, Jess always had a sunny expression, and to Jess's left stood a large, jolly-looking woman in her early forties whom Brianna didn't recognise at all.

Blankly, Brianna glanced back at Connor. Was this a deputation of some sort, a fundraising committee? Puzzled, she shifted her gaze back to the three women, and then she saw her. Standing awkwardly behind the jolly-looking woman, looking, oh, so shy and nervous, was a young girl. A young girl who couldn't have been any more than sixteen. A young girl with corn-coloured hair and large grey eyes, and Brianna dug her fingernails into the palms of her hands until they hurt.

'My name's Marina Hallet,' the jolly-looking lady declared, 'and this is my daughter, Nicola. She's the one who left the baby in the car park. She's Colin's mother.'

'Colin?' Brianna repeated, through lips grown suddenly dry.

'That's his name,' the teenager said softly. 'What I called him—after his father.'

'And we know one another, don't we, *Marcia*?' Jess smiled, and Nicola Hallet looked shamefaced.

'I'm sorry about lying to you that day in the hospital, Miss Carmichael—'

'Her name is Mrs Corezzi now, Nicola,' Rita declared irritably. 'Can't you at least try to get something right for once in your life?'

Nicola looked crushed, and Jess leant towards the girl, a gentle smile on her face.

'Nicola, please call me Jess. All my friends do,' she added, and Brianna heard Rita give a very deliberate sniff.

A sniff that everyone completely ignored.

'I should have told you my real name,' the teenager continued awkwardly. 'I should have said my name was Nicola Hallet, but...'

So Jess had been right, Brianna thought dully. The initial necklace that the girl she'd seen wearing *had* been either an N or an M. It was an N.

'Look, why don't we all go into the staffroom?' Jess suggested. 'It will be a lot more comfortable than standing out here in the corridor.'

'I'd really like to see my grandson,' Mrs Hallet said quickly, and Brianna saw Rita wince.

'And you will,' Jess declared, 'but I'm sure Sister Flannigan must have lots of questions for you.'

'Yes, of course,' Brianna said automatically.

But she didn't want to ask any questions, she didn't want to know anything at all about the teenager, or her family.

She just wanted them to go away, and give her back her dream.

'Aren't you coming in with us?' she said as the four women trooped into the staffroom, and Connor didn't move at all.

'I can't,' he said softly, 'you know I can't. Patient confidentiality, remember?'

He was right, she knew he was, but she suddenly felt so very alone, and he must have sensed it because he clasped her hands tightly.

'I'll be right out here,' he said. 'I won't go anywhere. I'll stay right out here, and wait for you in the corridor.'

Which was where she wanted to be, she thought as she stiffened her back and walked into the staffroom in time to hear Mrs Hallet tell Jess her family owned a fruit-growing farm near Penhally.

What difference did it make what kind of farm the Hallets owned? It wasn't important, it didn't matter, and before she could stop herself she rounded on Nicola.

'Why did you leave your son—abandon him?' she demanded.

Her words were harsh, she knew they were as she saw the teenager flush and heard Jess suck in her breath, but she didn't care. She wanted answers. Little Harry deserved them.

'The silly girl was frightened to tell us she was expecting a baby,' Mrs Hallet declared before her daughter could answer. 'We didn't even know she was going out with Colin Maddern from the garage, far less that she was pregnant. If only she'd told us. When I think of all those months when she must have been so frightened…' Mrs Hallet shook her head. 'I don't know how she coped, I really don't.'

'And you didn't realise—didn't notice your own daughter was pregnant?' Brianna exclaimed, not pretending to hide her disbelief even though Jess was staring at her with clear dismay.

'I know I should have done,' Mrs Hallet admitted, 'but what with the work on the farm, and my family of seven… You see, there's always something happening, some crisis, and Nicola… She's always been the quiet one, the one with her head stuck in a book, and…' She smiled apologetically at her daughter. 'She's always been a little on the plump side so I didn't notice any change in her.'

'I wore lots of baggy clothes,' Nicola murmured, 'and like Mum said, there's always so much going on in our house no one noticed I was getting bigger.'

And she looked so young, so very young, Brianna thought, feeling a hard lump in her throat that no amount of swallowing seemed to move. 'How old are you, Nicola?' she asked.

'Sixteen. Sixteen years and four months to be exact,' the girl added hurriedly.

As though those four months made any damn difference, Brianna thought. Nicola was still a mother, while she… She was never going to be one.

'Why did you leave him in the car park?' she exclaimed. 'Nicola, he could have *died* there!'

The teenager's eyes filled with tears.

'I was bringing him to the hospital because I knew there was something wrong with him,' she replied. 'When I tried to feed him he didn't seem to know what to do, and his breathing wasn't right, but the first person I saw was Grandma, and I knew she'd have a go at Mum, say it was all her fault that I'd got pregnant at fifteen. But it wasn't Mum's fault. Colin and I… We never intended to make love—we were going to wait—but…'

'These things just happen,' Jess said, shooting Brianna

a puzzled glance, and Nicola nodded and wiped her nose with the back of her hand.

'Colin…he said we'd get married if I found out I was pregnant, and I know we would have, because he loved me, and I loved him, but then…' The tears in the teenager's eyes began to spill over. 'He was killed, and he never knew… He never knew he had a son.'

And I think I knew him, Brianna thought dully as Jess leant forward and pressed a handkerchief into the teenager's hand, and she remembered the day she'd had trouble with her car months ago, and she'd stopped at the garage in St Piran, and the young mechanic there had mended it for her.

'Your Colin… He had black hair, and a lovely smile, didn't he?' she said, trying to keep her voice even but knowing she was failing miserably.

'You knew him?' Nicola said eagerly.

'I met him once,' Brianna replied. 'And I remember his smile.'

And how I'd thought that my Harry might have looked just like the young mechanic, if he'd lived and grown up.

'Why didn't you come back later, after your grandmother had gone?' Jess asked, and Nicola bit her lip.

'I meant to—I intended to,' she said, 'but Colin's breathing seemed to be getting worse, and then I saw you. I remembered how kind you were before, and I know I should have told you I was pregnant, but I was scared you'd tell Grandma, and she'd make me get an abortion, and I didn't want to have an abortion.'

'No one would have made you have an abortion,' Nicola's mother declared, shooting Rita a look that defied her to argue. 'You loved this boy, and he loved you, and your father and I would have helped.'

'But why didn't you just give the baby to Jess?' Brianna

protested. 'Why leave it where it might not be found for hours?'

'I guess I panicked,' Nicola replied. 'I recognised the car—I'd seen Mrs Corezzi—Jess—out in it, and I thought it was hers, that she was leaving the hospital so she'd be sure to find my son. I waited,' she added quickly. 'I didn't just go. I waited until you picked him up, so I knew he was safe.'

'And the first we knew of any of this was when she broke down in tears over that photograph in the paper,' Mrs Hallet said. 'That was when the whole story came out.'

'Can I see him?' Nicola asked. 'Can I see my son?'

'I'd like to see him, too,' Mrs Hallet declared, 'and I'm sure his great-grandmother would just love to see the newest addition to our family, wouldn't you, Rita?'

The ward clerk looked as though she would have preferred to have been force-fed poison, but she managed a tight-lipped nod.

'Of course you can see him,' Jess declared, 'but I have to warn you that you might find the sight of him a bit upsetting. He's been very ill, you see,' she added as Nicola looked from her to Brianna in panic. 'He had to have an operation yesterday, and though he's come through that well, he has a lot of tubes and wires attached to him to help him breathe.'

'You mean, he might…he could…die?' Nicola said, fresh tears welling in her eyes.

'No, he won't die,' Brianna said with difficulty. 'The tubes and wires are only temporary, a precaution.'

'And the important thing to remember is, under all the tubes and wires, he's still your son,' Jess said gently. 'He's still your baby.'

Your baby.

Not my baby, Brianna thought as Jess led the way out

of the staffroom, and she followed slowly. He was Nicola Hallet's baby, and she was happy about that—of course she was—because a baby should always be with its mother. It was the natural order of things, it was what was right.

'Are you OK?' Connor said the moment he saw her, his eyes worried, his face drawn.

'Of course I am,' she replied. 'Why wouldn't I be?'

'Brianna—'

She swept past him into the ward, her head held high, but, as she stood to one side of the incubator, and saw Mrs Hallet beam with clear pleasure at her grandson, and Nicola gaze down at him with such love in her eyes, she felt her heart twist inside her. Connor's eyes were fixed on her, she knew they were, but she couldn't meet his gaze, knew she would see sympathy there, and she didn't want to see sympathy, but when the baby stretched up one of his tiny hands towards his mother's face, she couldn't bear it. She just couldn't bear to be there, witnessing this reunion, and quietly she slipped out of the ward, needing to get away, to go anywhere, just so long as it was away.

'Brianna, wait!'

Connor had come after her, and she didn't want to see him, or hear his unease.

'You'll have to excuse me,' she said, turning her back on him, fast. 'I have things to do, paperwork—forms—to fill in...'

Quickly, she began to walk away from him, but he caught her by the elbow and steered her deliberately into the nurse unit manager's office.

'Brianna, sweetheart, you don't have to be brave,' he said, and she could see the anxiety in his eyes for her. 'I know how hard this must be for you.'

'It's not hard at all,' she said brightly. 'I'm fine, perfectly fine. It's great that Harry—Colin's—mother has come forward for him. Absolutely great.'

'She seems a very sweet girl,' he said carefully.

'And I'm sure she'll look after him perfectly well even though she's just sixteen,' she declared, picking up a piece of paper from his desk, then putting it down again, 'and it's not little Harry...' She bit her lip. '*Colin*'s fault he'll have the great-grandmother from hell.'

'I think we can be sure Nicola's mother will tell Rita to back off in no uncertain terms.'

She nodded. 'Yes, of course she will, but...' She picked up the sheet of paper again. 'Connor, how can we be sure this girl is his mother? I mean, what proof do we have?'

'Jess recognised her as the girl who came in that day.'

'But that doesn't prove anything, does it?' she argued back. 'Just because she's the girl Jess saw doesn't mean—'

'Brianna, she's his mother, you know she is,' he interrupted gently, 'and, though she's very young, I think she has a sensible head on her shoulders, and her mother and father will help her, make sure she does right by the little boy.'

'Yes, of course they will,' she murmured. 'And Mrs Hallet looked nice. Don't you think she looked nice?' she added, all too aware she was talking too much, but if she stopped...if she stopped... 'And the Hallets have a farm, so Colin will have all those wonderful places to play in, just as I did when I was a child, and I'll see him occasionally, won't I—around and about in Penhally. Not often, of course, but I might see him sometimes—'

'Oh, Bree—'

'And it won't matter that he won't remember me,' she said on a sob, 'because that's as it should be. He'll have his real mother, and lots of aunts and uncles, and probably grandparents—'

'Bree, I'm so sorry,' Connor said, his heart breaking for her, 'so very, very sorry. I know you wanted him, had grown to care for him.'

'But I'm not his mother, am I?' she said, as tears began to roll down her cheeks. 'And a baby…a baby should always be with his mother. Except he did look so much…so very much like Harry, and now…and now…'

And Connor reached for her, and she stepped into his arms, and he held her tight, and didn't tell her not to cry, knew better now, and thanked God that the tears she wept into his shoulder weren't like the tears she'd shed for their own Harry. That these were tears of regret, tears for what could never be, what he suspected she'd always known, deep down, could never be, and yet had still hoped.

'I'm OK now,' she hiccuped when her tears were finally spent.

'You're sure?' he said anxiously, drying her face with his fingertips, scanning her eyes with concern.

'Yes,' she said, beginning to nod, then shook her head. 'No, I'm not, but I will be.'

'Honestly?' he said, and she manufactured a smile.

'Honestly.'

'I think we should go home,' he said, and she closed her eyes.

'I can't—I have another two hours of my shift to work.'

'I'll square it with Megan—she'll understand.'

Going home sounded good. Getting away from the unit for even a little while seemed even better.

'OK. All right,' she said.

Connor made for the door, then stopped. 'You will still be here when I get back, won't you?'

'I'm not going anywhere,' she said with a trembling smile. 'Not without you.'

And he smiled. A wide, comforting smile that warmed her bruised and battered heart.

'Give me two minutes,' he said. 'I won't be any longer.'

She hoped he wouldn't be. She didn't want Rita to suddenly appear. The ward clerk might have been a thorn in her side ever since she'd come to St Piran, but she could not find it in her to gloat over Rita's clear discomfiture, though she knew many of the hospital staff undoubtedly would. All she wanted was to go home, to have some peace and quiet to come to terms with Nicola's appearance, but peace turned out to be in short supply when Connor returned and they walked together down the stairs towards the exit.

The nearer they got to the ground floor, the more Brianna became aware of the sound of angry voices. Voices that seemed to be raised in unison, in something that sounded almost like a chant, and when she and Connor reached the entrance hall to the hospital she stopped dead.

The forecourt in front of the hospital was a seething mass of people. People of all ages and sexes who were carrying placards with the letters 'SOB' painted on them.

'What in the world…?' she began, as Connor let out a muttered oath. 'It looks like some kind of demonstration, but what on earth are people demonstrating about, and what does SOB mean?'

'Brianna, come back into the hospital,' Connor said quickly. 'I need to talk to you. My report…it's nowhere near completed yet. I still have lots of departments to assess, and what I've written is simply an initial recommendation, based on my first impressions, not a definitive view.'

'But, how would anyone know what you'd written?' she said in confusion. 'Not even the secretaries in Admin are good enough to read your mind.'

'My notes were on that memory card—the one I lost

or…' Connor came to a halt and frowned. Kennie Vernon was amongst the demonstrators, notebook in hand, and he smiled when he saw Connor, a smile that was triumphant, and Connor swore, long and low, and fluently. 'He must have taken it. It was in the staffroom with my laptop yesterday when he came in to see Brooke. That low-life reporter must have taken it.'

'But what did your notes say?' Brianna demanded, still confused. 'What do all these banners mean?'

'Bree, I'm sorry, those notes were private, no one was supposed to see them yet, and they're only my thoughts, suggestions…'

His voice trailed away into silence, and as she stared at him blankly the penny dropped, and her blankness gave way to anger. A seething, furious anger.

'SOB,' she said. 'It stands for Save Our Babies, doesn't it? You've recommended to the board that they shut down the neonatal intensive care unit.'

'Brianna, it's not definite yet—'

'But you've recommended it,' she repeated. 'You looked at our unit, and you had the…the callousness…the insensitivity…to actually say it wasn't doing a good job!'

'It's not a question of whether it's doing a good job or not,' he said defensively. 'The work that's done in the unit is second to none—I would never disagree with that—but I have to go by the statistics—figures. The unit in Plymouth can cater for double the amount of babies—'

'Cater?' she exclaimed. '*Cater?* Connor, we're not some sort of fast-food restaurant, we're a specialist nursing centre!'

'Brianna—'

'And if you shut us down it's not simply a case of saying, well, all the babies can go to Plymouth. What about the winter, when the roads are icy, or blocked with snow? What about the height of summer when the road is packed with slow-moving caravans and sightseeing tourists? That thirty-mile journey could take an hour—more!'

'If it's a real emergency you have a helicopter service—'

'Which could be out on another call when we need it, or grounded by ice or gale-force winds.'

'Brianna—'

'It's always been figures and numbers, for you, hasn't it?' she said furiously. 'Forget about what people—real people—want or need. Connor, can't you see that not everything can be neatly tied up in a balance sheet?'

'But it makes good medical as well as economic sense,' he protested. 'Can't you at least see that?'

It also meant something else, she realised. Something that was altogether much, much closer to home.

'There'll also be no nurse unit manager's job for me either, will there, if you shut us down?' she said icily. 'Is that why you're doing this, because you think if I don't have a job I'll come back to you?'

'Of course that isn't what I thought!' he exclaimed, anger darkening his face. 'Brianna, listen to me—'

'And to think I told Rita you'd never let personal bias influence your work,' she continued, fury plain in her voice. 'You took one look at Penhally, and St Piran, and thought dead-end places. You thought no way would I ever want to live here, so let's make sure Brianna can't either, and then she'll meekly come back with me to London.'

'That never occurred to me for a second,' he flared.

'Just like it didn't occur to you last night to tell me what you were planning to do with my unit,' she retorted. 'You let me think you'd changed, Connor. You made me think you cared—'

'I did—I do—'

'Then how can you even *think* of shutting down an

NICU?' she cried. 'It's where Harry spent his few hours of life, where all these babies I look after get a chance to live. OK, so we couldn't save Harry, but just because we couldn't it doesn't mean you should deny all these other babies that chance.'

'Brianna—'

'I want you out of my house when I get home tonight,' she said, her voice shaking with anger. 'I want you, and your posh designer suits, and your expensive shirts and shoes, and your damn, all-singing-all-dancing phone out of my house by the time I get home, and if they're not I'll dump the whole lot in my garden.'

'Can't we at least sit down and talk about this like sensible human beings?' he exclaimed. 'If you would just let me explain—'

'There's no need to,' she interrupted, 'because I already know what you are. You're a bastard, Connor. A complete and utter bastard.'

And she walked away from him, pushing her way through the demonstrators who had now spilled out of the forecourt and into the hospital foyer, only to discover her way barred by Kennie Vernon. Normally she would have walked straight past him, but this time she didn't. This time she stopped and, sensing a scoop, he pulled out his pen.

'Do you have a comment for me, Sister Flannigan, for our readers?'

Brianna glanced over her shoulder. Someone in the crowd had clearly recognised Connor because he had been surrounded by demonstrators, and was being heckled mercilessly.

'Yes, I have a comment to make,' she said, completely uncaring of what Admin might say when they saw her words on the front page of tomorrow's paper. 'I think even the idea of shutting down our NICU is an appalling one.

We have an excellent unit here. A unit that serves the needs of the local community, and I am fully behind this protest, and I wish the organisers well.'

And she made for the stairs, looking over her shoulder only once, when a great cheer went up. Someone had thrown an egg at Connor. An egg which had landed smack-bang on the front of his smart city suit. And her one thought as she headed back to the unit was she wished she'd had an egg because she would have thrown it, too.

CHAPTER SEVEN

'WE NEVER thought this day would come, Sister Flannigan.' Naomi Renwick beamed. 'To be finally taking Amy home...'

'And I've taken a photograph of her—for your graduation board,' Naomi's husband declared. 'So other mothers and fathers can see there truly can be light at the end of the tunnel.'

'It's a lovely picture,' Brianna said as she took the photograph Mr Renwick was holding out to her. 'Thank you very much.'

'We were hoping we might see Mr Monahan before we go,' Naomi said. 'He's been so supportive over this last month, always stopping by for a chat whenever my husband and I have visited Amy in the evening.'

'He has—he did?' Brianna said faintly. 'I...I didn't know that.'

'He's a nice bloke,' Mr Renwick observed, 'and he seemed quite taken with our Amy. As I said to him, you're clearly getting broody, Connor, so maybe you and Sister Flannigan should be thinking about having kids of your own soon.'

'And...and what did he say to that?' Brianna asked through a throat so tight it hurt.

'He just smiled,' Naomi replied. 'Look, I know he got

a lot of very bad press after his notes were published in the *Gazette*,' Amy's mother continued quickly as Brianna took a shaky breath, 'but we can honestly say your husband never had anything but praise for the unit when he was talking to us.'

Connor hadn't simply got bad press, Brianna remembered. The board had been forced to issue a statement declaring no decision had been made about any cuts to services, but nobody in the hospital had believed that. Everyone simply thought that if NICU couldn't be closed because of the public outcry, it only meant some other department would be shut down instead.

'Connor did say he would definitely see us and Amy before we left,' Mr Renwick said, 'and I told him we'd be collecting her at four o'clock, so maybe we could give him another few minutes?'

The couple didn't have to. The ward door had opened, and Connor appeared.

'You made it, Connor.' Mr Renwick beamed. 'We thought you might have forgotten, or been too busy.'

'I'd never be too busy for such a momentous occasion, and I most certainly wouldn't forget,' he replied.

And his gaze was fixed firmly on the Renwicks, Brianna noticed, but what had she expected? He'd tried to talk to her over the past five weeks, had left innumerable messages on her answering-machine, had once even come to her cottage, and she'd refused to open the door. She'd been so angry, so very angry. A part of her still was, and yet, as she gazed up at him, all she could think was this was his last day in the hospital. Tomorrow he would leave St Piran, and, when he left, their marriage would be finally, and irrevocably, be over.

'Sister Flannigan, can we take a photograph of you and Connor together?' Mr Renwick asked. 'It would be something to show Amy when she grows up. A picture of the husband-and-wife team who helped her parents so much.'

'I really think it should just be a photograph of Sister Flannigan,' Connor said quickly, but Naomi shook her head.

'I want the two of you together,' she said.

Which was fine in theory, Brianna thought, but not so fine in practice. Naomi clearly wanted a 'happy couple' photograph, and neither of them fitted that bill any more.

'Connor, can't you at least put your arm around her?' Naomi protested. 'You're standing there looking like she's a complete stranger, and Sister Flannigan, a smile would be nice. I don't want Amy looking at this photograph in years to come and saying, "Yikes, they look grim", and I'm sure you don't want a picture of yourselves looking like a pair of stuffed dummies.'

And Connor dutifully put his arm around her, and Brianna forced herself to smile, and tried very hard not to cry.

All the dreams she'd had ten years ago on their wedding day. All the plans she'd made, the hopes she'd had, and now the last photograph of them together would be of her wearing a manufactured smile, and him not even attempting to smile at all.

Tell him you don't want him to go, her heart whispered. Tell him you want him to stay here, to try to make your marriage work.

But she couldn't. Connor and Cornwall were as compatible as cheese and gravy, and she couldn't go back to London with him. She knew she would just shrivel up and die in the city so, when the Renwicks carried their daughter out of the ward, she kept her gaze firmly fixed on them, and only let out the breath she knew she'd been holding when she heard the ward door shut.

'Colin's had three full bottles today,' Nicola Hallet said proudly as Brianna slowly walked past her. 'Dr Phillips said if he keeps on progressing like this she'll be recommending he's moved out of NICU and into Special Care, and after that…' Nicola beamed. 'Home. I'll finally be able to take him home.'

'That's terrific news, Nicola,' Brianna said, meaning it.

Young though the teenager might be, Nicola was proving to be an excellent, and completely devoted, mother, coming in every day to feed and bathe her son, and to talk and play with him.

'Your husband said he wants me to keep in touch with him, to let him know how Colin is, when he goes back to London,' Nicola continued, gazing fondly down at her son. 'Wasn't that kind of him?'

'Very kind,' Brianna said unevenly. 'When…when did he say all this?'

'On one of his visits to the unit,' Nicola replied. 'He's been coming here a lot in the evening.'

Who else had Connor been talking to? Brianna wondered, taking a shaky breath. First the Renwicks, and now Nicola, but *why*? What had drawn him back here, apparently night after night?

'Nicola—'

'How's my favourite boy in all the world?' Jess asked with a smile as she joined them.

'Dr Phillips said she's thinking of moving Colin to Special Care next week,' Nicola answered.

'That's wonderful news,' the counsellor declared, then glanced across at Brianna. 'Have you a moment?'

'Something wrong?' Brianna asked as she followed Jess across the ward, and the counsellor shook her head.

'I passed Connor in the corridor on my way in, and he said he'd like a word with you, if you've time.'

He wanted to say goodbye, Brianna realised, and she didn't want to say goodbye, didn't think her heart could take that.

'I'm afraid I'm rather busy at the moment,' she lied, and Jess sighed.

'Brianna, talk to him,' she said softly. 'What harm can it do just to talk to him?'

'Jess, what is there left for us to say that we haven't already said?' Brianna said sadly. 'I think a clean break, with no goodbyes, is best.'

'And you truly believe that?' Jess said with eyes that saw too much.

'Jess, just leave it, OK?'

'But, Brianna—'

She didn't give the counsellor time to finish. Instead, she walked over to one of the monitors, and swallowed hard. If talking to Connor would have changed anything, she would have done it in a minute, but it wouldn't change anything, she knew it wouldn't.

Determinedly, she picked up the pile of files stacked on the nurses' work station. She should have tackled them days ago, but she'd been so tired recently. Tired and uncharacteristically weepy, and she bit her lip. Maybe she should never have accepted the nurse unit manager's job. Maybe she just wasn't up to it, and she ought to simply tell Mr Brooke so.

'Brianna?'

She glanced over her shoulder to see Megan standing behind her.

'I've just passed Connor in the corridor,' the paediatric specialist registrar declared, 'and he said he'd like—'

'A word with me,' Brianna finished for her. 'Yes, I know.'

'I can hold the fort for you here, if you want. It would be no trouble.'

'Look, what is this?' Brianna exclaimed, taking refuge in anger. 'If it's not you, it's Jess, trying to push me out the door to talk to him.'

'I just thought that, as this is his last day…'

'I know what you thought,' Brianna said tightly, 'and, trust me, it isn't going to happen.'

'Brianna, don't you think you should at least let him say what he wants to say?' Megan said, her eyes concerned. 'You can tear him to shreds afterwards if you want, but, when he's been the one continually holding out the olive branch, couldn't you at least meet him halfway and hear him out?'

'Yeah, right. Like you do with Josh, you mean?' Brianna snapped. 'I can't say I've seen any signs of that.'

Megan flushed scarlet, opened her mouth, then closed it again tightly.

'OK, if that's how you feel,' she said, 'but I'm not going out there to tell him you won't see him. You can do that yourself, or you can leave him standing in the corridor waiting for hours in the hope you might change your mind. Your choice.'

'Megan—'

The paediatric specialist registrar had walked away, and Brianna started after her, then stopped. What in the world was happening to her? Megan and Jess both meant well, she knew they did, and yet she'd chewed their heads off. Chewed the heads off the two women she'd always thought of as friends, and she wanted to burst into tears again, and she really had to stop wanting to burst into tears.

Go and see him, a little voice whispered at the back of her mind. *You want to, you know you do, so go and see him.*

I can't, her heart cried. I can't. I don't want to say good-bye.

It will be the last time you ever see him, the little voice whispered. *The last time you'll ever see his face.* And before she was even aware she was moving, she was out in the corridor and he was there, waiting for her.

'Thanks for agreeing to see me,' he said.

Lord, but he looked so nervous, so awkward and un-comfortable, totally unlike her normally super-confident husband.

'Megan and Jess, seemed to think it was important,' she replied, only to realise, too late, just how awful her words sounded, as though her friends might care about him but she did not. 'I mean—'

'I thought you should know what's in my report to the board before it becomes common knowledge tomorrow,' he interrupted.

'You don't have to tell me the details,' she said quickly. 'I don't need to know before anyone else does.'

'Yes, you do,' he insisted. 'I've recommended no depart-ments, or wards, should be shut.'

She blinked. 'None?'

'I've had a lot of time to think over this past month,' he declared with a rueful half-smile, 'and I've realised you were right. Not everything can be measured on a balance sheet.'

'But, if you don't suggest any cuts, won't the board simply bring in someone else to audit us?' she protested.

'They need to save money, and won't they reason that if you can't find a solution then maybe somebody else might?'

'I've shown them how they can save money,' he replied. 'I've recommended cancelling the new, all-singing, all-dancing computer system they've ordered. Their old computer system—with some modifications—is more than up to the task.'

'Right.' She nodded.

He backed up a step. 'Well...that's all I wanted to tell you, so...'

He was going and, as she stared up at him, saw how careworn he looked, how very weary, she knew she still loved him. Despite everything he'd done, despite everything that had happened, she still loved him, and surely there had to be some way back for them, some way they could still be together?

'Connor...'

He stopped, and something that looked almost like hope stirred in his deep blue eyes. 'Yes?'

'I just wanted to say—you know—thank you,' she said awkwardly. 'On behalf of the parents, and the babies, I mean,' she added.

'That's OK,' he muttered.

Oh, Lord, but why had she said that? She'd always been the one who'd accused him of not talking, of not saying what he was really thinking, and now she couldn't seem to find the right words.

'You'll be going back to London tomorrow?' she said desperately.

'Not immediately,' he replied. 'I thought I might stay on here for a little while, have a holiday.'

Despite herself, her lips curved.

'You're not going to find much to do in Penhally in

April,' she observed, and saw an answering, hesitant, smile appear on his lips.

'Maybe I'll take up beachcombing,' he said. 'How's the new job going?'

'Tiring,' she admitted. 'I hadn't realised before just how much paperwork was involved.'

'You look tired,' he observed. 'Just don't overdo it, OK? I've had to learn the hard way that there's more to life than work.'

He's given you an opening, she thought, so use it. Use it now, but she didn't get a chance to.

'How's Rita?' he continued, and, when she rolled her eyes, he laughed. 'That good, eh?'

'She was pretty subdued for about a week, but she bounced right back again pretty quickly. As she said to me, "Sister Flannigan, the Bible does say that charity begins at home, so I'd hardly be a good Christian if I didn't find it in me to forgive my own granddaughter's transgressions."'

'She actually said that?' Connor gasped, and Brianna nodded.

'Yup, she did. I'm afraid nothing keeps our Rita down for long.'

'You know, in a weird way, I think I'm going to miss her,' he observed. 'Of course, it's going to be in a *very* weird way.'

Brianna laughed and, as he half turned, clearly thinking their conversation was over, she took a step forward.

'The Renwicks told me you've been visiting the unit in the evening,' she said. 'Nicola said you've been talking to her, too.'

'They're a nice couple, and she's a sweet kid, so…' His shoulders lifted awkwardly.

'But why, Connor?' she asked. 'Your assessment of

NICU was over weeks ago, so why did you keep coming back here?'

To her surprise, a deep tide of colour crept over her husband's cheeks.

'It's stupid—silly,' he muttered. 'Not worth talking about.'

'Tell me,' she pressed.

'You'll think I'm crazy.'

'Just tell me,' she protested, and saw him take a deep breath.

'Because it's where you work, and being in the unit… Sometimes I caught a hint of the soap you use, and it made me feel…close to you again, as though I was still a part of your life.'

Tears welled in her eyes. 'Oh, Connor—'

'Told you it was stupid, didn't I?' he said awkwardly, and she shook her head.

'No,' she replied with difficulty. 'I don't think it's stupid at all.'

'I'd better go,' he said again. 'I've taken up more than enough of your time.'

She put out her hand quickly.

'This holiday you're taking,' she said hesitantly. 'It seems like such a waste of money for you to stay in a hotel. You…you could move back into my cottage tomorrow, if you want. I mean, it would give us more time to talk,' she continued, feeling her cheeks beginning to darken as he stared at her, his face expressionless. 'And I…I would very much like for us to talk some more, if…if you'd like to, that is?'

A smile curved the corners of his mouth. A smile that grew, and grew.

'I would like that very much indeed,' he said, and she smiled in return, a suddenly shy, self-conscious smile.

'I'd better get back to work,' she said, 'otherwise they'll be sending out a search party for me.'

He nodded, and she turned, but she must have turned too fast because a wave of giddiness swept over her, and if Connor hadn't caught her she would have fallen.

'Are you OK?' he said anxiously.

'Rush of blood to the head, that's all,' she said, wishing the walls in the corridor would stop moving.

'You're sure?' he pressed. 'Hell, Brianna, you're chalk-white.'

'I'm fine—just fine,' she said shakily, taking several deep breaths. 'I shouldn't have skipped breakfast this morning, but I felt a bit queasy.'

'You'll have breakfast every morning when I move back in, and no arguments,' he said firmly, and she laughed.

'Going to be the flatmate from hell, are you?' she said, and he smiled but she could see his eyes were still concerned.

'When it comes to your health, you bet I am,' he declared.

She still felt slightly sick, and giddy, she realised as she walked away from him back into the ward, and it was weird. She didn't get sick—never had done. It had always been Connor who contracted every cold or infection going. She'd used to laugh, and tell him he could be the one-stop shop for medical students practising their skills, and he hadn't appreciated the joke. The only time she'd ever felt sick…

She came to a halt in the middle of the ward, her heart suddenly racing. The only time she'd ever felt sick had been when she'd been expecting Harry. The only time her emotions had been all over the place, as they were right now, had been when she'd been pregnant with Harry.

'No,' she whispered, as she desperately tried to count

back to the night when she and Connor had made love. 'I can't be. I can't.'

But she could.

Keep calm, she told herself, don't panic, keep calm. You could simply be late. You've only missed one period, and stress can do that. It took seven years for you to conceive Harry so the odds on you conceiving in one night are minuscule.

But not impossible.

'Chris, I just need to slip out for a moment,' she said, hoping her voice didn't sound nearly as strained as she thought it did.

It couldn't have done because the staff nurse simply nodded vaguely, and quickly Brianna left the unit and headed for Gynae.

No matter how long she stared at the thin blue lines they didn't go away. She'd sneaked three pregnancy kits out of Gynae, had been determined to leave nothing to chance, and each and every one of the kits said the same thing. She was pregnant.

'Brianna, are you in there?' Megan called, from outside the staffroom toilet.

'Yes…I'm here,' she managed to say.

'A and E have phoned. Four-month-old on its way to us. Mother seriously injured in a car crash, baby looks to have nothing more than minor lesions but they want us to check him out.'

And I don't want to do this, Brianna thought, squeezing her eyes shut. I can't deal with this, not right now, but she knew she must.

'I'll be out in a minute,' she said, and, when she heard Megan's footsteps fading away, she stared at the pregnancy kits on the floor in front of her.

One pregnancy test could get it wrong, but it was impossible for three to give the wrong result. A baby was growing inside her, and no amount of staring at the kits would alter that. No amount of willing the results to be different would change them, and stiffly she got to her feet, and even more stiffly walked out of the toilet, down the corridor, and into the ward.

The heat enveloped her instantly, but it didn't comfort her as it normally did. All she could see were the IV lines, tubes and incubators. All she could hear was the rasping sound of the ventilators, the constant bleep of the monitors, and in seven months' time, if she didn't go full term, as she hadn't before, she'd be back in here, not as a nurse but as a mother. A mother whose child's life would be attached to all those tubes and wires. A mother whose child would be clinging to life. A sob broke from her.

'Brianna, what's wrong?'

Megan was standing in front of her, her eyes full of concern, and Brianna shook her head.

'I have to get out of here.'

'But—'

'I can't bear this, I can't!' Brianna exclaimed, all too aware that Chris was gazing at her open-mouthed, Mr Brooke looked stunned, and Josh...

He was there, too, and he was walking towards her, worry and confusion written all over his face, and she turned and ran. Out of the ward, out of the unit, not knowing know where she was going, not even caring, just so long as she got away.

'Brianna, wait up a moment!'

She didn't want to wait as she heard Megan running after her. She was going to have wait for the next eight months, endure eight whole months of fear, and she pressed her fist against her mouth hard as another sob came from her.

'Brianna, what's happened? What's wrong?'

Megan had caught up with her, was trying to steer her into the on-call room, and she tried to pull herself free, but the paediatric specialist registrar was a lot stronger than she looked.

'Megan, let me go,' she said, her voice raw. 'Please, just let me go.'

'No way,' her friend replied. 'You're clearly very upset. Shall I get Connor? I can phone him—'

'No—no—don't get him!' Brianna begged. 'Please, don't get him!'

'Then tell me what's wrong, what's happened, because I swear I'll phone him if you don't,' Megan replied, her eyes dark with anxiety.

Slowly, Brianna went into the on-call room, and sat down heavily on the bed.

'I... Oh, God, Megan. I'm pregnant.'

The specialist paediatric registrar stared at her silently for a heartbeat, then sat down beside her.

'And I take it this is not good news?' she said gently.

'It's the worst news,' Brianna cried. 'The very worst news in the world!'

Megan's eyes darkened with an expression Brianna didn't understand, then she cleared her throat.

'The baby...is it Connor's?' she asked hesitantly, and when Brianna nodded she sighed. 'Look, I know you're not exactly on speaking terms with him at the moment, but you told me just a few weeks ago that you loved him, and maybe you can resolve whatever's driven you apart, and even if you can't, lots of women are single mothers—'

'I know,' Brianna interrupted. 'I know all that, but it isn't that simple, Megan, I wish to God it was. Three years ago Connor and I...we had a child. We'd been trying for a baby for seven years, and when I discovered I was pregnant it was...' She took an uneven breath. 'It was like having all of my birthdays and Christmases in one go.'

'What happened?' Megan asked, her eyes fixed on her.

'I must have had one of the worst pregnancies ever,' Brianna replied. 'I was sick the whole time, but I didn't care. I used to talk to him, Megan. All the time I'd talk to the baby, tell him what I was doing, what I could see, and tell him how...' Tears spilled over her cheeks, and she didn't rub them away. 'How he was going to be the most loved baby in the whole world, and when he was born... Connor—he says he looked like me, but he didn't. He looked like him, and he died, Megan. He only lived for twelve hours, and then my beautiful, precious son died.'

'Oh, Brianna, I am so sorry,' Megan declared, her own eyes filling, 'and discovering you're pregnant again... You must be scared to death, but just because your son died doesn't mean every other baby you have will die, too.'

'He had an inherited heart condition, Megan, and you know what that means. It means there's a very strong likelihood it will happen again.'

'Brianna, listen to me—'

'Why?' Brianna hurled at her. 'What's the point? You don't understand—you can't. You've never given birth to a child and been forced to watch him die. You've never watched your baby slowly slip away from you, knowing there was nothing you could to stop it.'

'I have.'

Brianna's eyes flew to her friend's, and she saw such an unutterable pain there that for a moment she forgot her own despair.

'You had a baby?' she whispered.

'A son, like you,' Megan replied, her voice low, but there was no mistaking the heartache in it. 'He was born eight years ago when I was a student doctor. His father was a doctor, too, working in the same hospital as me, and he was so handsome, Brianna. Handsome, and charming, and such fun, and I…' She closed her eyes. 'Even though he never seemed to notice me, I guess I was a little in love with him right from the first moment I saw him.'

'You're…you're talking about Josh, aren't you?' Brianna said hesitantly, and Megan nodded.

'I always thought I was too quiet for him, too studious, and then…' She took a breath. 'I went to a party, and he was there, and suddenly he seemed very interested in me, and…' A tear ran down the paediatric specialist registrar's cheek, and she brushed it away. 'It wasn't a one-night stand, Brianna, not for me. I thought it was the start of something special, but…'

'He walked away when he discovered you were pregnant?' Brianna said tentatively, and Megan laughed.

A harsh, bitter laugh that made Brianna wince.

'I didn't even get the chance to tell him I was pregnant. We were supposed to meet up the next day, and he stood me up, and when I saw him a few days later, he blanked me. He just walked straight past me as though he'd never met me, far less made love to me.'

'Oh, Megan—'

'When I discovered I was pregnant, my career was just taking off, and I thought, I can't give this baby a home. I can't give him the attention he deserves, so I was going to have an abortion until I saw the scan. When I saw this tiny figure inside me…' She shook her head. 'This tiny, oh, so perfect little human being inside me…'

'You couldn't go through with it.'

'He was my baby, Brianna, my little boy, and even if his father didn't want him, I did, and then…' Megan took a deep breath, and Brianna could see her friend's lips were trembling. 'I collapsed in the street when I was twenty-three weeks pregnant. Placental abruption, that's what the doctor in A and E said, and I was bleeding out, and I could hear someone shouting, "She has to be saved. The baby can't be saved, but we can save her", and I didn't want them to save me. I...' A sob escaped her. 'I just wanted to die, to be with my son, but they didn't let me die. They performed a complete hysterectomy, which means I can't ever have any more children.'

'Oh, Megan,' Brianna cried. 'I am sorry...so, so sorry.'

'I have relived that day so many times, Brianna,' Megan said, her voice shaking. 'Wondered so often if maybe Stephen knew I'd considered having an abortion, and, because he thought I didn't want him, he decided I was better off without him, but I wasn't. I wasn't.'

'But, having been through all that, having suffered the death of a child, can't you see why I can't face this again?' Brianna insisted. 'Can't you understand that I can't carry a child, grow to love it, and then have that baby die, too?'

'Brianna, statistically, the odds that everything might be all right—'

'*Might* be—*could* be. Megan I don't want *might*,' Brianna protested. 'I don't want *could*. I want you to tell me this baby will live!'

'I can't promise you that—no one can,' Megan replied. 'Brianna—'

She'd already got jerkily to her feet.

'I want to go home, Megan. I just want to get away from here, and go home.'

'But, Brianna...'

Her friend was already heading out of the on-call room, and for a moment Megan stared indecisively after her, then pulled her mobile phone from her pocket and dialled quickly.

'Pick up your phone, Connor,' she muttered. 'This is important, so pick up your damn phone!'

But he didn't. She'd reached his voice mail, and the last thing she wanted was his voice mail, but she left a message anyway, and then she left the on-call room only to stop dead. Josh was standing outside in the corridor, and his face told her everything.

'You heard,' she said flatly, and, when he nodded she shrugged, though her eyes were dark with shadows. 'There's no need to look quite so shocked. It's not as though you didn't already know about Stephen, and my hysterectomy.'

'Megan—'

She didn't let him finish. She simply walked back into the duty room and slammed the door, but he came in after her.

'Megan, if I could have saved Stephen, I would,' Josh said hoarsely. 'But he was too little, too premature, you know he was, and if we hadn't carried out the hysterectomy, you would have *died*, and I couldn't have borne that. Losing you as well as my son—'

'Are you asking me to believe you *cared*?' she demanded, her voice hard. 'If you are, then it's too little, too late.'

'Megan, listen to me,' he begged, his face white. 'You cannot possibly hate me more than I hate myself right now. When I held Stephen in my hands for those few brief moments, when I saw he wasn't breathing, knew he would never breathe—'

'Don't, Josh,' she protested, her face stricken, 'please *don't*—'

'And they rushed you to Theatre, and you were losing so much blood—'

'If you cared that much then why did you walk away from me?' she cried, her voice cracking. 'I thought we'd meant something to one another that night, and yet you didn't even turn up the next day as we'd arranged.'

'I was scared, Megan. My father…' He shook his head. 'He hurt my mother time and time again with his affairs, and yet she kept on taking him back, and taking him back, and I thought, if that's love, I want none of it. If that's what giving your heart means, I can't do that, so all my life I've refused to allow myself to get too close to anyone for fear I'd hurt them, or they'd hurt me.'

'And yet you married Rebecca,' she pointed out, and he bit his lip.

'I should never have done that—I see that now—but I married her because I was lonely. I married her because I was unhappy, and I married her because…' He sucked in an uneven breath. 'She wanted so little from me. I'm ashamed to admit that—I should never have married her when all I felt for her was a liking—but I thought she was happy. I told myself she was, but she wasn't.'

'Josh—'

'Megan, I have ruined three lives,' he said desolately. 'Yours, my wife's, my own, and though I deserve everything I've got—my wife walking out on me, you hating me— neither you nor Rebecca deserve the pain I've inflicted on you both.'

'I don't hate you,' Megan said, her voice trembling. 'I may have once, a long time ago. I may even have wished you'd never come back into my life, but I don't hate you. I don't think I ever could.'

'I know I can never make it up to you,' he said. 'I know I can never expect you to forgive me, or to care for me the way I care for you—'

'You care for me?' she interrupted, and he smiled, a lopsided, crooked smile.

'I realise now, though it's too late, that I always have, and I just want to say I'm sorry. I know that's a pathetic thing to say,' he continued, as a tear trickled down Megan's cheek, 'a completely inadequate thing to say, and I wish there were bigger words, better words I could use to convince you I truly am sorry for all the pain and heartache I've caused you, but there aren't.'

'I don't need bigger or better words,' she said on a sob. 'Those words are enough.'

'Are you saying…?' His eyes met hers, and he swallowed hard. 'Are you saying that maybe…maybe you could learn to care for me again?'

'Josh, I always have,' she said simply, 'and, God help me, I think I always will.'

And when he hesitantly held out his arms to her she walked straight into them, and when he kissed her it was as though the last eight years had never been. As though all the heartache and pain they'd both endured had never happened. And he'd said he'd cared for her. OK, so he hadn't said the 'L' word, but she knew he meant the 'L' word, he truly did, and the shiver she felt when she heard the lonely wail of an approaching ambulance, a wail that sounded so like a lost soul crying for the happiness it could never have, meant nothing. It didn't, she told herself, so when he deepened his kiss, held her even closer, moulded his body to hers, and she felt herself melting, and dissolving in his heat, she didn't stop him when he stretched behind him, and turned the lock on the on-duty call-room door.

* * *

Brianna's house was in complete darkness when Connor reached it, and if it hadn't been for her car parked outside he would have thought she wasn't home.

'Brianna needs you,' Megan had said, sounding frantic on his voice mail. 'She's gone home, and she really needs you, Connor.'

He'd driven like a maniac along the narrow Cornish roads, broken the speed limit the whole way, and now...

Hesitantly, he tried the front door, and it opened immediately. Was that good, or bad? He didn't know, and even more hesitantly he walked down the hall to the sitting room. The room was in darkness, just like the rest of the house, but moonlight was streaming through the window and he could just about make Brianna out, sitting motionless and hunched on the sofa.

'You know, you really should lock your front door,' he said, switching on one of the table lamps. 'I could have been anyone. A burglar, a serial killer, a door-to-door salesman trying to sell you a hundred and one things you never ever wanted.'

She didn't so much as turn her head, and he shivered. The room was freezing, and quickly he switched on the gas fire, and watched the fake flames spring to life, before turning back to her.

Had she moved at all? He didn't think she had.

'I expect I'm the last person in the world you want to see,' he said, walking over to the sofa and sitting down beside her, hoping to at least provoke a response, but he didn't. 'Megan rang me. She was worried about you.'

Still she didn't move, and tentatively he reached out, and took her hand in his. Lord, but her fingers felt like ice, and the shiver he'd felt earlier became more pronounced.

'Has something happened at the hospital?' he asked, wishing she would look at him, say something, anything.

'Has someone upset you, or is it one of the babies? Has one of the babies become very ill?'

Still she said nothing, and he gripped her hand tighter.

'Bree, for God's sake, say something, because you're scaring the hell out of me,' he said, and she was. 'Are you ill? You had that giddy spell earlier—is it something to do with that, and there's something wrong with you? Look, whatever it is, we can deal with it. I'm not going to walk away, I'm not going to leave you—'

'I'm pregnant.'

Her voice was so low, he wasn't sure he'd heard her correctly, and he half shook his head.

'I'm sorry, but did you just say…?'

'I'm pregnant, Connor,' she said dully. 'The night little Colin Hallet had his op, when we made love, I must have conceived a baby then.'

'But that's…' His face lit up. 'Oh, Bree, that's wonderful news, the very best of news.'

Her head snapped round to his.

'*Wonderful* news—*the very best* of news?' she cried. 'I don't want to be pregnant, Connor. Can't you understand, *I don't want to be pregnant*!'

'Bree, I know this is a shock, something you never planned,' he declared, putting his hands on her shoulders, 'but you're going to have a baby—*a baby*—and it's what you always wanted, and if…' His face twisted slightly. 'If you don't want me in your life to share this with you, I'll understand. All I'll ask of you is that you let me sometimes be there, for the child.'

'What if it dies?' she exclaimed, getting jerkily to her feet, her face white, her eyes desperate. 'What if this baby dies, too, Connor? Before—because of my job—I knew things could sometimes go wrong, but I only knew it in an abstract way, something that happened to other people, not to me, but it *has* happened to me, and it could happen again—we both know it could. Even if I do all the right things, even if I never take any risks, just like I didn't with Harry, it could happen again. This baby could have the same inherited heart defect, and it could die!'

'It might not,' he said, reaching for her only to see her evade him, 'and if it does we'll face it together.'

'That's easy for you to say,' she said, a tear running down her cheek, and she dashed it away. 'You won't be able to feel him, or her, moving inside you. You won't lie awake at night, thinking he hasn't moved in a little while, and does that mean he's not alive any more. You were right about Nicola's baby. I wanted him because he had no one. I wanted him because he looked so like our Harry, but I also wanted him because...' Another tear trickled down her cheek and she let it fall. 'He was *whole*, Connor, he was going to live, and to have to wait to find out if this baby...'

'So, you're going to have an abortion?' he said, watching her face. 'You're going to abort this baby, not even give it a chance to live, is that it?'

She stared at him, her mouth working soundlessly for a moment, then before he knew what was happening she was standing in front of him, pounding his chest with her fists.

'How can you say that?' she cried, hitting him with every word she spoke. 'How can you even think I'd kill my child? Of course I would never kill my child, never, *never*!'

'I know,' he said, quickly catching her wrists with his hands. 'Brianna, I *know* you wouldn't, and that's why the only thing you can do is to go on with this, and we can face it together, we can do it together, if...' He searched her face. 'You want me in your life, that is? I know I've made mistakes,' he continued as she tried to interrupt. 'I know I've got things wrong, but I have never ever stopped loving you.'

'And I haven't ever stopped loving you,' she said brokenly. 'I think…maybe…we just sort of lost one another somehow along the way, but I am so scared, Connor, so scared. If this baby dies, too…'

'I'm scared, too,' he admitted, taking her into his arms, and holding her tight. 'In the past, I always thought I had control over my life, my future, but now I know that was nothing but an illusion, that none of us have any control, that all we can do is hold onto one another through the good times, and the bad, and pray and hope.'

'I want certainty, not hope,' she sobbed into his chest. 'I want to know for sure, not have to pray.'

He tilted her head back so she had to look at him.

'I know, and I think that's what we all want, but life isn't like that. For such a very long time I thought, Why my son, why did this have to happen to my son? But now I know there is no answer to that. When Harry died—'

'You said the word,' she interrupted. 'Do you realise that's the first time you've ever said the word?'

'I couldn't say it before, because saying it…' Connor swallowed hard. 'It made it so final, so irrevocable. It meant I had to accept he was never, ever coming back.'

'And he isn't, is he?' she said, and Connor shook his head, a muscle in his jaw quivering.

'No, but do you remember when they took him off the life-support machine, and you were holding him in your arms, and I had one of his tiny hands in mine…? Do you remember him opening his eyes, and looking at us before he died?'

She nodded with difficulty. 'I remember.'

'I think now he was saying, "I love you both, and I know

you love me, but I have to go now. I can't stay with you any longer."'

'Oh, Connor…'

'Brianna, there was a time when I thought I couldn't face going on without him,' he said shakily, as tears spilled down her cheeks. 'I couldn't see any future without him, but he's gone on without us, and we have to go on without him. We won't ever forget him—we can't, not ever—and he will always have a treasured place in our hearts, but we have to look forward and not back.'

'I can't go back to London with you,' she said quickly. 'I know you love the city, but I love it here.'

'We're staying here. We might need to look for a bigger house once the baby comes, unless your landlord will let us build an extension, but we're staying in Penhally.'

'But you'll be so miserable,' she protested, 'and where would you work?'

'I would never be miserable with you beside me,' he said, willing her to believe him, 'and I've already got a job in St Piran.'

'You've got a job?' she said, and he smiled.

'The hospital board want me to be their financial advisor.'

'And you were offered this job, and accepted it, and never told me?' she said in confusion.

'I knew you didn't want to see me, to talk to me,' he said, his voice low, 'but I hoped, if I stayed here…' He lifted his shoulders awkwardly. 'Maybe in time you might grow to love me again.'

'I do, I always have, but…' She tried to stop her lips from trembling, but she couldn't. 'Will the baby be all right this time, Connor?'

He cupped her face in his hands, his blue eyes holding hers.

'I don't know, but whatever happens we're in this together. No matter what the future brings, we will *always* face it together.'

EPILOGUE

'AND how is my gorgeous wife this morning?'

'Your gorgeous wife feels like a barrage balloon that is about to burst.' Brianna sighed as she eased herself out of her seat.

'Back still sore?' Connor said sympathetically, coming up behind her and rubbing it gently.

'It must be the way I was sleeping—or rather not sleeping—last night,' she replied ruefully. 'I just couldn't get comfortable.'

'I'm not surprised,' Connor grinned, sliding his hands round to caress her swollen stomach. 'With two little munchkins in there, and only two weeks left until your due date, they're probably finding it a bit crowded.'

Brianna grimaced. 'Judging by how much they're kicking, that could be true.'

'Maybe they're both boys?' Connor exclaimed. 'Destined to be future world-class football players.'

Brianna closed her eyes. 'I just want them both to be all right.'

His arms tightened round her. 'They will be. Trust me.'

It wasn't a question of trust, she thought as she let her head fall back against his chest. It was a question now of luck, of the odds being stacked not once, but twice in their favour, and she didn't even want to think about what the chances of that happening might be.

'Stop worrying,' Connor said softly, clearly reading her mind, and she tried to smile, but it was hard.

She'd had a scan at twelve weeks, which had revealed she was expecting twins, but she'd refused to go for any more tests. She was more than happy to let the GP in Penhally regularly check her blood pressure, and to keep making sure there were still two little heartbeats, but she'd point blank refused to have any other kind of test, and Connor had backed her all the way.

'We'll deal with whatever happens when we have to,' he had told the GP, and, though the doctor hadn't been happy, he'd said no more.

'I was just thinking,' Connor continued hesitantly. 'Given that we're shortly going to be having two little babies in our home, are you quite sure you don't want the baby shower Jess and Megan want to throw for you?'

'Tell them I'm really touched, but no,' Brianna replied. 'I know everyone thinks I'm stupid, but…'

'You don't want to tempt fate,' Connor finished for her. 'Understood, though you do realise our children's first beds are going to be a couple of drawers because you won't even let me buy cots?'

'Connor—'

'And I'm sure they'll love the drawers,' he said, planting a kiss on the top of her head, then releasing her. 'I won't be late home tonight. I want to get the last of the onions, and carrots out of the ground before winter really sets in.'

She shook her head, and laughed. 'You and your vegetables. You'll be wanting us to buy chickens next.'

'Been reading my mind, have you?' He grinned, and she laughed again.

He'd taken to country living with an enthusiasm that

had amazed her. Never would she have thought her city-loving husband would have spent all of his spare time in the garden, creating a vegetable patch, but he had.

'No regrets?' she said. 'About living so far away from everything here in Cornwall?'

'Not a one. Everything I want is here.' He cupped her cheek, his blue eyes soft. 'I was just too blind and stupid to see it before.'

'And you're going to be late,' she said, catching sight of the kitchen clock. 'Give my best to the troops on the front line.'

'I will.' He nodded. 'You have my number in case you need me?'

She rolled her eyes.

'Connor, your number is the same number it was eight months ago, so get out of here.'

He turned to go, then came back, and took her in his arms. 'Have I told you this morning that I love you?'

'Twice.' She chuckled, as he kissed her. 'Though how you can love me when I look like a blob...'

'You have never looked more beautiful,' he said huskily, and her eyes filled.

'Lord, being pregnant isn't half playing havoc with my emotions,' she said tremulously. 'Now, will you *please* get out of here before I have to call the board and tell them their financial adviser is a fruitcake?'

'They already know that,' he replied, bending his head, clearly intent on kissing her again, and she fended him off.

'*Go!*'

She could hear him laughing as he went down the drive, and, when he drove away, she smiled as she absently rubbed her back. She hadn't ever been this happy, not even back in Killarney, and her pregnancy had been so much easier this time. She'd actually felt well instead of wretched, and all she needed now was…

'No,' she told the kettle as she made herself a cup of coffee. 'No thinking about what's going to happen in two weeks' time. Connor said it was forbidden.'

Which didn't mean she didn't constantly think about it, she realised as she drank her coffee. The nearer her due date loomed, the more frightened she was becoming.

'I'd much rather the two of you just stayed in there,' she told her bump. 'Where you're safe.'

One of the inhabitants of the bump kicked, and she winced slightly.

'I know, I know,' she said. 'You're eager to see the world, but stay where you are. You've only two more weeks to wait, and I have this laundry to do. Ninety-nine per cent of which,' she continued wryly as she bent to pick up the wash basket, 'appears to consist of your father's shirts, but I promise you I'll wean him out of his city suits one day.'

But not right now, she thought as a pain suddenly shot through her, and as she doubled up she felt something wet and warm trickle down her legs.

No! her mind exclaimed as she stared down and saw a bloody show among the liquid on the floor. Not now. She couldn't be going into labour now. It was too soon, too soon, and she took a deep breath and clutched the kitchen table tight, but the pain in her back was getting worse, a lot worse, and frantically she scrabbled for her mobile and dialled Connor's number.

He answered almost immediately, and she could hear the sound of traffic in the background which meant he had approached the town of St Piran.

'Connor Monahan here,' he declared cheerfully. 'World-renowned but also very modest financial advisor to St Piran Hospital, grower of the best onions in Cornwall, and lucky enough to be married to the most beautiful woman in the entire world, and, yes, I am remembering you want me to pick up some milk before I come home tonight.'

'Connor...' She struggled to keep her voice calm, but it didn't work. 'Connor, my waters have broken.'

For a second there was complete silence down the phone, then she heard him exhale, and the sound of his car accelerating.

'I'm on my way back. Stay where you are. Don't move.'

She wasn't going to, she thought as the phone went dead. She was going to stay right where she was and pray. Pray like she'd never prayed before.

'You're doing really, really well, Brianna,' the midwife declared encouragingly. 'Just a few more pushes and your first baby should be here.'

'Are...are the heart rates still OK?' Brianna gasped, trying to squint round at the monitor. 'No sign of any distress, abnormality?'

'Can you just concentrate on what you're supposed to be doing?' The midwife laughed. 'Honestly, you nurses and doctors make the worst possible mums-to-be. You know too much, that's the trouble. And, no, there's absolutely no sign whatsoever of either of your babies having difficulty,' she continued as Brianna made to interrupt. 'OK, another contraction's coming so work with it,' she added as Brianna let out a groan, and bore down hard.

'Is she OK?' Connor asked, his face chalk-white. 'My wife... Is she OK?'

'She's doing beautifully.'

'But it's been twelve hours,' Connor protested, wiping his forehead with one hand while holding onto Brianna's hand with the other. 'She's been in labour for twelve hours. Maybe you should be thinking of a Caesarean, or—'

'Shut…up…Connor,' Brianna said through her teeth. 'I…don't…want…a…oh…oh, my Lord…here comes another one.'

'Push, push,' the midwife ordered. 'The head's already out. We just need one more push, just one more, and… Oh, beautiful—just beautiful.' She beamed. 'You have a daughter, Brianna, a lovely daughter.'

'Is she all right?' Brianna asked, trying to lever herself upright, only to have to lie down again fast as another contraction rippled through her. 'Is she all right?'

'She's beautiful, Bree,' Connor said, his voice choked, his eyes shimmering. 'Just beautiful.'

But is she all right?' Brianna insisted.

'She's fine, just fine,' the midwife said reassuringly. 'You have a lovely, healthy, perfect baby. Now, keep on working with the contractions, keep working with them. I know you're very tired, but half the hospital staff seem to be outside in the corridor, desperately waiting for news, and we don't want to keep them waiting too much longer, do we?'

Brianna gripped Connor's hand again tightly, and heard him suck in his breath. He was going to be lucky to survive this without having any broken fingers, she thought, but the chuckle which would have broken from her was cut off as yet another contraction swept over her.

'Number two is on its way,' the midwife announced. 'Breathe with the pain, Brianna, go with it—don't fight it.'

'I'm…not…fighting…it,' Brianna protested, her face scarlet, her forehead beaded with sweat. 'I'm really not. I'm just…oh…oh, my…this is…'

'Hard,' Connor finished for her. 'I know it is, but you can do it, Bree. I can see the head crowning. You can do this. I know you can.'

And Brianna took a deep breath, and, with a harsh, guttural cry, pushed for all she was worth, and heard the midwife give an ecstatic whoop.

'She's here, Brianna. You have another little girl, and how you're ever going to tell your daughters apart... My heavens, they're like two peas in a pod, and the spitting image of their father.'

'Is she all right?' Brianna demanded. 'Is she...is she all right, too?'

'Absolutely,' the midwife announced.

For Brianna, all she wanted was to make sure her daughters were all right, to see for herself that they really and truly were all right, and when the midwife finally placed one of the babies in her arms she glanced quickly across at Connor and saw he was crying.

Crying and smiling at the same time, as he held their other daughter in his arms. A baby who was just as pink and healthy-looking as the one Brianna was holding. A baby who was breathing normally, and not erratically. A baby whose little face was screwed up in protest. Brianna let out a hiccupping laugh. A laugh that was pure relief and joy.

'Can I let the crowd outside in the corridor know the good news?' the midwife asked. 'The way they've been staked out all day, refusing to budge, you'd think these two babies were theirs. And, of course, they'll want to come in and see them, but...' She looked from Brianna to Connor, and smiled. 'Not yet, I think. The next few minutes are just for you. All four of you.'

And quickly the midwife bustled out the door, and Connor carefully placed the baby he was holding into Brianna's other arm, then sat down on the bed beside her.

'Oh, Bree, just look at them,' he said huskily. 'They are

just so…so…*beautiful*. And she's wrong—the midwife's wrong—they both look like you.'

'And Harry—they look like Harry, too, don't they?' Brianna said with an unsteady smile. 'I never thought this day would ever come, Connor. I never thought I would ever be able to think of Harry and smile. Every time I thought about him, I'd feel as though my heart was being ripped to pieces, but now… I just wish he could have been here, to see his little sisters, but I'm so grateful we had him even for that very short time.'

'I know,' he said softly. 'I feel the same way.' And then he laughed as an eruption of applause broke out in the corridor outside. 'Sounds like the midwife's just told everyone the good news.'

'We'll have to let them in soon, but do you realise we haven't even chosen names for our daughters?' Brianna declared. 'I didn't want to even think about names in case… you know…'

'Rhianna,' Connor said. 'I'd like to call one of them Rhianna, after your mother, if that's OK?'

'I'd like that, and I know she will.' Brianna nodded. 'And Aisling. Can we call our other daughter Aisling after your mother?''

'Are you sure?' Connor said unsteadily. 'It's a pretty old-fashioned sort of a name—'

'It's a beautiful name,' Brianna interrupted, planting a kiss on the top of each of her daughters' heads. 'Aisling and Rhianna. Our children.'

Connor delved into his pocket, and pulled out his wallet. For a second he stared down at it, then he carefully extracted a photograph and propped it up on the cabinet beside her.

'Aisling and Rhianna and Harry,' he said huskily. 'Our three beloved children.'

Tears welled in Brianna's eyes as she looked at the photograph.

'I didn't know you had that. You never said—never told me.'

'I took the photograph just after Harry was born, never thinking that…' He shook his head. 'And I couldn't throw it away, though even though looking at it always gave me pain, because it would have felt like I was throwing him away. I would have shown it to you, but…I thought…'

'I know.' She smiled tremulously. 'I know what you thought.'

From outside the labour ward they could hear the sound of raised voices, and Connor sighed.

'Sounds like they're getting restless out there,' he observed. 'Are you ready to let them in to see the new additions to the Monahan family?'

Brianna gazed down at her two daughters, then up at him.

'With you at my side, I'll always be ready for anything.'

And after Connor bent his head and kissed her, then slid off the bed to open the labour-ward door, Brianna glanced at the photograph on the bedside table and smiled.

'I love you, Harry,' she whispered. 'And I always will.'

LET'S TALK
Romance

For exclusive extracts, competitions
and special offers, find us online:

 facebook.com/millsandboon

@millsandboonuk

@millsandboon

Or get in touch on 0844 844 1351*

For all the latest titles coming soon, visit
millsandboon.co.uk/nextmonth

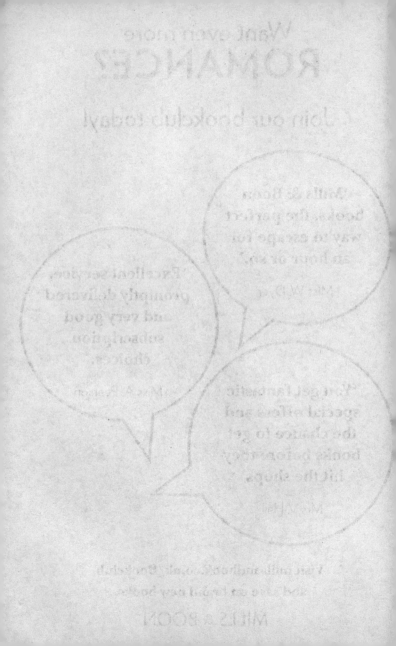